The Luck Penny

JOHN MAHER

BRANDON

A Brandon Original Paperback

First published in Britain and Ireland in 2007 by Brandon
an imprint of Mount Eagle Publications
Dingle, Co. Kerry, Ireland, and
Unit 3, Olympia Trading Estate, Coburg Road, London N22 6TZ, England

www.brandonbooks.com

ISBN 978-086322-355-6

2 4 6 8 10 9 7 5 3 1

Mount Eagle Publications receives support from
the Arts Council/An Chomhairle Ealaíon.

the arts
council
schomhairle
ealaíon

Cover design: Anú Design
Typesetting by Red Barn Publishing, Skeagh, Skibbereen
Printed in the UK

For my Grandmother,
Ann Howard,
Rathdowney

זכרונה לברכה

Acknowledgements

The author wishes to acknowledge the assistance given by the Arts Council of Ireland, the Tyrone Guthrie Centre at Annagh-makerrig and the Djerassi Resident Arts Program, California.

CONTENTS

PART THE FIRST

I

DR DREW ALONE

It was a morning on which a war might have started. The storm the previous night had all but stripped the lime trees, and the ground around the rectory was water-logged. There wasn't a sound of chick or child out on Sackville Square as the Reverend John Drew dragged open the flaking wooden shutters. He suddenly found himself wishing the three women were back again: Judith lolling about on the armchair, her nose buried in a book; Theodora tricking with some embroidery she had been set in Miss Markham's; and Eliza, in the background, calling out commands to Bridget Doheny in the scullery. But now he was alone with himself, with no warm words to soften the uneasy moments between dawn and dusk. And Westmacott's sojourn in Aghadoe had been deferred. His eye fell on the letter lying on the oak escritoire under the bedroom window.

Lanscombe Terrace
September 15 1849

My Dear John,
I hope this letter finds yourself, Eliza and the girls in good fettle. It is

with great chagrin that I have to tell you that I will be unable now to keep our assignation over the next two weeks.

He made his way down the creaking stairs. In the parlour, he surveyed the cold grate, the books strewn here and there and the half-eaten platter of pork on the table. He watched Bianconi swarm about the room, searching for a warm spot to settle down. It might be possible to do an hour's work before lighting the fire. Perhaps go over the syllable charts and the signs again. He could wrap his legs in Judith's fluffy mauve eiderdown and sit in at the drawing room table. But then that queer sort of sadness, a mill-stone pulling his soul down to the sinful depths of despond, over-whelmed him again. He stooped to pick up one of the copies of the Darius inscription, from Persepolis.

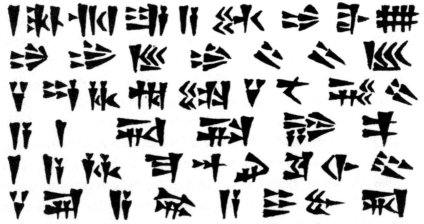

The legend, written in Babylonian over a palace portal, had sat out the centuries, waiting for the attentions of a woebegone, rheumatic cleric in a small damp town in the Queen's County. In a fit of pique, he suddenly screwed up the copy of the inscription and threw it into the empty grate. No, it wouldn't take much at all. Just a little spark from the box of matches Bridget Doheny had left on the mantelpiece. Then the vain words of a vain king would be sent roaring up the chimney of a vain cleric.

In the gloom of the early morning, it took John Drew a moment to make out the little silver locket lying beside the matches, and the silver chain dangling over the edge of the cold marble.

"She's forgotten the blessed thing . . ."

At first he stayed his hand from the locket, afraid, perhaps, to invoke an even greater evil by touching the thing. Then, he slowly reached out for the locket that contained the little wisp of blond hair. He fancied, for an idle moment, that the little silver locket was still warm from his wife's breast, but the cold metal case rebuffed his fingers, like the books and the script tables had already done. Slowly and deliberately, he set the little silver locket back down on the cold mantelpiece. He stood there awhile, lost between the locket and the scripts on the table—between the heart and the head—with the past washing over him, like the autumn rains that sluiced the choking dust down Sackville Square. He scarcely noticed Bianconi rubbing against his leg, and he certainly didn't hear the child's bony hand knocking on the bare wood of the scullery door at all.

"Dr Drew! Are you in there at all?"

John Drew crossed stiffly into the scullery. It must be one of Bridget Doheny's, come with the kindling. Despite the misunderstanding, Bridget Doheny wouldn't see him freeze. He opened the scullery door to the grubby, wizened little face of a ten-year-old boy.

"I brang the kippeens for you, Mr Drew."

"Oh, yes . . . the kindling . . . fine . . ."

"Do you want them left again the coachhouse wall?"

"Yes . . . by the coachhouse wall . . . that will be fine."

He watched absently as the boy dragged the bundles of damp faggots from the little handcart. How many were in the Doheny house? Eight or nine. Two dead during the height of the hunger, from fever, or so Mrs Tours had told Eliza. Not that he credited anything the Tours woman said. And Eliza was getting far too fond of visiting that quarter, in the dark of night: an unseemly thing for the wife of a minister of the cloth to be doing.

Bridget Doheny's boy smiled a gap-toothed smile at John Drew as they sauntered into the house. While the child set to clearing out the grate and arranging the sticks into a pyramid, John Drew cut a large wedge of bread and covered it in fresh salted butter: bread that Judith Drew had taken from the oven the day before; fresh, salted butter that Bridget Doheny had churned before her little temper tantrum out in the coachhouse. He set the wooden tray on the table and nodded to the boy. Easy seen that Eliza Drew wasn't at home. It would be wash your hands in the yard barrel and eat standing up in the scullery, boy. And maybe she was right at that. Too much familiarity complicated things with them. Hadn't he learned that to his cost the time of the business with one Mr Fox Keegan, all those years ago? He needed to know which way things stood with Bridget Doheny, though. Was the blessed woman going to reappear at all before Eliza came home? What a calamity! Hardly had Eliza and the girls left and Westmacott's letter arrived when Bridget Doheny turned on him and walked out. Misery comes in threes. The boy looked over the heel of bread at John Drew.

"What about your mother, then? What about Bridget?"

"I know nothing, Mr Drew. As God is me witness."

"Didn't she give you any message, then?"

John Drew cut another hunk of bread for the boy and larded it well with butter.

"I only heard her say to me father that she was rale put out."

"Is that so, now . . . rale put out . . ."

"Over them yokes she seen, above in the coachhouse . . . the ould cows' heads and them other yokes . . ."

John Drew thought back to the scene. Eliza had scarcely left with the girls in Willie Hill's pony-and-trap when he heard the clamour of Bridget Doheny in the scullery. Her face was all flustered, as though she had seen a ghost. He couldn't get any good of her at first. Finally, he had followed her out to the coachhouse, where the jaunting car was heeled up in the corner. But she wouldn't cross into the building.

"I'm not going in with them yokes in there, so I'm not!"

"What yokes, Bridget?"

"Them cows' heads and yokes. If I had've known they were there all the time, I would have went long ago, so I would."

And nothing would do her but to burst into tears, throw off her apron and storm out down Sackville Square. Such a scandal! It was all around the town now, of course. The world and his wife would know well that the matter wouldn't be resolved until Eliza Drew returned from London with Theodora. Even then, Mrs Tours would probably have to be prevailed upon to mediate.

There was no point in harrying the boy further, he realised, especially now that he had wolfed down the last of the bread and a large cut of cheese to boot. So John Drew showed him to the door kindly and then went back inside to stare into the fire. When the fire had found itself, he set a couple of damp culm balls on it and stood back to watch the coal smoke rise up the chimney. The house would still be cold without the women, no matter how many fires burned in it. Still, anyone strolling across Sackville Square that morning or coming out of the gates of Terry's brewery would at least know that, despite everything, the Reverend John Drew, among the clutter of rubbings and drawings and script tables that littered the drawing room, had made a fire. As he stood gazing into the flames, he recalled the precise moment, five or six years before, out in the coachhouse, when he had correctly read one of the first cuneatic words on a brick brought back from Mesopotamia.

Nabu-ku-du-ur-ri-usur

Syllables. Not letters. That was the key to it, of course. To think in syllables and, when the strange new Babylonian script demanded it, in ideographs. In ideawords.

The old blackness started sweeping over him then. He saw, in his mind's eye, dry piles of manuscripts with rough cuneiform scripts etched into them, blazing in the hearth. It would be a liberation from the past of ancient tyrants in the desert wastes of Persepolis. A liberation from the hours and days and years of study in dim light, away from the savants of London, in the manse in Aghadoe. But then the moment passed as suddenly as it had come. He knew it would come again, over the coming days though, now that there was no breakwater between him and despair. Now that the women were gone. But he must not give into despair. Must not commit the sin of Job. So John Drew, taking a deep breath, pulled his black frieze coat about him and made purposefully for the coachhouse in the pale midday light to read the brick again.

By Steam Train to Dublin

On the day before the storm, Willie Hill's man appeared with a bockety old trap in Sackville Square to bring Eliza and Theodora to the train and to bring Judith back out to Willie and Violet Hill's for the duration, so that John Drew and his visitor, Mr Westmacott, would have the peace and quiet necessary to carry on their work. It was all a bit of a squash in the trap with all the baggage. At the bottom of the square, a rust-coloured dray horse snorted in the cold September air as it drew a wagon laden with beer barrels past the gates of Terry's brewery. Theodora lisped the slogan on the side of the wagon to herself.

> *Guinness stout is good, no doubt*
> *In barrel or in bottle*
> *But Terry's Ale will never fail*
> *To quench the thirsty throttle.*

Eliza spotted Waxy Daly, cobbler and gossip, standing talking to a red-faced man in a topcoat near the brewery bridge. Both men nodded as the driver flicked the reins, goading the horse on up the hill past the squat Catholic church. Eliza Drew pulled

Theodora close to her, reminding her to keep the new cambric shawl pulled tight, because even in autumn a chill could knock you down, and quinsy was always lurking around the corner at the change of the seasons. Judith, dreamy-eyed and not yet awake, looked out vacantly on the street. They had all dressed by rushlight as John Drew carried their effects out to the gates and their eyes were still stained with sleepiness. Eliza and Theodora could catch up on their sleep on the train to Dublin, but the sleepiness in Judith Drew's eyes was something else. When that dreaming came into her eldest daughter's eyes, it always annoyed Eliza. She felt like shaking her and dragging her back to the world around her. Still, Dr Beatty's School for Young Ladies "especially suited to clergymen's daughters" at Mount Merrion, in Dublin, would soon bring her back to real life. The summer of idling and losing herself in unsuitable books would be over. There would be regularity, early mornings, a strict diet and a rod of iron for mind and morals. It would stand to Judith in later life, as her own boarding school, in Chiswick, had stood to Eliza.

As they turned down the hill, past the graveyard, Eliza Drew once more ran over all the arrangements she had made. She had set out a special routine for Bridget Doheny, with the "big cleaning days" and the "little cleaning days", marked with an X and a Y respectively, on a sheet of writing paper fixed to the pantry door. The house was to be kept in apple-pie order until she returned with Theodora, ten days later. When Mr Westmacott arrived over from London, Bridget was to take account of any particular needs the English scholar might have and make appropriate arrangements. On no account were the men to be bothered with unnecessary interruptions during the two weeks. Aside from his church duties, John Drew should be free to resume the previous summer's British Museum work with Mr Westmacott. A freshly painted jaunting car with a hunched-up figure at the reins approached them at a crook in the road. Eliza glanced across and caught the eye of Billy White, the postman, who was coming back from meeting the train. A burlap sack lay at his feet. Tidings of good and bad news.

"Are we in time, Mr White?"

"You needn't worry yourself at all, ma'am. Them trains does always be late out . . . on account of filling the boilers up."

"I see."

When they reached the mill, halfway between Aghadoe and the train station, Eliza Drew realised that, in her rush to have the girls ready, she had left her locket in the parlour. All of a sudden, despite her best efforts to staunch the flow of her thoughts, the Belfast days were in her mind again. The cold, damp house at Castle Place and the Union where John Drew had ministered to the poor, flooding into the town from the villages of Ulster, look-ing for work and sustenance. And the terrible disaster the Almighty had seen fit to visit on herself and her husband, the worst thing that could befall any woman or any man. A thing she would not name. They had placed an advertisement on the heels of the terrible visitation:

Clergyman will exchange living in Belfast for similar in parish in Wicklow or Wexford or similar.

Their flight, like that of the Jews of Egypt, had been a hasty one, with Theodora just a child and Judith fretting for the loss of friends. Of course, it mightn't have been so bad if they had been fleeing to Wicklow or Wexford, though England was what she herself had wanted. But John Drew had been offered only Aghadoe in the Queen's County, and since her objective was to get the girls out of Belfast as quickly as possible, they had accepted Aghadoe. The possibility of a post in the grove of Acad-eme was long gone. John Drew had been considered too High Church for that. So it was Queen's County, where no one could pronounce a "t" or a "th" to save their lives and the winters were wet and just as miserable as Belfast, if that were possible. But at least cholera and typhus had been kept at bay there.

When the trap crossed the railway bridge, it wheeled sharply right for the stone-cut train station at Ballydermot. Eliza called Theodora to settle her bonnet. Conveyances of every make and shape were drawn up to meet the steam train now taking water from the great green water tower. Eliza Drew spotted a few familiar faces. There was Twinkle Jameson, the wax chandler's daughter, and that English gentleman John Drew said had been sent over from Manchester to sort out some new chemical process in the brewery. She smiled at them vaguely as she helped her daughters down from the trap. They were all standing together on the platform, with Willie Hill's man minding the luggage, when she turned to Judith.

"My locket, Judith . . ."

"Pardon?"

"I've left my locket behind. Tell your father to take care of it until I come home."

And then there was a great fuss and a scene as the girls took it in turns to blame one another for the missing locket. Eliza Drew felt an ache cut through her heart. Then she rallied, hooshing Theodora aboard the trembling train, saying decisively, to no one in particular, "Yes, it will have to wait until I come back."

While the engine got up enough steam to chug out of the station, they waved farewell to Judith on the platform. Eliza reminded her, again, to conduct herself appropriately out at the Hills, and to remember that her return to Dublin and school was imminent. She might also look in on her father, the odd day, to check that everything was in order and that Bridget Doheny was carrying out her orders. The locket must stay where it was. Some things, perhaps, were meant to happen. At least, that was what Mrs Tours, the seamstress, made out. In uneasy moments, Eliza

Drew suspected that this sort of talk was only a stone's throw from papish superstition, the sort of hocus pocus that, when she was a child, had always roused her father to wrath at the dinner table. Isaac Cameron's sidelocks would bristle with anger as he stared across the table at Eliza, his eldest daughter.

"Reason, child! We are all creatures of reason or we are nothing!"

But wasn't reason, too, subject to the vagaries of vanity from time to time? Eliza Drew took out the tartan blanket and wrapped it around her daughter's legs, to guard against the chill of early morning.

What with the stopping and starting at this station and the next and the unexplained delays along the way, the journey to Dublin took about four hours, all in all. The only thing she was really worried about, though, was that the boiler would burst and shower them with scalding water. Rumour had it that it wasn't as much the heat of the water as the weakness of the boilermakers' rivets that accounted for the awful accidents you read about in the English papers. Luckily, she had managed to avoid Twinkle Jameson. With the exception of a crusty little woman in black widow's weeds, she and Theodora had no one to trouble them for most of the journey. Mind you, the old lady, when she spoke, was full of all sorts of morbid intelligences. Cholera was worse in Dublin than the papers were letting on, it seemed, and as for London! Eliza recalled the dinner in Gusty and Edith Lamb's, two weeks earlier, when they, along with the Willingtons of the Commons, had been subjected to a tour de force on the phenomenon of the disease, its provenance and remedies. The whole table had guffawed at the notion, proposed by no less a figure than Mrs Willington herself, that the sudden reappearance of the terrible disease from the East could be put down to divine intervention. It was Eliza who had brought Gusty Lamb to book for his pompous guffaw.

"And do you have a better explanation, Mr Lamb?"

"Well, I certainly don't have a worse one, Mrs Drew!"

Gusty Lamb's cheery, red-raw face couldn't hide the annoyance of being upbraided by a mere minister's wife, of course. They had all taken turns, as the sherry cobblers were served, at puzzling the thing out. Each had vented his own thesis. John Drew, a confirmed miasmatist, favoured the notion that clouds of contagion were at the heart of the whole cholera business. This would explain the movement of the disease from Bengal, right across Europe and the Lowlands, to the heart of the Empire. Edith Lamb, who was looking distinctly dowdy of late, felt that electricity might well lie at the root of the matter; galvanism was all very well, but it was still an unknown quantity. Which comment gave rise to the biggest belly laugh of the evening, from Philip Willington.

"Why, next you'll have the steam engine in the dock, Mrs Lamb!"

"Who knows, Mr Willington? Who knows?"

They all agreed, in the heel of the reel, that prudence was the most important thing. In cooking food, in drinking from strange sources and in mixing in unsavoury circumstances. Who could tell but that a simple handshake mightn't lie behind the transference of cholera between people? Even then, as she sat listening to the chatter at the table, Belfast had been at the back of Eliza's mind. But were such thoughts ever anywhere else? Mrs Tours thought not. She had said so in private moments, when Eliza Drew called into the seamstress's little house in Pound Street, on the pretext of dropping by to leave in some mending. The upright wife of a Protestant minister seeking solace in the hob philosophy of a Catholic seamstress! If anyone even suspected. . .

When they finally arrived in Dublin, a cold, raw wind was blowing up the river. Luckily, they managed to find a cab on the instant, and soon they were on the quays, past the Four Courts and the canvas-covered book stalls, heading for the hotel. The peace and stability that the Four Courts betokened was soon over-shadowed by what they saw further on. For Dublin's streets were a hotchpotch of horse manure, beggars and a few decent folk try-ing to clear a path between both. Hadn't they heard of crossing-sweepers at all here? In London, at least some effort was made to keep things clean in the better quarters. But that was the differ-ence between England and Ireland: Anglo-Saxon order was endemic to one and Celtic chaos to the other. As the cab turned up from Eden Quay, she thought of her sister Hetty Arkwright in the order and ease of her cosy house in Gower Street. That same Hetty, in front of the parlour fire, surrounded by her reading circle: Mrs Meredith, Mrs Rawlings and Mrs Collier. Charles Arkwright up in the study, chatting with a business colleague over some new project, or sorting out some problem at his corn factor's premises, down near London Wall. The sound of little Albert Arkwright above in the playroom, reliving the Napoleonic wars with the tin soldiers Eliza and Hetty's brother Walter Cameron had given him for Christmas.

When the cab pulled up sharply at the little hotel on Westland Row—recommended to Eliza by no less a figure than Edith Lamb—Eliza Drew didn't move until the porter had come down the steps to help with their baggage.

"You'll be Mrs Drew?"

"That's right . . . are our rooms ready?"

"Ready and waiting, ma'am!"

In a jiffy, she and Theodora were settled in their rooms. But after they had rested and freshened up, there was still the shop-ping to be done for London. There would be no time the follow-ing day, when they had to be up early for the Kingstown train and the Holyhead steampacket. There were presents for the Ark-wrights to be got, a couple of other bits and pieces to be tidied up, and then they could rest, once all the chores had been attended to. But first things first, as Isaac Cameron would have it.

III

PER TENEBRAS AD TENEBRAS

In the little two-up-and-two-down in Malpas Street, in Dublin, the whiff of paint spirits stung Fox Keegan into wakefulness. Dressing slowly, he recalled dimly Sam Parker's words as he stumbled up the stairs to bed the night before. His elderly host had been keen to impart the urgency of the message to him. The stranger who had called the night before was certain that Fox Keegan's father, old Jer Keegan down in north Kilkenny, was on his last legs.

"He said tell Fox to speak with Mr Larkin . . ."

Fox Keegan had spent the evening before in a pub off Thomas Street with the same Larkin. What they had all been talking about, he had now only the faintest idea. There was the usual political chit-chat, of course. There was talk of the tenant societies being formed down near Fox's own part of the country. Fox had grandly told the audience that only the wealthiest of farmers would sign up. In the wash of Victoria's visit, speculation was rife on the fate of the rebels of the previous year. Was some sort of pardon in the air? Or was transportation inevitable? It had all seemed so important the evening before, with each word and gesture charged with energy. The last thing Fox recalled was a gutty little man with a cloth cap pulled down over his forehead, going on about the fever sheds down in Kilmainham, where the cholera victims vented their bowels until their bodies finally gave up the ghost. The little man called them closer, in an earnest tone of conspiracy.

"You want to get the smell of the place! Worse than O'Keefe's the knacker's, so it is."

Far better, they had all agreed solemnly, to stick to beer and spirits, when water seemed so hazardous.

"You'll go back to the water, Fox, when it all blows over."

"I will all right."

Truth to tell, Fox had intended going straight home from the dispatch office in Pim's. Straight home to Sam Parker's house in Malpas Street, to settle down to think again about that book he had a notion of writing, the one he had been speaking to Casey about in Maguire's, in Mary Street. A sort of lead-on from *The Lament for Redhill* if, that is, a romantic story could be said to compliment a long ballad.

I will tell you a tale
Of truth and its foe
Round the green fields of Redhill
And the town of Knockroe.

But the need for company after a day in the hustle and bustle of the despatch office in Pim's had got the better of him. And now it was going on eight in the morning, and if he didn't clear his head in time, he wouldn't catch Larkin before work. Squashing a louse between thumb and forefinger, he looked into the speckled mirror on the dressing table, the mirror into which Sam Parker's late wife Sarah must have looked ten thousand times. He considered his own foxy red hair and the dusty brush of a moustache framing a face that smiled on the world, despite its own misgivings. The eyes didn't miss a beat. What was it Larkin said? "The Fox Never Rests."

On the way out the door, Sam Parker's phlegmy northern voice came to him from the little scullery: "You'll not forget the rent this month now, Fox?"

"'Deed and I won't, Sam."

"I don't want to be chasing after you now, like last month."

But the rent could wait. It would be straight to Mr Appleby in Pim's to arrange leave. At the corner of New Street, the stench of the chemical works in the fields behind Malpas Street finally dispelled that of the paint spirits. He found himself wondering at the smells of the world. If maybe you could make a big globe for children and stick the smells of each country on it, India would be spices, the Americas would be cigars and France could be bread and wine and flowers. And Ireland? Poor old Ireland would be the scutter sheds up in Kilmainham, O'Keefe's the knackers and the fine Celtic mist hovering over it all.

The Peasants' 1001 Nights—that was what he had told Casey he would call the blessed book, if it ever got written. It would be a sort of compendium of tales from the Irish countryside, drawn from his own days in Tullyroe and Aghadoe and all the other towns and hamlets he had visited. It would be a match for Mr Banim and Mr Carleton, who, when all was said and done, didn't have a knowledge of real life to rely on, like he did. The opening lines—he had written them only the month before—resounded in his mind.

I have often marvelled to myself at the store of lore and learning to be gleaned from an hour spent in the rustic company of the Irish peasant. Nor have I ever come away from such company, without owning that the singularity of nature and temperament to be found in the cots and cabins of the Irish peasant is second to none. The ancient nobility of the Gael is not to be gainsaid by rancour or spite!

That would set the tone and please any potential readers in London. He had a thousand tales to tell, each one more colourful than the last. Now that he had buried the troubles of more distant days, he could move on to what he imagined himself to be—a storyteller, in the old style. A clatter of little schoolchildren passed noisily by on their way to St Nicholas's. As he watched them gambol down New Street, Tullyroe was in his thoughts again. He pictured the rains lashing against the stone on a winter's morning and the school on the hill, outside Tullyroe, where he had once been monitor. A strange position it had been— working under the direction of a Protestant minister, teaching his tongue and his testament and, if the truth be known, his thoughts. Still, he had got used to it. Live with them or die with them: a thing that Larkin, for all his fine talk, would never understand. Fox Keegan imagined his friend's face looking at him over a guttering candle.

"We're peasants and they're planters, when all's said and done. And they'll never let us forget that."

"And we'll never let ourselves forget it, either."

Of course, that had been before his downfall in Tullyroe, before the first flight to Aghadoe, and the second flight to Dublin.

The Fox has no home.

At the corner of Fumbally's Lane, the smell of fresh bread caught his nostrils, but he ignored it and pushed on towards Cathedral Lane, by the back of the bone yard. If he caught Larkin in time, there might be a mug of tea and a cut of bread for breakfast, maybe. A little knot of scruffy children was gathered outside one of the tenements in Cathedral Lane. Unfortunate little bastards, whose peers down in Tullyroe would have a better chance of survival. He gave them a wide berth, though he was forced to pick his way through a rake of puddles in the filthy street. Better not be late into Pim's if he wanted old Appleby on his side. Who was to say that this wasn't just another false alarm? Maybe his father wasn't really dying down home at all. His father creaked more than a barn door in a storm, his mother always said. Which of these wretched houses was Larkin's? The one with the green door. He had seen it one summer's evening when he had shouldered Larkin to the corner of Kevin Street after a long, lachrymose session in Neary's. A hag in a shawl with her dull, suspicious eyes scrutinised him sharply as he pushed his way up the stairs. On the landing, a small boy was sitting crying, his knee cut open from a fall. Fox Keegan stooped over the child and patted him on the head.

"Would you tell me which is Larkin's door, like a good little man. . ."

"That one there, mister."

Larkin's wife opened the door to him. She had once been a fair-looking woman, Fox realised, but one whose features had long been done down by the burden of childrearing and the profligacy of her man. Over her shoulder, Fox could see Larkin lacing up his boots at the table. A right kip for any copy clerk to be living in, and especially one with a wife and children.

"Can I help you?"

"I've come to see Mr Larkin."

"There's someone here for you, Tom."

Larkin's head rose from the table.

"Tell him it's Keegan . . . John Keegan."

"So you're the bould Fox Keegan, then."

A weary, bitter smile tracked itself across the woman's face. An unwritten rule had been broken, after all: never visit the pauper in his hovel. Far better to spin grand yarns in the Castle Inn or gild the lily of an evening as he and Larkin stood spouting wisdom at the corner of New Street. But Fox had no choice here. He had to know the full story. If he didn't know soon, his father might be boxed and buried before he made Kilkenny.

As his eyes grew accustomed to the gloom, the light filtering through the little window at the back of the room revealed a large shock-headed youth sitting facing Larkin at the table. The boy watched Keegan suspiciously, obviously reading him for a boon companion of his father. The woman stood aside slowly to let Keegan in. A damp, rancid smell hit the visitor's nostrils. Though there was scarcely a stick of furniture in the room, Larkin's hoarse voice was all hail-fellow-well-met.

"You'll have a mug of tea, Fox?"

"If it's no trouble . . ."

"No trouble at all."

In a settle bed under the window, a younger boy was lying, coughing the croupy, hollow sort of cough that you didn't get in fresh air or a dry room. The woman crossed slowly to the fire to rise the teapot. There was no rush. Things would still be the same tomorrow and the morrow after that. The youth at the table pulled a cap down over his forehead and was out the door before she had returned to the table. He gave Keegan a scowl as he passed, but Fox ignored it and sat himself in.

"You'll have to have it black, Mr Keegan."

"Black is good enough, so it is, ma'am."

He glanced over his shoulder at the little boy in the bed as Larkin told him the whole story. Some young countryman, straight up from Kilkenny, had called in looking for Fox in the Horse and Jockey and been directed to Larkin. Fox's eyes tracked Larkin's woman as she went about the room.

"Anyway, we sent him on up to your lodgings. The story sounded serious enough."

"Well, I think he's on the way out."

No, this time it was no false alarm. It sounded as though his father would hardly last the night. Who had the messenger at Sam Parker's door been though? Larkin's memory was very vague: a tall, stooped youth. Probably one of his mother's cousins from the town. The boy on the settle bed started coughing again and called for a mug of tea. It seemed as though his lungs would rend themselves asunder with each bone-dry paroxysm. Fox glanced over his shoulder at the woman and the child.

"They say mountain air is great for that class of a cough . . ."

The woman turned around slowly to face him. Their eyes met. The bitterness welled up in the dark eyes.

"Well, if you hear tell of any mountain air in Cathedral Lane, make sure and be the first to let me know, Mr Keegan."

Larkin's chair screeched across the floor as he stood up. Fox Keegan threw back the last of the cheap, choking tea.

Neither Larkin nor his wife acknowledged one another as they parted at the door, and he and Fox Keegan were well out on Cathedral Lane before they uttered a word. Larkin told Keegan, in a confidential sort of tone, that although his wife could be a very contrary woman, she had her good days, too. Keegan said nothing, preferring the sanctuary of a distant gaze to dabbling in domestic matters. He recalled the cagey question Larkin had thrown him when they were in their cups one night, around the time of the Queen's visit.

"You never married yourself, Fox?"

"Only the once."

"Once is enough. Children?"

"I have a son."

"Begob, and aren't you the quiet man, now."

And with that, Fox had drunk deeper, unwilling to be drawn about the matter and cursing himself that he had responded to Larkin's foil at all.

As they passed Marsh's Library, nothing would do Larkin but to take up that ould sagosha story of his about the library, by way of distracting them both from the scene back in Larkin's hovel on Cathedral Lane. It was a yarn Fox Keegan had heard a thousand times before. How the door of the gentlemen's library had been shut firmly in Larkin's face by the foreigner, and all because he, Larkin, had demanded entrance to the library on the grounds of wanting to peruse some louse-ridden tome or other. Larkin's unshaven face grinned at Fox.

"Didn't our sort write the very books them bastards won't let us read? Eh? And that book of yours will be better nor the lot of them."

"When it's finished."

"That's a fact!"

The image of the woman back in Cathedral Lane came to Fox Keegan again. A bitter bedside companion to his friend's braggadocio. They paused a moment, alongside the Molyneaux Asylum, as though concluding some business deal. Fox Keegan allowed the other man to ramble on until the story had concluded with the usual bitter riposte to reality. Then he said softly, "I'll ask Appleby to let me out in time for the Carlow train . . . take the coach from there."

"And what if he won't leave you go?"

"I'll go anyway and hump the begrudgers!"

"No better man, Fox! Go bury your father and hump the begrudgers!"

Because, the truth was, Fox didn't care much. He had almost had enough of Pim's. If they didn't take him back after the funeral, what about it? There was always London. Or even further afield. The goldmines of California, maybe. They turned together to look up at one of the windows in the Molyneaux. An old blind woman, twice their age, was tapping at the windowpane. Her lightless eyes giving on to the street below.

"That swaddler's giving you the glad eye, Fox!"

"I could do worse, Tom."

Funny thing: a house full of blind women with sightless memories, all reminiscing to one another in their shared darkness. Childhoods lived out through their ears, through their fingertips even. Maybe the whole *Peasant's 1,001 Tales* could be told by a group of blind women. Boccacio in Ossary.

"Per Tenebras ad Tenebras, if my Latin is right."

"Here we go."

"When they die, you know . . . from shadow to shadow."

"Here, Fox, I'm not wasting the flowery days of me youth listening to bad poetry . . . come on."

They parted at the corner of Golden Lane, promising to meet up the following week when the sad business in Kilkenny was done. At the corner of Chancery Lane, Fox took stock of a couple of derelict house, with the grass sprouting out of the floors and the fireplaces still set into upstairs walls, open to the elements. Where was all that living gone now? All that love? Vesta, the goddess of the hearth, had fled beyond recall. Soon the old house in Tullyroe would be like this. The house itself would be for tumbling maybe. Before night was out, his father, a herdsman who could tend cattle better than the best animal doctor in all of Ireland, or England for that matter, would be away to the dark room, where all the blind women were headed. All gone, with the death of the hearth. As he passed down Golden Lane for Stephen Street, the sound of cattle lowing in Dublin Castle yard came to his ears, and he thought of that to which he would be returning before nightfall. An older world. Rude life ruminating in muddy autumn pastures. Ignorant beasts that knew neither day nor hour. And were better off for it, perhaps.

"I have a son."

Why couldn't he have kept his big mouth shut, that night with Larkin? Larkin probably had it all over Dublin the following day: "Fox Keegan has a bastard down in Kilkenny." Only the boy wasn't a bastard, whatever else he was.

He scurried by the double doors of Pim's and around into the alleyway. Hopkins, the little rat-faced timekeeper with the oiled back hair, was standing on the steps as he slipped by. Fox doffed his hat and settled his collar. Neeson, the chief despatch office clerk, was already in the little cabin when he arrived. He looked over his lunettes at Fox, his paunch pressed against the slanted writing table facing Fox's.

"Get a move on there, Mr Keegan."

"Shake of a lamb's tail: I have to have a quick word with Mr Appleby."

"You'll find him in Mr Hobson's office."

"Sound."

And then Fox was out like a flash through the double doors of the despatch office and across the floor to the offices by the haberdashery. He didn't even pause to give his customary wink to Dilly Shiels, she of the bright, Protestant smile. He didn't stop, in fact, until his fist was rapping on Mr Hobson the under-manager's door. It was stout, stentorian Mr Appleby who let Fox in to press his case for compassionate leave. Both men listened to him gravely, glancing at one another from time to time. With any luck, he might make the Carlow train and take the coach from there. Then a car from Kilkenny to Tullyroe. He might be in time for his father's last words. Or the first of the wake, at least. It all hung on jowly old Mr Appleby, with his striped waistcoat and his little, brass fob watch.

IV

LORNA LOVEGROVE AMONG THE MOORS

Mrs Tours looked over her glasses as she stitched, gawking out on to Pound Street. A couple of brewery men were standing over by the river, pulling on clay pipes, tobacco smoke curling into the bright, cold air. A thin, pale-faced boy in a flat cap was dragging a stubborn billy goat along on a rope and shouting at the little white head. One of the men nodded at the boy.

"You've a rale contrary one there, young Moran."

"He won't be so contrary if he gets my toe up his hole, so he won't."

Mrs Tours snapped a piece of thread with her teeth and went back to her needlework.

At the end of the day, everyone has to come to me to have an arse put in their trousers or a dress let out. Protestant and Papist, they all end up on my doorstep. Even here's-my-head-my-arse-will-follow Reverend John Drew that's so grand in himself, with all his quare studies. But I know the gallery that's going on up in his house. And his wife hardly on the train for London. Because Hoppy Fortune had it off of little Sarah Malone and her poor hunchedy back. And Hoppy Fortune told me everything. "Bridget Doheny is after running out on ould Drew, so she is."

All on account of the cows' heads and the sucked-out eggs that the Very Great Reverend John Drew kept out in the coach house. Hoppy Fortune said that Bridget Doheny was maybe thinking that she wouldn't be right in her woman's way if she came near any of those things. As if she could do with opening her legs any more anyway. And that youngest chap of Bridget Doheny's always reminds me of Tim Delaney, of the Long Road. It wouldn't surprise anyone if the good husband, Ned Doheny, was left out of that particular operation altogether. Anyway, I have to finish putting this hem in Sally Derham's dress or I'll be ate. More style than sense the Derham girls have, if you ask me. Make up for what God didn't give them in the face department. Of course, John Drew would really like me to beat Bridget Doheny back before Eliza Drew returns from London with little Theodora and raises all hell over the cows' heads and the eggs. Because he isn't man enough to do it himself. It vexes him that Eliza Drew comes up for a little chat with me, every now and then, letting on she's coming up to collect some mending. It's like this, so it is, Mr Dr Drew: men don't know and women don't tell. The minister's wife listening to sermons from a Catholic widow. Mrs Tours, the seamstress, and the minister's wife—all equal before God when the arse is out of your trousers.

Mrs Tours looked again at the bit of paper she had found in John Drew's frock coat that she had mended just before the last fair. Bit of paper she had meant to give back to him but never had.

Ideas-pictures-syllabary-alphabet
What is what?

Rale good English, that is. What is what?

It's that young one of his, Judith, he should be worrying about though, and not Bridget Doheny or all them quare words from the East. Because your daughter is in heat, Reverend Dr Mr Drew. Half the town can see it. Mrs Tours sees it. But then, Mrs Tours sees everything. And what she doesn't see, she hears. When I think of the lovely piece of embroidery Judith Drew gave me as a present from the Dame School, when they came here first. Gold thread on velvet.

Vade Mecum

Now, tell me this, and tell me no more, Dr Drew: did you know that your little Judith, staying innocently out in Willie Hill's while Eliza Drew and Theodora are in London, is keeping a nightly tryst by Taylor's well? I bet you didn't, sir. And who told me this? Dan Brady, the lodger, that's who. The other night, a moonlit night, when he crossed Campion's field to the well for me, he was stepping in by the ditch, and didn't he see the two of them: Judith, the minister's daughter from Sackville Square, not as big as a God's cow, and some other stookawn, and they holding hands beyond at the well. So Dan Brady stops where he is until they pass. She slips off back across the fields to Willie Hill's mansion and, I suppose, back in the window to Cassie Hill's bedroom, and me brave bucko goes back about his own business. Dan Brady didn't say who the great lover was, but then, how would he know and he only in the town a wet week. I told him to hould his whist and tell no one. And that he must be mistaken. But Mrs Tours will find out. By Jaesus and she will ! For I'll go and fetch the water myself tonight. Or tomorrow night. And I'll redden that fellow's ears when I catch him, because I swore a hole in a brass bucket I'd keep a weather eye open for Eliza Drew, just in case madame got up to any mischief. And Mrs Tours keeps her word. Always has. Even when it came to covering up for that blackguard Fox Keegan, all those years ago. For better or for worse.

Mrs Tours got up to rise the kettle from the hob. The spout was steaming and the cat sat puzzling to herself in front of the summer hearth. Another few minutes would finish the gingham dress. Then there were the couple of bits and pieces for the Leonards: a torn shirt, a fork for a pair of pants and a little fancy bonnet that needed a bit of braid put on it. She wet the tea then, mindful of the voices out on Pound Street once more. As the scalding water poured over the dusty leaves, she glanced at the newspaper on the table.

Eliza Drew must be in London by now. All those fine, wide streets and the grand get-up of the ladies. They have the cholera there, all the same, like the way it is above in Dublin. Worse it got, over the summer. The news-papers Willie Hill left in the other week are full of it. Isn't it well for my Paddy he is out of the whole whorin' place and over where they have gold in the mountains and the sun shines all the time. Where a man can grow three crops a year and more. But what good is a letter every now and then for an old widow woman like myself? Anyway, I have my letter written and ready to go by Billy White, if ever it gets to California with all the gold-mad men is in it.

Dear Paddy,

I received yours of the 6th of February on the 10th of August last and would have answered before now but you will be suprized when I tell you I had not the time to do so. I was glad to find by your letter that yee have arrived safe in San Francisco and are employed. I am not suprized as it is only what yee have always meritted. I don't know if the wayge you say is good, bad or indifferent. There is no great improvement in this country since yee left. Wee have still the potatoe blight every bit as bad. Jack Dollard ran off to America and hasnt been heard tell off since. Tom Nolan's place is gone and an English fellow has got it now. Many farms are idel. Butter is nearly 80 shillings a cwt. There is talk of the Cumminses going off to Sydney one of these days. Ned Phelan is after marring the Stokes girl from Gransha and there is great talk about the haste which is a thing I should not be writing at all, maybe. I am sending you on The Nation *and* The London Dispatch *with this. There is a poem of one Mr John Keegan in* The Nation. *The same "Fox" Keegan that nearly had us all in the barracks, once upon a time. There is great talk among the young ones of the gold out in California. I have not gave any of them your lodgings in case you are plaged with them in the future. The dearness of things here—is it the same or worse in California?*

I conclude this wishing you health, wealth and the blessing of the giver of all good gifts Almighty God is the sincere prayer of your mother.

Ann Tours

P.S. There is great talk of tennant wrights down in Kilkenny and they say the vexation of the whole thing will start off again soon. You are as well off above in California.

Mrs Tours set down her lunettes on the kitchen table and wiped her eyes. The cat was stretched out before the hearth now. Minding her mood. Waiting for a sign. Waiting until she had stopped crying.

There it is, Paddy—we will never meet again in this world anyway. And I am here and your poor father lies under the damp clay above in the graveyard. Killed cleaning out the lampers from the brewery horse's mouth with a wire brush. A little slip and he goes and cuts himself and the poison runs through him like the plague. Only lasted long enough to make my belly big with two sons. You and poor little Mike, God be good to him. So, Godspeed, Paddy. And God send you don't take up with a low woman there. At least you never got caught up with the Ribbon business here. Burning people out of their homes and cutting the legs of cattle, like that stookawn Keegan and his poem. A right rigamarole of a thing, it was.

And spare the land and spare the soil
The stealth of scheming Saxon toil.

Saxon toil, my arse. Now, how was it the Reverend Mr Drew and Fox Keegan ever took up together? And what did they talk about, all those years ago, up in that grand little house of his on Sackville Square? And Eliza Drew and her nerves at her because of the boy in Belfast. With Dr Drew and Mr Foxy Keegan scribbling notes and looking over maps and making big talk about the times that were in it, instead of living in the times that are.

A memory, from an evening a few years before, came tickling Mrs Tours' thoughts. She had been sitting working on a bit of mending as Eliza Drew looked on.

"Mr Foxy Keegan has a history, Mrs Drew."

"Is that so, Mrs Tours?"

The big childeyes of Eliza Drew. Like she was fit to cry.

"I had it from Waxy Daly, who has family in that part of the country, that he had a wife there, and left her . . ."

"Oh, dear!"

"Left her when she had this poor idiot of a child for him that can't put two words together."

The great patriot Mr Foxy-Loxy Keegan. The patriots with their great swagger and their little gentlemen saluting the Queen in their pantaloons. How well Fox Keegan scarpered out of his own dung heap when things got tough. Great fellow. Lodging with me and doing the books in the brewery for Mr Terry, and he out every night here in Aghadoe coorteekan in every cabin of the town. Then getting rale grand in himself and falling in with the minister.

"And what did he do in his own village, Mrs Tours?"

"He was some class of a schoolmaster. Not short on brains, anyway, Fox Keegan."

"A schoolmaster?

"That's the sort you get now. A lot of learning but no rearing on them at all."

"Indeed."

To tell the truth, I was fond enough of the Fox, behind it all. He put me in mind of my Paddy over in California with the other madmen. Sometimes I let on to Eliza Drew that I can't see some word because of my eyes and she helps me read it. A word like "obfuscate".

Isn't there enough to be going on with in the London Gazette *and the* Dublin Post *and* The Nation *without having to read all those strange signs, Reverend Mr Drew? Chamomile. Eliza Drew took the dried chamomile that I advised her on the journey. I'll have to put a word in her ear though about little Miss Judith Drew. A minister's daughter carrying on the like of that. But what is to be done if things gets out of hand? No use in talking to old bore-your-balls-off Drew up in his holy house. He wouldn't know what to do; he'd make a mystery out of it, and the next thing the girl has a touch of the other. The story is very simple, Reverend Dr Mr Drew: you lie down with dogs, you get up with fleas. I'll find out first of all who me brave bucko is that's tampering with the minister's daughter, and I'll lighten his load for him, so I will. Another Mr Foxy Keegan sweetalking a young girl into sharing her charms in the moonlight. Of course, it's all the reading of those romances that has the girl the way she is. That book she left behind her that day in the sewing basket.* Lorna Lovegrove Among the Moors.

> For Lorna, the dark Moor's touch was the strongest threat to her honour that she had ever borne. A shiver ran down her spine, and she drew the crocheted shawl tight about her tender person.

Talk in books like that puts a young woman in a strange way of thinking. You can be certain sure a man wrote it. What happens to us early marks us for life though, that's one sure thing. I lost my mother, and Mr Fox Keegan saw the great scrap with the peelers at Redhill, the skulls being cracked all around him and the bodies buried in secret at the dead of night.

Vade Mecum. *It was far simpler when Judith Drew stuck to her embroidering. But that's the way of things. Young women gets quare notions of themselves. But then, that's what keeps the world turning.*

Mrs Tours stood up from the table, shifted her weight from one leg to the other and called to the cat.

"Whisht till I get you a sup of milk, alanna."

She lifted out the shiny gallon can from the safe and crossed out into the yard, through the scullery. There, she poured a saucerful for the cat, mixing it with water from the rain barrel by the back door. Then, when the cat began lapping at the water-milk, Mrs Tours crossed back into the scullery again, pulling the door behind her. As she crossed into the parlour, she saw a slightly stooped figure in a top hat pass the window on the way out of town.

I declare to Jaesus, if that isn't Mr Reverend Dr Drew out on his parambles again! Will I call him? Let on I want news of Eliza? Bring him in and ask him about Bridget Doheny and his daughter? Probably walking out to Willie Hill's place to see the little vixen sunning herself in the drawing room, all sweet and cosy and innocent for Papa. It's easy fool men. No, I'll leave it. Tonight though, I'll slip out across Campion's field and hide in the bushes with the bucket. And if Missy Judith Drew turns up, there'll be a right vade mecum. I'll get the measure of the whole thing then, and sort out that little gold digger with his eye on her drawers. And by the time of the next pig fair on Tuesday, I'll have settled for them both. Because I still can't credit it really is Judith Drew. I'll have to see her with me own eyes, so I will, before I make any spake.

When John Drew was safely out of sight and the danger of an audience was past, Mrs Tours attended to the fire, rising up the ashes and bedding down a few sods on top to keep it in for the night. Then, while the last light of the evening was still in the window, she sat down to finish off a bit of darning she had neglected that morning.

V

AN ENCOUNTER IN DUBLIN

George's Street was full of shawlies and their squawking children, wretched women with barefoot urchins who clogged up the streets and the little alleyways around Dame Street. Eliza Drew pulled her daughter close to her. Once inside the door of Pim's great store, the smell of the beeswax and the starch reassured her. If business was slack though, the drapery assistants weren't exactly falling over one another to catch her eye. Their arms rested on the counters with the big brass measuring rods, and their tone was languorous in the extreme. Well for them, Eliza Drew thought to herself.

"Can I help you at all, ma'am?

Theodora was full of chat about the colourful cloths and the material at the haberdashery counter. They eyed the bales of tweed and cavalry twill on the great shelves. Theodora ran her hand along a bolt of navy serge lying on the counter. A little chit of a girl, hardly the size of Theodora herself, smiled at her from behind the counter, but Eliza Drew gazed over the girl's head and caught the eye of the middle-aged man beside her. If you wanted something done in business, the authority of a man was required.

The man was over in a flash. She told him that she wanted to be sure that everything would be delivered to Noonan's Hotel by that evening, at the latest. The draper's assistant, in his grey waist-coat, made a great show of reassuring her, but she insisted on further clarifying the matter. She was to catch the train to Kingstown with her daughter the following morning and, from there, the steampacket to England. Any delay in delivery would cause great inconvenience. It was settled that, when Eliza had made her purchases, a direct arrangement would be made with the despatch office at the back of the store.

On the way upstairs to the linen department, they glanced in at the despatch office through the sombre double doors behind the staircase. There were racks and racks of parcels tied in twine and sealed with wax. A couple of handcarts lay against a far wall. At the street side of the despatch office, in a little wooden cabin, a heavy-set man with a fair moustache was writing down names and numbers into a great ledger. Every so often he would call out a number, and a voice from somewhere among the racks would reply.

"Three hundred and twenty six, Mr Moran."

"That's for Mulkerns . . . Capel Street."

They watched as the stout man called through the little hatch in the wooden cabin for one of the delivery boys. A little rascal with a jaunty cap appeared then, grabbed his allotted parcel, and was off into the laneway like the wind. It all appeared brisk and businesslike.

They proceeded to the first floor to choose the linen from Belfast that was to be Hetty Arkwright's family present. Eliza recounted for Theodora, as in a school lesson, the day trip they had once taken into the countryside of Antrim, before Theodora was born, to escape the loathsome atmosphere of Belfast. She and John Drew and Judith had watched the harvesters, knee deep in the mire of the ponds, as they drew the bundles of flax out of the foetid water. And the whiff of the retting ponds!

"Was Edward alive then?"

"Yes . . . yes, of course."

Eliza pulled her thoughts back to the clean, white, fresh linen, a symbol of purity from humble beginnings. In those days, it had seemed as though half of Ulster was covered with bleaching greens. As though the Almighty Himself had somehow dropped these enormous handkerchiefs on to the fields of Ulster so that they might all marvel at them. When she had paid for the linen, she hurried downstairs with Theodora, leaving strict orders that the linen be sent down to the lace counter, so that both could be delivered together. At the lace counter, a stout woman in a ruffled collar drew out a great number of samples from a glass case. Eliza finally settled on the Carrickmacross work. She knew she would in the end, having first admired the material the night of the Christmas ball in Eastholme, Captain Neal's house, beside the brewery. She chose a mantilla and a table set in it for Hetty. The mantilla might never be worn and the table set never used, but it would be displayed as a keepsake of her visit and a sign of sisterly affection. A tall youth appeared at her shoulder with the heavy parcel of linen sheets. He spoke deferentially to the lace woman.

"These have to go with the lace."

The boy was asked to go and fetch someone directly from the despatch office. The lace woman told Eliza she understood the worry of the whole thing.

"It wouldn't do to arrive in London with one arm longer than the other."

Eliza Drew flinched at the familiar turn of phrase and fixed her eye on Theodora, who was sitting on a chair by the counter, fidgeting with the little parcel her mother had asked her to hold. Hearing the heavy tread of the despatch clerk behind her, she turned about slowly.

Busy remonstrating with Theodora for taking the small, red

abacus she had bought for Albert Arkwright out of its wrapping paper, she didn't recognise him at first. The lace woman was whispering to herself as she checked the sum Eliza had laid out, but Eliza's thoughts were all in a spin.

"Three pounds four and sixpence . . . as it happens, there's a small reduction this month . . . let me see, now."

She should have recognised Fox Keegan's eyes, if not his face, and that awful moustache of his which was better suited to someone of superior age and station. How long had it been? Three or four years. She knew by the narrowing of the eyes that he had recognised her immediately. It was the same type of look Waxy Daly had given them that morning, as they passed out of the square in Aghadoe. Country cute and always watch your back with them. Never forget that we settled their land. "Not by the sweat of your brow have you inherited this land . . ." If a thousand years passed they wouldn't forget. Not that they had bothered working it in the first place.

The voice of the little lace woman came to Eliza Drew from a great distance now.

"Mr Keegan here will sort out everything, madam."

Mr Keegan indeed! The last night they had met in the rectory in Aghadoe was the day after the awful business at the new train station, the night the unfortunate ganger-man was beaten to death. Mr Willington had said it was party spirit, pure and simple. Some Ribbon shenanigans behind it. Or maybe an old debt being repaid, perhaps. Hadn't it come out in court—or had she imagined it?—that the dead man had once been a bailiff in Kilkenny? Whatever the reason, the affair had ended in death outside one of the big grey canvas tents set up for the railway workers at Ballydermot. Two of the scoundrels had been caught. One had been hanged and the other released, for lack of evidence. The Judas who had hidden beneath the railway parapet and given the signal had never been satisfactorily identified in

court. But Eliza Drew knew, as did half of Aghadoe. She was looking at him now. Fox Keegan's little mouth opened at the corners.

"Mrs Drew!"

"Mr Keegan."

"And that must be little Theodora. My, how she's grown. And
how is Mr Drew?"

"Busy at home."

"I'm sure. And how can I be of service?"

They had first met Fox Keegan at the summer fête in the
brewery, when Theodora had just turned two. He had been taken
on as a clerk in the brewery. Mrs Tours had it on cast-iron
authority that he really had abandoned a wife and child in north
Kilkenny. A nice recommendation to have for a visitor to the rectory. And John Drew, more fool he, had lapped it up, all the
charming stories and yarns, like some ridiculous explorer in the
depths of Africa. There were snatches of conversations Eliza
Drew had overheard in the dining room as the men sat at a table
crowded with papers and maps.

"You see, Fox, these Gaelic sounds, I suspect, may be very old
Hebrew words. Tullach looks very much like Tel."

She was brought back to the moment by Fox Keegan's
chuckle as he watched Theodora calculate the change on the
abacus.

"She'll mind your money for you, Mrs Drew."

"I can manage that for myself, thank you."

And all the while, Fox Keegan just stood there at the counter,
as though waiting for her to say something else. It took all day, of
course, to fold the spider-web mantilla and the table set and pack
it neatly in the brown paper, then to bind it and seal it just so.
She heard the assistant whisper to herself as she counted out the
coppers and the silver.

"You have too much here, madam."

"Really?"

And then there was the whole rigmarole of recounting the silver and the copper. Fox Keegan smiled with his wide blue eyes at herself and Theodora. It was the smile of the native all right. Concealed behind those eyes were cunning and artifice and God-knows-what. It was the sort of devious, two-faced, silver-tongued cunning that made the likes of Fox Keegan collaborators by day and conspirators by night. The lace woman slid a shiny shilling back across the counter. Theodora reached for it and handed it to her mother. It was in that instant Eliza thought of saying it. She straightened herself up, looked the tall, thin man before her in the eye and said, "The luck penny, Mr Keegan . . . here you are."

That took him aback all right. The smile on the lips suddenly gainsaid by the anger in the eyes, the sort of vengeful anger the likes of Keegan couldn't hide, no matter how they dressed it up in all sorts of smooth talk.

"Are you sure it's not the Queen's shilling in disguise, Mrs Drew?"

The lace lady interjected at that point, her plump, puffy face pushing over the counter at them. Just to clarify, or so she said, that the linen and lace would be delivered to Noonan's Hotel on time. Fox Keegan spoke to the woman out of the corner of his mouth, keeping his eyes fixed on Eliza Drew. They heard the lace lady's breathless voice from the side.

"Will you be dealing with the delivery yourself, Mr Keegan?"

"As Mrs Drew knows, we have servants for that sort of thing."

"I beg your pardon, Mr Keegan?"

"Hewers of wood and drawers of water. That's the Book of Deuteronomy, Mrs Drew, isn't it? Or do I have that right?"

Eliza Drew turned on her heel and was out the door of Pim's again, ignoring the impulse to call for the manager and have Fox Keegan upbraided for his tongue. She practically wrenched the arm off poor little Theodora in her haste to put Grafton Street between herself and Fox Keegan. She wouldn't put it past him to find some pretext for leaving the store and following her, but he would hardly be so bold as to appear at Noonan's. Yes, her words had galled Fox Keegan, because she knew the secret: that the rectory and John Drew had been Fox Keegan's alibi that wet, windy night. And Mrs Tours was part of the same scandal, too.

When Theodora was in bed, Eliza Drew sat in the lounge under the coloured lithograph of Queen Victoria arriving at Kingstown, writing a couple of letters at the bureau in the corner. She had promised herself an evening promenade along Brunswick Street and up across Carlisle Bridge, which she now had to forego out of fear that Fox Keegan might accost her if she ventured out of the hotel. When she kissed Theodora in sleep, later that night, a frown flitted across Eliza Drew's brow as she recalled, once more, her older daughter's strange smile at the train station, a smile that betrayed a new guile in Judith Drew. Eliza Drew didn't know what it meant exactly. In sleep, she clutched her pillowcase anxiously, as the locket on the cold mantelpiece in Aghadoe wove its way into her dreams and a voice whispered to her, over and over again: "Filium non habeo . . . filium non habeo . . . filium non habeo."

Unknown to Eliza Drew's waking mind, the image of her dead son, Edward Drew, was roaming across the fields of unreason, despite the hardness of her own heart and the rein she thought she had on her thoughts.

VI

DR DREW IN PURDAH

John Drew awoke to the sound of hooves on the square and the thwack of Jer Dooley's ashplant across the backs of the cattle he was herding out by the Burrow. If it hadn't been for the lowing of the cattle, he thought to himself, he wouldn't have known it was so late in the morning, because he had quite forgotten, despite Eliza's explicit instructions, to wind the great clock in the hall. In the parlour, the pile of papers was exactly where he had left it the night before. Why had he stayed his hand at the last moment and not consigned the whole lot to the fire? he wondered. Perhaps out of fear of that which he was to preach about on the Sunday. The prophet Habbakuk's plaintiff whine: "Oh, Lord, how long shall I cry for help. And thou wilt not hear?"

There were leaks in the roof, in the little valleys facing the square. On windy days, the rain edged its way in under the lead flashing. It would be another extraordinary debit from the parish account books. Bianconi appeared at his feet, rubbing against him in an earnest of goodwill, wondering where the three women were gone, no doubt. He thought the creature had somehow sensed their imminent departure from the air of anticipation and the strange clothes. Theodora, too, had been more solicitous of the creature's comfort than usual, which had probably made the animal all the more suspicious. Hard to think of a cat as a man-thing. Inscrutable orientals, they were. Small wonder they had come from the East.

He set about a desultory clean-up of the parlour. He left the dinner plates and vessels out in the scullery and made a great effort to rouse himself out of a lethargy that now seemed almost sinful. There were voices out on Sackville Square and the sound of a cart coming in from the Burrow. That's what he needed: a brisk walk to shake off the cobwebs and to drive away the spectre of self-pity and remorse. He was still clearing up when he heard the latch lift on the back door.

"I'm back, Dr Drew."

"And what about your mother?"

"She only said for me to come up and light the fire."

He watched the boy set the bundle of faggots down on the stone hearth, half-listening to him.

"Tim Delaney's above on the roof, Dr Drew."

He left the boy to set the fire and made for the front garden to watch the man on the roof, in the breeches and bowler. Tim Delaney's ruddy face turned slowly towards him, from the top of the ladder.

"I didn't want to be putting in on you, Dr Drew, so I just started off."

"Quite so."

A cart was drawn up outside the barracks, its driver in deep conversation with Henry Arkins, the sergeant. From where he stood, John Drew couldn't hear a word, but the man at the top of the ladder had the whole story anyway. There had been a bit of a to-do in John Gordon's at the bottom of the square, the night before. Something over a right of way. Words had been exchanged and a mêlée had ensued. Tim Delaney spoke between a mouthful of nails. Had John Drew not heard anything, and he only at the far side of the square?

"I was in the Land of Nod, I'm afraid."

"Where's that, now, Dr Drew?"

"Asleep. I was asleep."

He watched the hammer tip-tap the flat-headed nails through the lead flashing. The man with the mouthful of metal eased himself further on to the roof. The valley nearest the porch looked very patchy, he noted. It would need a proper job before winter set in. Henry Arkins, catching John Drew's eye from the barracks, nodded at him, and John Drew smiled in return. Behind the sound of the tap-tapping hammer, he heard the crackle of the parlour fire taking. Telling the man on the roof to call him when all was done, John Drew went back into the house to hunt for the accounts ledger.

There was no doubt about it—Bridget Doheny's little labourer really was worthy of his hire. Not a feckless fool, like the father. The boy had coaxed the fire into a real blaze. The flames flickered brightly, throwing shadows on to the walls of the parlour and sending the aroma of bracken about the whole house. When the boy was gone, John Drew sat down to the plat-ter of meat and bread that he had put aside for himself. He was musing over the whole question of telling the time—wax candles as against the coils of the clock as against Jer Dooley's cows—when his eye fell once more on Westmacott's letter, and he was drawn back to the balmy summer days of the previous year in London. Eliza and he had put up with the Arkwrights, on Gower Street, while the girls had spent the couple of weeks with Willie Hill's family outside Aghadoe. There had been panic about the streets of London though. Even behind the solid stone of the British Museum, you could feel it. Sandbags around the muse-um—wasn't that overdoing it a little? Westmacott had asked—because of the great protest down on Kennington Common. The government had blocked the bridges across the Thames to stop the Chartist leader O'Brien and the rabble. Imported extremism was always the worst kind, especially French. Strange to say, the real enemy had been within the walls of the museum itself: two of the curators had been carried away, not by agitators and latter-day Chartists, but by cholera. How he hated all that self-righteous anger though. Why wasn't it possible just to sit down and sort things through? Of course, the Irish business was just as bad. One extreme wanted to have all the Protestants in Ireland extirpated, while the other side wanted the natives kowtowing for eternity. But these were different times. Playing Israelites and Philistines was a poor way to do things. Yes, all extremism was bad. *Res ipsa locutor.* Like the copy of *Pastorini's Letter* that Hardwicke had shown him in Belfast. A great Catholic diatribe about how the Day of Judgement was nigh for the Protestants in Ireland, when they would be vanquished and Rome would reign supreme. Its author had calculated the expected year with all sorts of suspect jiggery-pokery. Turning letters and words into numbers. What year was the great revenge to be? 1832 or 1833? Got that wrong, my learned friends. We're still here. We need one another too much now. Mind you, peasants will believe any sort of nonsense if they are encouraged by their leaders. Gives them hope. Dignity even. A thing Eliza would never understand. Whip a dog and it bites back when you least expect it. Planter and peasant. Numbers and letters business in *Pastorini's Letter* was stolen from the Jews, like so much else. Of course, a letter is a number, when all is said and done. Babylonian. Cold letters on colder stone. On rock faces in Persia. East India Company inscriptions from Lake Van. Layard's miracle work at Nineveh. Others skulking in the shadows to glean all the credit, for his, John Drew's, endeavours. But was he now to add the sin of pride to the list of other failings? He found himself reading Westmacott's letter again.

My Dear John,

I hope this letter finds yourself, Eliza and the girls in good fettle. It is with great chagrin that I have to tell you that I will be unable now to keep up our assignation over the next two weeks. If this notice takes you by surprise, it is so because the intelligence has just been communicated to me. I have been prevailed upon to be part of a delegation to Paris, in connection with the Turkish business, of which I can speak little in a letter such as this. It is quite a bolt from the blue. All my protestations have been in vain. It seems that matters in that area have become fraught, of late, and that the Foreign Office insists on sending my good self as part of the diplomatic "expeditionary force" to seek some temporary resolution. Although I will gladly do my duty, for Queen and country, it comes as a great blow to my hopes of capping the good work we had done on cuneatics last year.

Layard's book has fired the popular imagination, of course, and made ancient Assyria a place of great intrigue and speculation. An empire as ancient as Egypt or Greece. A civilisation that was great before Rome. Of course, Layard had given a good account of himself and his researches in the book. A brave man, no doubt. Even Westmacott had agreed on that, having met with Layard at one of Lady Dunboyne's soirées in Hampstead. But the real work of unravelling the words of the Chaldean ancients would not be done in fancy drawing-rooms but in darkened studies, in England and France and Germany. Aye, and in a small rectory in Aghadoe, in the Queen's County. There was enough heart in the parlour fire now to settle the matter, if he really had the courage to. To consume a hundred books and a thousand deluded pamphlets.

John Drew crossed slowly to the fire and threw a fresh log on. He took up the locket on the mantelpiece. The locket snapped open. His son's serious little face looked out at him from the cold calotype of the picture. Strong features, yes. Eliza's dark eyes. Little like Judith, all told. Bridget Doheny's son came to mind then. A good-humoured little soul. Who wasn't to say but that he was every bit as clever as Edward Drew had been? He snapped the locket shut suddenly, wondering to himself whether a letter wouldn't arrive from Eliza in connection with the locket. But no, she would play it down for herself, consign her feelings to the flames. But feelings and memories would, like the fabled phoenix, rise from the embers. Bridget Doheny's son had stirred something in him, and he fought back the tears in his eyes as he pretended to himself that he was looking for the accounts ledger.

Late that afternoon, Willie Hill fetched up at the rectory. John Drew had just finished with Mrs Morehampton, of the Commons, in connection with arranging a visit to her sick mother, when he heard Willie Hill's heavy fist on the porch door. He had come directly from the boulting mill, by the Beggar's Bridge, and he looked quite comical, carrying the little wicker basket of provisions that his wife had sent over, covered in a charming red-and-white gingham cloth. The basket was full to the brim with more than John Drew could possibly eat: hard cheese and oatmeal cakes, pies and spotted dick and a dozen fresh eggs. The big man set the basket down on the table.

"Violet sent this over by me, John."

"Well, isn't that very thoughtful of her."

In a moment, they had left the outside world behind them. Willie Hill had brought over a bundle of newspapers—the *London Gazette*, the *Dublin Chronicle* and the *Belfast News Letter* among them—and they sat to reading and rummaging through the news of the past weeks as they chatted. They were both agreed that there would be hell to pay over the riots at Dolly's Brae, up in Ulster, now that the assizes were in session. Party spirit on both sides had been responsible for the deaths in Armagh on July twelfth.

"Will there ever be peace in that quarter, do you think, John?"

"Not in our lifetime, I'm afraid."

"My mother, God rest her, used to say the same—thirty years ago."

"And our children will still be saying the same, three hundred hence, mark my words."

The London papers were saturated with the Bermondsey murder. It was clear that the Manning couple had done away with that poor man, Murphy—was that his name? Willie Hill wasn't sure, only that it made a change from reading about suicides by drowning and Prussic acid and the latest figures for the cholera epidemic.

It was as he was setting the black-bottomed kettle on the hob that Willie Hill noticed, for the first time, the pile of manuscripts by the hearth. He didn't say anything at first, just went about, humming and hawing to himself, until the kettle started gurgling. Having taken down two big porcelain mugs from the dresser in the scullery, he sat in by John Drew at the fire.

"'Fornenst' the glow', as they used to say up north."

"Indeed."

Willie Hill tapped his foot on a spot in front of the pile of manuscripts. John Drew looked over his lunettes at his companion. Willie Hill said that he didn't mean to be presumptuous, but was John Drew seriously contemplating doing what he thought he was: burning the fruits of a score years and more? Was this to be the action of the *Pastor Fido,* who had not only defended the faith at the famous debate in Dungannon, all those years ago, but whose name was now beginning to appear in the mouths of the savants of the Academy? John Drew shifted awkwardly under the stern gaze. He suddenly felt like a little boy caught out for some trifling misdemeanour. He took a gulp of the hot, sweet tea.

"Things were clearer in Dungannon. We knew where we stood. We could take down the Roman edifice, brick by brick."

Willie Hill didn't speak for a moment. He busied himself with perusing some manuscript which was quite beyond him. He glanced at one of the cuneatic tables, with its wedge-shaped icons, then he cast an eye over a couple of offprints from the Academy in Dublin. His eyes fixed on a sheet of jottings and a sentence which read: "Some signs = 2 or 3 different sounds? / 2 or 3 different meanings? c.f. Van and Persepolis tables."

Now his hand was resting on John Drew's shoulder; the older, frailer man looked up. Willie Hill said, in the severest of tones he could muster, that if he thought John Drew was about to consign his life's work to the fire, he would cart it all away until such time as John Drew came to his senses again. All he wanted, he said, was a sign. Some token that his companion would not send the whole lot roaring up the chimney. John Drew reached out for the Bible on the parlour table and he opened it at Habbakuk as an earnest of his good intentions.

"I have passed through my despair . . . like the venerable Habbakuk."

"And glad I am to hear of it!"

They talked a little more of the glory days of Dungannon, then, when three Romish priests and three ministers of the Established Church were lined up, facing one another, on the stage of the local hall. The *Evening Standard* had carried a full account of the great debate. But the event that had stuck in both their minds was not the preening reverence of the priests or the priggishness of one of their own ministers, but the drunken gentleman who had wandered in late, on the second night, and thrown an empty bottle of *uiscebaugh* at the stage. There was a swish of frock coats as Catholic and Protestant tried to shield themselves. After the gauche intruder disappeared into the dark of the night, none of them had been able to ascertain, in conversation among themselves, the creed of the miscreant. Willie Hill rapped the grate three times with the long poker.

"These sorts are all religions and none," he said "And we have a few of them down here, too."

Willie Hill stayed until the light was beginning to leave the sky. He offered the services of Heather, his middle daughter, to come and keep house for John Drew in the afternoons until such time as either Eliza Drew or Bridget Doheny reappeared, but John Drew would have none of it. It would cause more aggravation, both inside and outside the rectory, than it cured. If Bridget Doheny were to see a strange woman replacing her, she wouldn't cross the threshold again. And where would they be then? When all was said and done, Bridget Doheny, with all her moods and moments, was a capable, managing woman. In the end, it was settled that Alice Hill would have a basket sent up every other day and that Bridget Doheny's boy would keep on with his chores. Anything more or less would be a costly *causus belli* for all concerned.

John Drew walked with Willie Hill across Sackville Square, the basket jiggling about between them.

They parted at the brewery gates where Willie Hill had some business in the office. John Drew carried on, in order to walk his thoughts, back across the Beggar's Bridge and up towards the pound where Micksie Sullivan was filling up a horse trough with a pail of water. They nodded to one another. At the tanyard gates, John Drew paused to remove a stone from his shoe. Up the hill he went then, bearing left for the brewery cottages, so as not to pass by Bridget Doheny's cabin or have any of her children spot him. He heard the beating of a hammer on an anvil in Dinny Grey's forge, below Bridget Doheny's. Hammer, iron, gods. Haddad, god of Phoenician thunder. Also, a blacksmith, for the Arabs. But it wasn't the god Haddad that bothered the likes of Eliza Drew and Bridget Doheny, John Drew understood, but Mot—the god of death. Of primeval fear. The fear of fears. The lord of the whole pantheon, who had a thousand names over time. Who knew but that Eliza might take Bridget Doheny's side? Why did the silly woman have to walk out at all!

At the crossroads, he wheeled left and headed back down into the town by Pound Street. The Worthingtons' eldest son, Sylvester, the one who wore the fancy get-up like a Hussar's cast-off, saluted him as he passed on a jaunting car. He suddenly found himself in front of Mrs Tours' window, with the woman herself smiling out at him over her spectacles as she worked away at the hem of a dress. For a moment, he was tempted to call into the whitewashed cottage on some pretext or other, but then he thought the better of it and continued on for the sanctuary of the square and the fire in the parlour. Jer Dooley was driving the cattle back down the Burrow into Sackville Square as he reached the church gate.

"Hardy weather, Dr Drew."

"Hardy weather, indeed."

When night fell on the parlour, John Drew sat a long time by the fire puzzling over things. When he was nodding off in the armchair, all thought of Bridget Doheny and Mrs Tours deserted him, and he was left wondering about certain signs that still foxed him in one of the Persepolitan inscriptions. In particular, he pondered the end of the first line, with the name of Darius written out in syllables and his designation written in two ideographs: LUGAL GAL—Great King. What did the little sign signify at the end of the line? John Drew closed his eyes slowly and, by the throbbing heart of the fire, summoned up the image of the first line of the inscription before his mind's eye.

His lips moved as he read the ancient pronunciation of the name of Darius and its royal designation: "Da-ri-ia-a-mush LUGAL GAL . . . Darius, the Great King . . ."

Yes, but what did the trellis-like sign mean? It wasn't just a question of the powers he and Westmacott had assigned to some of the signs, because, besides the whole business of syllables and ideographs, there were clearly some signs that were indicators of class or type something. Like the plural sign in the second line.

Some signs, of course, must explain the mode or reading or interpretation and weren't actually meant to be pronounced all. Perhaps, they indicated that the ideographs from the more ancient language were to be pronounced in the newer Babylonian. These were the sort of questions about which Westmacott and he could have finally come to some resolution. With the image of the plural sign in his mind, John Drew nodded off in the warm gloom. When he did awake, cold and pale and confused, with the oil flame guttering gently in the lamp on the parlour table, he found the locket he had taken down from the mantelpiece still clasped tightly in his hand. But if his son's image had sidled in beside the image cut in stone, there was no trace of it left in his waking mind.

VII

THE TRYST BY TAYLOR'S WELL

Mrs Tours set down the piece of boiling bacon into the bubbling water and watched a moment as the piece of flesh gurgled in the pot. Then she tidied the fire around the grate and set the lid at an angle so the steam could escape. When she was sure that all was right, she took her coat from the scullery door and made out into Pound Street, telling Tadhg Doheny, who was breaking sticks in the yard, to watch the fire while she was out. A couple of children were playing hop-scotch near the Beggar's Bridge as she passed. She called out to a girl with a ponytail standing alone at the edge of the group.

"I haven't seen your mother all week, Peg Ryan. Is she not well in herself?"

"She has a touch of a cough, so she has."

"Tell her I'll send her up a bottle by one of the Dohenys this evening that'll see her right."

"Right you are, Mrs Tours."

Mrs Tours spotted Annie Dowling and another woman at the foot of the square. She was going to call out to them, but they rounded Gordon's corner and disappeared just as Mrs Tours reached the square. Waxy Daly was tap-tap-tapping away in his little booth. A pair of big brewery boots, by the sound of it.

Said it out plain and straight to Annie Dowling, I did, while the both of us were standing in front of Waxy Daly's hut, a few weeks ago, and he hammering away at Jem Dowling's boots and letting on not to be listening to us. Plain and straight, I said it to her. "Let your Jack marry her! Let him marry her!"

And Mrs Jem Dowling got all upset, on account of her little Jack wanting to marry Mary Saunders of the cottages who had this child only last year, by one of the English foremen in the brewery. Grand and mighty in herself, and going on about Fr Farrelly this and Fr Farrelly that. "Let him marry her," I said again, if she shits a bucket a day itself. And lucky the little useless gom will be if it's only the one bastard she has by the time he gets her to the altar. The whole town can mount her after that, if they have a mind to. Though I didn't say that part to her, of course.

Mrs Tours crossed over to Terry's, for the post. A drayhorse was tethered to the tree opposite the shop. It gave off a great thunderclap of a fart as she reached the door. Billy White had a letter for Mrs Tours, in Eliza's Drew's spidery Protestant handwriting. All the way from Dublin. John Terry smiled at Mrs Tours from the sanctuary of his counter.

"Anything strange, Mrs Tours?"

"Divil a thing, John."

"They say the weather's to keep up."

"We'll have to put up with it, one way or the other."

Mrs Tours slipped the letter into her coat and nodded back at John Terry.

And many's the arse I put in your trousers too, Mr Terry. Could do with a bit of reinforcement in the fork too, like all of the men. I know what'll be in the letter of course. A little P.S. about keeping an eye on madam, out in Willie Hill's mansion. And many's the day I spent out there too, years

*ago, fitting up their drapes. I know every nook and cranny in the Hills'
house. From the sunroom to the bedrooms. And every hill and hollow in
the gardens, too.*

*Would have went out last night only for that Mrs Moore and Mrs
Nolan, of the Lanes, appeared in, looking for the croup cure. All on
account of the little Harkins baby coming down bad with it, and he
hardly six months old. They were at sixes and sevens, the two of them.
Wondering if the weather had anything to do with it. Or bad water,
maybe? Dan Brady was in the parlour at his dinner. I gave him a wink
and asked him to step out and fill the bucket from Taylor's well later, the
way I'd have fresh water for the morning. Then I sat in with the two
women and rose up the fire and boiled up the brew. And, I declare to Jaesus, when the two of them had gone home, didn't Dan Brady appear at
the back door with the same news.*

"They were there again, Mrs Tours."

"Are you sure it was Judith Drew, it was?"

*"Don't I know her from seeing her in the square. And I know the 'ould
Protestant spake of her too."*

"And do you not have any idea at all who the chap was?"

"Not a notion, Mrs Tours. As God is me witness."

*And that's why I had to leave it all till today. Slipped up by the forge
this morning, letting on I had to leave a parcel of mending into
Sullivans'. As I passed the top of the hill, who do I see scooting back in
the door with her broom only Bridget Doheny, and that tribe of hers running around like the red Indians you do hear tell of over in America. A
pity that stook of a husband of hers doesn't put himself out a bit more,
and she wouldn't have need to scrub and scrape for the likes of the Drews.
Less mickey and more money is what is needed in that quarter. I let a roar
at little Tadhg Doheny, who was standing scratching himself by the wall.
I asked him to call down later because I had a few messages for him.*

"No bother, Mrs Tours."

*I heard tell that Bridget Doheny was sending him up to light the fire
in Drews' and do a few bits and pieces. A right hames of a place it must*

be now, without a woman keeping a firm hand on it. If the English scholar had arrived, it might all have worked out all right. Maybe Bridget Doheny wouldn't have got notions into her little head. Tadhg Doheny stared up at me like I was going to hit him a scelp.

"Tell me this and tell me no more, Tadhg, alanna."

"Yes, Mrs Tours?"

"How is Dr Drew getting on up there?"

"He's getting on grand, so he is, Mrs Tours."

"Is he, faith? And has that mother of yours not been up there since?"

"I don't know nothing about that now, Mrs Tours, so I don't."

In the high hole of my arse, says I, in me own mind. I left him and he promising to call in on me to do the few messages later on. You won't credit this: as I was coming back down over the river, who do I see in a grand pony-and-trap and she out for a jaunt with Cassie Hill, only Missy Judith Drew herself, with Willie Hill's man at the reins. Little Lorna Lovegrove, as she probably thinks herself. The dark hair peeping out under the bonnet and those heavy eyebrows of hers. All got up in the purple dress her mother had me make up for her last Christmas, when she was still half-innocent, and she sitting up, bold as brass, on the side of the car, cocking a snook at the whole town. Sitting on a fortune and she doesn't realise it, but do any of them? How they change in a year. Eliza Drew won't be sorry to have that one back up in that fancy boarding school in Dublin. Put a bit of manners on her. And Cassie Hill could do with a little order too. They waved at me as they passed. At Mrs Tours, the old fool. Taking out, letting in. A couple of darts and pleats here. A dab hand at the gusseting and hemming. Make you up as fancy a dress as you'd get in New York from an old pile of rags. Put a new arse in your man's pants, too, so he doesn't disgrace you at mass of a Sunday. Or service. Wouldn't I like to put that up on a sign outside the door:

Master Bespoke Seamstress

All Arses Equal before the Lord

In the afternoon, Mrs Tours sat down with a couple of old newspapers that Willie Hill had left in, the previous week, and read through the headlines slowly. There was more about the cholera in London, of course, and something about the trouble in the Punjab. When it was getting dark, she sat over by the window and did the letting out on the dress Mrs Seavers had been promised. Tadhg Doheny arrived back at the door with the last of the light.

"Me mother said I could lave coming home till late."

"Did she, faith? And tell us this, will you find your way back in the dark?"

"No bother to me, Mrs Tours. Didn't I often bring me father home and it pitch dark."

"I'm sure you did."

Mrs Tours watched the boy as he went off with the gallon can to Jer Dooley's for the milk and with the parcel for Mrs Seavers under his arm.

God be good to Celia Seavers' backside and send it doesn't get any bigger or there won't be a chair in the whole town that will hold her. Of course, all those children. The hips. Though, there's Bridget Doheny with her brood and she hardly spread at all. Women come in all shapes and sizes. And you have to get on with everyone in a small town. Like my mother, the big widow, God rest her, used to say to all us girls and boys when we got vexed with anyone down the town, "Keep in wud 'em all!"

Mrs Tours set Dan Brady's supper and Mr Somers' supper on the table in the parlour and called up to the men. Then she put away all the bits and pieces and settled down by the window until it was time to go spying. She found herself nodding by the candlelight and wondering whether the whole thing wasn't just Dan Brady's imagination.

All the times Eliza Drew sat by the window with me. At first, she used to come with the girls, letting on it was for a cure or to pick up some mending, though she knew well I could have sent that up by one of the Dohenys. She would sit there, asking about the cure for this and that as I finished

*off whatever little piece I had to do for her, but the cure for what Eliza
Drew has won't come out of a bottle. As time passed, of course, Eliza Drew
started to come without the girls. She would come when she was sure none
of the other women would be around, in the late afternoon or very early
in the morning. I would stitch away and let her talk things out for herself, because I knew she needed something from me, something more than
cures or curses. And then, one day, around Easter time, she dropped in to
collect a couple of his lordship's linen shirts, and it all came out then
about the boy, and those awful days when they lived in that curse of a
town, Belfast. Bad cess to it. It was the little boy's anniversary, do you see,
April 8th. I looked out over my glasses and then I left my hand on her lap.*

"What is it, alanna?"

And then the crying started. Deep, mournful, animal sort of cries.

"Whisht! Whisht, alanna! Won't you tell me about it?

*And when Eliza Drew was done and she had told me everything, she
was the minister's wife again and I was the Catholic seamstress. I said to
her then, real soft like, "I had a child die on me once, Eliza . . . a little
boy, too . . . the twin of my Paddy, that's over in America . . .*

*I had never called her by her first name before. I laid my hand on her
head, like you would with a little child. And, ever since that day, when she
comes back, there is no talk of the boy or of the days in Belfast and all that
sickness. I know well there's no talking between herself and ould Drew about
it. It's not right for men to talk about that sort of thing anyway. It's for the
women to do the crying. Maybe that's why he prefers to live back with the
bulls with the wings and all those arrowhead signs on that bit of paper.*

It was dark when Mrs Tours headed off across Campion's field.
Dan Brady was gone to Gordon's for a drop, and Mr Somers was
up in bed. There was a moon about, but the clouds kept coming
and going. She walked through a great big pile of piss-the-beds
with their heads all closed up in the moonlight, smelling the
dung from Jer Dooley's cows. As she reached the line of trees at
the corner of Campion's field, a fox slipped in across the ditch,

with its head bobbing up and down, this way and that, like it knew she was there but couldn't exactly say where. She was crouched down by the trees, suddenly feeling the need to make her water, when a voice called out in the gloom.

"Are you there?"

It was a man's voice—a sort of out-of-town voice, but not that far out.

"Are you there, Judy?"

Judy, bejaesus! That's a good one. Ould Drew and his wife send that one to the dame school, then the boarding school in Dublin, feed her and rear her well, and she ends up in a dark field being called Judy, like some streel from a London street. She must have arrived in from the Bawn side. A right midnight tryst it is too. Still wearing the dress she had on in the jaunting car today. Judy! And now they're giggling. The minister's daughter and one of our own, out gallivanting in the night air, without priest or padre to keep an eye on them. I have a good mind, to run over and tear them apart, but I'll have to make me water soon. I'm cut in two with the pain. I'll kneel down here and do it with me legs crossed, like the old women used to do if they were out in the fields working away from the house. Here it comes. Warm and welcome.

"You'll be back in Dublin in two weeks. At school, Judy."

"Oh, Michael."

Michael, by Christ! Now I'll see who it is . . . the moon is on his face. I declare to Jaesus, if it isn't one of Joe Hennigan's boys. Michael.

They're off home now. I'll wait until the moon is gone, just in case. Now, isn't that a good one. Dan Brady was right. That little streel is carrying on behind everyone's back. Her mother in London and her father lost in his books, but now Mrs Tours knows what's going on, and I'll knock the nonsense out of her. Little Lorna Lovegrove is right.

It wasn't so much the thirst or the hunger that so upset Lorna now, but the intelligence that she was sailing far from the shores of Christendom. That ahead, without a shadow of doubt, lay the land of the Moor and his seraglio. And it was only by dint of a cool nerve and a steady heart, that she kept her thoughts in check during those long nights in the rat-infested hold of the Corsair's ship.

I'll go to sleep tonight, full of the fear of what young women may do. And how the heart gets in the way of the head always, when we are young. What am I to do to stop those two stookawns? What is it ould Drew wrote? "What is what?"

Maybe he's as well off with his dreaming of bulls with wings and old stones. With the dead. But I'll have to do something. It's up to Mrs Tours to do something soon, because the rooster never sleeps. The big widow told me that, many's the time. The rooster never sleeps, and many's the woman learned that to her cost after she got a belly on her as big as a harvest frog.

VIII

THE FOX GOES SOUTH

It wasn't to be that handy for Fox Keegan to get from Dublin to Kilkenny after all, because both Mr Appleby and Mr Hobson had other matters to discuss with him: in particular, lax timekeeping and being too forward with some of the female counter-staff, which would mean Dilly Shiels. Fox Keegan glanced at the wall clock behind Mr Appleby's barren head. It was ten of nine, which meant that the Carlow train was now out of the question. Better to leave all haste aside then and humour the two men with a show of humility. If you could fake that, you were away in a hack. Mr Appleby pursed his lips and ran a bony finger over the felted crown of the hat lying beside the brass inkpot. Mr Appleby's clear blue eyes looked from Mr Hobson to Fox Keegan, hat in hand before the desk.

"Mr Hobson tells me that you're quite handy with accounts."

"That would be from my time in Terry's, Mr Appleby."

"The brewery in Queen's County, you mean?"

They wouldn't deign to drink the stuff themselves, of course, but they were handy enough at brewing it and dispensing it to the natives for a few coppers. The clock was now at nine. God knows how he would make Tullyroe and his father's farm by nightfall. A straight run to Kilkenny from Dublin would have taken only ten hours, but now he would have to do it differently: maybe a covered car as far as Carlow, then pick up some sort of contraption heading south to Kilkenny. Shank's mare from Kilkenny, if neccessary. Or he might get a lift off someone going out the Freshford road. As he was totting up the hours in his head, the brittle English accent of the older man leaning on the desk cut through Fox Keegan's thoughts. Mr Appleby said that the fat could still be pulled from the fire, somehow; if whatever was troubling Mr Keegan could be sorted out, there were great prospects of success in the future. Mr Hobson nodded to his superior. The tufts of hair in his nose. The timid little accent of the under-manager before the great one.

"Mr Appleby is right. It's all down to your attitude, Mr Keegan . . ."

Mr Appleby took up his hat and dusted it on his sleeve. He glanced at Mr Hobson again.

"I'm sorry to hear about your father, Mr Keegan, but, when all this is sorted out, we expect a great improvement . . . otherwise . . . do I make myself clear?"

"Yes, Mr Appleby. Very clear. And I appreciate your taking the time . . ."

"Mr Hobson here will deal with the matter of time-off, in lieu of wages. Mr Hobson . . ."

"Yes, Mr Appleby?"

"I shall be in the despatch office, if I'm needed. Good day, Mr Keegan."

Out on Burgh Quay, he settled for the first covered car going to Naas.

A fine summer drizzle was falling on the canvas as the car drew up Winetavern Street under the cathedral arch. He glanced around him at the company—a couple with a small boy, a middle-aged gentleman with a bulbous nose, an elderly couple and a little cricket of a man who insisted on lighting up his noxious dudeen without as much as a by-your-leave. He buried himself in the newspaper.

Day of Humiliation-Prayers Offered in Several Quarters Against the Cholera

At all costs, he wanted to avoid intercourse with the querulous little man with the restless tongue, who would have his life's story out of him in an instant. He had already sorted out seed, breed and generation of the couple with the child. When the little man with the dudeen turned his prying eye Fox's way, Fox said simply, "You're a terrible man for questions, so you are."

"Ask and ye shall know, so says the Lord."

"I don't recall the Lord saying that anywhere."

"You must be reading one of them bargain Bibles, then."

Car journeys always stirred up the past for Fox Keegan. Whether by interrogation of himself or others. Memories of the small holding in Tullyroe, that his grandfather had migrated to from Callan. His father and brothers trying to make a living out of twenty acres of middling land, a couple of cows, a few pigs and endless drills of bothersome potatoes. He had always felt awkward in their hearty company. The Joseph who had to go down to Egypt. Who couldn't stay still and talk old men's talk in the evening. At first, after the wild days, there was some sort of surrender to house and hearth. That was when he was given the position of schoolteacher up in Minister Rodgers' little school on Kilgarran Hill, up the road from Tullyroe, because there wasn't another master available in the locality to learn the little swaddlers their own prayers. A queer deal it was too: Minister Rodgers would appear at the tigeen near the Protestant church, every Monday morning, with the orders for the week. Fox Keegan would set to teaching them their own tongue and their own creed. A tongue that was fast swallowing up the remnants of his mother's and grandmother's tongue because there was no business to be done in it. What you bought with in Callan, you bred into your children in Tullyroe. Mouths and minds followed the money. That was the way of the world. He mused over the names of the children: Marshall, Willington, Holmes, Holland. Terence and David and Edith and Violet. Not a Bridget nor a Tadhg among them. Little Oliver Edwards and his sister Sarah looking up at his beer-sick face on a Monday morning. Noting the little trace of bread soda at the corner of his mouth to settle his stomach-ache after the night in Matty Fitz's.

He heard his own voice, from memory, against the sound of the covered car crawling along the Naas road.

"Also, we have to come to some arrangement over the new primers, tell ye'er parents . . ."

There were books with stories about clever foxes and foolish crows and little ditties in praise of the virtues of honesty, thrift and hard work.

Labour is the handmaiden of Thrift

Laboremus in pace. Miss Holland came in every Tuesday and Thursday, in her little black bonnet, to take the girls for needlework and embroidery. He himself sought to drill some sense of fair play into the boys in the rough-and-tumble of the schoolyard. It was a strange set-up, when you thought about it. In his father's house, the school was scarcely mentioned except in a rough aside from his father or his brother Tom, after they had dragged themselves in from a day thinning turnips or coaxing the scratch plough behind one of the mares.

"Well for you, Fox, up there in the heat with that lot."

Odder still was the growth of that new feeling: of being lost between two shores. Between his father's hearty humour and the sharp-minded words of Minister Rodgers. One thing he was sure of though—even if he couldn't explain it to himself at the time—there was no going back. When you had left your own, you could never get fully back. Or belong to the other crowd either. It was around that time that he first started to make poetry, small bits, at first, as his mother's tongue began fading more and more into the background until it seemed no more to him than a strange shadow. The tongue of the old and the dying, fading away, like the late snow on the bushes around Tullyroe. He scribbled down poems about nature and God and animals. Harmless ramblings, if the truth be known. Before things got tricky and he started to think too much about being caught between the two shores and what it meant in the greater scheme of things. Before Mary Macken shared her charms with him, after the Pattern, one long August day.

They pulled into Naas around two in the afternoon. There was a great commotion going on near the market house. A cart had broken an axle and blocked up half the street. A man in a little velvet jacket seemed to be in charge of clearing the street. Fox Keegan made his way through the carts and the beasts tethered to posts, and ducked into Bergin's, near the Castledermot road, for company. The last he saw of the little man with the dudeen was as he looked back over the heads of the crowd. The little man's glance seemed to say

"You won't last, me bucko!"

No, he would never last at anything, either the schoolmastering on Kilgarran Hill, with the scholars lisping out their tables, or the farm itself. Even the handy number in the brewery in Aghadoe, he had to go and lose. Feckless and footloose he was. Rhyme without a reason. Bergin's was full to the door with dealers and small farmers bemoaning the price of this or that. He called for a bottle of Terry's ale. It had been given out by the driver of the covered car that the Kilkenny caravan wouldn't leave before three. In the end, he cut it too fine. Got caught up in a contretemps about the visit of H.M. Queen Victoria and all to that. The stookawn behind the counter reading the account out, blow by blow, to get them all at one another, of course.

> *The excitement now became really intense, every eye is strained towards the landing. For a moment expectation hushed the voices of the spectators. A peal of guns, a grand crash of music, a long, loud, and deafening cheer, and Queen Victoria lands for the first time on Irish shores. The enthusiasm was immense. Everything but the joyous and happy nature of the occasion was entirely forgotten. The Queen advanced leaning on Prince Albert, attired in simple costume, in a dress of brown and white spotted muslin, with a visite, of pearl-coloured silk and Limerick lace, and white crepe bonnet; she looked youthful and animated, smiled, and acknowledged repeatedly the plaudits of those who had the privilege of being near the royal presence, and it was at once evident that her expectations in respect of the country were more than realised. Cheer after cheer burst forth; crowds of gentlemen rushed forward to the covered platform which extended from the Jetty to the station; groups of elegantly attired ladies were in every available standing place, and the general feeling among our fair friends was one of unmixed pleasure and loyalty, if we could judge of it by eyes sparkling almost beautiful with delight, by smiles of cordial welcome, and handkerchiefs waved in repeated bursts of enthusiasm*

The ignorant yoke beside him gobbed on the floor. He said it was all fine and well but what had it to do with the price of oats or beef? Fox Keegan hadn't intended stepping into the fray but, in such company, even a show of indifference counted for a comment. Soon, the whole debate was being led along by a thick-looking type in a battered hat whose wife Fox Keegan instinctively pitied. When he looked down into his own glass though, it was the image of Mary Macken that smiled back at him. Neither the harp nor the crown seemed of much moment when love lost was the question. He wondered idly, for a moment, where love went when it disappeared. Did it go up in the air, like a vapour, to join all the other vapours? Or was it like galvanism itself—a sort of power of its own? A faint memory stirred in his mind then, of stealing away from the graveyard after the dressing of the graves one fine Pattern day. He had arranged to meet Mary Macken up at the back of Porter's Hill, where they knew no one would be. One touch borrowed another. There was the sound of skylarks in the air above Tullyroe when they made love.

The man on the stool beside him nudged Fox Keegan.

"I thought you had to catch the Kilkenny car?"

"Jesus, Mary and Joseph! Is that clock right?"

"More right than that newspaper our friend is reading out of."

The spiny finger jabbed at the newspaper on the counter. Then it was out the door like the clappers and off through the market crowd to find that the Kilkenny car had gone a full ten minutes before. A woman at a flour stall tipped her bonnet to him.

"It does always leave that little bit early of a Friday, sir."

He wandered round then, the beer swishing about in his belly, until he came to some arrangement of things in his head. He would take the first caravan going south. This he did, pushing his way to the head of the line and tipping the driver. He slept most of the way, despite the bad road, only waking up when they had crossed the Heath, outside Maryborough. He was out of the caravan in short order then and caught a connection for Abbeyleix. That would be as far as he would get that night. If only Appleby had let him out earlier, he could have made the Carlow train and at least be in Kilkenny by now.

The jaunting car that took him out of Maryborough was a sorry affair. A rickety class of a thing that took every rut in the road to heart.

As they pulled into Abbeyleix, he called out to the driver, "E'er a notion where I might get lodgings for the night?"

"I'll tell you what you'll do, now. Go down by the weighing-house until you get to the public house by the pump. Drennan's. They'll put you right there, so they will."

He was sore, after the day's journey. Godspeed the day when the whole country would be covered with steam engines, from top to bottom. There would be no more looking for grace-and-favour from cantankerous drivers. He heard the car pull away as he crossed the street. Then he slung Sam Parker's satchel over his shoulder and made, post haste, for Drennan's, by the pump.

IX

LUGAL.LUGAL.MESH.LUGAL

F or good luck, the roof of the church held. Because, when John Drew was going over the vestry registries that afternoon, a veritable monsoon storm brought a torrent of rain down. The sky darkened so much, just before the deluge, that he was obliged to sit over by the vestry window to read.

Emerson, Henry James. August 8th, 1849

He had neglected to fill in the baptismal register, until prompted by Eliza in the letter he had received just that morning. Still, Aghadoe was in the Queen's County, and just as the main road had gone around it, so too did the diocesan principals, in their infinite wisdom. The same neglect served him well he understood. What would he do if he had a real congregation to attend to? It would leave little time to pursue what he perceived to be his true duty before God and man. A death here, a birth there. There was the odd squabble with the authorities over the living provided or the upkeep of the church and burials. But Eliza had settled into things. The memories of Belfast seemed, finally, to have been put to rest. She had her routines and he had his. Even if she did seem to spend too much time with the Tours woman, was it really such a bad thing? Eliza's face was before him now. She left a wicker basket down on the kitchen table between them.

"Mrs Tours suggests Yarrow . . . a strong infusion."

"Yarrow? Is there some scientific basis to this, Eliza?"

Eliza's arched eyebrow. The sign that said *nolle me tangere!*

"Everything isn't science, John. If that were so, then what would we make of all our scriptures? Can you prove them scientifically?"

"I try to. In Habbakuk, for example, are we speaking of the Chaldeans or the Assyrians? Or both?"

Eliza Drew began sifting through the mending. Her words were firm. Mrs Tours' words were stronger than scripture itself.

"Yarrow it is, then."

When the rain had abated, he locked up the vestry books in the oak press and slipped back to the rectory. The worst of the weather seemed to be past. If he took his coat with him, a short walk might still be possible.

He swung right before the brewery and up past the Beggar's Bridge. The following day's sermon was fresh in his head now. He was mindful of Eliza's caution in the letter.

"Be prepared, John. You don't want to leave them snoozing in the pews."

At Beggar's Bridge, he realised that he hadn't taken in the gallon that Bridget Doheny's boy had left on the back doorstep. The thunder might well have turned the milk by now. He pressed on, nevertheless, the prophet Habbakuk firm in his thoughts now.

O, Lord, how long shall I cry
And thou wilt not hear?
Even cry out unto thee of violence,
And thou wilt not save!

From the far side of the road, Tim Delaney called out to him, "Soft day, Dr Drew."

"Indeed and it is. And a fine job you did on the roof, if I might say so."

"Sound."

A group of men stood by the horse pound gates, discussing a beast tethered to a post. They appeared to be haggling over money. John Drew smiled at them and they doffed their caps in response.

When he reached the corner of the Long Road and the houses thinned out, John Drew felt his thoughts loose themselves with the pace of his feet and the lack of humankind around him. He paused to pluck a couple of early blackberries from a bush and stood a moment, staring at nothing in particular. The Lake Van inscriptions, which he had worked on the previous year, were as clear as they would ever be and his notes had been received well at the Academy, in Dublin. The language in which they were written—and the particular cuneatic script—had clearly been borrowed from another people. A dark people who had lived in the Land Between the Two Rivers before the Bablyonians and Assyrians had uprooted them. The people of Sumer? Was that who they were? The dark people were the same source, perhaps, as the Babylonian script of the Darius inscription, at Persepolis, with its intrusive ideographs and class determinatives. The last tokens of a dying tribe. Because the syllables—as they were written in the newer Babylonian language—simply did not fit as well in the cuneatic script as the earlier language. Like Lord Palmerston's words in the mouth of, say, Brigid Doheny. Or trying to write the Gaelic words stranded in her speech with the orthographic logic—or lack of it, indeed—of English, with its hotchpotch of Anglo-Saxon and Latin and French. In the clear autumnal air, John Drew rolled the names of the Tigris and the Euphrates on his tongue, savouring the sense of the exotic that they imparted.

In principio erat verbum

He pictured the wedge-shaped impressions on the clay tablets, baked hard in the Mesopotamian sun. Yes, the third language of the Darius inscription from Persepolis was the real prize. The Babylonian. Not the inscription written in the Old Persian of Darius himself—though that was a great help in the translation and the transliteration. Nor indeed the second inscription—the Elamite. As he walked along, the second line of the Babylonian version of the Darius inscription welled up in John Drew's mind again.

He decoded the ideographs as he walked along, for the thousandth time. The fruit of many hours spent over other inscriptions brought back from the Land of the Two Rivers by the likes of Layard, in London. Signs he had decoded by analysis and analogy and the sheer serendipity of intuition.

LUGAL. LUGAL. MESH. LUGAL. KUR. KUR. MESH

King. King. Plural sign. Land. Land. Plural sign.

King of Kings. Of all the lands.

A necklace of thoughtpictures modified by other syllabic signs. He would show, in different tables, the scripts that were to be read as syllables and the ones that were really ideographs and could be read in either the older or the newer language. He would nail his colours to the mast on the matter and damn the begrudgers.

The just shall live by his faith

He would stand himself upon the watchtower of his own investigations. He would live by his faith and let the slings and arrows rain down on him from London, and Paris and Berlin.

A light shower began falling as he approached the crook in the road. He pulled on his coat and stood in under an oak tree for shelter until the rain had passed.

A horse-and-cart was approaching from the direction of the Commons. In the silence after the shower of rain, you could hear its creaking wheels from half a mile away. Far above John Drew's head, on the wind, black sickle-shaped swifts were slewing about in the clear sky. Their wings could pass for scimitars, seen from below, he thought. He pictured the swift's wing impressed in clay then. An image that could be read as a scimitar or a sword or even a sickle. Or even a soldier. If you doubled the swift sign, it might became a general. Soldier of soldiers. King of kings. Two scimitar wings, side by side, on a clay tablet. So the swift's wing could be

> A swift
> A scimitar
> A sickle
> A soldier
> A general

You could read it in whatever language you chose. The language you actually spoke or an older, dead language. A venerated language. Latin, Greek, Gaelic, Sumerian. The picture could represent a syllable as the writing developed, over the generations. So the meaning of the original picture would be lost in the mists of time. Some signs, at one time or another, might have represented both sounds and ideas. Traditions passed from scribe to scribe, over the generations. Until only the scribes could tell whether a sickle-shaped impression was to be read as swift or scimitar or a plain syllable, *swi-*. Or even a different syllable, from the older tongue. Yes, the principle of polyphony, in the Babylonian Darius inscription, had to be addressed, one way or the other.

John Drew realised suddenly that, if he had read the second line of the inscription correctly, he had read the skies around Aghadoe wrong. Though the fickle southern Irish sky was still not quite as bad as the Ulster one, both were less faithful than the skies over somewhere like London, or the far south of England.

Things were taking a bad turn in the heavens. Dark, brooding clouds were bearing up from the south again, from the borders of Queen's County and Kilkenny. The horse-and-cart passed him as he wheeled about for the town. A brockman, as they used to say in Belfast, gathering scraps to feed pigs. The sickly sweet stench stayed with him until he reached Mrs Tours' cottage, where he scurried by, in haste both to escape her gimlet eye and to get back to the house before more rain. When he arrived home, it was to find that the milk had soured in the gallon at the back door but that Bianconi was busy lapping it up.

LUGAL. LUGAL. MESH. LUGAL.

King of Kings.

But how to proceed? Only this much was sure—the final work on the inscription would probably come in an instant, or not at all. Still, all the painful plodding must come first. Finger-sifting words, dead to the tongue and the ear, for nigh on two millennia. Words that were dead, even as the ancient scribes scored them into the soft Mesopotamian clay, over two thousand years before. Even the dead, thought Dr John Drew, have their language.

X

WE READ A BRICK

John Drew looked down over his spectacles at the congregation, scattered among the cold pews. As the harmonium groaned into life to his left, he glanced over at Mrs Gilford. There was never any question of changing the blessed woman's style of playing. It was as bold as it was firm. She would simply take up her position by the side of the altar and proceed without as much as a by-your-leave to minister or congregation. Nor did the generality show much enthusiasm for the prophet Habbakuk that morning. Although the Eversham sisters, as always, were bolt upright in the family pew, so recently surrendered by the untimely deaths of their parents the previous year, from a double dose of consumption. To their side, sat the Stewarts and, beside them again, Miss Hamilton and her squint-eyed niece, Emily. John Drew spotted Willie and Violet, Cassie Hill and his own daughter, Judith, halfway down the church. The rest of the congregation was a vague sea of Sabbath worshippers. John Drew noted that Habbakuk's warnings, re the Chaldeans, didn't seem to cause any great unease in Aghadoe.

Their chariots are swifter than leopards.

Aghadoe had never seemed more distant, in that instant, from Mesopotamia and the ancient kings. It was only when Mrs Gilford drew them all into the final hymn that there was any sense of the torpor of the Sunday sloughing off. He hadn't neglected to mention the Days of Fast and Humiliation in various parts of England: from Eastbourne northwards. Or the great mercy done to the likes of Aghadoe, in not having to bear the burden of the cholera which had been the lot of Dublin and London and Manchester. He did not mention, however, for fear of being misrepresented in the mouths of his parishioners, that he himself thought the illness more a matter of human neglect than divine intervention. As he heard the last chord die away on the harmonium, he recalled *The Times'* lofty words on the matter.

> *The Cholera is the best reformer of all sanitary reformers; it allows of no mistakes and overlooks no indiscretions.*

After the service, he disrobed in the vestry before slipping back into the rectory. Willie Hill would chat with the few parishioners standing about at the Sackville Square gates. In the gloom of the parlour, he started when a voice spoke to him from the shadows.

"Father . . ."

His eyes struggled as he strained to seize on what little light had managed to break through the barrage of trees surrounding the rectory. His eyes seized on the white shawl about her shoulders and the pink bonnet tilted jauntily to one side.

"It's me . . . Judith!"

He floundered about for a moment, trying to gather his thoughts together. There was something he had wanted to say to the girl, but he just couldn't put his finger on it. They spoke for a few moments. Desultory conversation. What had Mama said in her letter to him? Was there anything he needed done in the house? (Not that Judith Drew would have a mind to do it, if there was.

That was more Theodora's way). His eldest daughter followed his footsteps into the drawing room. Yes, it was true about Bridget Doheny, he told her. But the boy—Tadhg, was that his name?—still called with the kindling, helped with the chores and did a few messages for him. Things weren't all that bad, and Violet Hill was good enough to send over any extra provisions needed. He hoped Judith was behaving with due respect over in the Hill household. Judith Drew lay her book down slowly on the table. Her eyes were full of something he seemed not to have a name for.

She began fidgeting with her bonnet. As though to pull the peak down over her eyes and shield them from her father's scrutiny. Had he upset her? he wondered. Had he spoken too harshly with her? You couldn't be up to daughters. If you were too lenient, they thought you didn't love them any more. If you spoke too harshly with them, you were taken for an old ogre and they would fall into the trap of the first fine gentleman with a silver tongue who presented himself at the door. Judith Drew bit her lip, making out, all of a sudden, that they were holding up Willie Hill and Violet Hill and Cassie Hill. It was a bad thing to be unpunctual. Hadn't her father always said that?

"You really should try and keep more order in the house, Father."

The brazen little miss! He had hardly got his breath back when she was out the door and cosying up to Cassie Hill and company. It wasn't enough that Bridget Doheny had walked out on him. Now his own daughter was giving him insolence.

They rode in silence out to the Hills' house. Out by the Beggar's Bridge, for the Commons road. Judith kept a stiff silence and Cassie Hill did the same. The whisper had obviously been put in her ear at the church gates. Even Violet Hill couldn't get a word out of them. It was "yes, ma'am" and "no, ma'am" and "three bags full, ma'am". It was all too sweet to be wholesome, in other words. Before dinner, John Drew and Willie Hill went around the back of the great house to the harness room. Although there was no one available but the serving-staff, they heeled up the jaunting car for the wheels to be checked the following morning. The jaunting car had been making that odd kreak-kreak sound that, according to Violet Hill, usually presaged a broken axle or a cracked wheel. Willie Hill would leave John Drew back to town in the side-car, after dinner.

Dinner was a pleasant enough affair. It wasn't like one of those great events they had out in the Willingtons', where everyone was obliged to have a witty word on their lips. Nor was it the stolid, somnolent affair it was in John Drew's own household, when the ever-simmering row between Eliza and Judith threatened to erupt at any moment. The two young ladies persisted in their show of silence though. Miss Morgan was still on the staff, John Drew was glad to see. She had been laid low for a while, but was now fully recovered from some unspecified ailment. It was goose and all the trimmings. And a fine goose it was too. Miss Morgan, a little chit of a woman who was sixty, if she was a day, recommended the specially prepared sauce, the recipe for which she had acquired, many years before, from a cousin in service in Maryborough. She didn't hold back on chat either, as she dished out the steaming Brussels sprouts.

"We haven't seen you for Sunday dinner in a while, Dr Drew."

"Yes, indeed. Quite a while."

Violet Hill wiped her lips with a napkin.

"John, you know you're more than welcome to dine with us, any time you wish."

"That is very kind of you."

"Especially . . ."

She glanced at the far end of the table, where the girls were giggling over some trifle or other.

"Especially in the light of present circumstances with the Doheny woman."

Violet Hill went on to mention Mr Mayhew then. Talk had it, that he had scarcely a day or more in him. John Drew remembered then, almost by way of an afterthought, that he had promised to drop by the house that afternoon to offer whatever slight spiritual relief he might provide. Then they spoke about the vexed matter of the proposed workhouse out near the train station. A proposal had just been completed, that very week. The number thrown on the mercy of charity alone was no longer sustainable. The poor rate would have to be better administered. Willie Hill informed the table that a design for the new buildings was already being drawn up by competent hands in Dublin.

"Our own poorhouse. Is that an advance, William?"

When Miss Morgan served the blancmange, the workhouse question seemed to fade with the clatter of dessert spoons against the china.

After dinner, the girls scurried off to the drawing room, Violet Hill busied herself with arrangements in the kitchen, and John Drew and his host made for the larger study, at the far end of the house. As he passed the open door of the drawing room, they caught a glimpse of the two young women in the bay window, giggling, over God-knows-what, as they leafed through a flower album together. Though it was really quite vexing, John Drew knew he wouldn't get a straight answer about anything from Judith Drew in this mood.

Miss Morgan brought in strong coffee then, and they sat across the great oak table, facing one another. A pile of Dublin and London newspapers lay to one side. As they spoke, each man took his cue from whatever tittle-tattle his eyes happened upon. There was more agitation going on in Tipperary. It was beginning to look like the tithe business, all over again. Had John Drew not heard? John Drew looked over his companion's shoulder at the portrait of William Hill, *Père*, sawmill owner and breeder of fine hunters, over the cold grate. An Englishman to the bone. Willie Hill leaned across the table.

"I have heard they're even haughing cattle. Isn't that cruel? Cutting their tendons, so the beasts can't walk and have to be put down."

"Terrible!"

"Aye and feeding ragwort to them too."

"Dreadful!"

While evil must be punished, Willie Hill noted, reform must also come. Dissent usually sprang from empty bellies. Though many, of course, wouldn't agree with him, Willie Hill had found his own tenants, even in the worst of '47, more sinned against than sinning. The new workhouse might just take the edge from much of the local unrest. But John Drew's mind was away some-where else now, and Willie Hill's enthusiasm was beginning to tell on him a little. The kind, smiling, sidelocked face beamed at him across the table. A good man, John Drew thought. A solid pater-familias. And where did he, John Drew, come in that particular race? What kind of father would he have been, in the longer term, had his son survived.

"I hear the Dippers have been sighted in Roscrea, John."

"Dippers? The good weather must bring them out."

"Total immersion this time, it seems. Lead the gullible down to the river, baptise them in that muddy little Jordan of theirs and Hey Presto! They are saved. I wish it were so easy, in reality."

"God send we don't get them back again in Aghadoe!"

"I think the stench from the brewery fields would put them off, don't you?"

"I will say this much, poor Father Houlihan was only too glad to join with me in condemning the whole circus, the last time."

"There you go! We have interests in common . . ."

John Drew glanced again at the face of William Hill, senior, in the portrait on the wall. He may not have had quite the noble visage of his son, but the same bright, life-seizing eyes, were there.

In was late afternoon when both men rose from the great oak table and left the newspapers to one side. The girls were still in the drawing room. Willie Hill rapped with his fist as they passed.

"Judith, your father is leaving."

Judith Drew popped her dark-haired head out then, promising to drop by on the Tuesday afternoon, when the market was winding down. That same light was in her eyes now. But John Drew read it clearly this time. It was a sort of innocence that wasn't that innocent. Eliza had been right about that too, only he hadn't wanted to see it. His daughter's distant smile stayed with John Drew all the way back to town. He had Willie Hill drop him at the Mayhews' stone house, near the Catholic graveyard. A small group of women was gathered in the sitting room, like so many carrion crows. The widow-to-be was sitting in their midst. He knew, from Eliza and others, that the marriage could scarcely have been called a happy one. Still, death in as much as it divided all, united all.

De Mortui Nil Nisi Bonum

It was, John Drew thought, the type of scene that was as old as Biblical times. The women at the well, bearing the burden of their sister. The man in the sick bed approaching his maker in a delirium of fever and anguish. In the bedroom, the Mayhews' eldest son was sitting by an oil lamp. Thomas Mayhew stood up awkwardly when John Drew entered. Neither he nor his father would have worn out their welcome in the premises at the top of Sackville Square.

"Thomas, isn't it?"

"That's right, Dr Drew."

Still, form had to be followed. Spiritual balm was needed, when nature, like the terrible Chaldeans, came wielding her sword. The breathing of the man in the bed was scarcely perceptible. He might have been dead already but for the occasional sigh or fluttering of an eyelid. In the rude light of the oil lamp, his skin seemed strangely translucent. John Drew stayed in the house the best part of an hour, hearing the women come and go in the next room, attending to Mrs Mayhew's rambling narrative of hope lost and found, then lost again. When he finally took his leave, refusing all entreaties to take tea as he was so fearful of the company of the women in the sitting room, Thomas Mayhew drove him back to the rectory. He understood that the young man was only too glad of the respite from the house of the dying.

In order to clear his thoughts a little, he made for the chicken coop and the coachhouse. The loose plank in the near wall of the chicken coop bothered him. Perhaps Mr Reynard had already had his wicked way with the fowl inside. But, when he stooped his head to enter the chicken coop, he found the half-dozen hens there sitting in mute indifference on their perches with the cock-of-the-walk preening himself at the far end. He pushed the rain-water barrel, which Eliza and the girls used for soft water to wash their hair, up against the loose plank. It would keep until morning, when he could get Bridget Doheny's boy to put a few nails in it. In the coachhouse, he fussed about with the two sets of harness and collar and then set about clearing out the dust and debris from the trap. Only when he had trotted Evie back into the coachhouse and settled her down with a bag of Terry's best oats, did he venture to where the little collection that had so upset Bridget Doheny was located.

He ran his fingers over the cow skulls and examined a couple of the eggshells. Thrush, blackbird and sparrow. Things that little Theodora found amusement in. How could a grown woman, the like of Bridget Doheny, take exception to such objects? In the fading light, although it caused him no terror, he let on to himself, for a moment, that he could indeed see the image of the evil one in the cow skulls. To try and see what Bridget Doheny might have seen. A pooka, as they called it in Aghadoe. But then he realised that this was not what had troubled the woman at all. She was more bothered with the notion that the skulls and the eggs, by their very nature, could put some sort of a curse on her. This was more priestcraft, of course. More of the sort of superstition that caused uproar when the rath that was at the top of Sackville Square was levelled by John Howard, all those years ago, to build the Protestant church that he, John Drew, would one day come to preside over. Of course, the priests took advantage of this type of folly in the Queen's County. He knew, though, that some sort of accommodation would have to be reached with Brigid Doheny, sooner or later. He lifted up one of the wax-bound bricks from the rough-and-ready workbench to his left and snuggled it under his arm. Then he made for the house as Evie snorted and grunted in her thrall to the fresh feed of oats.

He left his boots inside the front door so that he would remember to leave them in for heeling at Waxy Daly's little booth, the following morning. Then, lighting the oil lamp, he sat in at his desk, unwrapped the brick and ran his finger over the ancient symbols.

Nabu-ku-du-ur-ri-usur

And there he sat, until the wick began to gutter in the oil lamp, rolling the brick about in his hand and puzzling over the way one sign could mean a number of things. Dimly apprehending that, behind his conscious thoughts, speculations in the third language were churning about. Later that evening, he sat down at his desk and scanned the third line of the Darius inscription.

𐎺 𐎩𐎡 𐎤𐎣 𐎫𐎡 𐎵𐎡 𐎺 𐎼 𐎶𐎣 𐏐

His lips read the syllables aloud, without fear that someone outside on Sackville Square might hear him.

Sha-nap-ha-ri-li-sha-nu-gab-bi
Totality of tongues. All.

He drew, idly, the cuneiform symbol for Sha, repeated twice in the line. With its three inverted triangles.

Then he read aloud the translation he and Westmacott had agreed upon, for the first three of the six lines.

Darius the Great King.
King of Kings. Of all the countries.
Of the totality of languages. All.

It matched the Old Persian parallel inscription all right. Right down to the last syllable of li-sha-nu. Tongue. Same word in Hebrew and Arabic. No ideographs here. Just plain, uncluttered syllables to represent yet another language—the Babylonian— fading out as the Old Persian of Darius and the Achmaenids took hold. Just as the Babylonian had, a thousand years earlier, crowded out the older, darker language of the ideographs. Yet again, the scribes were the real high priests of change. The ones who knew the past, represented the present and left a record of both for posterity. Satisfied with his reading, and having correct- ed, for the umpteenth time, the new syllable sheet he hoped to append to the translation, he stood up and stretched himself.

Too tired to track his own thoughts any further, John Drew pushed the script tables to one side and made his way wearily up the stairs for the subterranean speculations of deep sleep. Unaware that, among the signs and symbols of the Land Between the Two Rivers, the image of his dead son would soon appear. A brick in an ancient, sun-baked wall. Now here, now there. Each time, meaning something different and something the same.

XI

ELIZA AND HETTY IN GOWER STREET

An early morning mist was sweeping in from the side-streets around the station as the steampacket train drew up alongside the platform. Those in the closed carriages were disembarked first. There was a great scurry of porters as bonnets and top hats clambered out. Eliza waved to a boy with a tartan king's man about his neck. She nodded to indicate the small brown trunk and the rather worn-looking portmanteau waiting in the carriage. A stout gentleman in a flat cap shouted at no one in particular.

"London! London!"

When she finally managed to make her way through the sea of faces, with Theodora at one side and the chirpy little cockney porter with the handcart at the other, Eliza momentarily panicked. What if Hetty hadn't managed to make it to the train? She instinctively touched her breast only to find, yet again, that the token she had kept there so long was still in Aghadoe. But Hetty Arkwright was there all right, decked out in a dress of dark green with a cambric cape. A come-as-you-please sort of hat with a gay feather topped off the whole display. Plump little Albert

Arkwright was standing beside her. Hetty Arkwright rushed forward and embraced her sister. It had been over a year, but the chill, cruel waters between their respective islands seemed less menacing now, with the steampacket and the train threading a path between them. The children eyed one another cautiously. Eliza remarked to herself at how pasty-faced little Albert Arkwright looked. Not at all like Theodora, with her country complexion and sturdy gait. She knelt down to examine the boy's plum-coloured suit and cap.

"What a fine little gentleman you're turning into, Albert!"

Albert Arkwright smiled vaguely and continued staring at her. Then it was a hansom through the crowded streets of the metropolis. They marvelled at the gaslamps still lighting and the costermongers setting out their stalls with mussels and whelks and fruits and vegetables. It wasn't hard to find beggars though. Hetty Arkwright leaned across to her sister

"Mostly Irish beggars, if you please. As if we didn't have enough of our own."

The Irish were everywhere, it seemed. In the slums and tenements and the gin palaces. You could, according to Hetty, hear their cries on each street corner. Albert Arkwright twisted his mouth in an imitation of an Irish brogue.

"Spare a few coppers for the child, ma'am!"

Although Eliza blushed, there was no getting away from them, whether in Aghadoe, in Dublin, or London. They were probably roaming the streets of Chicago, New York and Boston too, if the truth be known. And California gold would bring even more to that quarter. Eliza drew Theodora close to her. The girl was already nodding off with the motion of the carriage. And then, in a thrice, they were crossing Russell Street and the stentorian, Portland Stone edifice of the British Museum. The cab jerked to a halt outside the great terraced house in Gower Street. What might it have been like if she, Eliza, had married in London?

Even a minister's wife wouldn't have been stuck for congenial company in London. There would be books by the dozen and theatrical experiences too. If that was what one wanted, of course. Belfast, above all, had been the worst move. Dour, provincial Belfast, a sort of mealy-mouthed Manchester where even the Presbyterians and the established Church couldn't see eye to eye on anything. As they ascended the granite steps of the house on Gower Street, Eliza overheard the mangling woman singing to herself in the basement. The rough-and-ready north-of-England accent seemed singularly suited to the words of the song.

> *Sitting on his own in the oakum shed*
> *Is a little old man who nods his head*
> *A little old man who nods his head*
> *Sitting on his own in the oakum shed*

The great black door of Hetty Arkwright's house opened to them, and Kitty McCormack, the maid-of-all-work, with a brogue on her as broad as a tinker's tongue, helped them carry the luggage indoors. The trunk was set down in the hall, to be brought upstairs later by Kitty and the musical mangling woman. First things first though. Eliza carried Theodora up to the bedroom on the second floor, where they would both sleep. There was grand blue-striped paper on the walls, a lilac rug on the floor and the pink drapes wouldn't have looked out of place in Her Majesty's quarters. It was, Eliza secretly felt, the bedroom of a much-wished-for daughter who had never been born. Drawing the curtains, she popped off Theodora's patent shoes and pulled the eiderdown over her so that the child might rest from the noisome train journey. Then she slipped back down to the parlour, where Kitty was already serving tea.

It was so refreshing to be back in London, all the same. London, with all its chaos of cabs and omnibuses and constant movement. The broad streets suddenly seemed a great break from the dismal sameness of Aghadoe. Of course, there was a sense, in London, that you were at the very heart of things. Eliza sat Albert Arkwright down beside her and gave him a spoon of the senna pod oil Hetty handed her.

"Poor Albert gets colicky at the slightest upset."

Then it was back to his own room for a nap, for Master Arkwright, with firm instructions given to Kitty McCormack to look in on him, from time to time. Because you could never trust boys with windows or gas taps or faucets. With anything, in fact, that had any sort of a switch. Because it was still too chill to sit out in the garden, the two sisters stood awhile in the sun room as Hetty pointed out all that had been done since Eliza's last visit.

"Albert's cherry tree still has pride of place. The raised flower beds are a new idea, of course."

"And that machine over there?"

"It's a type of mechanical water fountain that Charles tells me is worked by gravity."

"Gravity must be having a day off today."

They allowed themselves a small giggle, then Hetty was on to how things had mended greatly, since the previous year and all the Chartist disturbances. Though a corn factor like Charles Arkwright was at the mercy not only of the weather but of parliamentary debates, price changes and unrest, things seemed to be on the up.

"Do you know, Eliza, we thought there was going to be a second French Revolution here, last summer, just after you had left. With all the agitation down in Kennington Common. There were even dragoons called in to keep an eye on things in the city."

"So I read."

Eliza Drew pictured Charles Arkwright, seated among his peers, in a stuffy office near London Wall. A little cramped office, where a fortune might be made or lost. She imagined a group of men in confab, shrouded in smoke, their top hats resting on the great oak table before them. A tall bewhiskered man was haranguing the gathering, banging his table with a clenched fist. Coal, trains, steam, steel and cotton. There was power in every single thing, if only one knew how to manipulate it. Power, even, in the cuneatic inscriptions her husband was content to blind himself perusing, in the darkened study in Aghadoe.

Hetty's words faded back into her consciousness. But they were little more than a faint, distant buzzing in her ears.

"Go up and rest a little, Eliza. Don't fight it. You can freshen up afterwards and then we'll pay our respects to Father."

It was about noon when Eliza Drew finally woke to the tap-tap-tapping of her sister's white-gloved hand on the bedroom door. She could hear the laughter of the children in the room above her and, mixed in with their laughter, Kitty McCormack's voice. Little Albert seemed to have got over his bout of colic. They could slip out now, while Kitty kept an eye on things, Hetty ventured.

"Are you sure?"

"I have her well trained, believe you me."

It was only then that Eliza Drew noticed the oddly shaped receptacles on the windowsills. They were, for all the world, like the little boxes a shoe-black might use. They were the sort of thing that Bridget Doheny, back in Aghadoe, would have called, feckydos. (And, by the by, Eliza thought to herself, wasn't it odd that the letter from John Drew waiting for her on the table in Hetty Arkwright's, which must have been written just after she had left, made no mention at all of the same Bridget Doheny? Women noticed changes more than men, she told herself. A painting out of line, a strange smile, a child's sudden change of temperament. Surely the wretched Mrs Doheny wasn't ill again, with more of her little aches and pains?)

"Those things are fumigators, Eliza. Charles insists on having them in all the bedrooms, against the miasma coming in from the streets."

They took a walk then, crossing briskly through Russell Square and the midday bustle. Gentlemen and ladies were out strolling and nannies with perambulators. She must return there for a walk with Theodora, in the afternoon. A little constitutional would do the child good, after being cooped up in the boat and train. Perhaps too much time in the presence of steam was bad for the health too. On Bernard Street, they paused to speak with Mrs Meredith, from the ladies' reading circle. Mrs Meredith was a tall, mannish woman whose waist was bisected by a none-too-kind corset. Her purple cape didn't find favour with Eliza at all. There was something too falsely penitential about it. And Mrs Meredith didn't seem like a woman who believed in either penance or punishment. Mrs Meredith wondered whether Hetty was sure this evening was convenient for the reading circle. What with it being her sister's first day in London, after all.

"Actually, it was Eliza here who insisted on keeping arrangements just as they are."

"I would like to sit in on the circle this time, Mrs Meredith."

"And you are more than welcome!"

The foppish hat seemed a little off, in a woman of such substance—a physician's wife—but Eliza put it down to a certain innate flightiness exacerbated by too much novel reading. Which put her in mind of Judith, back in Aghadoe, who probably had her nose, at that very moment, stuck in some unsavoury book, out in Willie Hill's mansion. Would she ever forget the travesty of a tale she had caught her reading, at the start of summer!

> The hot winds coming in over the desert sands burn the soul and singe the senses. It is only the very hardy who can withstand the torture of the long, searing days of the summers of Araby. On the most terrible of those days, when even the yellow scorpions of the desert cowered under rocks, Lorna took refuge in thoughts of England with its green swards and fresh pastures. The haywain

making its merry way along a rustic track, to the singing of a rosy-cheeked farmer. But, most of all, when her thoughts sought to wrench themselves free of the terrible drought without, she thought of Roddy. Of Roddy Dunbar, in his fine frieze coat and jet black top hat, with his hand outstretched, waiting for her to descend from the London coach, in the little village of Minch Hampton. Nor could Roddy know that his true love was still alive. Or that her thoughts were of him and him alone, in the days of hell, when the khamsin blew in from the desert, scorching everything in its path and burning the very breath in Lorna's breast.

Mrs Tours had said she would keep an eye on Judith. No more than that could Eliza Drew ask for.

They passed in slowly through the sombre gates of St George's burial ground. Truth to tell, Eliza could have found the headstone blindfolded with the winged angel atop the plinth. A vain memorial to a man who hadn't an ounce of vanity to his name. They read the sombre, curt legend

Isaac Cameron
Aet. 3rd October 1775
Mort. 10th April 1835
Requiescat in Pace

A party of mourners was standing to their right, the remnant of some earlier burial. Not quite as bad in St George's as in the burial ground up in St Pancras, where the old dead were pushing up the newly dead and the stench of the bodies swollen with the illness was too much for the stoutest of mourners. Perhaps healthier to burn people, like in India, as John Drew had suggested at the Willingtons' table, at Easter. But where did that leave one on Resurrection Day then? Eliza watched the black hats and the silk ribbons of the mourners. Noting that she must clean her shoes of the graveyard dirt as soon as she got back to Gower Street. Never bring dirty shoes into a house, after a funeral. Was this superstition? Perhaps this had something to do with the great sickness itself. According to John Drew, Mr Chadwick's report was all about this sort of thing: sanitary burial grounds, clean water and the proper disposal of sanitary waste. But what if the other theory held out? What if the contagion really was caused by some sort of miasma, stealing over the land, in the dead of night? Then, fumigators or no, there was really no protection for the likes of herself and Hetty and their children. What caused the sickness in the rookeries of St Giles—just the other side of Oxford Street, after all—would surely cross over on the wind, some foul night. They lingered a few moments by their father's grave, reminiscing over days long gone and speaking about their childhood. Not a gilded childhood, by any means, but one that was, for the most part, safe and secure and warm. Because of their father. Eliza Drew thought of the Frost Fairs on the Thames. Trips down the river to Richmond, trips into the countryside. Eliza turned to her sister slowly. The plump face put her off for a moment. But then she spoke. Her question was a simple one but one to which she really required no particular answer but the sound of her own voice.

"Are we good mothers, Hetty? Better than our own mother?"

"That's not really a fair question to ask, Eliza."

Hetty Arkwright smiled back uneasily at her sister. For Hetty Arkwright, whatever else she was, was a woman who expected good of life. And who mostly received it, in consequence of making those around her happy. She wasn't the sort of woman who was always waiting for an ambush around the corner, or bad news, with every knock on the door, like her sister.

They waited until the children were in bed, later that evening, before dining on turtle soup and pheasant, followed by strawberry compote. It was the sort of rich fare that scandalised Eliza, at the Worthingtons' table. Theodora had read Albert to sleep with an illustrated version of the Joseph story, and Eliza had then read Theodora to sleep with the tale of Sindbad. When the dinner things had been cleared away and Kitty McCormack had retired to her bedroom, beside the playroom, the ladies started to arrive. First came Mrs Collier, her great frame filling the room with laughter and lightness. Then Mrs Meredith appeared in. The quorum was sealed with Mrs Rawlings, with her continental umbrella and cape, who was full of chat about the doings of the day. In truth, there was but a small reading session with Mrs Meredith intoning the fourth chapter of *Jane Eyre*. They spoke a while of the young heroine's trials and of the condition of her heart. At one point, Eliza was almost tempted to make mention of Judith's obsession with the unsavoury Lorna Lovegrove but thought better of it, believing that such low forms of narrative were scarcely to be mentioned in such august company. All were honour bound to read only as far as the specified chapter. So that none would have a lead on the others and so that their specula-tions on the possible outcome would be fairer and fresher. The talk opened out somewhat when Mrs Collier began asking Eliza to give some account of matters in Ireland, especially concerning the new agitation, Her Majesty's recent visit and the terrible scenes that had taken place in Ulster, a while previously. What was the location called again? Mrs Meredith wondered. Eliza coughed and glanced over at her sister.

"Dolly's Brae, I think."

"Shocking! Appalling! Party spirit, of course."

Mrs Collier was a woman who was constantly appalled by things. By the weather, by the overcrowded streets and the price of victuals. When Eliza confessed to having no special under-standing of the whole situation, the talk moved on to the matter of her journey from Dublin. Eliza found herself slightly aghast at the frankness of the ladies and the forthrightness of their opinions, feeling, not a little, like the country mouse come to town. Mrs Rawlings was full of praise for the whole railway enterprise, of course.

"Soon you will be able to make the journey from London to Glasgow in a single day!"

"But who would want to visit Glasgow, Mrs Rawlings? Even for a single day?"

There was a sustained round of laughter then before talk turned to John Drew's work. Mrs Meredith knew the provenance of his studies on cuneatics. The accounts of Mr Layard's travels in Mesopotamia had excited the whole thinking population of London. His brave endeavours among the savages on the Euphrates and the Tigris were the subject of many a dinner party conversation. There were tales, too, of monuments unearthed that could rival those of Greece and Rome. Soon the British Museum would be full of artefacts from that quarter, if what Mrs Meredith had been told was half-true.

The evening finished off with a good-humoured rubber of whist. As they played, the smell of the camphor in the fumigators in the upstairs bedrooms caught in Eliza's throat. Mrs Rawlings came down firmly on the side of the miasmatists, feeling that the fumigators strategically placed at bedroom windows might still do some good by combusting the toxic component of the air as it reached the house walls. But Mrs Meredith, whose husband, after all, was on the board of the Foundling Hospital and had something to do with the corporation, said that water lay at the root of the whole matter. Boiling the water, especially in the height of summer, was the best defence of all. Hadn't it been proven among the soldiers, during the Sikh rebellion?

Charles Arkwright appeared in around half past nine. He kissed his sister-in-law on both cheeks, after the continental fashion, and made for the kitchen to eat a late supper. He popped his dark mane of hair through the door, a short while later, to suggest that if any of the ladies needed a cab, he would fetch one. But said ladies had already decided to walk home as the summer light was still in the sky. Eliza found herself shocked, once more, at their candour. As she and Hetty stood on the steps to bid them farewell, Mrs Collier said, "This isn't Drury Lane, Eliza. There's no need to worry."

The sisters were alone again then. Fussing about in the parlour, re-arranging things. In the cosy room where she and her daughter would sleep, her sister undid Eliza Drew's stays. Then they quenched the fumigators at the windows. They regarded one another silently as they heard Charles Arkwright climb up the stairs for bed.

"Are you glad you came, Eliza?"

"I always come on Father's anniversary."

"Yes, but are you glad you came?"

"Yes . . . yes . . . very glad."

Hetty Arkwright didn't notice the locket missing from her sister's breast. Or think too much about little Albert Arkwright's odd pallor, as the boy's face was to the wall, in sleep. She was, after all, a woman who was full of good cheer and a lover of life and all its conceits. Nevertheless, the sisters slept, that first night, not quite free from concern about the evils concealed in the night air over London and in the waters below her. Or the badness harboured in the foul, foetid closets and privies where, in the dead of dark, the nightsoil men came to cart away the humus that would be used to liven up the ground where the finest of fruits and vegetables thrived.

XII

MRS TOURS IS VEXED

Mrs Tours opened the scullery door to let out the cat who was pawing at the leg of the chair. She glanced over the back gate, out into the field, then emptied the tea-leaves out on to the little pile of ashes over in the corner. A couple of children were out playing in the field. She could hear them in the distance. Connie Kavanagh was one. The other seemed to be one of the Moores. She shouted across the gate at them, pointing to the dip in the field.

"Mind ye don't go near that ould well, like good children!"

But the children were away with the wind before she could raise her voice again. She stood a moment, watching their progress through the long grass, before turning back for the scullery again.

I was vexed on account of Judith Drew avoiding my eye and she tipping out of town in the jaunting car with her father and the Hills, after service. I was walking up Pound Street, after second mass, when the jaunting car comes trotting by. The Hills nodded to me. You're made up with them two lassies, says I, in me own mind. Many's the day I spent up in their palace, on the Commons road, sewing the drapes and mending one thing and

*another. And, if I needed the money again, or the lodgers walked off on me,
I'd be back up there in the morning. I wouldn't mind ould Drew not giving me the time of day. Will you whisht! He probably didn't see me at all.
But Judith just looked the other way. Eliza Drew must have let her know
that I was keeping an eye on her. Probably thought, do you see, that as long
as she played along at the fair on Tuesday, that I wouldn't look any further. Well, think again, missie!*

Mrs Tours pulled the door to and, crossing into the kitchen,
reminded herself that there was still work to be done before she
could put on the lodgers' dinner. She sat herself at the kitchen
table and pulled across an old copy of the *London Evening
Standard* that she had been reading. Her lips moved as her eyes
tracked the letters. It was an account of the bad sanitation system
in London and the terrible frights people had when a child fell
ill, with cholera in the air. She crossed herself absent-mindedly as
she read, raising her eyes only once at the sound of a dog barking out on Pound Street.

*There was no point in making a show of myself trying to talk to the Hills
that day. And no point at all in bringing the matter to the attention of
Mr Dr Drew, who couldn't mind mice at the crossroads. The only thing
for it was to catch Violet Hill at the fair, on the Tuesday. Because she
always comes into town, of a Tuesday, with that little hoppy maid of
hers, to shop for fruit and vegetables and anything fancy that might be
about. So, I held me spake a few more days. Dan Brady slipped out the
two nights to keep an eye on them. They were out by Taylor's well on the
Saturday, but not on the Sunday. I was beginning to wonder whether the
passion was cooling or whether someone had found out on the Hennigans' side. Mind you it's easy to see how she fell for Michael Hennigan
with his big dark eyes and his Italian skin. Many a girl would. A great
gob for a beer bottle too, of course. And hardly gone twenty. But what if
the whole business went too far and young Hennigan got into her
ladyship's drawers? Well, by Christ, if I thought there was any notion of*

that in young Hennigan's mind, I'd give him a grumbling in his grul-locks that he wouldn't forget in a hurry. To tell you the truth, I had a little cry over the whole business. When the lodgers were in bed. Then I smartened up and thought over what I would say to Violet Hill when I met her. Maybe shove that book of Judith's into her hand. A fine whore's prayerbook for a young woman to be reading. Show Violet Hill where madam's thoughts really are.

It was Layla who broke the news to Lorna on the night of the full moon, when they could hear, from the battlements above, the Moorish singers chanting their hypnotic songs in the streets below. Lorna wept bitter-ly, her face pressed against the damask pillow, her mind's eye filled with the torment of what was before her and the memory of what she had left behind. Eng-land: its green pastures and gay swards. The village green and the yeoman, walking home at sunset from the ploughed field. The lowing of cattle in the distance.

It was sometime after midnight, when the sound of the musicmakers had died away, that Layla was sent for. She embraced her sister tenderly. The chamberlain snapped his long fingers and two of the Emir's hand-maidens drew Lorna's only friend away. It was not long after that, when Allah's call to prayer was being sound-ed from all the minarets around the city, that the heavy wooden door of the chamber swung open and the great Moor's dark eyes flashed at his unfortunate prey. The hour had come . . .

I was worn out by the worry of it all. There was a great rush on for the two bridesmaids' gowns for the Mitchell girl and—would you credit it?—didn't Mrs Mitchell arrive in at the last minute and declare that she wanted to add a few blue bows to the gowns. Not at all tasteful, if you ask me. I was near going blind in the bad light—it was very overcast that day. I had to get the little Doheny chap to thread the last needle for me after he did the messages. I slept the sleep of the dead that night. But the sound of the cattle being driven down Pound Street for the square and the shouts of all the farmers woke me up handy enough. As I lay on the bed, I could hear the chat of the farmers outside the door.

"Be Christ and they'd better be offering more than the last day."

"You'll have to take what you get, like the rest of us."

"Deed and I won't . . . is it for nothing they want them?"

There were dogs barking and bonhams squealing. By the time I had dressed and come down the stairs, there was a solid line of cowshite all along the whitewashed wall of Pound Street. The same every fair day. And they don't bother cleaning it off afterwards either. There was no point in cleaning it up until the evening, when all the beasts had gone home. The two-legged ones as well as the four-legged ones.

Mrs Tours stood up to wet the tea. The kettle was hissing on the hob, and she groaned slightly as she stooped to lift the blackened vessel from the flame. She stood a moment, looking out the window, letting it draw, before pouring herself a mug of tarry tea and sitting down again to the newspaper. But her mind found no purchase on the words and, without noticing it, she took off her spectacles and laid them down on the table in front of her. In an instant, she was nodding off, her plump frame supported by the kitchen wall and the stern upright of the chairs Willie Hill's wife had left in the Christmas before last, on foot of a last-minute job she had done on Cassie Hill's party dress.

It was all go down in the square. There was a rake of stalls over by Terry's shop. Terry himself was out standing at the door, watching the trade pass by. There were big country women selling eggs and apples and God-knows-what. There was a couple of stalls with a few cute boys selling little fecky-dos. To tell the truth, if it wasn't for the cowshite, I'd have a fair every week. Just for the bit of chat. No matter if I have a basket of work itself waiting for me at home. Sergeant Arkins was standing over in front of the barracks, and he having a good chat with Nolan, the head foreman in the brewery. All grand and aisy like. Never know when they would need one another. One of them makes the beer; the other keeps order after people has drank too much of it. Well and if I didn't run into old ladies, I declare to God, I hadn't seen in a year. Their men well dead and buried. The sons helping them down out of jaunting-cars. Ould sticks of women you'd think should be long gone out of it, to leave room for everyone else. There was a great crowd inside and outside John Gordon's shop at the bottom of the square. Always plenty of money for beer. It would all end in tears, anyway. When a few of the wild boyos had too much porter under their belts and they lost the run of their mickies and their mouths.

Violet Hill didn't show up until well eleven. I nearly missed her. And I thinking I'd spot her a mile away. She had left that great jaunting car of hers inside the brewery gates. They're so well got with Terry, do you see. She appeared out of the blue, with little missy mouse maid dragging two big baskets. I started walking down past the barracks. Nice and easy like. I was in no great hurry. She was talking to that Quinn woman—the one with the gammy leg—when I got to the corner of the square. I could hear the ould Quinn one, lawdy-dawying away in that rale put-on Englishy accent of hers. As if she wasn't born out the road in the bog, like the rest of us. Only difference was she had a Protestant prayerbook put in her paws the day she was born.

"Don't you know we love to have a party at the end of every summer, Violet?"

"Isn't that grand? I'm sure William and I would like to come along, so."

Violet Hill caught sight of me then. Maybe she thought I was looking for fresh custom. The Quinn one got the message, in the end, and started to pack her bags. I smiled sweetly at her.

"Them's two lovely young boys you have, Mrs Quinn."

"And right terrors they are too, Mrs Tours!"

"That's lads for you . . . all go."

Violet Hill just stood staring at me for a moment. With little goodie-two-shoes standing beside her with her two baskets full.

"Was there something you wanted to see me about, Mrs Tours?"

"Faith and there was."

And then, would you credit it, doesn't ould Drew come along on his perambules. Surprised he would risk getting cowshite on his boots on fair day. He stopped right in front of us and looked at me as though he had never met me in his life.

"Mrs Tours . . . I wasn't sure it was you."

"And who did you think it was then, tell us?"

You ignorant black fucker you, says I, in me own mind. Has it got so bad now that they don't even see us standing in front of them? Of course, he's so gone into himself with all them books, doesn't even see his own flesh and blood.

What is What?

It's a wonder he even notices poor Eliza Drew and the girls. He was full of the business over Bridget Doheny that day, of course. How would he get the woman back into the house before Eliza Drew came home? Axe me arse, Dr Drew, I felt like saying. But, says I, I'll put a word in, in that quarter. Don't you worry there. I couldn't very well bring up the business of Judith Drew with Violet Hill, and he standing there. I could hardly tell the Reverend Dr Mr Drew that one of the sons of the biggest Catholic farmers had a notion of throwing the leg over his eldest daughter. And that little Miss Judith was only too happy to give him a rub of the relic in return. I heard him ask Violet Hill how things were with Judith out in the house though. And, when Violet seemed at ease with everything, I said to myself, Am I putting too much store by all this gallavantin' by the well?

Because, when I looked at Violet Hill and her nice hair and the way everything was in order with her, I didn't know what to be saying. Still and all, says I to meself, I'll wait by the well tonight and see if little Lorna Lovegrove turns up for her appointment or if love has gone cold. Then I said good day to herself, and myself and ould Drew walked on towards Pound Street. He was off out for his constitutional, as he calls it, and I was going home to finish a bit of mending for Nan Seavers. I pointed out the line of dirt along the wall of the house, just to get a rise out of him.

"Isn't that a disgrace, Dr Drew? All that cowshite there."

"Yes, indeed, Mrs Tours. Those gentlemen with their cattle should be

jollywell made clean it all off . . . all that."

"What, Dr Drew?"

"All that dreadful . . . cow dung."

Jollywell is right. Nice answer you'd get if you asked that crowd of bog-men to scrub off their own scutter. Maybe in England they do that, Dr Drew, says I, in me own mind. But it'll be a long time before it catches on here. And I bade him good day and went inside to have a little nap, to get me strength back so I could finish the mending and be ready for the well.

Mrs Tours awoke sharply to the sound of a caller at the door. She took a moment to compose herself, threw back the last of the mug of tea and settled her spectacles on her nose again, then rose stiffly to answer the door.

"Are you in, Mrs Tours?"

"Don't knock the door down on me, will you."

She opened the door to Nan Ryan, in all her finery, who was holding some class of a fancy costume in her arms. Would Mrs Tours have a minute to fix a dropped hem on a dress? It was for her daughter, Mary, and there was a train to catch tomorrow morning. Mrs Tours took the dress in her hands and called the other woman in.

"Wet the tea there, Mrs Ryan and I'll have that done by the time we have a mouthful drunk."

"Ah, you're very good, Mrs Tours. I knew you wouldn't let me down, so you wouldn't."

Mrs Tours looked over her spectacles as she snapped a piece of thread.

"Tell me this and tell me no more, Nan, did that husband of yours ever buy that bit of land, out by Keeley's?"

When Mrs Tours had finished touching up the hem on the dress, she sat over with her companion and questioned her more on her husband and children. The better to get the price of the intrusion out of her, before turning back to the basket of mending she had to finish before dark.

XIII

OF SHANAVESTS AND RIBBONMEN

There was nothing for Fox Keegan to do but pass the night in Abbeyleix. He had no difficulty at all in finding Drennan's shop; the sound of conversation inside and the smell of cheap porter on the warm evening air was enough. When he stooped his head to enter the bar, all eyes turned towards him. A few old lads were drinking at the long counter. Over by the huge chimney breast, another couple of worthies were hatching over a little turf fire, in deep conversation with a dark-faced gentleman who hadn't troubled to take off his hat. Deciding to return for a few scoops later, Fox Keegan asked directions from the sour-faced woman behind the bar to Reilly's lodging house.

"O'Reilly's is just after the laneway . . . on the right . . . you can't miss it."

O'Reilly's was a tidy-enough gaff. The widow woman led him up the stairs, then left him there to sort himself out. The lodger who occupied the other bed was out at a threshing and would probably sleep the night in a barn. Fox Keegan lay down on the bed to compose himself and fell into a short sleep. Waking out of sorts and out of place, it took him a moment or so to get his bearings. And then the image of Drennan's was in his mind. The smell of porter and the warm buzz of loose, useless conversation. He pulled on his boots again and threw the satchel over his shoulder. You wouldn't know who might stray into such a house. Maybe the widow woman herself was a little light-fingered.

He settled in quite happily at the long counter, in between the two old boys at the bar. The woman behind the bar finished clearing up and went off into the house itself. The two on either side of him sat there, pulling on their pipes, talking across him, without turning towards one another. Although it was all grand and easy, he was faintly mindful of the three creatures behind him around the fire. Especially the older one with the black hat. One of the old men asked where he was headed for. When he said Kilkenny, the other spoke.

"Is it gone astray you are?"

"I missed the Carlow train and then the Kilkenny car in Naas."

"Aren't you the right gom altogether!"

As the porter weaved its subtle magic on his tired senses, he let several cats out of several bags. He mentioned that he had once been a schoolmaster down in Tullyroe, his home village. That he had then been a clerk in Terry's, in Aghadoe. And, finally, that he had gone to Dublin and ended up in Pim's, a great store in Dublin. The man with the black hat sitting over by the fire gobbed a ball of tobacco juice into the flames. It sizzled as he spoke.

"Did I hear tell you used to live in Aghadoe?"

"Aye, that's right. I was in the brewery."

"And you gave up that grand job to go and work above in Dublin? Is it mad you are?"

The pair at the far side of the fire joined in the general mirth. Fox was a funny class of a fellow, they said. What made him leave his schoolmastering job in Kilkenny anyway?

"I didn't have the patience for it."

"Pity about you!"

The man in the black hat went out to relieve himself against the yard wall. The woman behind the counter winked at Fox as she passed him a fresh bottle of beer.

"Steer clear of that fellow. The Bowsy Murphy we call him. This is the only shop will let him in, in the whole town."

One of the old boys got down from his stool then. It was time for home, he said. Fox watched him amble out into the warm August air. The tap-tap-tap of the blackthorn stick on the flagged floor. The other old fellow turned to him, nodding towards the etching of the great Daniel O'Connell on the far wall, in between the bottles and jugs.

"There's the boy that stood up to them!"

Fox smiled at the old face beside him.

"And without a drop of blood being shed."

"Well, faith and he threatened it often enough, so he did!"

And then, just like that, the company was all talk about the great harm done, in every quarter of the world, by the English. The Sikhs were named and the Hindoos and all the tormented tribes of the world and they only wanting to be left alone to their own devices. When the Bowsy Murphy returned and resumed his place by the fire, he picked at his teeth and threw a couple of sods on the fire, as though indifferent to the whole conversation. His two companions opposite didn't hold back, however. If it wasn't the plight of the Sikhs, it was the past year and the great rage all over Europe. The smaller of the two nodded towards Fox as he spoke.

"You had them all last year, mister . . . Rome and Milan and Venice and the Hungarian crowd . . . all up in arms . . . same as us. Isn't that right, Mr Murphy?"

But the Bowsy Murphy just carried on picking at his teeth by the fire and nodding to himself as though working out some secret puzzle. Fox could feel his thoughts slipping away from him now. The journey and the little snooze and the porter had combined to dull his senses. He tried to shut himself up but wasn't quite able to. He heard his own tremulous voice, as if from a distance now.

"And what about Pio Nono, then? What about the pope? He doesn't seem to have any great love for the nationalists."

The big man in the black hat looked over at him. A dour, wicked sort of look that had little good in it. Fox nodded at the woman behind the counter.

"Sure didn't he side with the Italians first and then with the Austrians?"

The Bowsy Murphy stirred himself. The two at the far side of the fire were watching for a stir in his rheumy eyes. For some class of cue. Bowsy Murphy didn't look at Fox Keegan as he spoke, but went on staring into the fire.

"Aren't you the great fellow? Making game of the pope of Rome. That's what has you well got with the other crowd of swaddlers."

Fox looked up at the woman's face behind the bar. Her eyes said: Drink up and go home. Which was what he had decided to do now. If you wanted trouble, you were never stuck for it in a small town. Especially if you were a stranger. But first he had to go and pass water. He felt weak as he stood watching the water spray against the outside wall. He smiled as he thought of Dilly Shiels in Pim's. Such fine thoughts beat politics and God-talk hands down. He longed to be as one with her. To wake to her smile, on starched white sheets. A thing that would never be. Across the divide. Commerce was one thing; love was another.

He sat himself back down to finish up his drink. The talk at the bar had turned to the harvest now. Would the weather hold or would it be like the previous year? And what news was there of the potato crop? Fox Keegan slipped down from the stool and picked up his satchel. The Bowsy Murphy made a great show of calling for Fox Keegan's attention. There wasn't a sound from the others.

"Tell me this and tell me no more, Mr Schoolmaster . . ."

"Yes?"

"Did you ever hear tell of a fellow from Aghadoe, be the name of Jer Hynes?"

Fox glanced at the other eyes. Wide boys. Waiting for him to move. No, Fox Keegan said. He had never heard tell of that name.

"Now, I find that very strange, so I do. For he would have been in Aghadoe around your time. Same age and all . . ."

Bowsy Murphy nodded at the woman washing the glasses behind the counter.

"Would you ever give us another bottle there, like a good woman."

What to do: to walk, run or stand still? To leave now would be an admission of guilt. Better brazen it out. It had worked for him before. The Bowsy Murphy stood up slowly and advanced towards the counter. He took up the open bottle and the glass and looked right into Fox Keegan's eyes. There was a smell of sour beer and bad teeth.

"You might know his friend, then. Pat Dempsey, of the Green Roads. They both worked on the ould railway, a few years back. Pat Dempsey got into a bit of bother."

"Is that so, now?"

"And do you know what?"

"What's that?"

"Didn't they go and hang him for it."

"Is that a fact now?"

"It is so, sonny boy. And you fuckinwell know it is, so you do."

The two by the fire were stirring in their seats now. The taller one making a scraping sound with his blackthorn on the hearth as though trying to scratch out a letter or a word. Bowsy Murphy pushed up the brim of his hat with the open bottle. Fox Keegan was making him out to be a liar, he said. And he didn't like any man doing that. He would get very vexed if any man called him a liar. Or even thought he was a liar. Behind him, Fox Keegan heard the other two stand up from the fire. The old man beside him moved along the counter. Maybe this was it. A sharp crack of a stick over the head. Or a broken bottle rammed into his face. But instead, the two by the fire said they were for home. He felt relief surge through him but tried not to show it. Bowsy Murphy looked from one of the men to the other.

"Why hast thou forsaken me, boys?"

"We have to be on home. I said I wouldn't be out late."

"I said I wouldn't be out late! That woman of yours has you turned into a rale maneen, so she has!"

Fox Keegan should have been uneasy about the grand exit. Hadn't he been told often enough in Dublin that if someone left the company suddenly, he should watch out on the street? But this was Abbeyleix, after all. Not the Liberties of Dublin or the Quays. He looked through bleary eyes at the ogre in front of him. His own words were slurred now.

"The past is the past. What's done is done."

"Is that a fact now? And I still say you're making a liar out of me, in front of my friends. And I don't like that one little bit, Mr Schoolmaster!"

"I think you've misunderstood me."

The Bowsy Murphy looked across the counter at the woman. He seemed to be softening somewhat. Or tiring of the game.

"That's what comes from not mixing with your own kind, Peggy."

"Is that right, now?"

"You do get notions."

And that seemed to be that. But he should have known better.

Maybe left the shop and headed back up towards the town. God knows, it was warm enough out. It might have been Italy or France. He could have gone a bit out the Kilkenny road and curled up out of sight, in a ditch for the night, then walked on in the morning until he spotted the Kilkenny car coming out of Abbeyleix. But he was dog-tired and the cheap porter had taken its toll on his legs. All he wanted was a clean bed, with no lice, and a good sleep. He made slowly for the door.

Bowsy Murphy went back to his seat by the fire then, not looking back at Fox Keegan at all, as he left the pub. He seemed to be talking to himself now. Reprising the whole conversation as though his two companions were still in front of him.

Still and all, Fox Keegan thought afterwards, he should have sniffed danger in the air. Especially when the voice called out to him, from the darkened laneway at the crook in the street. It wouldn't have been too late to make a run for the town then. But, like the tired, drunken gom he was, he had to go and stick his nose down the laneway. In a flash, he was dragged into the dark and the hammering started. He curled up like an autumn hedgehog as the kicks rained down on him, along with the blows from the knobbly blackthorn.

"Go back to your fancy friends now! Let them mend your broken head! You fucking turncoat!"

How they kept at it, winded and all as they were, he didn't know. But every bone in his body felt broken. Every muscle felt like it had been flayed. His head alone escaped unscathed. He had managed to tuck himself in by a rain barrel next to the gable wall.

Needless to say, the canvas satchel was well gone when the pair finally ran off. And, with it, the few shillings he had brought for the journey, along with a clean shirt and a few odds and ends. There was no going back to the lodging house now. He had no money for one and he couldn't show up in this state. So he moved closer to the rain barrel and slept a painful sleep. And there he lay, drunk and bleeding, while the rest of the town slept. Not even noticing, an hour or so later, the Bowsy Murphy planting his big brogue in his backside as he spat on him.

XIV

THEODORA SEES A WOLF

When Eliza Drew left the house in Gower Street that morning, Theodora was still fast asleep. It appeared that Albert Arkwright was feeling a little peevish. Eliza thought she should say something about the boy to Hetty, later on, after she had visited the British Museum to collect the copies of the inscriptions John Drew had requested. Maybe the boy had worms? It could happen in the cleanest of households. Eliza had breakfasted, if you could call it that, with Charles Arkwright. While Kitty McCormack slipped up and down to them with tea and toast and muffins, Charles worked his way silently through the *Morning Chronicle*. It was no intention of Charles Arkwright's to slight her, of course. Far from it. Hetty had told Eliza that her husband preferred to steer clear of early morning conversations. There was just the morning newspaper and, beyond that, the sound of tea being sipped and toast being munched. When Charles Arkwright left down the newspaper all of a sudden, Eliza thought there was going to be some sort of conversation. But the man in front of her just smiled and said, "Time to go, said the crow!"

There was a little peck on the cheek for Hetty, and then Charles Arkwright was off in the cab to London Wall. Following a few minutes after him, Eliza left to meet Mr Allison, one of the Eastern curators in the museum, to collect the package for John Drew.

Gower Street was alive with the grinding of dozens of wheels. Eliza Drew took her time though, happy to have the leisure to watch others going about their business. Smiling at babies in great perambulators. Minding the high fashion she saw around her, in hats and dresses. A woman at the corner of Store Street was selling flowers from a great wicker basket. Eliza reminded herself to pick up a bunch on the way home. She crossed into Montague Place and entered the new museum from there. How imposing the whole edifice was. The hallmarks of empire and learning in each column and arch. The majesty of empire would not be so easily mocked, now that Victoria's reach extended as far as the Orient and the lands of the East. The world was in thrall to London, its engines and devices. And yet, for all of that, a humble cherry tree could still blossom at the heart of the empire, in Hetty Arkwright's garden in Gower Street. The simple thought pleased her, for it betokened a certain humility that must guide the reins of empire.

How Are the Mighty Fallen

If it were not for agitators like the coalman Murphy up in St Pancras or Agar town or wherever it was—the women in the reading circle seemed to know all these sordid things—life would be much better for the generality. Inciting the unlettered could scarcely improve things. She ascended the great steps, lifting her skirt so as not to trip herself. John Drew had given clear directions as to where to go. At the corner of the second-floor landing, she asked for more specific directions. A surly looking porter, with a moustache that almost smothered his mouth, inclined his head towards her.

"Mr Allison's office, madam? Is it a general query?"

"I have an appointment."

"This way then, madam."

Their feet rang out as they walked along the chill corridor. Eliza Drew was wandering among her own thoughts when she suddenly stopped in shock, for there, at the far end of the corridor, was the very last person she had expected to meet in London. The ruddy cheeks, the hat set at a raffish angle. The excitable gait put the seal on it. He was in conversation with Mr Allison, whom she recalled having met briefly the previous summer in London. The gentlemen stopped just in front of Eliza and the moustachioed porter.

"Mr Westmacott!"

"Mrs Drew!"

"But I thought you were supposed to be in Ireland with my husband?"

She heard the porter retreat behind her. Then that giddiness came over her again. The presentiment that all was about to fall apart. Mr Allison took her by one arm, Westmacott took her by the other.

"Are you all right, ma'am? Mr Jenkins!"

She heard the porter scurry back to them.

"Mr Jenkins, fetch a glass of water for this lady! Quickly!"

And the next thing she knew, she was in Mr Allison's office. With Mr Westmacott tending her a glass of water wrapped in a silk handkerchief and the two men fretting over her like mother hens. Things began to clarify slowly then. It appeared that Mr Westmacott's trip had been cancelled, at the last moment, because of urgent government business. There was no more to it than that. Would that Aghadoe had the new electric telegraph! Then there would have been time to make other arrangements. Perhaps leave Judith in Sackville Square, where Bridget Doheny could keep an eye on her. She felt foolish now. Flustered and foolish, in front of the men. She tried to regain her bearings by ignoring requests to rest, and insisted on collecting the copies of the inscriptions she had come for. She struggled hard to give the impression of order.

"I have a copy of the list my husband sent last month. There was some problem about the quality of one of the Persepolitan inscriptions."

"Ah, yes. Mr Westmacott mentioned that already."

"He is working on a new set of Babylonian tables at the moment, he asked me to say . . ."

Mr Allison was all fuss and bother, but there was something in the tone of condescension that cut her. A certain lowering of the voice, as though he didn't want to be overheard talking about such grave matters to a mere woman. She was beginning to think like one of Hetty's reading circle, and she wasn't back in London a wet week! Hadn't John Drew said to her, many's the time, in one of his own little piques, that the London savants imagined themselves to be something they were not. Westmacott was different, of course. Perhaps because he had seen the world and been humbled by the ancient civilisations of the East. When Eliza took the parcel and, very ceremoniously, ticked off her list, Mr Westmacott insisted on accompanying her to the Russell Street entrance. He apologised, yet again, for startling her. She had suffered, he noted, the same shock the Caliph's servant had suffered in the thousand and one nights.

"You mean an appointment in Samara, Mr Westmacott?"

"Precisely!"

"But, thankfully, there is no death involved in this tale."

The evil eye again. You had to say against a thing said immediately in order to nullify it. Like a sort of verbal fumigator. Like the Catholics did in Aghadoe. More priestcraft. Westmacott fixed his hat at a more civilised slant. It was funny Eliza Drew should say that, he volunteered, but, just the previous week, one of his acquaintances, a parliamentary secretary no less, had been carried off by the disease. It was clear, Mr Westmacott went on, that even great stone fortresses like New Houses of Parliament weren't immune to the fickle finger of fate.

"Don't you call that God's will, Mr Westmacott?"

"Perhaps. But I'm not a fatalist, Mrs Drew. And neither, I suspect, are you."

They walked together as far as Duke Street where, Mr Westmacott told her, he must catch a cab for a meeting with some government functionary. He would be sailing for Turkey, the following week. Into the heart of the Ottoman Empire itself. It was a shame that the sojourn in Ireland had been cancelled. He and John Drew had held themselves back in their individual studies so that they both might complete the translation of the Babylonian version of the Darius inscription.

"It's an ill wind, Mr Westmacott . . ."

"My, my, Mrs Drew, I believe I do detect an undercurrent of superstition in your words."

"Nothing more than the wisdom of the ages."

"Indeed."

And there she went again. More peasant talk. She was beginning to sound more and more like an Irish washerwoman, with her halfpenny wisdoms and her fatalism. Not to mention the strange sessions she had had, of late, with Mrs Tours. She resolved, there and then, to put some sort of distance between herself and the seamstress as soon as she returned. Listen a little less to Bridget Doheny's ravings as well, about pookas and the like.

They all had a little picnic in the garden in Gower Street, later that morning. Kitty McCormack baked scones for the children and Hetty and Eliza had a platter of tongue and cold potato salad. The clouds had cleared by then and the sun was at full strength. Nevertheless, when it was time for the little outing they had planned, they took care to bring cloaks with them. Eliza dressed Theodora in the pinafore with the Holland pockets that Judith had once worn to the dame school. A straw bonnet with calico strings was enough to keep either sun or rain off. Then the four of them headed off up Gower Street, crossing by the New Road for Regent's Park. It was as well they had eaten before, as it was quite a walk to the Zoological Gardens. Not at all as near as it had seemed in the guidebook Hetty had given her. They stopped to purchase some pears from a clean-looking woman in a tartan shawl, saving them until they should be inside the gardens. They didn't know what to see first. Hetty had a mind to see the camels though, and so it was settled.

"Ships of the desert, the Mohammedans call them, Eliza."

Eliza was most taken with the eagles' aviary. Mighty, frowning birds that gave no quarter to friend or foe. Little Theodora's eyes started out of her head as she watched them fly from branch to branch. Then it was off to the llama house, Master Albert's favourite. The child seemed not as taken with the creatures as his mother had expected. If anything, Eliza thought, he looked even pastier than he had the morning they arrived in London. The wolves' den was the *pièce-de-resistance* of the whole trip. The wolves really were the mean, grey-coated creatures of myth and legend. Theodora clung to her mother's skirts, fearful, yet fascinated by the spectacle. There is something primitive in all of us, Eliza Drew thought then, that makes us afraid of wolves and rats and spiders. Some learning from thousands of years ago. Else, how would a small child know to be afraid of such creatures? Maybe it was like a secret script, written inside the brain. As hard to read as one of John Drew's cuneatic lines. Harder perhaps. Poor little Albert was so worn out at the end of the walk that Hetty insisted that they take a hansom cab home. The Arkwrights used cabs as though they had no legs. No wonder Hetty was so heavy around the haunches. Perhaps, all in all, the air in Aghadoe was better for a growing child than that in London.

It was an early night for the children. Little Albert came down with a sudden case of the runs, and there was great toing and froing from his bedroom. Hetty was adamant that it was the sharpness of the pears they had eaten in Regent's Park.

"The slightest thing gives Albert a nasty tummy, Eliza."

All the while, Theodora sat up in bed, reading *Rosie's Voyage Around the World* and drawing pictures on a slate. Then she nodded off, just like that, despite the chatter from the next bedroom and the sour stench from the fumigators by the open window. Albert Arkwright had finally settled down and Charles and the ladies were sitting down to dinner when who should walk in, a day earlier than expected, but their brother, the bold Walter Cameron himself. He looked like someone fresh off a boat, though, truth to tell, he couldn't have travelled that far. The two sisters fell on him at once, making a great fuss of their brother while Charles Arkwright called to Kitty McCormack to bring an extra plate. He had, of course, dropped into a taproom or two, on the way and had a thousand yarns to tell, each one more scandalous than the next. Eliza scrutinised the silk waistcoat, the fobwatch and the pressed trousers. A railway man, all right. Better that, mind you, than being at the bottom of the pile.

"Have you any new sweethearts, Walter?"

"None that quite match up to my standard, Lizzy."

Lizzy! She hadn't been called that since they had last met, two years previously. Even Hetty didn't call her that. Elizabeth, Eliza, Lizzy. The childhood name charmed her, as long as there was no one on the street to bear witness to it. Walter had brought a new plaything for Albert. Had almost fallen in the door with it. A little globe with the shadow of empire marked out in red. Pride of place, of course, going to India. Walter was waxing loud on the subject now.

"We will fill India with railways! From Kashmir to Malabar!"

Nothing would persuade Walter Cameron, of course, but to

leave the little globe beside the boy's bed. Though, by this time, Albert Arkwright should have been in his second sleep. Hetty called down to the kitchen.

"Kitty, would you follow that fellow up the stairs, like a good woman, and see he doesn't tumble in on the child?"

A few minutes later, Kitty McCormack came running back down the stairs and Walter Cameron was right behind her. There was something odd, they said. Would Hetty Arkwright come up? Hetty and Eliza made for the bedroom as one. It was a strange sight to behold, all right. The half-naked boy lying on the bed, like a Hindoo savage, with an army of lead soldiers—Wellington's finest—strewn all over the carpet with their heads pulled off. As though some strange notion had seized the boy, in his fever. Hetty put her hand on little Albert's forehead. It was cold and clammy. They pulled down the windows and closed the curtains against the night air. Then Kitty was sent out, post haste, for Dr Downs. In less than ten minutes, they were back. And, what with Walter Cameron fussing in the background as he held the globe and Hetty mopping the child's brow and Charles Arkwright muttering to himself, Eliza was surprised the doctor could get near the child at all. Dr Downs seemed less concerned than might have been expected. Eliza kept track of his eyes to see that he wasn't just trying to re-assure her sister. There had, he said, probably been a little stomach upset over the past few days. He had seen quite a few cases in his rooms. It was something associated with milk, perhaps, or the warm weather. Things were apt to go off in the beat of a heart. But the boy appeared to be over the worst of it now. The fever seemed to be breaking. The sheets were changed then and a cold compress placed on the boy's forehead. Dr Downs prescribed sips of chilled water, every couple of hours. But no food. So that the system might flush out whatever was plaguing it. The main thing was to keep the fever down. He left word with them to call him should there be any sudden decline in the boy's condition. At any rate, he would drop by first thing in the morning.

Hetty hushed the men downstairs and she and Kitty and Eliza started seeing to things. Kitty McCormack laid out a mattress on the floor, by Albert's bed, so that Hetty could spend the night with her son. Eliza fetched fresh towels from the linen press and made up another cold compress. In the heel of the reel, because she was so fearful for her, Eliza took Theodora into the bed with her. Whispering to her, as she slept, over and over again.

"It's all right, alanna! It's all right!"

As though she were whispering some sort of charm. Like Mrs Tours had done to her, the day she had first spoken of Edward's death.

Eliza Drew fell into a fretful sleep that night, to the sound of the men chatting below in the drawing room, their banter fuelled by the couple of bottles of claret Charles had brought up from the cellar. Sleep solved nothing though. Nor concealed anything, the way it usually did. For Eliza Drew flew over the skies of Belfast that night. From the Cavehill, looking down on the great town of Belfast, through its narrow, northern streets. Over the gasworks and the iron works. Where the Blackstaff spewed its foul waters into the Lagan. Over the Linenhall and the little streets off the square. Until she was hovering over the workhouse, on the outskirts of the town, with its grim, grey buildings. Then back down into the town again, her body hurtling along the streets, looking for him in every alleyway and lane. For Edward, in the jacket and breeches she had bought him for his sixth birthday. But Edward kept disappearing around corners, goading her into following him. And then she was suddenly hovering close to the streets. Hurtling over the cess ponds and sewers and shoughs. And now, he was finally turning to face her. Only he was a man now. And his face had changed. And he wasn't Edward any more. At a corner where two stinking streams met, she hovered in front of him. A rushlight in her hand. Thanking him profusely. But for what?

"Mr Chadwick, my husband and I . . ."

But then Mr Chadwick, the sanitary reformer, was gone again. Scouting out fresh sewers. Shouting at the dark-suited men trudging before him through the foetid waters. She awoke, sometime around midnight, to hear the two gentlemen on the stairs, with claret-clouded tongues. Walter's voice was the more strident of the two. With the certainty of steel and iron running through it.

"It is a miasma! Pure and simple. Mark my words. The filthy air of this city is the cause of this cholera business."

"And I tell you, Walter my friend, that the water below these streets is at the heart of it."

And then she fell back to sleep with Theodora's head against hers, glad that Mr Chadwick was gone. Glad that Belfast was gone. But knowing, in a way without words, and in that sweet, unreasonable region between sleeping and waking, that she must bury her son.

XV

THE FOX AND DR DREW

The day of Peter Mayhew's burial was uncomfortably hot. During the service, the side doors were left open to refresh the building. John Drew could see the scattering of Catholics standing outside under the plane trees, unable, naturally enough, to set foot inside the church. All, that is, save Mrs Nan Tours, who wouldn't be said or led by anyone but kept her own counsel and sat, trim and prim, like the most proper protestant in the last pew.

After the service, John Drew took a lift in the Templetons' jaunting car, with Cyril and his wife Betty two cars behind, and the commonality following on shank's mare to the little burial ground, down near the Brewery Fields. As they drove off, John Drew noticed the blinds down in Terry's shop and John Gordon's public house at the lower end of the square. Even Waxy Daly's tip-tap-tapping on his cobbler's last wasn't to be heard. Though the little man was probably inside the booth, busying himself with something or other until such time as the last of the mourners had passed by and he could open up. And a good crowd it was too, thought John Drew.

There was a fair scattering of Catholics too, at the graveyard, for old Mayhew had drinking companions from both sides of the fence. And every town needed someone who could read the law. Another diviner of obscure scriptures, like himself. The earth was bone dry, after just a few days of sun, and Sparky Sullivan and his son had a hard time turning the sods for the grave. He had passed both gravediggers, sun-weathered and stiff, only the day before. A pity planter and papist couldn't be buried together in the field. If they couldn't live together, surely they could share eternal rest together? There must be a better shape to things than the murderous party spirit that came out at Dolly's Brae, in Ulster. There had to be.

In a dusty laneway, in Abbeyleix, Fox Keegan was roused by the sting of stones being thrown by a little group of children. A big brazen girl of about ten or eleven gave him a root up the backside with her bare foot.

"Get up out of that!"

He stirred himself slowly and gazed at the gallery of grubby faces around him. One of the boys raised his fist with another stone. Fox's voice was a hoarse rattle.

"Will you stop pegging them stones, will you?"

When he shook himself out and stood up fully, they all backed away. All except one young boy. The wild hair and the cheeky face sneered at him.

"You . . . what time is it?"

"Axe me arse, mister!"

"I'm only asking, you little fecker, you."

He dusted off his coat. The children were all eyes now, wondering what he would do next. He ignored their taunts as they followed him along the street. Past Drennan's, where the woman of the house was out scrubbing the doorstep in the bright sunshine. A few of them were still behind him as he wheeled right towards the old town. He bent over and picked up a stone from the rutted road.

"Shag off, the whole lot of ye, will ye!"

What was it to be then? Head out on the Kilkenny road or take the shorter road to Aghadoe and, perhaps, some sort of assistance? Wasn't that pushing his luck a bit, returning to a town he had once fled from? If he didn't make haste though, he would be too late to say farewell to his father. He could sort out what to do, when he got to Aghadoe. Maybe slip up to Mrs Tours and get around her to arrange something. Better to get out of town anyway, before his erstwhile assailants rose from their lousy beds or the Bowsy Murphy passed by in his jaunting car and came at him a second time.

As he turned right for the Aghadoe road, a stone whizzed by his ear. But he didn't look back. Looking back was always a mistake, in life and in love. The couple of coppers left in his pants pocket wouldn't have bought any distance from the Kilkenny car anyway. It wasn't that far of a walk to Aghadoe. If he took it handy enough, he might be there before six, with a couple of breaks along the way. He headed down towards the Oldtown bridge. There would be fewer cars on the Aghadoe road, of course. But you never knew. For good luck, just outside the gates of De Vesci's estate, he managed to get a jaunt from a farmer with an ass-and-cart who was going about a mile up the road. Fox Keegan pitied the poor ass, tormented with flies. He sat dangling his legs over the edge of the cart, trying to avoid conversation with the driver. He could scarcely understand what the old boy was saying anyway, as he hadn't a tooth in his head. When they parted, Fox Keegan pushed himself for a good mile until a cart, on the way to Ballacolla, stopped for him. At the far side of Ballacolla, a farmer he had known from his days in the brewery gave him a jaunt as far as the bridge below Aghadoe.

"You're not in great shape, Fox."

"No. A bit of a wild night."

"Aren't you an awful divil! Will you ever get sense, do you think?"

"Bit late now, Tom."

"You might be right there, so you might."

He hopped down from the jaunting car at the stone bridge and made his was into the town, by the Burrow.

Then he made slowly for the house of John Drew.

John Drew was obliged to present himself at the funeral meal in the Mayhews', after the burial. It had not been a wake, strictly speaking. But a goodly spread had been laid on in the Mayhews' house with the Evisham sisters—first cousins of Mrs Mayhew, after all—doing all the coming and going with pots of tea, plates of cold meat and the like. For the gentlemen, of course, there was a small drop of whiskey. Notwithstanding the fact that the same liquid had blighted the Mayhew household for the previous thirty years and put paid to what might have been a very lucrative legal practice. John Drew ended up, in the finish of things, stuck among the ladies, in a high-backed chair. It was hard to make conversation but he did his best. Yes, he said, Mrs Drew and Theodora were all well in London. The crossing had been easy. Mrs Derham, of the Grange, a long-faced woman with a persistent cough, mentioned that an uncle of hers had taken a turn, once, on the steampacket to London. So they all proceeded to quiz her on the details and John Drew was left alone for a while. Tilly Evisham leaned over to pour him a hot sup from the teapot. There was a soporific smell of lavender from her purple dress.

"They say, one day, we'll be flying through the air, Dr Drew. Thanks to steam."

"Really?"

"I read it in the *London Gazette.* It appears that some gentlemen are already assembling machines . . . somewhere . . ."

While they were all gnawing on this intelligence, Cyril Templeton gave him the nod and offered to drop him back home. The fresh air was a great relief after the stuffy parlour. He climbed out of the car just before the brewery, anxious to stretch his legs. The pungent smell of malt came to him as he walked up Sackville Square. John Gordon's public house was open. Through the half-door, the tubby little publican nodded at him. Peter Mayhew's purse would be sorely missed in Gordon's. Still, there would be someone else to replace him, before long. Outside Terry's, a little knot of women was gathered. He overheard them talking as he passed by.

"The chest went again him, in the end."

One tongue buried beneath another. *Untersprache.* A memory of the Gaelic their grandparents spoke secreted under their awkward English. Like the hidden language of the third Persepolitan inscription, buried beneath the Babylonian, in ideographs. One tongue lurking beneath another. And what was he, John Drew, doing in his rectory in Sackville Square but superimposing his own vision of things on an older culture? Sometimes though, it felt to him as if it were the Catholics of Aghadoe who were swallowing him up. On other days, he had a sense of a certain loss in their eyes. That it was he and his ilk who were doing the devouring. As he passed the barracks, he noticed Sergeant Arkins talking to a man holding the reins of an ass-and-cart. Arkins nodded towards him, as though there was something on his mind, then turned back when the man spoke. The side gate was open. Odd; he thought he had shut it as the last of the mourners filed out of the church grounds. He pushed on ahead, ashplant in one hand, Bible in the other. John Drew was just inside the gate when he became aware of a form to the left of him. He turned slowly to see an unkempt-looking man, in a tattered frieze coat and a battered hat, staring at him. He stood back, instinctively raising the ashplant above his head and covering his breast with the bible. He glanced through the gates, in the direction of the barracks, ready to call out to Sergeant Arkins. In truth, he didn't know what to say.

"Who are you? What is it you want?"

The stranger's smile hardened.

"Do you not recognise me, Dr Drew?"

"Who the devil are you?"

"And all the grand evenings we spent in that nice study in there. And we going over old maps and inscriptions."

"Who are you, sir?"

"Eaten bread is soon forgotten, Dr Drew!"

Damned if it wasn't Mr Fox Keegan! That he, John Drew, had hoped never to set eyes on again.

Fox Keegan stepped forward unsteadily, from the shadow of the lime trees. His eyes seemed much darker to John Drew now. He had aged a lot since they had last met. Too many nights in rough company. John Drew lowered his ashplant. At least Eliza wasn't here. Or the girls. At that moment, they both noticed another person at the gateway. Sergeant Arkins stared through the bars at Fox Keegan, his eyes full of venom.

"Is this gentleman bothering you, Dr Drew?"

John Drew looked at both men over his spectacles. Sergeant Arkins stood back from the gate, with his thumbs in his belt, still staring at Fox Keegan.

"No, sergeant. Thank you. I had been expecting him."

"Well, if there's any bother at all, Dr Drew."

"Thank you, sergeant. I appreciate that . . . Mr Keegan and I are friends of old."

"Is that so, now?"

John Drew turned back to his companion.

"Follow me into the house, sir, if you please."

He smiled benignly at Sergeant Arkins, who kept his place until both men were inside the door. Fox Keegan took off his cap and left it down on the dining-table. What a ruckus awaited him,

when Eliza got to hear of the visitor. As she surely would. Bianconi leapt up on the table as they entered the room, and John Drew began tidying up the papers on the floor. He spoke without looking at the younger man.

"What brings you here, Mr Keegan? In other words, what are you looking for?"

"I'm on me way home to me father. He's on his last legs, so he is."

John Drew noted, for the first time now, the bruised face and the bloodshot eye. Where was this all leading to?

"I'm sorry about your father."

"And I ran into a bit of bad luck in Abbeyleix."

"Bad luck, like good luck, Mr Keegan, we tend to make ourselves."

John Drew went into the kitchen, returning with a basin of water and a flannel-cloth and invited Fox Keegan to clean his wounds. When Fox Keegan had tended to himself, they sat across the oak table in the dining room. What was to be done about things? John Drew said. Had Mr Keegan no means at all of getting to Tullyroe?

The Sojourner, the Widow and the Blind Man

The three classes of people to whom the prophets entreated one to show charity. Yes, but that was all very well in the time of the patriarchs and so on. We weren't living in the desert now. John Drew was puzzling over what the right action was when there was a knock on the door. He rose stiffly.

"Yes? Who's there?"

"It's me, John. Willie Hill . . ."

The door opened and Willie Hill strode in with a fresh basket of provisions for the house. Apples and plums, a meat pie, a loaf of soda bread and a large round of hard cheese. Fox Keegan didn't rise from his chair. He just sat there, looking at his hands, keeping his gaze from the tall man standing before him.

"You know Mr Keegan, Willie . . ."

"Indeed I do. We all do. And what brings you back to these parts, sir?"

"I'm passing through, so I am."

"With great despatch, one hopes."

"Not fast enough for me neither, sir."

While John Drew and Willie Hill were all hugger mugger at the door—with Willie Hill counselling John Drew, most strenuously, against the notion of giving the vagrant a bed for the night—Fox Keegan busied himself setting a fire in the living room.

When the whispering died away and Willie Hill departed at last, Fox Keegan and John Drew went about the house, as though each had, independently, been given a list of chores to do. Fox Keegan cleared away the detritus of three or four meals, while his host gathered together the notes and books he had scattered around the room, leaving them on the newly cleaned table. When the fire was settled in and the room looked a little like it had done before Eliza Drew left for London, they sat back at the table again. Although it would cause blue murder when Eliza got to hear of it, John Drew offered to drive Fox Keegan the twenty or thirty miles to Tullyroe the following day, on account of it being his father. There were a few conditions attached to the offer, however. Fox Keegan was to go and have his pants and coat mended by Mrs Tours, to ask her for lodgings for the one night (all of which he, John Drew, would pay for) and, in return, Fox Keegan could help John Drew copy out some tables that evening. There was to be no drinking either. If he caught the scent of alcohol from Fox Keegan's breath, when he came back from Mrs Tours' house, he would consider the deal void. He could make his own way to Tullyroe, father or no father.

Dan Delaney's wife, Cissy, and some of the other women were sitting in the parlour drinking tea when Fox Keegan arrived at

Mrs Tours'. Mrs Tours made a great show of not being shocked to see the traveller, sending him off in a pair of pants left behind by the late Mr Mayhew, while she took in Fox's own garments to be mended. She told Fox Keegan he was lucky she had only a little work to do. The ladies all stayed still until the door pulled after him. Then he heard them fall to talking.

"Is that the Keegan chap I heard tell of, from the brewery?"

When night set in and both men had eaten their fill, John Drew and Fox Keegan sat facing one another, across the great dining room table. While John Drew guided him, with the oil lamp between them, Fox copied out the signs and letters allotted to him by his companion. Not understanding one of them, of course. But arranging them in clear, sharp rows for transmission for correspondents in all corners of the world.

John Drew read aloud the transliteration, syllable by syllable, running his finger along the inscription and getting Fox Keegan to voice it after him. As though the younger man, by chanting the secret of the syllables, might somehow come to copy them better.

"*A-ush-ta-as-pa* . . . it means the son of Hystaspes . . . go on, try repeating it."

"*A-ush-ta-as-pa* . . . and each one of these is a sound?"

"Most are syllables and some seem to be letters . . . not like the second line you copied . . . they were really sort of pictures . . . ideographs, in fact."

"So how do you know how to read the pictures, then?"

"From other inscriptions that show parallel lists . . . in fact, you can probably read the picture signs in two ways . . . in this Babylonian language and in the older language . . ."

Fox Keegan dipped his pen in the inkwell.

"They must have got fierce mixed up sometimes."

"Sometimes they did. Many of them were probably like you, Mr Keegan."

"From north Kilkenny, is it, Dr Drew?

John Drew winced and looked down over his spectacles at the grinning man.

"Scribes, I mean . . . they may not have actually known what they were copying."

"Writing without reading, you mean?"

"Something like that, I fancy."

As they toiled, John Drew spoke late into the night, as though to no one and everyone, of tongues and signs and languages dead and gone, as though the years had not passed between them. They spoke about the great rivers, the Euphrates and the Tigris, and about ancient cities, lost to memory in the minds of men. It was like the olden days.

There was no drinking that night. Either down in Gordon's or anywhere else. After the episode the night before, Fox Keegan was happy enough to seek sanctuary in the rectory. Mrs Tours was still up when he arrived in to sleep on the settle bed. Her hearty voice called out to him from the kitchen.

"Is that you, Fox Keegan?"

"It is, Mrs Tours."

"Would you ever bolt that door, like a good man, and quench the lamp?"

In the early morning, Fox Keegan swapped the late Mr Mayhew's pants for his own, buttoned up his coat and made for Sackville Square. But not before Mrs Tours, in her nightgown, had sat him down at the breakfast table to hear his story, and, in particular, the full details of a drunken night, a long time before. Because Fox Keegan would confess only to someone who would listen and not tell. As she had done once before, the night of the fatal engagement at the railway encampment near the Green Roads. Because there were a few details Mrs Tours needed to know. It was always handy to know things other people wanted kept secret. It was like having a bit of material put aside, for patching. You never knew when it would come in handy. Mrs Tours looked down over her spectacles.

"But there were four of ye that night. Am I right or am I wrong?"

"Four of us. That's right; not three."

"And tell me this now and tell me no more . . . who was it the fourth one was? Because I think I have a notion, so I do."

And when Mrs Tours had completed her intelligences, she set to rising up the fire and getting on with the day. As though she was putting no pass on it. As though Fox Keegan hadn't mentioned the name Fonsey Hennigan at all, at all.

PART THE SECOND

XVI

LORNA LOVEGROVE IS A RIP

Mrs Tours hunted a wild cat out of the yard, firing a sod of turf at it as it disappeared over the gate into Campion's field. Then she lifted up the pail of water and made back into the scullery. As she turned to wash the vessels, her eye fell on the book she had been half-reading and she smiled at its innocence and vanity.

> The wind was savage, the night Lorna made her first attempt at escaping from the Alcazaba, the Moor's fortress. The gales, blowing in from the sea, carried great clouds of sand, smothering the city of Makathir in a choking dust. The guards on the palace gates and at the smaller portals had wrapped their faces in burnoufs, the better to shield themselves from the fury of the storm. It was hard to see who was coming or going in the night. On such days, Layla had told Lorna, the guards had the habit of settling themselves in the little alcoves and recesses around the palace grounds, until the worst of the tempest had passed. It was early in the morning, while the storm still raged, that Lorna heard Layla's fearful knock on the chamber door. A

knock that signalled flight and escape from the clutches of the Moor and all his retainers.

Mrs Tours went into the kitchen and sat at the sewing table by the window. As she threaded the needle, she thought once more of Fox Keegan.

He was very quiet in himself, the next morning, at the table. He was worn out, I suppose, between the hammering he got in Abbeyleix and the work Drew had given him, the night before.

"How would you like your egg, Fox?"

"With another one, Mrs Tours."

"You never lost the lip, anyway."

If he wasn't such a clever fool, he could be well set up somewhere now. That grand, handy schoolmaster's job in Kilkenny he gave up. What did he ever go leaving it for? Though I know the answer to that, of course. The woman and the child. He was running away from them. I sat down at the table with him and let the tea draw.

"Tell me this and tell me no more . . ."

"What's that, Mrs Tours?"

"What sort are you at all, Fox? What do you be at?"

His eyes looked the other way.

"Would you not think of settling, Fox?"

"Too late now."

"Even below in your own place?"

"Me brother has the farm. And sure, I'm not a farmer anyway. Nor never was."

I know the whole story of the railway incident, I needn't tell you. And whatever little bit I didn't know, Fox Keegan came out with it then. Like he was making his last will and testament. I knew Fox wasn't directly involved in the killing. That wouldn't be his sort. He was tricked into keeping lookout, and he full of beer, by some of the smart boys. Of course, all those poems about our native land and all that class of carry-on went to his head too. And maybe the eviction he seen, years before, when the constabulary came along to turf out that family, down in Knockroe. He often told me about it too. Militiamen and ordinary people were killed that day. Their skulls cracked open like eggshells. That wouldn't do you much good, if you were a small child watching it. If he hadn't to have seen that, he might never have got involved with all the other lunatics. No, I had no call to ask Fox Keegan about the railway business because I heard every bit of it from those who wouldn't tell anyone else but Mrs Tours. In the dark, like a priest I am, sometimes. A woman priest. The scullery is my little confessional. They come to Mrs Tours for absolution as well as an arse in their trousers. But, still and all, I wanted to hear the other bit from his own mouth. The bit about the Hennigan chap.

He golloped down the egg and I cut him a few more slices of soda bread. There was a bit of talk about the father then and the brother who would take over the farm. It seems the brother is to marry some local woman that the mother isn't too pleased with. Keegan got all high and mighty in himself, then.

"Mothers is very funny, when it comes to their sons. No woman is good enough. They'll let their daughters marry the tinker but the son brings a woman on to the land."

He had this grand notion in his head of writing a big book of stories, he told me. A collection of yarns, you might say. If he ever had a sober day to do it, that is.

I interrupted him.

"And tell me this . . . how is ould Drew, up there on his own? As contrary as ever, I suppose?"

It seems that Drew got the price of bringing him to his father's funeral out of Fox Keegan by having him copy out his meanderings until the poor man's eyes were nearly falling out. I thought it was the drink that had given him the big red eyes. That maybe someone down the town had taken pity on him and filled him full of beer. It was only at the door, and he putting on his long coat, that Mr Foxy Keegan let on what his plan was.

"I have to lave Drew's horse up to Dinny Grey. He lost a shoe, the other day."

"You were his scribe last night; now you're his stable boy."

"He's going to give me a jaunt over to Tullyroe. To me father's house."

"Is that a fact, now? You must be well got with him, so you must."

And sure enough, not long after, and I out sweeping the hall, didn't I see the bould Fox Keegan leading ould Drew's horse up by the pound to Dinny Grey's forge. It had hardly sunk in, what he had said to me, when Ker Costigan's car appeared, for to bring me out to his wife for a fitting. As she was down with her chest again, she had to stay indoors. It didn't take me ten minutes to pin her and measure her. I've made that many dresses for her now. And she isn't a woman that's inclined to put on weight, even after three children. Ker Costigan was driving me back into town and didn't we run into little Miss Judith and Cassie Hill and they coming back from a trip into town. When Ker Costigan pulled up, I leaned over the side of the car.

"Your mother said you were to call in on me, Judith."

"I never got round to it, Mrs Tours."

"Did you not, faith? You must be woeful busy, then, so you must."

And the Cassie one sniggering behind her little white gloves. All sweet as pie. That horse-faced driver of Willie Hill's fiddling with the reins. They were in a great hurry to get home for lunch, it seems. Lunch—a great name for a bit of cold meat and bread on a plate. Judith Drew promised to call in on me then. I tell you this much, if I got five minutes with her away from that Cassie one, in the parlour, I'd redden her ears for her. Put a few queries to her, such as, what were you doing with young Hennigan, by Taylor's well? And do you want to lose your good name and worse? Let on to her that I would write directly to her mother, in London, if she didn't leave off. Because it's only mothers who can put order on their daughters. And if they don't, no one does. That's how you get whores, like Maggie Mitchell, up in the Commons. A man only has to look at her and her hole opens.

I was over by the river, a while later, throwing out a bucket of offal, when I heard a clip-clop up the street. I look out over my spectacles and don't I see Dr Drew and Fox Keegan and they driving up the road in the *jaunting car. With Fox Keegan shouting giddy-up and his lordship sitting back in great style, in his farting jacket and his high hat, and he thinking his fine thoughts to himself.*

What is What?

John Drew pulled up, as I was tipping the last of the offal into the river, to have a little chat. To see if I could set things right. So I said I would do what I could. It was only then that it hit me that I was on my own. Eliza Drew was gone. John Drew was gone. And Bridget Doheny hadn't been heard tell of in days. That night, Dan Brady slipped out to the well, but he didn't see a thing. Later on, I slipped over by Campion's field myself, but I didn't see anything either. Though I went to bed thinking things was easy again, I woke up thinking different altogether. And that's the why I made up my mind to go out to Willie Hill's. To stand my ground in front of that little minx. Because I felt, to tell the God's truth, that little Lorna Lovegrove, out in Willie Hill's, was making a right gom out of me. And I would be blamed, in the heel of the reel, if she ended up with a belly on her. Mrs Tours, the lady priest.

XVII

ELIZA'S FLIGHT NORTHWARDS

Kitty McCormack was run off her feet that morning. There were basins of hot water to be fetched and fresh towels to be brought upstairs. Dr Downs insisted that fumigators be lit throughout the house. No one mentioned it, of course, but by the time Charles Arkwright left, for a brief visit to the London Wall offices to leave instructions with his second-in-command, Mr Cranbourne, the dreaded word was in everyone's mind. *Cholera.* The previous week in London had been as bad as any that summer. The heat certainly seemed to have something to do with it. Otherwise, why would the illness have travelled across Europe from the Orient? Was this to be the true price of Empire, then—the release of some malignant Hindoo or Mohammedan genie that punished those who trespassed on its demesne? The numbers of dead recorded down in St Giles and up in Belle Isle, at St Pancras, were shocking to behold. It was like a roll-call of the war dead. While the dispute between the miasmatists and their opponents raged in the papers, in the taprooms and in hushed conversations in drawing-rooms, the deadly pestilence was slowly threading its way through London's streets. Nor did class or creed seem to afford much protection. That it had penetrated the stout walls of the British Museum, the previous summer, was still a sobering shock to commoner and gentleman alike. Even Theodora had become caught up in the terror, asking Eliza, after her bedtime story a few nights before, "Are we all going to die, Mother?"

"No. Not at all. Mr Chadwick is working on the problem at this very moment."

Eliza went on to paint a picture for the girl of a morose-looking gentleman in a top-hat, scouring the streets and sewers of London for the source of the pestilence. It was an illustrated extract from the dream she herself had had, the night before.

By the time Dr Downs arrived, the soiled sheets, the ashen pallor of the boy and his incoherent ramblings all seemed to add up to something very sinister. When Charles Arkwright arrived back, around noon, the boy's fever had turned to delirium. Dr Downs was to return at three. He left explicit instructions to give the boy only boiled water, and to change the sheets as often as necessary, with gloved hands. On no account were they to give the boy food. There were secret words with Charles Arkwright on the return. Kitty McCormack raced by Eliza, for the basement, with another load of soiled linen. The mangling woman was up to her elbows in work. Hetty Arkwright came to the top of the landing. Her voice was full of an authority not usual in a younger sister.

"Eliza, are you going to take Theodora out, as promised?"

"I can't leave you alone, Hetty."

"Please, Eliza! The girl needs fresh air. It will help all of us. Please!"

Eliza Drew looked through the dining room doors at her daughter, in the pink bonnet. Theodora Drew was picking over the pieces of a wooden jigsaw of the Battle of Waterloo, on the great dining table. Eliza Drew understood what her sister was saying.

"All right so. All right, Hetty."

Charles Arkwright led herself and Theodora to the little cabman's shelter at the corner of Russell Square, where a red-faced jarvey tipped his cap to them. Charles Arkwright gave clear instructions. It might all have been the start of a jolly family outing, but for the fact of the sick boy back in Gower Street.

"Please leave these two ladies to the New Houses of Parliament."

"Certainly, sir."

Charles Arkwright waved to them distantly. His long, patrician face looked grimmer than Eliza had ever seen it.

There was a great crowd in the grounds of the New Houses of Parliament. People arriving from all quarters, by steamer, by omnibus and by hansom cab. As though, by mutual agreement, the centre of empire and of the world had suddenly been settled, on that very day. They bought a bag of roasted chestnuts from a clean-looking costermonger and munched them as they walked along.

As she watched Theodora, Mrs Tours slipped in among Eliza Drew's thoughts. And that first day, the previous year, when Eliza had told Mrs Tours about Edward. It was profane, what she had let herself be drawn into. And she had repeated the session a number of times, flying in the face of God and reason and her religion. All because of the pull of the light.

The seamstress's gnarled hands held Eliza Drew's hands, across the kitchen table, in the light of the guttering oil lamp.

"Give me your hands, alanna."

"What are you doing, Mrs Tours?"

"Whisht, now. Just give me your hands."

Mrs Tours looked over her spectacles as she laid Eliza's hands flat on the table. Then she asked Eliza Drew, very softly, to close her eyes and let on there was nothing in her head. No words and no pictures and no sounds. Mrs Tours had drawn the drapes and trimmed the lamp. The lodgers wouldn't burst in on them, as they kept to their own side of the house in the evening. At first, Eliza resisted closing her eyes. Then, slowly, the room fell from view. Fell from mind. The sounds about became more indistinct now. She could feel the warmth in the older woman's hands. An energy without a name. Mrs Tours' calm voice seemed to be coming to her from another room altogether. She felt her thoughts slowing down. It seemed as though she had stopped breathing, that her heart had stopped beating, even. A dog barked in the distance, though she could not tell where. She heard two men talking on Pound Street, as they passed the house. Their gruff words.

"Lave him go. Lave him go, so! That's what I say."

Eliza Drew shuddered slightly as though someone had sent a galvanic charge through her body. And then that light was there. It was the very first time she had seen it. Not a face, as she might have expected, but a light. The radiance of a child's soul, she was sure. It was in her and she was in it. The only sound she could hear was that of her own heavy sobbing, like an infant troubled in sleep, frowning to itself. Mrs Tours held her hands tighter now, bidding Eliza to still herself, but letting her vent her heartbreak as the light danced about inside her. And then the sounds out on the street started to filter back again slowly. Horses' hooves, out near the crossroads. A dog barking in Campion's field. As Eliza Drew slowly opened her eyes, Mrs Tours began to release her hands. The darkness was receding now and, with it, the odd light that had hovered around its fringes. Mrs Tours was looking straight into her eyes. The older woman stood up slowly, without as much as a word, and went to settle the black-bottomed kettle on the hob. When Eliza Drew was back out on Pound Street a short while later, having taken a stiff cup of tea, she was suddenly overwhelmed by a morbid sense of wrongdoing at having crossed into the fields of fancy. She said nothing of the whole affair to John Drew, that night or any other night, because there were some things husbands did not need to know. But she understood that, despite everything, she must see the light again, when the time was right. Mrs Tours would know when the time was right. Mrs Tours always knew.

Instead of taking the steamer back up the river as Charles Arkwright had recommended, they walked up Whitehall for the Strand. In Trafalgar Square, they paused to see Admiral Nelson's column. Had Judith been there, Eliza would have brought them both into the new gallery. But the exhibition would have been wasted on Theodora. So, they bought a bag of dried bread from a chirpy little man near by and fed the pigeons instead. It was almost three, by the time they made the Strand.

A few minutes later, they crossed into Covent Garden. The market was winding down for the day. Discarded flower and fruit boxes lay all along the pavements. Even the porters had slowed to a trot. At the corner of James Street, she bought a bunch of nice red roses from a young girl, not much older than Theodora. Both girls eyed one another, ages and stations immediately apparent.

"That'll be tuppence, ma'am."

"Is that an Irish accent, I hear?"

"Yes, ma'am. I'm from County Cork."

"And we're from the Queen's County."

"Is that what they sound like there, ma'am?"

"Some of them."

She felt a sudden twinge for the girl, something she had no wish to feel at all. Too much softness was a curse. It merely succeeded in opening the old wound once more. They passed an Italian knife-grinder on a corner, a rough-looking cove with a wall eye. Sparks flew in all directions from the spinning whetstone. Fascinated, they watched him awhile, from a discreet distance. It was at that point—when she thought about it afterwards—that Eliza Drew first began to feel a little feverish. They crossed into St Martin's Lane, heading back in the general direction of Gower Street, via Oxford Street. She would take her time getting back, hoping that things would have settled by they time they reached Hetty's house. But now Theodora was complaining of a need to make water. It was too unsavoury to go into one of the chop houses, and a taproom was quite out of the question. Better to find an alleyway for the girl. That was really why she had taken to the side-streets at that point. Because it wasn't as if Eliza Drew couldn't find her way back from Covent Garden to Oxford Street. The Lord knows, she had walked it often enough, as a child. This was her city, after all. Not Dublin or, God spare us, Belfast which, when all was said and done, was just a glorified industrial town. All the same, the streets and the slums that had sprung up in the wake of the Irish hunger were foreign to her childhood. Somewhere just below the Seven Dials, she drew Theodora down a laneway.

"Be quick, like a good girl."

A door opened on the laneway. A heavy-set, ignorant-looking woman threw out a pot full of cold tea leaves. Both women exchanged glances. An Irish voice shouted at Eliza. An angry, Irish one. But then, were the Irish ever any other way?

"Madam, I'd be very grateful if you stuck to pissing on your own patch, so I would."

Eliza Drew grabbed Theodora by the arm as the door slammed shut behind them. It was walking through Seven Dials itself, a few moments later, that Eliza took the notion that she was being followed. Perhaps some blackguard after her purse. She seized Theodora's hand and made off with her into the rabbit warren of streets over by St Giles's church, a place she had only dimly heard about, at the Arkwrights' table, a place that had formed no part of her own childhood. She looked over her shoulder, through the anonymous faces of the jostling crowd.

"What is it, Mother?"

"We're taking a short cut. Come along, Theodora!"

It was the stench of the streets that first alerted Eliza. She should have turned around and retraced her steps, at that point. Because these were the infamous rookeries of St Giles. Full to overflowing with the detritus of life. Mostly Irish, needless to say.

Too busy stirring sedition in their own country to make something of it, unlike the loyal elements in Ulster. The children she heard around her still carried the curse of the brogue with them, like some malign birthmark. Lines of clothing were strung across the streets, in a haphazard fashion. She watched the barefoot children scurrying between the puddles of water. The sulphurous stink of cinder heaps at the corners of the streets stung her nostrils. She felt the dizziness at her again now. And that breathlessness too, as though something heavy were pressing on her bosom. A blind man, sitting on a stool outside a rickety tenement door, turned when he marked them approaching.

"Spare a few coppers, ma'am!"

She swung away from the creature and drew Theodora away. But now they were in another alleyway that surpassed even the other streets for squalor. A child was bawling in an upstairs room. She heard a woman's care-ravaged voice soothing it in a strange tongue. Gaelic perhaps. There was an odd tingling in her breast, as though the child's cry had stirred something without a name there. They began making their way back through the streets, until they reached the spot where the woman at the door had shouted at Eliza. She knew where she was now, more or less, and swung right into Compton Street, past a house standing curiously silent among the others. She didn't pause to read the notice on the door, because she knew what it must say. The house would have been cleared by the curse. It would be filled back up within a few weeks with more unfortunates, unaware of the fate of the previous tenants. Mrs Luttrell had told her about such things. She upbraided herself, on the spot, for what Isaac Cameron would surely have called Chartist thoughts. Nevertheless, it still seemed a callous thing to do.

Eliza Drew was suddenly stunned by the strange march of her own musings.

At the corner of the street, she paused once more to catch her breath and get her bearings. Theodora's shoes were filthy from the puddles and the hem of her pinafore was splattered with dirt. But it didn't matter. It didn't matter any more. As she watched a group of women at the public pump, she fancied she felt something pushing her forward again. But it wasn't a face in the crowd now, it was something else altogether. She watched a large, red-faced woman filling a pail of water while another woman worked the pump handle.

"I'll give you a hand with them clothes, so I will."

"Will he be all right, do you think?"

"A touch of the colic is all it is."

Women, children, sickness. Birth and death. There was a little queue of women forming behind the two women. Some of them had children in tow. Others just stood there, scarcely uttering a word. A youngish woman, of twenty or so, was washing a sick child over a pit, not ten yards from the pump. Eliza paused a moment, affecting to settle her skirt, and her eyes moved between the women at the pump and the woman with the sick infant. The sickly smell of diarrhoea was in her nostrils. The dream she had entertained, the previous night, was pushing its way in among her thoughts now. Belfast and all its black memories. She could feel herself flying again, in over the Lagan and up by the confluence with the Blackstaff. Careering over Donegall Square and the little streets around it. She could feel her body lift, even as she stood there with Theodora. Being there and not being there. It was just then that she first perceived a sense of something leading her rather than driving her. A sensation of something drawing her on, like the odd light in Mrs Tours' kitchen that first evening. Just at the edge of her field of vision. She turned and crossed over into Oxford Street. The crowd was all around her now. But yet she felt strangely free. Because Theodora was no longer at her side. There was no one holding her hand and dragging her down now. She had the odd desire to unburden herself of everything now before lying down and sleeping. At the corner of Museum Street, she placed the freshl wrapped roses she had bought for Hetty in a crossing-sweeper's cart.

"You're throwing your lovely flowers away, ma'am."

"They're too heavy for me."

Roses amid the squalor seemed wrong. It was much nicer on the other side of Oxford Street, all the same. There were no smells or loud noises and no foul rookeries with hundreds of sick children hanging out of her, demanding suckle. At the far corner of Museum Street, she undid her bonnet, letting it rest on her neck. The desire to sleep seemed to be passing now and she felt altogether better. But, somewhere inside, the light was still calling. It appeared to depend on which way she faced. If she looked back in the direction of Oxford Street and St Giles, it faded to the edge of her vision. If she turned back north, towards St Pancras, it drew in from the edges. A subtle, silent glow. At the corner of Great Russell Street, she stood a moment, smiling at the vanity of everything. In the distance, standing talking to another man, she spotted Mr Westmacott. She carried on by his blind side, so as not to risk engagement in conversation. Because that would have weighed her down. It occurred to her, at that point, that everything and everyone, from John Drew and his machinations to those of her own flesh and blood, might really be part of one great joke. That they might all really be playing charades and that only she, Eliza Drew, was the real one. What if John Drew and Hetty—and even Judith and Theodora and little Albert Arkwright—were all actors, sent to try her? Eliza Drew accepted the possibility calmly, now that she felt lighter in herself.

When Westmacott had moved off up Great Russell Street, Eliza Drew crossed between the carriages and strode purposefully up the steps of the British Museum. This was empire, all right!

This was eternal empire! The giggling that had beset her a few minutes before seized her again. The vanity of everything seemed suddenly so amusing and so naïve.

Vanitas Vanitatem
A year comes and a year passes
And there is nothing new under the sun.

Did they all not realise that they would soon be dead? That nothing awaited them but the sorry end of a wooden box and the corruption of their mortal bodies? She toyed with the idea of seeing some of the wonders sent back from foreign quarters, in the British Museum. But that too would have weighed her down and she was less convinced now that there was a Mesopotamia or that the Greece she had heard about from her father, as a child, was anything more than a fraud dreamed up to distract the credulous, back in London. Perhaps John Drew's precious inscriptions, for that matter, were a lot of hokum. She found herself walking briskly through the great building, then exiting on Montague Place. She wondered to herself, once more, whether Mr Westmacott's appearance wasn't some sort of crude joke. If it was a joke, it was a jolly good joke! She had to admit that much. Perhaps Westmacott was waiting for her at the cemetery. Perhaps they would all be there, waiting for her. John and Judith and Theodora and Hetty and Charles and Albert. But not Albert. Because Albert was probably dead by now. Like Edward. He was somewhere else. In the dead place. Like the spirits of the black and bloated bodies in the churchyards that kept pushing one another up out of the grounds, as though to look for air. For relief. Bodies that the cholera still tormented, even in death. So much so that the stench of their corruption reached into the churches, even as the funeral services were being held. She seemed to perceive the sickly sweet smell whichever way she looked now. She was glad that someone had taken Theodora away. To mind her. Because she was a weak mother. A weak mother whose children always died on her. She felt lighter now. Yes: the main thing was to feel light. To float, in a way. Without roses or papers or the pressure of a small hand. Or the worry of Theodora's touch.

She crossed into Russell Square, where she took a seat by a park bench to watch the nannies and the ladies and gentlemen out walking. Of course, all of these children might well be hers. From the little boy in the navy-blue sailor suit, with the hoop, to the girl with the golden tresses, walking by the jingling perambulator. She sat some time in the park, just watching the other actors. No one would find her there, even though it was only a stone's throw from Hetty's house, in Gower Street, because she was easy in herself now and it was just a matter of floating towards the light. When she finally stood up, composed and refreshed, she knew where she must go. So she crossed towards the northern end of the square and out along Bernard Street. There were children's voices in the air, as she passed along the walls of the foundling hospital. The children of sick and dying women and dead women. Some of them born into bastardy. She thought vaguely of Theodora and tried to picture her daughter's face again. But the light was too strong now so she had to desist. Girls' voices, came floating across the walls to her, chanting in unison.

Hip-hop two times
Hip-hop three times
Hip-hop four times
Back you go!

She realised sadly, that she would never be able to explain the light to anyone else. Even though the light was even more real than the jarvey's crude shout as she crossed into St George's cemetery and caught the death smell in her nostrils again.

"Mind out, ma'am! Mind the cab!"

She was looking down on herself now like in the Belfast dream. She was, to all intents and purposes, still Eliza Drew. That much was clear. But what did it mean? A woman in a purple dress turned and smiled at her as she made for the plot. Eliza Drew smiled back, not quite knowing why. She stood in front of the tombstone and, crossed herself.

Requiescat in Pace

Who was buried here? She struggled to remember. Not Theodora and not Albert Arwkright either because they were back in Gower Street. Nor even Edward Drew. He was buried in Belfast. She slowly mouthed her father's name. Reading the syllables like a child with its first primer.

Is-aac Ca-me-ro-on

She wondered whether she should read some of the syllables as open and others as closed syllables. John Drew seemed to be having the same problem with the cuneatic inscription on which he was working. It was an important problem. Because syllables were at the heart of everything, as she had overheard John Drew say, more than once.

She fluffed out her skirt and sat down on the dusty ground near the tomb, her legs crossed beneath her, in an attitude of composure and bliss. She tried, as best she could, to remember who exactly her father was again. The quick and the dead, following one another about. After a few minutes, she rose slowly and moved away from the tombstones. She considered the incident she and Hetty had been reminiscing about, only the other day. The day their father had brought them, on his own, to the Frost Fair down by the Thames. Why wasn't their mother with them that day? Eliza Drew recalled something about a special dinner and Mother staying at home with the day-maid while Father took them off. There were crowds of people milling around the stalls. She was holding Hetty's hand, like she had held Theodora's today. Feeling brave, but secretly afraid that the skaters they were watching on the ice might tumble into the Thames or they would lose Father in the crush. Hetty could have been only two or three, at the time. Her puckered, winsome little face, looking up at her, Eliza, for strength and reassurance. Because Mother wasn't there. A light dressing of snow had fallen during the night and they crunched along through the crisp white powder in their winter boots. But why wasn't Mother there? Eliza paused a moment at the gates of St George's to consider her own question. Because Mother was down with a bout of melancholy again. That was the reason. She had been laid low with one of those humours that took her, every so often. That was the real reason they were at the Frost Fair with Father. Because Mother was bedridden. Father seemed somehow different to her that day. As though he too had been relieved of a great burden. At a stall along the riverbank, he bought each of them a straw dolly with a little dress of calico. Hetty said that she would call hers Sarah, after the character in the Bible. But Eliza still couldn't think of a sensible name for her own straw doll. A name that made sense. A name. Everyone must have a name. Especially the dead.

With the caution of someone afraid of stumbling, Eliza Drew stepped out on to the pavement. The light the day of the Frost Fair had been different. That was the thing about it. The light was like the light she had seen in Mrs Tours' house. The same light, which she had followed northwards, to where she was now standing. She knew, without fouling her thoughts with mundane words, that the day of the Frost Fair must have been the happiest day of her life. With her father holding one hand and she holding Hetty's little mittened hand, and Mother safe, being looked after. For ever.

Gray's Inn Road was awash with omnibuses and hansom cabs flowing south for Holborn and north towards St Pancras. She should have turned home then, but she knew that she must continue northwards for a bit longer. At least until the light had faded in the corner of her eyes. And so she did, in the general direction of King's Cross, where the barred and bolted edifice of the old smallpox hospital rose up before her.

She realised that she was walking, more or less, towards St Pancras old church and Belle Isle. The grimy landmark of the gasworks lay to her right. It was somewhere around the gasworks that Eliza Drew suddenly began to feel that she was losing her bearings, that she was no longer very sure where north was any more. The way back south, back home, became suddenly confused. She made her way up a long, badly surfaced road, thinking to ask directions back towards the more verdant squares to the north of Oxford Street. Because the need to sleep was on her again. The need to lie down and let her mind undo the day.

She found herself, all of a sudden, in the middle of a little settlement of cottages, quite apart from the main road. An inn with the name The Good Samaritan caused her to smile a moment. A couple of labouring men were sitting before a great trestle table in the sun, drinking ale. They looked at her oddly as she passed, but it caused her no worry. She scarcely seemed to notice the hem of her dress dragging in the dried mud as she skirted the pools and rivulets in the road. She needed to drink something though, what with the sun and the walk and the salted chestnuts she had eaten with Theodora earlier on. She couldn't bring herself to enter an inn though, even one called The Good Samaritan, so she carried on through the huddle of cottages, trying to get back to the main road again by inscribing a great arc. An old lady carrying a rush basket stopped to gawk at her as she passed. Thinking, perhaps, that she was some Lady Bountiful come slum-gazing so as to write an account in one of the newspapers, for the entertainment of the quality. A scream suddenly rent the air, and a little boy, of seven or eight, came running around the corner with a hoop and stick. He wore patched trousers, and his torn shirt was almost beyond washing. He took a tumble and collided with her. She bent down slowly to help the boy to his feet. Her voice was warm. The voice of Mrs Tours, it seemed to her.

"Are you all right, alanna?"

The boy sniffled and raised himself up slowly. He frowned, like boys tended to do when they were mollycoddled too much. Then he was gone, like the wind, down the street. She watched the boy until he disappeared into a whitewashed cottage, the bright halo of light around his shoulders. Eliza Drew picked up the metal hoop and called after the boy.

"Boy . . . your hoop . . . here it is . . . Edward!"

A woman's head peeped out of the dark inside the cottage. The women's eyes met. For the same instant that they were one woman, with one child with a halo of light around his shoulders. The woman went back inside the house and the half-door closed over. She could hear voices from within. And then they faded away as she moved off, vaguely heading in the direction of the canal.

It was only when she gained the back of St Pancras old church itself that Eliza Drew regained her bearings. The journey appeared to be nearing its end now. Eliza Drew was thankful for that, because the light was fading fast now. Even though she aligned her eyes at the correct angle, its luminescence was dimming by the minute. She had worked out north and south again now. If she continued to the top of Somers Town, it would be possible to strike south in a straight line, for Russell Square. It was just then that she caught sight of the Southampton Arms at the crossroads and knew she must sit inside, scandal or no scandal, and let her thoughts arrange themselves once more.

She looked in through the oak doors at the front of the tavern. A man with a great broomhandle of a moustache was standing wiping glasses behind the bar. He gazed out at her, expressionless. Though the sultry heat of the August evening was giving way to a chill, there were still a few venerable gentlemen sitting out at the long tables. It must be late now. She hadn't been aware of the time when she was trudging through the muddy lanes to get there. There had been a sense, indeed, that time had been abrogated until that point when she placed her feet out on the main road again. She waited a moment on the pavement, just staring through the doors of the ale house. As she stood there, Eliza Drew became faintly aware of a piano tinkling lightly on the evening air. The music had an odd, ethereal quality to it. It seemed at a tilt from the common world around her. Without willing it or wanting it, she followed the bidding of her ears until she found herself walking down a little laneway, alongside the tavern, to the side-door of what seemed to be a sort of taproom. A man in a fawn waistcoat was sitting just inside the door. He frowned as he looked at her.

"Can I be of service, ma'am?"

She ignored the question and carried on inside. Some forty or fifty patrons were parked at tables, chatting and singing and drumming on the tables with their fists. A young lady was standing on a tiny stage over by the back wall of the great room. A sign over a primitive proscenium arch read:

All Pals Together!

The young woman was got up in a most extraordinary fashion. She might have been, Eliza thought, one of the streetwalkers who frequented Drury Lane and the Strand. She was dressed in a coquettish bonnet of pink trimmed with purple, and wore several petticoats of the most garish colours, topped of with a pair of patent boots that had certainly seen better days. Her accent was that of the lower orders. Eliza strained to catch the words of the song over the din.

I'm as impudent as I can be
I sips me gin like I sips me tea

> *Oh, I'm a naughty one but I don't care*
> *'Cos I'm just a bachelor girl*

There were other unsavoury verses about love and marriage and sailors and secret trysts. The words had a queer sort of fascination for Eliza, and she looked around, as though to ascertain that no one who might recognise her was present. But no one among the throng paid her much heed. Even the little man at the door soon lost interest and went back to staring out on to the little laneway. Eliza Drew turned back towards the stage. The singer had disappeared now. As a man turned up the gas mantles at the side of the room, two gentlemen, thin as lathes and clad only in loin-cloths, appeared on the stage with a basket in between them. It was a sketch that had the two dark-skinned rascals vying with one another for the ownership of a rubber snake in a basket. Each played on a little wooden flute to coax the wily serpent to his side. Surely they weren't real Hindoos? At the end of the little sketch, a string was tugged from behind a curtain and the snake disappeared off the stage, sending the two fakirs scurrying after it to cries of, "Goodness gracious! Mr Singh has stolen my serpent!"

The next on was a dusky Arabian who sang a jolly ditty about his camel. A real brigand in a turban, whom you wouldn't like to run into down a dark alleyway. He teased the crowd with catcalls and jibes.

> *And when I go into the suq*
> *My camel follows suit*

She noticed, for the first time, people slipping in and out through the curtain between the little taproom theatre and the tavern itself. Her throat felt raw now and, with the tears streaming down her cheeks from the Mohammedan's manic face, she felt even drier. When she brushed aside the curtain and passed into the taproom, there was a collective silence from the men positioned along the length of the counter. One of the younger bar-hands crossed to her, perhaps thinking she was going to ask for directions.

"I would like to have a drink of mineral water."

"A mineral water, madam?"

"Yes, you do have mineral waters?"

The younger man, after a nod and a wink from his senior at the far end of the counter, fetched a glass of carbonated water but refused to take a single penny for the drink. She made straight back for the little music hall where a pedlar was playing Mr Shylock to the crowd.

Ve go and get our money's worth
From efery von ve meet

The little goatee beard genuinely amused her. But these people weren't real, of course. The naughty girl, the Hindoo, the Arabian or the Israelite pedlar. Yet still, they seemed to have some sort of truth about them. Even Pat Denny and his Pig, the next act on, who stood at the centre of the stage with his big jaw, battered bowler and shillelagh and a stuffed pig under his arm. This wasn't Waxy Daly, from Aghadoe, right enough. And it certainly wasn't Mr Fox Keegan either. But it still bore some relation to them, in a way. The way a joke can only be predicated on reality or a parody can only mimic something stronger. Eliza Drew was about to set her glass down on one of the tables, when a pretty young woman kitted out in pinks and sky blue took the stage. It was the sort of outfit she might once have wanted Judith to wear, as a girl. The woman was, for all the world, the picture of a real little English lady. Even in the sombre glare of the gaslight you could see it.

An English rose by any other name
An English rose still looks the same

Gentle and innocent
Tender and pure
An English garden rose

It was only when her eyes adjusted to the gloom again that Eliza Drew apprehended that the English rose was the same person as the naughty girl who had appeared at the start of the show. She was surprised that she could have been so easily taken in by the simple addition of a few fancy garments. And that was really the last large thought Eliza Drew recalled entertaining before she found herself sitting at the little table in the laneway with the doorkeeper man calling out to the crowd.

"Give the lady some air! Give the lady some air!"

Someone introduced smelling salts under her nostrils, at that point, and her head jerked backwards violently with the sharpness of the retort. Then there was more clear, honest-to-God mineral water. As the last of the patrons vacated the little theatre, passing by her on their way into the lane, the older bartender from the taproom appeared beside her. She looked over her shoulders at the little stage. The gaslights were fully up now, the crowd was gone and the actors were divesting themselves of their costumes and make-up. There had been only two men and a woman all along. Paddy and the Hindoo and all the rest were really the charades of just two men. One of them, a chirpy young fellow, in his early twenties, shouted over to the bartender.

"Good door, Mr Newell?"

"Best this summer, me old china."

The bartender turned back to Eliza. They would fetch a cab for her. But they must know where she needed to be left off. South was not a sufficient address. Eliza relented then, knowing that she must surrender her address to the stranger. And so, in a thrice, she was sitting inside a well-appointed hansom with a tartan quilt around her legs, heading ever southwards, ever southwards, for Gower Street. She must have slept during the journey, for hardly had she been helped into the cab than Kitty McCormack was skipping down the steps of the house on Gower Street and running towards her.

"Lord God, it's Mrs Drew!"

Hetty and Kitty McCormack led her back up the steps, and the cab went clip-clopping off in the direction of Oxford Street. In the parlour, Hetty took off her sister's coat. Eliza looked up into the worried eyes.

"What about Albert?"

"Eliza, you had scarcely walked out that door when his fever broke. Dr Downs says he should be up and well by tomorrow."

"And Theodora?"

Kitty McCormack took the coat and disappeared downstairs. Hetty Arkwright knelt down in front of Eliza Drew. Her eyes fixed on her sister's eyes as though trying to read the ciphers behind her words.

"Theodora is a great girl. She walked straight home from Oxford Street on her own . . . after you became . . . separated. I think we should fetch Dr Downs again, Eliza.

It was to be Dr Downs' third visit that day. Eliza knew he was being sent for as soon as she heard the door slam behind Kitty McCormack and the little boots race down the granite steps. Hetty poured tea into willow-pattern cups. She sat opposite Eliza as though they were drawing up a battle-plan for a picnic.

"What happened to you, Eliza? Do you remember?"

"I don't recall very much, actually."

"Can you remember nothing at all? Were you accosted by someone?"

Hetty told her that Theodora had scarcely spoken a word when she came back. The girl had told Hetty, in point of fact, that Eliza had let her go home on her own and said she would be back soon. Which couldn't have been true, could it? Eliza Drew smiled, neither confirming nor denying anything. Anyway, Theodora was fast asleep, as though her mother hadn't gone missing at all and all was well with the world. What was the meaning of it all? Hetty wanted to know. Charles Arkwright arrived at the door, breathless, in the same instant as Dr Downs. He had been out scouring the streets around Russell Square, with a constable, to see whether Eliza had met with an accident. Through a gap in the parlour door, Eliza saw the two men in earnest conversation with Eliza. Charles Arkwright withdrew to his study, leaving the doctor and Hetty to speak with Eliza. Dr Downs explained gently to Eliza that she had suffered from some sort of heatstroke, a thing that was well understood now because of the soldiers in the sub-continent. He prescribed a sedative powder, suggested Eliza take bed rest the following day and ordered a halt to any strenuous exercise until the brain-pan had time to regain its equilibrium, as regards water.

Eliza passed by Charles Arkwright as she made for bed, a little later. His voice was gentle. There was a kindness in his eyes.

"Everything in order, Eliza?"

"Yes, thank you."

"If there's anything at all I can do . . ."

Eliza Drew slept with Theodora again that night, whispering comforts into her ear and telling her she was back and that she would not be going away again. Just before sleep, she heard Hetty and Charles' voices in the far bedroom. Charles Arkwright's deep baritone sounded comical against Hetty's lighter register. Eliza resolved, as she slipped into sleep, that she would talk with John Drew when she returned to Aghadoe. She would set down the locket with the lock of Edward's hair on the table and, when the girls were in bed, begin to talk to John Drew, whether he listened or no. For not talking, she now understood, would not stop the evil eye from striking. This was a matter for God and nature and design. Her sleeping dreams that night were all-a-jumble. When she awoke with Theodora's head cuddled on her breast, she could remember only bits and pieces. The flower-girl in Covent Garden. The grimy steam-boats on the Thames. Pat Denny and his pig looking down at her from the little stage. And Mrs Tours looking at her over her spectacles as she stooped to help the child with the halo, in the rough little colony near St Pancras. She heard her own voice then. Mrs Tours' voice.

"What is it, alanna?"

The next thing, she had fallen back to sleep and, when she awoke for the second time that morning, it was to hear Theodora and Albert's agitated voices in the playroom as they fought over the globe Walter Cameron had brought a few nights before. Eliza Drew longed for the light again and knew that, somehow or other, she must soon pay another visit to Mrs Tours. Now that she had come to some sort or reconciliation with the light. Now that she had finally come to admit that it really was there.

XVIII

OVER THE HILLS TO TULLYROE

John Drew caught sight of Mrs Tours as she was tipping the last of the offal into the brewery river, across the road from her cottage. It was just as well, because he needed to speak to the blessed woman. Eliza would be home in two days and the matter of Bridget Doheny had still not been sorted out. He signalled to Fox Keegan to pull up. The trap shuddered to a halt. Mrs Tours wiped her hands in her apron and looked up at them, squinting in the strong morning light.

"Mrs Tours . . ."

"Is it yourself is in it, Dr Drew?"

"I wonder if I might have a private word with you?"

John Drew cast his eye on the lumps of offal floating downstream. Mrs Tours must have been too busy to dump her rubbish in the river the night before. He stood outside the house, beside the pony-and-trap, gazing down Pound Street at Mary Begadan making her way down the town with her little tribe. Fewer children, less porter and more work needed. The wisdom of Eliza Drew and of Mrs Tours.

"You were going to say, Dr Drew?"

John Drew looked into Mrs Tours' broad face. Was she going to let him stand there and speak his piece—right in the middle of the road? Her smile was sweet, he thought, but the eyes behind the spectacles betrayed shrewdness. The cunning of the native who dealt with both sides. Like the clever fool holding the reins in the trap could never learn to do.

"Bridget Doheny . . . you've probably heard about the whole affair by now."

"Faith and I have. Would you like me to have a word in her ear, Dr Drew?"

"If you wouldn't mind awfully. Eliza will be back the day after tomorrow . . . and Judith."

"Well, I can call out to Mr Hill's and ask her to return by tomorrow."

"Tomorrow, so."

John Drew felt the weight of the locket case in his frock coat pocket as he stood staring at Mrs Tours. The locket with the lock of Edward's hair. A morbid keepsake but strangely comforting. All that is left of our bright boy. A lock of hair.

"It's settled then?"

"All settled, Dr Drew."

As he watched Mrs Tours make her way back across Pound Street into her house, he fancied for a moment that he saw her smile to herself. It was the sort of smile a grown-up might give an errant child. He realised once again, with a certain amount of distress, that Mrs Tours' knowledge was of another type altogether. It was the wisdom of the ages, gathered at countless hearths through myriad conversations. Like the tales of the Patriarchs, handed down from mouth to mouth, until some Hebrew genius began writing them down. Only no one would ever write down Mrs Tours' wisdom. Fox Keegan snapped the reins and John Drew was thrown back in his seat as the trap pushed on for the crossroads.

Just after they had passed out of the town, the talk started up. The night before, in the solitude of the rectory, had been just like the old days, with Fox Keegan as John Drew's rustic amanuensis. It was as though a spirit of those old days had been visited upon them when John Drew and Fox Keegan would make little forays out into the countryside. And Fox Keegan was good at Gaelic place-names, all because of some Kerry schoolmaster he had had as a child and the scraps he had picked up from the older people around Tullyroe, where the last whisper of the dying language could be heard. Aghaboe was cow-field and Raheen was hillock. That was how their relationship had started. It was the sort of harmless antiquarian diversion John Drew used to lighten the load of his own cuneatic studies. Eliza was always uneasy in the young man's company though. Not at all amused by his turn of speech or his lack of deference towards her. Yes, that was it.

"I wouldn't trust your Mr Fox Keegan as far as I'd throw him, John."

"Really, Eliza."

"Fox in name and fox in nature, John."

And yet the great Mrs Tours spoke well of the man, even after the terrible events at the railway camp. But for her, John Drew wouldn't have been persuaded to stand by him. Because a doubt was a doubt. Even the greatest rascal must be given the benefit of the doubt. But he resolved to have it out with Mr Fox Keegan before they reached Tullyroe. What was there to lose? He should ask him straight out: were you involved in the killing of that poor man? And the devil be damned with the answer, one way or the other!

John Drew regarded Fox Keegan out of the corner of his eye. The battered cawbeen pulled down over the eye as he sized up the road ahead. Now wasn't the time to ask. Further on. John Drew coughed a dry, brittle cough.

"Has your father been ailing long, Fox?"

"All his life. I'll tell you a good one, Dr Drew."

"Yes?"

"We only had goose the once every year, at Christmas, do you see. Well, this once didn't me father make a big show of coughing at the table and he telling us all that he mightn't be around for the following Christmas."

"I see."

"So me mother says, faith and we'll have to get a smaller goose next year, so we will."

"Bit of a creaking door, then?"

"You might say that, so you might."

"Still your father, though,"

"That's right. Still me father, bad and all as he is."

The fine mist that had shrouded the autumn hedgerows was now lifting. As the road rose before them, meandering its way out of the bogs of Queen's County for the limestone soils of north Kilkenny, the sun grew even stronger. We are leaving the bad land my ancestors fought for, thought John Drew. Making for the better land the shrewd Normans seized, hundreds of years before them. Good grazing and tillage. Not like the isolated patches of good land, in Queen's County, cut off from one another in the middle of the bog. The natives crossing in from the wilds to harry the planter, an alien entity in a strange landscape. Aghadoe wasn't Sussex and would never be. Without intending to, John Drew spoke his thoughts to the man beside him.

"I enjoyed our work last night, Fox."

"And so did I, Dr Drew. So did I."

"You're a clever man, Fox. But you know that, of course."

"Then what has me the way I am? Without a farthing to my name?"

"Awkwardness, I would say."

"Aye, you might be right there, so you might, Dr Drew."

John Drew sensed the man beside him straighten up.

"Is there something wrong?"

"This ould jennet of yours is pulling sideways, so it is."

With that, they were both down out of the trap while Fox poked about at everything, from the harness to the shafts and the axles. Maybe it was the road, if you could call it a road, because everything else seemed in order. Before they clambered back into the car to resume the journey, John Drew scoured the bushes at the side of the road and came back with a hatful of blackberries.

"Nature's bounty, Mr Keegan."

"Aye."

While they were standing there, wolfing down the blackberries, an ass-and-cart came around the crook in the road, at Castletown. Fox Keegan nodded ahead of him.

"That's old Miss Cunningham. She lives out on the moor."

A crabbed-looking woman was sitting hunched over the reins on the side of the cart. The donkey plodded on past them slowly but the woman scarcely looked across at them as she passed. Fox Keegan nodded towards the ass-and-cart as it rounded the corner for Aghadoe.

"Women who don't have children do go mad, Dr Drew. Did you ever hear tell of that?"

"And some women who have children go mad too."

"I suppose you're right."

"But you never . . . Fox?"

"Come on, or me father'll be well boxed by the time I get home."

There was silence then, for a few moments. John Drew realised he had crossed too far into his companion's acre. Out of the noisy town of Aghadoe, in the Queen's County, into the misty past of his companion, in north Kilkenny. He was distracted a moment by the sudden realisation that the locket was missing from his frock coat.

"The blessed thing was in my pocket a moment ago!"

Fox Keegan reached into the trap and lifted up the little silver locket, dangling from its chain. The silver case glistened in the noon-day sun. John Drew nodded at his companion.

"Perhaps you could mind it for me, Fox. I shouldn't have brought it with me at all, of course."

"No bother."

They were hardly back in the trap when the horse began to pull to the right again. Fox said they should carry on as far as Johnstown and stop in at the forge there, just in case. The sun was high in the sky now and all around them the early autumn light was in the bushes. The final gasp of an indifferent summer. It was the last Queen's County would see of blue skies before the dark, dank days of winter set in again. At the bridge near Gawl, a boy was herding a brindled cow that was strip-grazing along the side of the road. He looked up at them as they trotted past, sensing the odd match they made. John Drew wiped his spectacles.

"That was one of my first follies, Fox. Gawl . . . do you remember?"

"What's that, Dr Drew?"

"A false etymology. I broke my father's rule, when he taught me my first Hebrew word. Never trust the vowels."

"Never trusted them much meself anyway, Dr Drew."

"I thought Gawl must mean foreigner, you see, because of all the Protestant farms around here."

"It does in some places, Dr Drew. Baile na nGall . . . The town of the foreigners."

"But it was really Gabhall . . . fork . . . the fork in the river . . . across from here . . . don't you remember, Fox?"

"Oh, I remember it well, so I do. The two of us standing out in a field, looking at that ould bit of a stone there, in the lashings of rain."

John Drew looked over at the man snapping the reins. But

Fox Keegan kept his eye on the road. John Drew's voice had a note of gentle puzzlement in it.

"What does it feel like to see a language dying around you?"

"Well, it's like this, Dr Drew, if you can't sell a cow in it, there isn't much call for it."

"I suppose so. I suppose so."

Fox Keegan flicked the reins and the horse picked up speed again, though he was still pulling to one side. They weren't too far from Johnstown now. They could see what the matter was there. It would be another couple of hours before they crossed over the hills and down into the valley of Tullyroe. John Drew would make his way back again before nightfall, having left Fox at his home. He would feed and water the horse in Tullyroe and get back as far as Johnstown, where he could sort out lodgings for the night. John Drew put the matter out of his head then, just as the horse shuddered to a halt, snorting in the warm air. In a flash, Fox Keegan was out of the car. It could be only one thing really. The horse whinnied as he ran his hand along its legs. Sure enough, the creature had thrown a shoe. Now they would surely have to stop at the forge.

"He's lost a shoe, so he has, Dr Drew."

"Dear me!"

"Sure maybe it broke a bigger cross."

"I beg your pardon?"

"Well, if it had've happened up in the hills like, we would have been rightly bunched."

"Yes, I see what you mean, Mr Keegan. I see what you mean."

They walked the next half-mile or so into Johnstown, flanking the horse, to give it a rest from drawing the two of them. At the pump, at the edge of town, some children were playing tig. They stopped to gawk at the two men strolling beside the horse.

"E'er a chance of a jaunt, mister?"

"Go on out of that!"

The forge was on the Cork road. They could hear the hammer clinging off the anvil as they rounded the corner. A rough-looking, heavy-set man with a mouthful of nails and a heavy leather apron came out to inspect the horse. They led the horse round into the yard, unhitched it and heeled up the trap. The blacksmith's boy was as black-faced as his father.

"Me father says them shoes he has on him isn't worth a shite."

"And will your father be long, do you think?"

"He says he'll do him as soon as he has Tynan's ould mare done."

Fox elected to go and stretch his legs while they led the horse back round to the forge. John Drew glanced around the yard and eyed an old abandoned carriage, over by the ivy-covered gable wall. The carriage looked altogether out of place in a small town like Johnstown. It was the sort of ancient brougham you saw on the streets of Belfast, years ago. And even then, it was a little too grand for poor old Belfast. John Drew considered the carriage a moment then glanced at his fob-watch. There was easily a half an hour to go before the horse would be set to rights. Maybe an hour even. He could catch forty winks in the big carriage maybe. The late night toiling over the cuneatic tables was telling on him. He was ten or more years older than Fox Keegan. Ten years nearer the grave. In the shake of a lamb's tail he had settled himself into the dusty old carriage with its tattered velvet upholstery, having first driven out a grey-and-white cat that was happily sunning her person on the seat. He pulled his hat down over his forehead and huddled into the corner. Just half an hour would freshen him up for the journey ahead. As he slipped towards sleep, John Drew felt the chill of autumn steal its way into his bones, despite the sluggish sun. He wondered momentarily where Fox Keegan had gone. Maybe off to have a little jorum in some shebeen. As he nodded off, he was vaguely aware of the cat insinuating its way back in beside him. He let it settle and made no move to shift it. A cousin of Bianconi's. All cats are one.

They were hazy at first, the symbols that floated in front of his eyes as he slipped towards sleep. It was a series of symbols from the first line of the inscription. He transliterated the first line again, in half-sleep.

Da-ri-ia-a-mush-LUGAL.GAL

And that odd sign at the end of the line. He still hadn't reached a decision as to what it must signify. A word dropped into the new language from the older one, like LUGAL or GAL? Maybe the sign was an indicator. A determinative? Suggesting what, then? Class? Case ending? He thought about Darius the Great, probably illiterate himself, ordering his scribes and stone-masons to cut out the royal dedication in three languages. The mighty Darius, who had lived in a period of great change with the Persians taking over the reigns and the Babylonians only a literary memory, in the minds of scribes. Words half-remembered, old rites and customs neglected. In his mind, John Drew heard the voice of Mrs Tours to Eliza, out in the pantry.

"That fella does be out *koorteekin* half the night."

Koorteekin. Old language in a new one. An older idea: night-visiting. No word for it in English. Like *gallivanting.* Was that French? Maybe. What would *koorteekin* be like as an ideograph then? A man walking, maybe. Or a moon. Which could also be used as a syllable. *Koo.* In sleep, John Drew's eyes tracked along the first line of the Darius inscription. There was no Westmacott now. He had been left on his own to come to a conclusive reading of the inscription, form a definite syllabary and list the ideographs secreted in the older, extinct tongue. With the help of the Old Persian version, things had been made easier, of course. And some of the earlier syllabaries had been a help too. His eyes jumped to the fifth line of the six-line inscription.

In the deserted white room of his sleeping mind, John Drew read the line to himself once more, syllable by ancient syllable.

"a-ha-ma-an-ni-ish-shi-i . . . the Achaemenian . . ."

His eyes opened slightly. He was vaguely aware of the black-smith's boy whistling to himself in the yard. A tune that weaved in and out of his thoughts. A tune that seemed, somehow or other, to have a similar rhythm to the line he was reading in his dreams.

"Lillibullero Bullenalla . . ."

An Ulster song from the troubles of '98. Ideasounds. Odd to hear it here. Travellers on the Cork road, of course. Boy knowing he was a minister. A little joke in song. Ideaword. Ideapictures. He looked over his shoulder at the blacksmith's boy. Their eyes met for a moment.

"He's shoeing the horse now, so he is."

John Drew crowded himself back into the corner of the old brougham and fell to his second sleep. But the boy's face was etched in his mind now, among the symbols. The same fair hair as that in the little locket and the same childish devilment in the eyes. He pretended to resist the pull of the notion that had way-laid his waking thoughts but he didn't have the heart to. And so, when his fingers felt for the talisman, for the little silver locket with the lock of blond hair, he found himself suddenly falling past the crossroads of consciousness again.

He was in grey, provincial Belfast again. With Judith and Edward and Eliza, walking together towards the Music Hall on Arthur Street. It was a summer's evening, like this one. The harsh, guttural thrust of northern voices was all around him. Straight talkers, straight dealers. No room in their harsh, stran-gulated vowels for equivocation. Of course, there was plenty of party spirit on the streets, especially then, as the hungry ones came in from towns and villages all over Ulster to work and feed and fight. There were brawls down around Peter's Hill and that nasty murder near the gasworks. But they had remained aloof from much of the spite all the same. There had really been only the one incident, and on the Sabbath too, when some miscreant had stolen into the vestry, and cut up John Drew's clerical collar, perhaps thinking that his sermon that day had been a little too high church. A little too close to papist whimsy for comfort. But he and his family hadn't managed to stay aloof from the sinister finger that sought them out within their own house. The pestilence that came *koorteekin* that awful week had never been named. Just one of the many nameless diseases of the poor that he, John Drew, must have carried home.

He recalled little Edward Drew's pale face against the pillow, the last evening of his life. Dr McCracken's useless ministrations. The pills and the potions and the cupping. Then the terrible realisation that, despite their best efforts to provide a veritable citadel against the world outside, some invisible hand had seized the boy. Eliza Drew, distraught and inconsolable, mopping the child's brow with a sponge filled with valerian while he sat with Judith at a game of battledore in the kitchen. The county jail, the hospital on Frederick Street—maybe even the Union, off the Lisburn road—was this where he had suckled the sickness to bring it home to Edward? John Drew recalled a sort of queasiness and dizziness a few days before the boy came down with the thing. Was this it, then? The malign sickness passing from himself to Edward? Perhaps the misguided philanthropy that Eliza was always chiding him for had occasioned his son's death. Those laborious visits to the wards in the Union building, assailed by all kinds of coughs and chills. In his own guilt and Eliza's grief, a whole saga had been played out. Silent evenings by the study fire. A brooding that sometimes left Eliza bedridden for days with a sort of melancholy that Dr McCracken could no more cure than he could Edward's illness of the body. It was the same sort of melancholy, Charles Arkwright had told him, in a private moment in Gower Street, that had bedevilled Eliza and Hetty's mother, some forty years before. Because it had all been too much for Eliza Drew. A splinter of sadness had entered into her heart that would never be removed. John Drew watched his son turn to face him now, as they both sat before the study fire, the *Belfast Newsletter* laid to one side. Edward Drew, standing there in the little patent shoes Eliza had bought him. Shoes that would never see a year's wear. There was a quiet smile on his lips, a token of the tranquillity within. Edward's eyes were looking at his father now, fixing him in a gentle gaze. John Drew felt his hand reach out to touch his son's hair. His dried lips stirred themselves to whisper the boy's name.

"Edward . . . are you?"

The boy smiled. His pale, soft face paler still in the soft light of the oil lamp on the study table.

"I'm all right now, Father."

"Good . . . good."

Edward Drew was laughing now, laughing for them both. As though it had all been some sort of joke. A misunderstanding. Beyond the window of the study, John Drew could hear the sound of hammering. The heavy fall of Odin's hammer on the anvil. Of Haddad, the god of iron and war.

KEDOING KEDOING KEDOING

Metal on metal. There was a smell of burning in his nostrils. Then shouts somewhere near him. A boy's voice. But not Edward's voice.

"Are you all right there, sir?"

He opened his eyes painfully to the purple braiding on the inside of the car and the stray cat curled up at his feet. The sound of iron on iron was still ringing in his ears.

KEDOING KEDOING KEDOING

The boy was looking up at him with Edward's quizzical smile on his lips.

"My father has the horse done, sir."

John Drew moved himself stiffly and clambered down on to

the rough ground. The day seemed even more unseasonably warm now. A swarm of horse-flies was gadding about the dung-heap in the corner. In another corner, over by the horse trough, a stray chicken was picking at pebbles. He shook himself into wakefulness and followed the boy back to the forge. Fox Keegan was standing to one side of the anvil, mesmerised by the flying sparks. The horse was tethered to a post at the entrance, indifferent to all the comings and goings. He would need a good drink before carrying on. The blacksmith's boy led the horse around to the trough while John Drew rooted about in the little purse affair Eliza had given him for coins. Metal exchanged for metal. Silver for iron. An expensive metal for a base one. And what was the differ between them?

"Are we right so, Dr Drew?"

"Yes, Mr Keegan. Right and ready."

When the horse had drunk its fill, they hitched him to the trap and pulled off across the Cork road towards Freshford. They spoke little, each man working away at his own thoughts, until Fox coaxed the trap to the right, on to the little road that would lead them up over Knockamuck and down to where Tullyroe lay, silent to the world, in a valley the Norman lords of Kilkenny had once seen fit to settle. Graces, Bennetts, de Burgos. Aliens in an alien landscape. Like John Drew himself, in Queen's County. Drew, Featherstonehaugh, Carter, Thompson. Saxon, Norman, Gael. And a few other blow-ins, here and there. Each leavening the dough a little more.

As the curved road rose sharply, both men descended from the trap to ease the load on the beast. It was a poor road, little more than a track really. A dry road, with a little line of grass running down the middle, that the winter rains would wash away in a couple of months. But now, with the last of summer, there was still enough purchase on the stony ground for the horse to keep up a reasonable pace. Near the top of Knockamuck they rested for a while, seating themselves on the grass like nature's gentlemen, to eat the soda bread and eggs Mrs Tours had sent with Fox Keegan that morning. While Fox slipped off into a little copse to attend to his business, John Drew chewed away at the dry bread and salted butter. There wasn't a sound to be heard in the still air. Not as much as a cow lowing or a sheep bleating. John Drew watched his companion re-trace his footsteps until Fox Keegan was standing behind him as the horse champed away on the grass. What possessed John Drew to break his silence then, he would find it hard to say afterwards. Perhaps the unexpected journey had touched something off in both of them. Or the dream of the boy, back in the blacksmith's yard. For there was suddenly no fear on John Drew's tongue. He wiped the crumbs from his mouth and turned to face the man standing beside him with his hands in his pockets. His voice was gentle. He might have been mouthing some harmless afterthought.

"Mr Keegan . . . Fox . . ."

"Yes, Dr Drew?"

"Tell me this and tell me no more."

Mrs Tours' turn of phrase in his, John Drew's, Protestant mouth.

"Were you or were you not involved in that poor man's murder at the railway camp, all those years ago?"

John Drew looked up at the man standing beside him, chewing on a blade of grass. It was some moments before Fox Keegan answered. When he did open his mouth to speak, his catchlight eyes remained fixed on the horizon, as though he was speaking to no one and everyone.

"I didn't have hand, part or act in his death."

"But you were the lookout, weren't you?"

"I thought they were only going to give him a few flakes of a stick, on account of he didn't want to give the boys any more work on the railway job."

"How many ruffians were there?"

"Three . . . two . . ."

"Well, was it two or three?"

Fox Keegan looked about him a moment, then turned back to his interrogator.

"Three."

"I see. And they knew him from before, as a tithe proctor? Is that right, Mr Keegan?"

"Aye."

"And that's where you knew him from too . . . from the Knockroe incident?"

"Could be, all right."

There was no more to be said on the matter. It was all very simple: either John Drew accepted his companion's word or he didn't.

They climbed back on to the car at the top of the hill. Below lay the little nooks and crannies of the valley in which Tullyroe sat. Grace's land, now broken up into little tenant farms like that of Fox's father. Maybe, like the tithes once paid to the like of John Drew himself, the tenant farmers would one day rule the roost and lord it over their own little patches of land. The last they spoke of the whole business was as the car breasted the hill and the horse gathered pace for the downward trot.

"Why did you get involved in all that agitation then, years ago?"

"Because of what I seen at Knockroe, Dr Drew. You know that well."

"But you don't believe in agitation any more . . . am I right?"

"I believe people came and took land what didn't belong to them. That was a wrong thing to do."

"But what's done is done, Fox."

"Well, pretending it never happened won't help anyone either. The truth has to be told, Dr Drew. Them that tumbles raths has to pay for it, in the heel of the reel, one way or the other."

"Does that mean the rath must be re-built?"

"Can't be, can it, Dr Drew? And anyways, it wasn't all bad what ye done . . ."

The horse paused a moment, before turning into the downward track, as though sensing it was entering another world. There were only a few miles to go before Tullyroe and the cottage hidden in the glen, but these miles were further from his own world than John Drew had been in an age. The hedgerows were wilder here and things progressed slower. A trip into Kilkenny would be a great affair in these parts and news, by and large, travelled on foot rather than on horseback. It felt as though the horse was making strange now for it seemed to shy at every crook in the road. As they crossed a little stone bridge, about a mile further down the road, they spotted a man strolling home with a sort of spade affair over his shoulder. He nodded at the two men in the jaunting car. John Drew noticed the labourer's eye fall on him and felt the eyes on his back as they drove on. He reached for the dog collar and slipped it off. His frock coat and waistcoat would pass muster.

"There's no call to leave your collar off, Dr Drew."

"Best keep things simple, Fox."

"You'll have to stay the night anyhow. It's too late to make your way home over Knockamuck."

It was a few moments before John Drew committed himself, as though he were enjoying the silent debate with himself. Not that there really was any debate. He wouldn't make it back to Johnstown by nightfall. And getting caught out in the chill air of an autumn evening could be fatal.

"Yes, I suppose we'll have to make some arrangement."

At the crossroads in Tullyroe, an old crone in widow's weeds was standing in front of Daly's, the shop. She squinted as she watched them approach, then beckoned to Fox Keegan to come over to her. They whispered together for a moment, then Fox climbed back up on the jaunting car and, with a flick of the reins, they were out on the road for the farm.

"What did the old lady have to say, Fox?"

"She says me father passed away yesterday, so he did."

"I'm very sorry to hear that."

"He had the priest and all. They'll bury him tomorrow morning."

"I'm sorry."

"Do you know what that means, then, Dr Drew?"

"I'm sorry? I don't understand."

Fox Keegan glanced sideways at the older man with the spectacles. The gaps in his teeth were more apparent when he grinned. He looked like a little boy about to play a nasty prank.

"Have you ever been to a wake, Dr Drew?"

"Well, I . . . no, actually . . . I . . . haven't."

"Well and you're going to one now, so you are."

As the horse's hooves gathered pace, John Drew's eyes caught the dog collar resting on the blanket under the seat. This vanity too would fade. The vanity of a cleric deducing the words of a Galilean divine who died almost two thousand years earlier in Palestine. And what was left, when all the vanities were swept away? Love, perhaps. Kindness and compassion. Perhaps there was no more purpose to life than the acts of life itself. A passage from shadow through light to shadow. From the dark glade whence the ensoulment of Edward Drew had taken place to the still darker glade where his childish soul now reposed.

They pulled in from the road on to a track that rose towards the low hill at Lismore, where the family cabin was located.

"There's your namesake, Mr Keegan!"

And sure enough, there, as brazen as you like, was Mr Reynard out patrolling the ditches and drains in search of a foolish hen maybe or a rabbit out sunning itself.

"You can't bate the fox for cuteness, Dr Drew."

"Indeed."

As they rounded the great rath at the butt end of the farm, they saw the figure of a man driving a couple of cows back in from the higher ground for milking. He was wearing a battered hat and goaded the beasts ahead of him with the broad of his hand as they shuffled along. Fox Keegan raised his hand in salute.

"That's my brother Tom. He do have the farm now."

"Do you know something, Fox . . ."

"What's that now?"

"Your accent has changed since we came over that hill."

"Well, it's like this, so it is. If I came back with any airs and graces, they'd soon knock it out of me, so they would. Me mother said to me, in the letter she wrote before I came down last year, leave ye'er fancy accent at the railway station in Kilkenny, John. Wasn't that a good one?"

The horse-and-trap pulled into the farmyard, with chickens scattering to left and right and a bad-tempered collie bitch snapping at the cartwheels. John Drew stooped down and slipped the dog collar into his frock coat.

"You don't want me to call you Dr Drew, so?"

"Just say I'm someone from the brewery . . . a manager."

"The brewery? Aye, fair enough so."

Three neighbour women were sitting at the long table in the kitchen with Fox's mother, a solid-faced, serious-looking person. The wake would start up soon enough. There were rounds of soda bread and cake at one end of the long table, a couple of jugs of whiskey and stout in a creel on the floor and the smell of tobacco already hung in the air. Was this what they might have done once in old Babylon? Made a feast after the death of a loved one? Who knew where peasants got their traditions from. It certainly wasn't from the island across the water. From the Saxons.

Or the Normans, for that matter. When the awkward introductions had been done and the neighbour women had finished sizing him up and down, it was agreed that a straw bed would be made up in the loft. Then it was into the little room off the kitchen, where Fox's sister Mary was sitting with the cold body of her father. The young woman stood up as they came in, her eyes making a sweep of both men at once.

"We thought ye would never make it, Fox."

"I got held up."

"Is that the way it is?"

When Mary Keegan left, John Drew followed Fox to the bedside and watched him place a snatched kiss on the dead man's brow. Jer Keegan's face was tranquil. A face framed by sidelocks and jowls, it was one that had lived a life.

When he had drunk his fill of tea out in the kitchen and eaten a few slices of fresh soda bread, John Drew took leave of the little gathering in the kitchen to take a constitutional before the light left the sky altogether. He parted with Fox Keegan at the haggard and watched him make his way across the muddy track towards where his brother was leading the two cows back up into the pasture after the milking. Neither man appeared to speak to the other as they sauntered along behind the cattle. Fox Keegan's gait seemed to have changed too now, along with his speech. If one person could accommodate so much change in such a short time, how much more so a great language? With this awkward thought, John Drew pulled his black frieze coat tightly about him and made steadily for the higher ground beyond the little orchard in order to sort his thoughts before sleep.

XIX

LORNA LOVEGROVE IS NOT AT HOME

Mrs Tours ran her hand along the lining of the velvet jacket. It would take only a minute to stitch up the hem again. She looked down over her glasses and took up a thimble. Jack Kavanagh would be calling in for it the following day. They would have a grand cup of tea, and she would get a bit of news about matters out beyond the brewery fields. A tired frown passed over Mrs Tours, all of a sudden, and, not minding herself, she pricked her middle finger with the needle. She spoke softly to the cat on the floor, at her feet.

"That's for luck, so it is."

Now, as God is me witness, I didn't know what was ahead of me out in Willie Hill's mansion. Maybe if I had've, I wouldn't have gone. I thought the whole business with Judith Drew and her beau had faded out. Eliza Drew would be back in a few days, Missie Judith would be shipped up to Dublin and it would all blow over like a bellyful of bad wind. As if the Hennigans didn't have enough to do minding their own children without letting their eldest get involved with the minister's daughter. And the grand house the Hennigans have, out there in the Bawn. Oh, stick to your own side. Born, bred and buried with the one lot makes it all simpler. Not that I did, of course.

I was walking out the road, with the little red scarf tied around me head, and doesn't Jer Dooley comes by on his ass-and-cart. So I took a jaunt off of him, out as far as the turn in the road. But I paid well for the journey because he had more talk in him than an ould one at Maryborough market.

"Any strange, Mrs Tours?"

"Just meself and yourself, Jer."

He went on about the railway, then the visit of the Queen and where did I stand on that? And then he was off about the union they want to build out by the four roads.

"We could find ourselves in it, handy enough, if things go bad again."

"'Deed and I'd throw meself in the river before I entered any union."

"Oh, now, Mrs Tours, that's terrible talk altogether, so it is."

Away from him, I thought I would never get. He left me at the Commons bridge and I trotted off up Willie Hill's driveway with the grand trees and the bushes. There was hardly a stir when I got to the place. I was surprised I didn't see the two madams gadding about or sitting in one of the long windows, admiring themselves. One of Willie Hill's men was out cutting logs at the stables. I nodded to him and made my way up the big granite steps. No servants' entrance for Mrs Tours, thank you. The lovely red drapes I made up for them were still up on the windows, as grand as the day I first ran them up. I rang the bell and stood back to have a look around. That little hoppity maid of theirs appeared at the door—the Morgan one. She was all mistress-of-the-house with me. Far from it she was reared. There's only one thing worse than a Protestant master and that's a Protestant maid. I smiled sweetly at her. Many's the fork I put in her father's trousers. And handy enough he was at wearing them out, in his youth, by all accounts.

"Is Mrs Hill at home?"

"Is there something the matter, Mrs Tours?"

"Well, and if there is, it'd be none of your affair, would it?"

"I'll go and fetch her so."

Fetch, is right. I stood in the hallway, looking around at all the grand bits and pieces. At the big brass gong and the glass case with the stuffed pheasants and the long swords up on the wall. I could hear a great lot of fussing and foostering going on in the breakfast room and then Violet Hill appears, in all her finery. A grand white gown on her and her hair done up with pins. A real whore's handbag of a get-up it was.

"Mrs Tours . . . can I help you?"

"Dr Drew asked me to drop out, the way Judith would be back in time to get the house ready for her mother when she gets home."

"So the Doheny woman never returned?"

"So I hear tell."

Then, didn't I hear this woeful scream. Well, I declare to Jaesus, it put the heart crossways in me. It was like the sort of scream you'd give if you saw something in a ditch at night. We all turned to look back up the big stairs, myself and Violet Hill and little Miss Countrymouse, the maid. And there, at the top of the stairs, was Cassie Hill and she roaring like a bull. Standing there in her flowery shift, like all belonging to her was dead. Her mother made a run to calm her down, and myself and the Morgan one just stared.

"What is it, Cassie? What's the matter, pet?"

Pet is right. I'd have reddened her arse with a kick if she was mine, the same cheeky little rip. It's too much fussing they get nowadays. Cassie Hill just stood there, sobbing big sobs until her mother finally got it out of her.

"Judith is gone! She's run off."

"What do you mean, Cassie . . . run off?"

"She's run away!"

"Where? Where to?"

"I don't know . . ."

And then we were all hooshed into the breakfast room and Violet Hill and her potscrub scuttled off to get some potion or other and I was left alone for a moment with the little miss. I stood myself in front of her and lifted up her chin.

"Never mind them ould tears, girl!"

"Mrs Tours, please leave me alone! My mother will . . ."

"Now, you'd better come clean with me, girl, or I'll make it worse for you when Eliza Drew gets back, so I will."

"Please!"

"Where has that tramp gone off to?"

"I don't know!"

"You have one minute to own up or I'll tell your mother the whole story about the midnight gallivanting, that you knew about all along."

There was a little sniffle. Cassie Hill glanced back at the door. She could hear the ould one coming back.

"Is she run off with that Hennigan chap?"

"Yes."

"To where? Answer me, or I'll give you the back of my hand!"

"To Hennigans' farm."

"In the name of Jaesus! Do they want every Protestant from here to Bedlam down on top of them? And Arkins and all his men too?"

"Judith said she was nearly eighteen now so they wouldn't be able to touch her soon."

"That's the game then, is it?"

And, with that, doesn't Violet Hill arrive back with a bottle of medicine to settle missie's nerves. Toe up the high hole of her arse is what she needs, says I, in me own mind. But you couldn't say that to a mother, of course.

There was great commotion then, with Cassie Hill turning on the tears and Violet Hill getting herself into a great lather about what was to be done. She gave Cassie a great gulp of this yellow stuff from a bottle and looked over at me. She wasn't playing the lady of the manor any more now. She ordered the Morgan one to go out and tell one of the men to get the pony-and-trap ready. Mr Hill in the boulting mill, by the Beggar's Bridge, would have to be told straightaway. He would surely know what to do.

"I will stay here with Cassie, Mrs Tours. You can go back by the car, if you like."

Which she thought was putting me in my place. But I was in a panic too. Judith Drew must have worked out her plan well in advance. I would have to strike while the iron was hot. I wished to God Fox Keegan was back again so I could check all he told me. But I had the gist of it, all the same. Knowledge is a great thing. Not just book learning, but the bits and pieces you do pick up when you're putting an arse in a trousers or letting out a dress. All ready for barter, if you like. Cassie Hill was quick enough to talk when she knew what I had on her. But I wasn't so sure about Kate Hennigan at all, at all. But one thing I knew was that Willie Hill wouldn't get far bringing Sergeant Arkins and his men out to that lot. Respecting the law wasn't in their nature, whether it was Irish law or English law. That crowd would blackguard Jesus Christ down off of the cross itself, charge him for the nails and say they done it for Ireland.

I got off of the Hill's trap at the Commons crossroads and walked in the rest of the way to do a bit of thinking. I cut across the bridge and up by the brewery cottages. Then I made me way up that dirty ould lane Bridget Doheny lives in, past Dinny Grey, the blacksmith's. I could see him peeping out from the forge. He looked like one of them Hottentots, in that cave of his.

"That's a grand day, Mrs Tours."

"It is, faith."

His eyes followed me all the way up the lane. Knew well where I was going, of course. The Doheny tribe were out rolling around in the muck like pagans from Africa. His royal highness was sitting inside at the table, smoking a pipe, if you please. Lord of all he surveyed. He put on a great show when he saw me.

"Mrs Tours!"

"Is herself in? I wanted to have a word with her about something."

"She's above in her Aunt Mary's, that's where she is."

"Well and would you ever tell her to call in on me later, if she has a minute? Maybe Tadhg there would go up and set the fire in the Drews'."

"*Grand, so.*"

I left him then. Mickey tit, that couldn't stir his shite to do an honest day's work. If it was bulling his wife he got paid for, he'd be like one of them American millionaires, over in New York. Plenty of time for that, of course. The youngest one was sitting on the floor, chawing on a bit of mouldy bread I wouldn't give the dog. And big baldy bollox puffing away on his pipe. Plenty of money for tobacco and beer, of course. It was him started the row down in the square the other night too, I hear tell. Fit him better now to be out doing an honest day's work.

I went straight back to the house then because I had a basket of mending to get through and a dress to let down for one of the Stensons of the back road. A flowery sort of affair. The sort of get-up my grandmother would have given away to the tinkers. Yes, that's what it was like—a tinker's dress. And talking of tinkers, didn't one Hoppie Killeen, with the big tinker's gob on him, appear at the door a while later, looking for pots to mend.

I let him take away the colander that got broke last Christmas and one of the old pots that had lost a handle. Off he goes across the road, and sits himself by the river to do his bit of soldering. I kept an eye on him through the window, all the same. It isn't easy to come by a good pot and you can't do without a colander, so you can't. I took a walk down the town in the afternoon to get the milk from Jer Dooley's, of the Burrow.

I had a little rest in the afternoon, with the worry of it all. I put me legs up on the old couch in the sitting room. When I woke, I could hear one of the big brewery drays clip-clopping by. There was a sudden chill in the air and I realised I had nearly let the stove go out. So I raked it up and had it roaring up the chimney in no time at all. By the time Dan Brady came in for his dinner, the house was warm and snug again and I settled down to the last of the sewing. It was just after dark when the knock came on the door. How well she left it until it was dark to turn up. Afraid anyone would see her, you see. But everyone comes to Mrs Tours' door in the end, priest or preacher.

"*Is that you, Bridget?*"

She had Tadhg with her. I cut him a slice of bread and sat him over in the corner, near the range. When Dan Brady came down to polish his boots, the two of them chatted happily and had a game of soldiers with some of my empty spools. I showed Bridget Doheny the dress Mrs Seavers had left with me, that she has no use for. And the couple of pairs of pants that would do for the biggest lad, Christopher.

"Thank you very much, Mrs Tours. I couldn't."

"Whisht now! There's many would be glad of them."

She began to look all worried then. I hunted Tadhg out into the scullery with a cut of bread. Him and Dan Brady were all chat out there about horses and machines and fights.

"I'm after making a stookawn of myself over the Drews. I don't know what to do. But them yokes he has out in the coachhouse. It isn't right, Mrs Tours."

"Sure the man himself isn't right, but we still have to live in the same town as him, Bridget."

We had a nice sup of tea then, that I had slipped a little bit of chamomile into. It was all grand and aisy. She looked over the dress again and said it was a fine dress. And well for Mrs Seavers she could give nice dresses like that away.

"It was belonging to the sister that died on her, so it was."

Then Bridget Doheny went on about that layabout of a husband of hers. "He's very bad with a cough, Mrs Tours," says she. "That'd be on account of smoking too much tobacco," says I. "And his legs do be at him too, Mrs Tours." "That's on account of he never gets up off his arse, my good woman," says I. I didn't put a tooth in it, so I didn't. No fear he has a pain in his mickey, says I to meself. That particular instrument is never short of exercise. "I do have to look after him more than the children," says she. Men are like that, says I, in me own mind. If you let them.

"Would he not think of looking for work down in the brewery itself?"

"He would, only the left leg is gone again him again."

"It isn't his middle leg that's bothering him, anyway, alanna."

She started laughing then a bit, so I knew I had her with me. The little lad had fallen asleep across the table, and Dan Brady slipped off to bed with instructions to call me just before light, when he was up for the early shift at the brewery. I was thinking to myself that if Willie Hill didn't show up with news, I might have to go out to Hennigans' alone. And then Bridget Doheny starting crying, all of a sudden.

"There, there, alanna. Me and you can sort this all out rale aisy, so we can. What does ould Drew have up in that coachhouse anyway?"

"All sorts of eggs and animals' skulls. Even a badger's skull."

"Well now, I have a message to go up there tomorrow, so I'll throw the whole bleddy lot out and leave them in a big sack, the way he can dump them down the fields himself."

"But what will Dr Drew say, Mrs Tours?"

"He won't say a thing, because I'm after telling him, if he wants the hardest-working woman in the town back, he'll have to get shut of the lot. It'll all be fixed up by tomorrow night and you can get up to the house and have it sparkling for when Eliza and her long face comes back that evening."

"I don't know what to say."

"Say nothing at all is what you'll say. That lot hates to be under a compliment to anyone. And another thing . . ."

"What's that, Mrs Tours?"

"You can leave young Tadhg down to me tomorrow, to chop a few sticks. That'd be a great help to me."

I had to nearly push her out the door, so I did. I'm sure she was in great form when she got back up to her lord and master. He'll get a good run at her tonight, says I, in me own mind. Everyone goes to bed happy.

Well, I declare to Jaesus, I had hardly sat down again when there was a rap on the window. I heard the pony-and-trap from down the road but I didn't know who it was.

"Who's that, at this hour of the night?"

I pulled back the curtain and there, in the moonlight, was Willie Hill's face looking in at me. I let him in as quiet as I could, so as not to wake the lodgers. He was very aeriated altogether. In a great state over little Lorna Lovegrove out in Hennigans' and how he had let the Drews down.

"You had a right to pull her out by the hair of the head, Mr Hill."

"But procedures must be followed."

"Well and I have a few procedures in me own mind. The truth is, Mr Hill—"

"Yes?

"Judith Drew has made a fool of you and run rings around the two of you."

He was quiet for a moment. He knew well enough to keep his mouth shut.

"Do you have any idea how we might settle this matter, Mrs Tours?"

"I might, so I might. But there's to be no Sergeant Arkins."

I let him stew in it while I went to wet the tea. I got him to fill up the oil lamp and make himself generally useful. I let him get rale agitated in himself, the way it would be easy to persuade him, in the end. He was fidgeting and foostering with my needles so much, and he drinking the tea, I spoke slowly to him.

"Are you thinking of becoming a seamstress, Mr Hill?

He smiled at me. The cup of tea settled him a bit.

"Now . . ." says I.

"I'll tell you what we'll do . . ." says I.

When I put the whole scheme to him, he was full of ifs and buts, of course. Then I said, "Fair enough, Mr Hill. You and Sergeant Arkins can sort it out yourselves and see what Eliza Drew makes of it when she gets back."

"I didn't mean to be rude, Mrs Tours."

"Whisht and I'll tell you something, Mr Hill. When you're dealing with ignorant bog-farmers like the Hennigans, you have to be rude. That class doesn't understand . . . procedures."

By Jaesus and he listened then. I went through my little scheme again because he didn't have a better plan. I gave Willie Hill strict instructions to be back by four in the morning. I didn't go into details with him. All the iffing and butting would have put me off. All I knew was that I had to catch Kate Hennigan on her own. Willie Hill went off home then, to tell his wife that everything was under control. I said there was no point in panicking her with the truth. You have to be very careful with the truth, sometimes. It can catch you out as easy as telling lies can.

I dragged myself upstairs then and climbed into bed with all me finery on. The way I wouldn't have to dress the next morning. It was no time at all before Willie Hill was back at the door in the pony-and-trap and Dan Brady was calling into me from the landing.

"Are you right, Mrs Tours? It's Mr Hill at the door."

We all sat down in the kitchen and had a mugful of tea and a couple of slices of soda bread, without a word between us. And then Willie Hill and me set off in the moonlight for the Hennigans' farm.

XX

DAWN IN HETTY'S HOUSE

Still groggy from the infusion of laudanum Dr Downs had given her the night before, Eliza Drew reached for the locket on her breast. Her fingers finding nothing, however, she lay back again and closed her eyes. She told herself firmly that she must write a letter to John Drew before her feet touched ground in Ireland again. What she had to say must be hinted at in writing before it could be spoken of. She sensed somehow that something nameless had resolved itself in her heart. It wasn't the cold resignation one heard so much preaching about but something more like an acceptance of destiny. The idea, in its own way, was faintly upsetting to her.

Eliza Drew fell back to a third sleep then and, when she awoke, it was to hear the children's voices out in the garden as they pranced around the little pear tree. Hetty arrived up in the bedroom then, having heard her stir. They said little to one another, just held hands and smiled. When she rose, Eliza Drew made her toilet at leisure, taking more time than usual in fixing her hair. If a woman lost interest in her hair, it meant she had lost interest in herself. That was what she remembered most, as a child, as a symptom of her mother's distress. Hetty, of course, didn't miss a thing.

"You should keep your hair up like that, Eliza. It makes you look . . ."

"Younger?"

"I was going to say happier. It brings out your features."

Hetty Arkwright wanted to fuss and fooster over her hair then but Eliza Drew had a letter to write. When Hetty bade Kitty McCormack bring breakfast to them in the garden, they sat out in high style, watching Edward and Theodora gambol about in the sunshine. Hetty, as always, couldn't stop talking for a moment. As though talking would somehow stifle any chance of a re-occurrence of the illness that had seized little Albert a few days before. Or the spell that had come over Eliza, on her great tour.

Hetty crunched on a slice of toasted bread as she spoke.

"Walter is working on one of the new lines now. He's in charge of all those new cuttings and tunnels, it seems."

"Really."

In the letter, Eliza would be forthright. She would out with her thoughts and feelings, regardless. They would sit down beside the fire, back in Aghadoe, and face one another. Judith would be packed off back to Dublin, in a few days' time, and there would be time for quiet talk, in the evenings. Things had to be said. Mrs Tours was right: what isn't said eats a person up, causes sicknesses and gloom and unhappiness.

> *Dear John,*
> *This is just a short letter to let you know Theodora and I are both well and will arrive back at the train station at half past five on Wednesday afternoon, God willing. We have had a wonderful week with Hetty and Charles. Everyone is in good fettle. The weather here . . .*

Hetty poured tea from the little blue willow-pattern teapot. She said that the reading circle was to meet that evening in Mrs Stewart's, off Russell Square. She wouldn't be going herself as she must make sure that Albert suffered no relapse, but perhaps Eliza would like to deputise for her? Eliza found herself oddly agreeable.

"I would love to."

"It's settled then . . . Kitty can walk you over to Mrs Stewart's at eight and you can take a cab back."

Hetty licked her fingertips and ran them through a stray lock on her sister's forehead.

"See, that's what tending to your hair does. It cheers you up."

All of a sudden, the children spotted a red squirrel over by the laburnum tree—Eliza had suggested Hetty cut it down years ago because of the poisonous pods—and went whooping around the garden like Hindoo savages. The little creature shinned away up the tree and, in a flash, was gone from sight. They went back to the game of hoop again. Eliza composed as she listened to her sister.

The weather here has been, all in all, quite splendid. London is really much drier than Dublin or Queen's County. I met your Mr Westmacott, by chance, a couple of days ago, and you can imagine my shock at seeing him here and not in Aghadoe. I hope your work hasn't suffered too much by his absence. It has been a week of strange encounters. In Dublin, I met up, quite by accident too, with an old acquaintance of yours—Mr Fox Keegan—in Pims, when I was in buying some lace for Hetty. He looked well fed and watered, but ever the rogue, I needn't tell you.

John, there are things of which we must speak when I return to Aghadoe. While the fear is gone out of me, I feel I must mention them here, just to put you on notice. How many days have now passed since . . . ?

Kitty McCormack appeared with a fresh pot of tea. Was Mrs Drew feeling better now? There were some of the powders left that the doctor had prescribed.

"He does always say to finish the dose."

"That's fine, Kitty. I think we can sort that out ourselves."

Hetty Arkwright buttered a third slice of toasted bread. It was all she could do to hold the question back until Kitty McCormack was back in the scullery.

"Eliza, do you remember where you went yesterday?"

"I'm not sure."

She recalled losing her grip on Theodora's hand as she crossed Oxford Street all right. The weight being lifted from her and throwing away the flowers she had bought for Hetty. She recalled seeing Mr Westmacott near the British Museum, a man who should not have been there at all. Then visiting the cemetery at St George's, where her father lay, the rush of the horses and cabs on the Gray's Inn Road and the child she had found up near Agar Town. A child that was all children. Whom she had succoured.

"Eliza? Are you all right?

"The letter, Hetty. I want to catch the afternoon post. I must go and finish it now."

"Why don't you finish it in peace, in Charles's study?"

Hetty Arkwright opened the door to the study.

No one entered Charles Arkwright's study, except by invitation. It was a square, sensible room, book lined and altogether airless. By the walnut desk, a great globe sat in a revolving cradle with the empire marked out in red. The fire was dead in the grate but there scarcely seemed any need for a fire in a room at the centre of the house. A print on one wall depicted a scene from the Battle of Trafalgar while, on the wall opposite, a drawing of a railway terminus hung in an ostentatious gilt frame. Eliza Drew turned to her sister at the door.

"Are you sure Charles won't mind?

"What he doesn't know can't hurt him, can it?

The heavy oak door swung to and she crossed the dark floor to the desk. It was a tidy desk, with bills-of-lading laid in one stack in a wooden tray and an accounts ledger open for all to see. Eliza Drew set the ledger to one side and took out the embossed paper she had bought in Dublin, on a whim. She ran her finger over the creamy paper, savouring, for a moment, the sensuous burr of its surface. Then, without further ado, she dipped one of the ink pens in the countersunk pot of royal blue ink and began writing. Her hand didn't pause until she had delivered herself of the more mundane details of the previous days. She made no mention at all of Albert Arkwright's illness. To do so, in light of what she had to say next, would only give John Drew a pretext for considering her request a vagary occasioned by upset. She tapped the pen twice to remove the excess ink and continued.

It is clear that we must sit down and speak of our loss. Edward is gone and we will meet him only in the next world. We must reconcile ourselves to our loss and choose the best way to carry on. You are my husband, John, and it is with respect for your station and love for you that I beseech you not to spurn this mother's request. We must be helpmeets to one another in this matter. If we cannot know one another's feelings, we surely cannot help one another. Our grieving period must end now. It has already gone on far too long. We must get on with life, even though our wounds will never fully heal. Therefore, I propose that when Judith has returned to school in Dublin, we sit down at the first opportunity and begin to lay bare our thoughts and feelings. Much has changed with me over the past week. Dear John, whether you are willing or unwilling to speak your heart as regards our lovely Edward, I do not know. One thing is sure, however: I must speak mine.

For I can no longer keep silent about the hurt that has chilled my heart. I am writing this in confidence to you, the better for you to be prepared on my return to Aghadoe.

Please have Judith at the house for our arrival and give Bridget Doheny instructions to give the house a thorough going over and to have the fire well in, now that autumn is upon us. Both Theodora and I are looking forward to being home again

Your loving wife,
Eliza

By the time Eliza Drew went to catch the eleven-thirty post at the receiving office, the day had already turned chilly. Hetty walked with her as far as Russell Square, not wishing to leave Albert on his own with Kitty McCormack for too long. They sat together on one of the long seats in the park, watching the ebb and flow of life about them. A woman in a great black hat wandered by, selling flowers from a basket.

"Lovely blooms . . . fresh blooms."

They strolled about the great square for a while then, remarking on all of the changes that had come about in the quarter over the past ten years.

"Father would scarcely recognise it."

It was when Eliza fell to talking about her hour in the tavern up past St Pancras that her sister got uneasy, feeling, perhaps, that another burst of hysteria was about to overtake Eliza.

"The Hindoo gentleman was not a Hindoo at all."

"I see."

"And the Mohammedan was an actor too. And Paddy, with the pig . . ."

"Just an actor too? Surely there are plenty of the real thing about?

"I suppose, but you see, they were just a simple view of things."

"I don't know what you're driving at, Eliza

"Well, there is no Hindoo really like that. Or Pat Denny and his pig. As for the naughty girl . . ."

"Well, there are plenty of those about, Eliza. Just take a stroll down to Covent Garden after dark."

"You're missing my point, Hetty."

But Hetty Arkwright made no show of understanding what her sister was trying to explain. Eliza Drew insisted that all such portrayals—right down to daguerrotypes—were only part of the tale.

"So, even Mr Fox Talbot's pictures tell lies, then?"

"No, not lies exactly, but not the whole truth either. It depends as much on the position of the beholder as on the position of the subject."

"Really, Eliza, one of us must be confused, because I haven't the faintest idea what you're talking about."

In fact, it was easier explain it all to Theodora, over lunch. Theodora understood that the pictures in her storybook weren't the whole truth. That nothing, in fact, short of the Almighty Himself, could ever be the whole truth. Theodora sipped at her eggnog.

"Is that why you left me yesterday, Mama? To look for the truth?"

"Perhaps . . ."

"Were you sad over Edward again, Mama?"

"What's that?"

"Over Edward . . . were you sad?"

"Yes . . . sad. But I'm happier now."

"I know that, Mama . . . your face . . . your hair."

Little Albert Arkwright was well out of earshot, having been put down for a restorative catnap by Kitty. But Hetty signalled to her sister to turn away from the subject, all the same. Only Eliza wouldn't be halted. In an instant, the whole putrid mess of Belfast came tripping off her tongue. The hovels where disease and foul air and drunkenness and debauchery reigned. Hot-beds of pestilence and misery, into which she and John Drew and their three children had been dragged.

"How old was I, when Edward died, Mama?"

"Two years . . . just gone."

The story was told in a matter-of-fact manner. A terrible tale told at arm's length.

"Eliza, don't you think that's enough for Theodora for one day?"

"Have you heard enough, Theodora?"

"Just the locket, Mother . . . where is it?"

"I left it behind me in Aghadoe."

"On purpose?"

"Who knows, dear . . . perhaps."

The day was growing steadily duller now so that, by the time four o'clock struck, a great grey barrage of clouds was blocking out the sun. Eliza might have called off the engagement with the Ladies' Reading Circle had it not been for the new resolve that welled up in her again.

It was wet underfoot and a wind was blowing up Goodge Street when Eliza and Kitty McCormack closed the door behind them. They were practically blown off their feet, by the time they reached Mrs Stewart's house. Eliza waited until Kitty McCormack had slipped away before crossing the threshold. All the ladies were there, despite the inclement weather. Books were then ceremoniously opened at the required spot. There was to be no chitterchatter until after the chapter had been read. When Eliza was encouraged to read aloud, for the company, another chapter from *Jane Eyre,* Mrs Meredith took pains to compliment her on the clarity of her voice and the confidence of her presentation.

"Perhaps I should be on the stage, Mrs Meredith?"

They all had a grand laugh at that as the glasses of Madeira were handed around. The very thought of it! Still and all, in a curious way, as she rode home in the cab to the Arkwrights' that evening, Eliza Drew knew that, should she choose to, such a thing would never again seem beyond her. Because life was simply too short for prevarication. Life must first be lived on this side of the grave.

XXI

A LITTLE SIEGE

I wrapped meself up tight, so I did, when I climbed up into Willie Hill's trap, the way the damp wouldn't get in on my chest. Many's the one got her death walking out of a night and her chest bare to the world. There wasn't a single soul in Pound Street at that hour of the morning. You could hear the horses' hooves a mile away as we went clattering off down through the town. At the Beggar's Bridge, and we turning down towards the brewery, Willie Hill says, "Are we doing the right thing, Mrs Tours?"

"Faith and we'll see soon enough."

Jimmy Prendergast was standing at the brewery gates as we passed. Much of a gotchee he'd make. Couldn't run ten yards to save himself, never mind catch a couple of cute lads making mischief. Dangerous job, all the same. You have to be everyone's enemy, keeping L.O. on the property all the time. I thought of that poor bastard Fitzsimons, at the railway camp, who didn't deserve what he got. Isn't that right, Mrs Hennigan? But by Jaesus and she knows the whole story all right.

I said to myself, I have a riddle for Eileen Hennigan, out in her big farm with the Protestant minister's daughter hidden up in the loft. And I thought to meself as we passed the graveyard: you'll hop to my tune this *morning, madam. I'll soften your cough for you, so I will. See how smart you are, when one of ye'er own is threatened. Pat Dempsey hanged for the killing. Jer Hynes acquitted. Fox Keegan not charged. And a fourth man—that no one mentioned at all, because they were afraid of the family. A fourth man, who was probably the biggest blackguard of them all.*

We didn't speak to one another, me and Willie Hill, as we rode out to Donaghmore, by moonlight, until we turned over the bridge and up by the mill. It wasn't far from first light, but there was just enough dark left for all sorts of divilment. Now Hennigans' farm isn't that far from the village itself. A good bit of land they have too. When all around them was dropping with the fever and the hunger a few years ago, they had barley and oats to spare. The Hennigans always managed to have their share of bonhams and sucky calves too. Great ones for the big talk about Ireland this and Ireland that. But there was many a black Protestant gave more in the hungry times than those bastards ever did. Even if some of them did it just to get us to read their ould bible. No, the Hennigans never wore out their pockets digging in them. Feed your own, keep your mouth closed and your ears open. That's the way of the world. We didn't go into the farm by the long lane; instead we went around by Nan Kearney's old cottage—God be good to her. The way the pigs wouldn't raise a racket. We got out of the trap at the ditch and left Willie Hill's man with strict orders not to budge.

You could see a little lamp upstairs in the farmhouse window, across the fields. How well they were able to burn tallow and keep fires on all night, bad and all as times are. I pictured the layout of the house to meself, from the time I used to go out there to help Eileen Hennigan with her work. The downstairs rooms and the kitchen and the scullery and where the bedrooms were upstairs. Judith Drew was probably in the room with the lamp so as loverboy could keep his eye on her.

I slipped off then, letting on I was going to make me water. I could still hear Willie Hill muttering away as I slipped along by the ditch. There was a couple of cows lying about in the near field and if I didn't nearly kill myself walking into them, I was in such a rush. But cows are easygoing creatures, not like pigs. They were the ones that started making the real commotion when I banged myself against the water-barrel and I crossing the haggard. All of a sudden, there was murder everywhere. It was great gallery altogether! The collie dog started barking like a lunatic and the ould rooster started the hens off. I heard one of Eileen Hennigan's sons shouting.

"Quench the light! Quench the light!"

If I had known what was coming next, I would have gone back over the same ditch as fast as I came. The lamp went out upstairs all of a sudden. Then the back door opened very slowly. I could half see a figure of a man in the doorway. I knew by the gimp of him that it was Joe Hennigan, all six foot and to spare. I saw something pointing up into the air, like a class of a stick and then, as God is me witness, wasn't there a great roar and Joe Hennigan let loose with this big blunderbuss of a thing, right over my head. Well, if I didn't have a weakness on the spot. Then a voice shouted at me.

"Stop where you are!"

When I got my breath back, I got very cross and I let a great roar out of me.

"You bad bastard you, Joe Hennigan, and you firing on a poor widow woman!"

There wasn't a stir for a minute. I spotted missie's face in one of the bedroom windows, with Michael Hennigan behind her. I could see the gun being lowered and I heard Eileen Hennigan's voice.

"Who's that out there?"

"It's Nan Tours. Is it trying to kill me ye are?"

"Go on off with yourself, Nan. We have no row with you, so we haven't."

"Well, I'm coming in to visit you, so you may lave me in or shoot me."

"Go on off home with yourself, Mrs Tours."

"I will, when I've got over the shock of you trying to kill me."

I kept on walking towards the house. I knew well they wouldn't shoot me, of course. I was just at the door, and Eileen Hennigan looking out at me with a puss on her like Jesus raising the Jews from the hot ashes when Joe Hennigan raises the gun again.

Oh, Jaesus, says I in me own mind, we're all bunched now. So says I, real easy like, "Mrs Hennigan has invited me in for a cup of tea and a little chat. Isn't that right, Eileen?"

I could see Joe Hennigan whispering in her ear, but Eileen Hennigan just shrugged her shoulders and ignored him.

"Isn't that right, Eileen?" says I again.

Like a flash, I was in the door. The door closed behind me. Eileen Hennigan looked me straight in the eye as Joe Hennigan left the gun down on the table.

"You're a very foolish woman, Nan."

"Well, and if I am, and you're twice as foolish, Eileen Hennigan."

I turned around to face Joe Hennigan. A thick, ignorant go-be-the-wall he is too. Says I, "Have you the tea wet yet?"

He didn't know whether to shoot me or leave me be. Then he took up the gun and disappeared into the parlour. So it was just myself and Eileen Hennigan in the kitchen together. She rose up the kettle from the hob to wet the tea. Then we sat down to talk things over. I knew well she wasn't a stupid woman, though there's many a woman married to a stupid man. Every time old bollox stuck his head in the kitchen door, she ran him. When lover boy appeared on the stairs, she hunted him too. Her hands were shaking when she poured the tea. I knew I had her, easy enough. It was her stookawn of a husband I had to sort out. But she had to be the one to deliver the message to her lord and master.

Eileen Hennigan was like a hen on a griddle. She couldn't sit and face me when we were talking, so I did all of me talking as she trotted around the kitchen rising up the fire and letting on to be tidying the place. She hardly said a word as I spoke. First of all, I made a little spake about Bridget Doheny walking out on ould Drew on account of the cows' heads and the eggs and that class of thing. Eileen Hennigan didn't put any pass on that. Then I mentioned the matter of her ladyship above in the bedroom and the ructions it would cause everywhere if a finger was laid on the minister's daughter. Eileen Hennigan's voice was real low, like she was talking to a priest or making a wish at a well.

"I didn't bring any of this on us, Nan."

"'Deed and I knew that all along, Eileen, alanna. Everyone knows that."

"Everyone?"

"Sure the whole town will have the story by this evening, unless something is done now."

I didn't lift a finger to help her as she threw the sods on to the fire and drew it out. I didn't stir either when she went over to the dresser, letting on to be sorting out the vessels.

"E'er a chance of a drop of tea there, Eileen?"

Eileen Hennigan poured me a strong cup of tarry tea. I noticed her hand wasn't shaking as much now. She realised that there was a way out of all this bother. I don't know exactly when I mentioned to her about the little boy the Drews lost. But it was my final shot at Eileen Hennigan.

"You know the Drews lost a child once, Eileen."

"What's that?"

"A little boy. When they lived in the north."

"I never heard tell of that, now."

"So, I suppose, they're especial nervous about the two that's left. Do you follow me?"

And with that, she started crying big tears, like a blabbery baby. "Come here," says I. "Come over here, now. Arrah, sure haven't we all made mistakes, Eileen? And some mistakes can be put to right easy enough, before more damage is done." I put my arm around her and she sobbing her heart out.

"Whisht, alanna! Whisht!"

"It was the goodness of Michael's heart made him take in that girl, Nan."

"Of course it was, sure."

Goodness of his flute more like it, says I, in me own mind. Just then, didn't ould bollox appear back in the kitchen. Eileen Hennigan gallops out the door then and leaves me to face him. He didn't make any attempt to stop her. He just closed the door over and crossed the flag floor slowly. For a moment, I thought he was going to take off his belt and horsewhip me. Which I'm sure he wanted to do, the way he does to poor Eileen. The whole town knows that. But he pulled up a chair instead and sat staring at me. Threatening, like.

"You have no call to come meddling in other people's affairs, so you haven't, you ould bitch, you!"

"And you should keep more order on your sons and not have them running off with other people's daughters, so you should!"

"Is she too grand for the likes of us, so?"

"You know well what I mean."

"Ye'er all the one between the legs, missus, and don't you be gettin' no notions about yourself. You're only a feckin' dressmaker and you lickin' their Orange arses for them."

The hand was raised again. I ducked back a bit, though I knew well he wouldn't hit me. Joe Hennigan carried on like that for a while then, storming around the kitchen. I just sipped away at me cup of tea and let him get on with it. There wasn't a stir anywhere in the house. They were all too afraid to stick their noses in. Willie Hill's horse gave a kind of shriek in the distance, at the far end of the haggard. Joe Hennigan turned around to me. You could see the animal behind his eyes. Great lad for beating women, says I, in me own mind. That's what his son will end up doing with madam upstairs, if I don't put a stop to his gallop. He raced over to me again and stuck his dirty finger in my face.

"Arkins and his cowboys better not try anything clever!"

I didn't know where the cheeky words came from, but I just left down my cup of tea and said, "You're putting the fear of God into me, you great big man you!"

"I'll shoot the whole bleddy lot of them if they show their noses around here!"

"Sit down and take the weight of your legs, Joe, like a good man."

I saw the beast behind his eyes again then. He was within an ass's roar of hitting me a flake that would drive my jaw across the floor.

"I mightn't lay a finger on you, ma'am . . . but I have friends who might."

I took up the cup of tea slowly and took a big gulp out of it. I drew a deep breath and let it out slowly.

"Like Fonsey, that killed the poor watchman out at the railway camp and got away with it? Fonsey that ended up over in American, rale sudden, like?"

"Fonsey done nothing, so he didn't!"

"Would poor Pat Dempsey that got hung say that? But, sure, dead men don't talk, do they?"

The eyes narrowed down. That was the most dangerous moment. Suddenly Joe Hennigan's hand shot out and he scattered cups and saucers and all, smashing them to smithereens against the wall.

"You dirty ould bitch, you! Comin' out here to make game of us for your fancy friends!"

I let him ramble on like that for a few minutes. I could hear Judith Drew whispering upstairs in the bedroom, realising, maybe for the first time, the sort of crowd she was getting involved with. If Joe Hennigan did a reel on the floor, he did ten jigs too. But I just sat there, letting on I wasn't one bit afraid of him. And me shivering in me boots. When he came back to the table again, I took another deep breath.

"Now, I think it's time yourself and myself got down to a bit of business, Joe."

He said nothing. The sun was up at that stage. The light was coming in through the flowery curtains I had made up for the Hennigans ten years before. I stood up and went over to the fire, very come-as-you-are like, and started raking the ashes. I threw a couple of sods on to the fire then and pulled my chair in close.

"Let you sit down now and we'll see if we can sort things out."

He didn't sit down, of course. He stood behind me, trying to menace me, but I just carried on talking. I gave as good as I got. You'd think I was telling the story to a child, I told it so easy.

"It was a very stormy night that night, Joe. Do you remember?"

"I don't know what you're talking about, woman."

"Don't you, faith?"

I talked about Fox Keegan meeting up with Joe Hennigan's brother, Fonsey, out in O'Keefe's of the Green Roads. All the drinking they did that night until they started getting thick about the way Fitzsimons, the watchman, was going to let some of them go, on account of the work being nearly finished. Fox, of course, like the idiot he is, got dragged into it, to keep lookout while the boys taught Fitzsimons a lesson. One word borrowed another anyway and, before you knew it, hadn't my brave boys decided to sort Fitzsimons out sharpish with a few belts of a blackthorn stick. Fox didn't expect it to be anything more than a few flakes of the stick. The truth of it was though, Fonsey Hennigan and Pat Dempsey and Jer Hynes had already been given their marching orders for stealing material from the railway. Nails and iron rods and that class of thing. Fox Keegan, smart and all as he was, didn't know this, so they walked him into it. Pat Dempsey called Fitzsimons out of the tent and him and Fonsey Hennigan and Jer Hynes started laying into him. And when poor Fox was trying to to stop them beating the poor man to death, he was told feck off with himself and keep his mouth shut. So he ran. First to me and then to John Drew, the next morning.

I turned back to Joe Hennigan.

"Your brother Fonsey and Pat Dempsey and Jer Hynes killed that poor man. Fox Keegan is a witness to it, so he is."

"Well and if Mr Keegan ever opens his fuckin' mouth to anyone . . ."

But I butted in.

"He won't need to, Joe. I have it all writ down and sealed in an envelope that's left with a certain Father Farrelly."

"How well you keep in with both sides, you ould whore you!"

"I've left an envelope with Father Farrelly, and if a hair on my head or on Fox's is harmed . . . What I'm saying to you is this, Joe, no one need ever know about it. If things are settled right this morning, with Drew's daughter. She should go home to her own."

"And are we not good enough for her, then?"

And with that, didn't Joe Hennigan storm out of the room and into the parlour, where Eileen Hennigan and one of the daughters were sitting huddled together. I could see him through the crack in the door, standing over them. But they didn't have anything to barter, not like me. I could barter one story for another. I knew he would probably give Eileen a good hiding on the head of it, later on that day. But that wasn't my concern. If he beat up the whole blessed lot of them, it wasn't my business. I sat there, pretending to be real cool and calm like, until big bollox came back into the kitchen. I didn't stir. One move might ruin everything. When Joe Hennigan came in, he closed over the parlour door slowly. He was sucking his lips like a child with a sweet, weighing it all up. Then he got all nice and friendly with me. The big eyes were staring at me. That's the only time I felt really afraid. That smile of his put me on edge, so it did. Anyway, he sits down real careful and says to me, "I've decided the Protestant biddy will have to go back, so she will."

Then he repeated the message again, so all could hear. So they would all think what a great fellow he was and that he had decided it all by himself. He did a thing that unsettled me then. He laid his big ugly hand on my shoulder and pulled me towards him. His voice was very soft.

"And if you ever say another word against our Fonsey, I'll pull those beady fuckin' eyes from that scrawny head of yours."

XXII

A Wake and Other Shenanigans

John Drew carried on over the stile, towards the higher fields. A great track of mud and cow dung ran along by the bushes and he was forced to keep to the part of the field that was covered in thistles and nettles. He was winded by the time he got to the great shattered oak tree at the heart of the field and paused to catch his breath. Down below, in the little valley, distant figures were making their way into the haggard. These weren't simply neighbours dropping in to pay their respects, he understood, but the cast and chorus of the wake itself. A fine jig Eliza Drew herself would dance if she found out he had enmeshed himself in the goings-on of a Catholic wake. The valley of Tullyroe seemed, in that moment, as remote from Aghadoe and Queen's County as the wilds of Persia or Afghanistan. A sudden movement in the bushes caught his eye and he turned to behold a young fox loping along, hunting for innocent grazers sitting out in the last of the September sun. The animal paused a moment to look back at John Drew. Man and beast observed one another for a moment. Then the fox drew in closer to the ditch and disappeared through a gap.

At the top of the hill, John Drew found he could look across the fields and see the village of Tullyroe itself. It was just an aggravated crossroads really. A scatter of houses that chance had thrown up in the valley.

The smell of chamomile came to him just as the melancholy notion wandered in among his thoughts: this can never be mine. It is another world. If we stay a thousand years, we will still feel ill at ease here. At a spot on the hill where the mud had congealed into something approaching solid ground, John Drew down sat on a lichen-covered rock and poked at the ground with a stick. Although he had no mind to tackle the true compass of his thoughts, for fear of disturbing something that was being turned over in the background, a certain presentiment of knowing began to well up in him. Idling, like a child lazing over a school slate, he scratched out shapes in the mud and dust with the sharp end of the blackthorn. First a triangle, the rude token of the female in the primitive script.

It was something Westmacott had pointed out to him shyly, the year before, on a Mesopotamian tablet, in the British Museum. It was an early cuneatic symbol. Momentarily stunned by the sensuousness of the minute, he glanced about, fancying for a second that he was being observed. But no eye fell upon him and his eye found no one either. He was present in the knowing of neither man nor beast. John Drew had a sense, at that moment, of all creation lying within him and without him. A sense of ancient days began to infuse his thoughts now. Of men sitting under the Assyrian sun, looking out over the land and the mountains from the royal edifice of Persepolis. He saw a pointed reed gouging out a picture-word in a dun-coloured tablet of clay and heard the concussion of a chisel on warm stone. The language of empire sliced into syllables, in clay and stone. And the hidden, silent language in between. A language of signs, not sounds. Of crude pictures. Like the one he had just drawn in the mud. Of primitive minds. LUGAL. King.

But he must avoid troubling his thoughts with too many demands. The muddy water would clear soon enough and when that cleared, there would be something new. The thing was not to worry it now. To let matters churn about within, wherever they might fall. Like a fox loping along by a ditch, on the prowl, not knowing what he was looking for until he found it. Until nature met its prey.

John Drew retraced his footsteps in the growing gloom, down towards the lower fields. At that point where the haggard met the first of the muddy cow-tracks, he noticed the figure of Tom Keegan tinkering with a bolt on the scratch plough. It was an awkward moment. Should he pass on for the house and the music or pause to speak with the man? And if he did speak to Fox Keegan's brother, what on earth would they have to talk about? The shock-haired man turned from his task and nodded towards the house.

"They're starting early Mr . . ."

"Drew. Yes, I suppose they are."

"And Fox is in the middle of it, of course. All great men for talk."

When Fox Keegan's brother straightened himself up, John Drew could see that he was quite unlike Fox in demeanour. Someone whose great grandchildren would work the selfsame soil in a hundred years. They will dispossess us as we dispossessed them once. If the merciless advance of steam and galvanism hasn't destroyed the whole world by then. John Drew wiped his glasses with one of Theodora's embroidered handkerchiefs. The other man grunted.

"That's a grand fancy handkerchief for a brewery man."

"It's my daughter's, from the Dame School."

"I never had much schooling myself. Fox, of course, could teach the scholars."

"Oh, yes, your brother is a smart man all right."

"A clever class of an idiot, if you ask me."

Jacob and Esau. Who was first out of the womb? Tom, it would be. He had the manner of an older brother. The sense of resentment towards a younger, sharper upstart. John Drew replaced his glasses on his nose.

"Where do you think your brother will end up?"

"Dead in a ditch, probably. On the head of too much drink."

"Do you mind my asking . . ."

"Come again?"

"Fox's wife . . ."

Tom Keegan took up the hammer he had left on the ground. His eyes fixed on John Drew.

"Aye, he have a wife all right, but he ran away on her, like."

"Maybe a wife would have settled him down."

"You can't tame a fox, so you can't."

The younger man gave a laugh. It was a cold, cheerless laugh, the laugh of the brother left behind to tend the farm.

"Didn't no one ever tell you that, sir?"

"I'm sorry?"

"You can't tame a fox, so you can't."

John Drew followed Fox Keegan's brother across the haggard to the dead house, from where a squeeze box was playing what sounded to John Drew's ears like a jig. John Drew waited a few moments outside the house, in the dark, just listening to the clamour inside, while his companion bolted the stable door and heeled up the jaunting car. There were loud voices inside the house. He could hear Fox's name being thrown about.

"Give us an ould come-all-ye there, Fox!"

That odd melancholy flowed through him again. The same sort of bittersweet rush that he had felt up in the far fields: the notion that he would always be alien in this land. The only ones he would ever be close to would be the likes of Fox Keegan or Mrs Tours. Individuals who, one way or the other, were caught between two shores. Flawed gems, like himself. As he felt for the locket in his pocket and realised that Fox Keegan was still minding it, he suddenly felt an overwhelming impulse to weep. For everything that had passed and for everything that was to pass. The world suddenly seemed altogether beyond his ken. Life and death and the dazed progression of the days in between. What was the purpose of things, if everything must come to an end? A nice notion for a minister of the cloth to entertain. A great fear seized him now, for his wife and daughters. A fear of what the world might do to them and the demons that waited around every corner with a malevolence he couldn't hope to neutralise.

As he stood leaning against the wall, in the fading light, he became aware of a grunting noise over to his right, by the stable. At first, he thought it was Tom Keegan. Then there was a long deep moan as of a man on the threshold of lust. The sound grew louder now and, when he sought to stand away from it, he knocked over a pail of rainwater set on a plank under the gutter. Someone drew back the mottled kitchen curtains. The lamplight that gave on to the haggard blinded him for a moment, but when his eyes reached an accommodation with the light, he beheld, trapped in the shadows between the house and the stable, the renegade smiles of a courting couple. Behind him, he could hear Tom Keegan's boots on the hard ground. He looked over his glasses at the woman. She put her fingers to her lips, imploring him not to give the game away, but the man seemed not to care. John Drew turned back to face Tom Keegan. The couple ducked back into the shadows. The curtain was drawn over again. Tom Keegan took his arm

"Can you not find the door, Mr Drew?"

"The dark . . . I got mixed up."

"Faith and it's easy mix you up now, so it is."

The kitchen was steeped in tobacco smoke and the smell of strong spirits pervaded the whole room. The man playing the squeeze box had retired to his pipe and the whole room seemed to have broken up into little cabals. Through the open bedroom door, John Drew saw the dead man, the rosary beads entwined in his fingers. The wake wasn't at all what he had expected it to be. Certainly, there was something primitive about it, even grotesque. But it was probably a ritual that was as old as the Mesopotamian clay tablets that swamped his thoughts daily. There was something strangely whole about it too, though. It was as if, by dint of making a great feast in the company of the dead, the people were saying: life goes on. Or, at the very least, life does not end here. But he was beginning to tire of his own thoughts now. When the party made room for him to sit on the long bench by the kitchen table, John Drew affected more fatigue than he really felt. For that sense of not belonging was in him again and the knowledge that he must not overplay his hand. There were eyes on him too. The men whispering to one another, "And who would the lad in black be?"

The women, as always, were more circumspect, their eyes sweeping about the room. They would save their speculations for a later hour. He allowed himself eat a little brack and had a cup of tea. A small, stooped man at the far side of the great kitchen table, who looked as though he wasn't long for the world himself, took him to task.

"Musha and would you not have a drink itself, sir? And you after travelling all the way from . . . where was it again?"

"Aghadoe."

"Aghadoe. I'd say you're not a native there. Would I be right?"

"London. I was brought over by the brewery."

"You work in the brewery and you won't touch a drop. Now that's a quare one, if you ask me."

He suddenly felt like a small boy in the middle of the gathering. He nodded over at Fox Keegan's mother then made his way up the ladder for the straw pallet in the loft. It was as well to go to bed and escape it all. Let them say what they liked behind his back.

It was the vicissitudes of age and the pressure on his bladder that made John Drew wake sometime around four o'clock in the morning. He lay there for a while, listening to the chat downstairs and watching the fug of tobacco smoke rising to the ceiling. There was laughter from one corner, the sound of a scratchy fiddle in another. But it was only when the woman's voice penetrated through the mists of his early morning thoughts that John Drew's mind came to life. It was an unusually clear voice, he thought. He lay there for a little while, debating with himself whether to rise or no, until nature got the better of him and he was forced to leave the rough bed. As he made his way unsteadily down the ladder, the last of the song faded away. He turned at the bottom of the ladder and looked about the room. But he might not have been there at all, for scarcely anyone paid him heed. At the far side of the room, next to where the dead man was resting, a woman of around twenty or so was standing erect, her hand resting on the back of a chair. Her voice seemed at once happy and sad.

And this was my grief and my shame.

When the melody faded away on the heavy air, there was silence for a moment. An old man sitting over by the fire tapped his pipe against the wall.

"Maith thú, Mary Fleming!"

John Drew's eyes fixed on the singer. It was the same woman he had seen outside courting, caught in the coarsest of positions in the shadows, between the house and the stable. How could such sensitivity and coarseness be married together in the one woman? He thought of Judith, she of the dark eyes and the moods to match. It upset him to think that one of his own flesh-and-blood might stoop so low. But who was he to say? Perhaps all women—and all men too, for that matter—were nothing more than a meeting of the coarsest and finest sensibilities. And wasn't the love act itself scarcely above the random rutting of the beasts of the field? As he made his way through the little gathering, he puzzled over the provenance of man and those things which set him above the animal kingdom. He pulled the half-door closed behind him, his face stinging in the cold, fresh air, and crossed the haggard towards the shed with the suckling calves. Maybe what separated us from the creatures of the fields was both love and intellect together, John Drew mused. A mixture of low senti-ment and high thought. As he relieved himself against the back wall of the calf house, John Drew savoured the elemental silence in the field behind him. It was the sort of peace you couldn't find even in Aghadoe and, most certainly, not in London. As he made his way back across the haggard, he spotted a large creature scur-rying away into the dark. A badger or a fox, maybe. If it were a fox, it would be cute enough to avoid him. But if it were a badg-er, it might well seize his leg if he stumbled upon its shelter. He was glad to get back into the warmth of the house again.

When he appeared in the kitchen, Fox Keegan's mother strolled across the floor and took him by the arm.

"You must have a drink with us before you retire, Mr Drew."

Despite all his protestations, and thinking it the better part of courtesy anyway, he allowed himself be seated by the old gentle-men near the fire who had scarcely half-a-dozen teeth between them. The shorter man was the quiet one, but his companion made up for it.

"You're not from these parts."

"I come from Aghadoe . . . Queen's County."

"And is that how they spake up there, is it?"

The other old gentleman laughed out loud.

"I'm originally from London."

"Well and I'm originally from here, so I am."

"I work in the brewery."

"Begob and you must have a right snout on you for drink, so."

"I . . ."

Before he could stop them, there was a tumbler of rough whiskey in his hand. The sort no one bothered to pay tax on. The two old men seemed to forget him then, for they fell to chatting among themselves again. It was only as the whiskey bit into his throat that he realised they were muttering to one another in a mélange of English and Gaelic. He affected not to be listening, especially when he noticed Fox Keegan's mother regarding him strangely across the room. But he couldn't help catching some snatches.

"Nach gcrochann an tóin sin an gúna go h-álainn?

"She have a fine arse for that dress all right, God bless her."

The shadow of the older tongue fell hard on their English. In the order of the words, in their articulation and in the curious twist they put on the grammar of his, John Drew's language. Yes, it was in their English that you saw the true shadow of the older language. The second line of the Darius inscription. The one written in ideographs. The dead language. Old Chaldean.

LUGAL. LUGAL. MESH. LUGAL KUR. KUR. MESH

A different way of seeing the world. Maybe it was even responsible for the way they thought. No wonder he and they would never feel completely at ease with one another. It was these notions John Drew carried with him back up the ladder to the loft, a little while later. He glanced back over his shoulder as he reached the top rung and noticed, for the first time, Fox Keegan lying fast asleep in the settle bed in the corner. His eyes crossed the mother's eyes momentarily, but there was nothing to see. He lay down on the straw pallet again, without bothering to remove his boots. As he lay on the bed, his thoughts turned, now drowsy with the day, to the last line and he bade himself consider it carefully so that in sleep his undermind would work on it and alert him to any misreading in the morning.

With his eyes closed and the sound of the chatter from below still in his ears, he read the line slowly and carefully.

"Sha-E-a-ga-a-I-pu-ush . . . who built this house . . ."

When John Drew awoke, some hours later, it was to the hammering of nails into the deal coffin down below. A mighty, savage sound that spelled the end of the old and the commencement of the voyage to the next world. A tri-literal hammering on the wooden coffin. The basic sound of life and death, of fate knocking on the door. All life comes in threes, John Drew thought to himself. Birth, children, death.

XXIII

A Day of Humiliation

Even if a Day of Humiliation had not been called, all over England, to offer atonement in the face of the cholera crisis, Eliza Drew would still have started an altercation with her sister. The storm clouds had been brewing since the night before, with the worry of the previous days now subsided. Charles Arkwright had remained in his study, working his way steadily through a sheaf of papers. This, in itself, had put Hetty in a bad mood. Eliza could hear Kitty McCormack playing Fetch the Thimble with the children, in the drawing room. The giggles came to Eliza through the walls as she sat in the easy chair, reading and re-reading John Drew's letter. What her husband had to say was strange to her eyes. All the more so, because their letters had crossed and his words could not have been prompted by her own.

She glanced across the room at her sister. Something unsettled her about Hetty now. A sense that her sister must always be in the right. She put the bothersome thought out of her mind and turned back to John Drew's letter. She could scarcely believe the words she was reading. The man behind the written words seemed altogether like another person.

I am minded of our days in Belfast, Eliza. Each day you are gone has brought back fresh memories of the good times and of the terrible times. I am reminded of our walks in Donegall Square and the concerts we attended. Our friends, too, come to mind. Old Dr McLoughlin of Castle Street and the Harrises, of Glengall Street. Each time the unpleasantness rises up in my thoughts, I banish it as quickly as I can. And yet, I know I cannot put a stay on such speculations indefinitely. Perhaps it was the locket you left behind that started the whole cascade or the mere fact of my enforced solitude. Whatever the cause, I find I cannot dodge the past any more. In fact, though I have sought to hide from my thoughts in sleep, sleep has proved a scoundrel and given me no refuge whatsoever. This is the third night of my torment. It grieves me to put such matters in writing, Eliza, but I feel I must do so. There are some things it is easier to write of than to speak of.

Edward has been contiguous to my dreams these past few nights. I have seen him in the little garden in Belfast. I have an image of him playing with Judith in the dining room. I have awoken in the middle of the night, almost expecting to find our lovely little boy asleep in the next room. There is no blaming the Almighty for this. These visitations are of man's making. However, in as much as we cannot let Edward go, he must constantly haunt our very dreams. I have come to accept that now—to welcome it, in fact. Although I know that women must conspire with women to order the world and care for their children, I beg of you, in this instance, to keep this matter between ourselves. For we alone must have the burying of dear Edward. Ourselves and no one else. It is a terrible thing to speak of but speak of it we must—between ourselves. When you return, therefore, I propose . . .

Eliza Drew's eyes turned away from the page again and caught her sister's smile. There was a flash of sisterly suspicion in Hetty Arkwright's eyes for a moment.

"Does John have much to say?"

"Oh, he's complaining about his gout, as per usual, and Mr Westmacott not appearing, of course."

"Nothing else?"

"Isn't that enough, Hetty?"

The children were put down to sleep around half past eight. Hetty read to them from *Tommy's Voyage to India*. Theodora wondered whether Eliza was going to light the little burner to stop the illness creeping into the house."

"It is nothing to do with the air, Theodora."

"But Kitty says . . ."

"Never mind Kitty McCormack! It is all in the water."

"Is that what Mr Chadwick says?"

"That's exactly what Mr Chadwick says. And Mr Chadwick knows best."

She had to sing Mrs Tours' mouse song for Theodora then.

There was a little cobbler who lived in a house
There was a little cobbler who had a little mouse
The mouse had a master
And the master had a maid
And they all played together in the little shady glade

She lay beside Theodora, until the child had fallen to sleep. Down below, she could hear Hetty and Charles chatting away in the dining room. Husbands and wives. A world of wisdom and a sea of sentiment. A strange thought set in on her then: John Drew would die before her. He would pass over into the land of shades and she would be a widow then, like Mrs Tours. As the living of Aghadoe would no longer be hers, she would have to move to some little cottage or back to London, even. She pictured herself for a moment, living in a little house in Aghadoe, with her daughters gone to the far corners of the world. Then she sorrowed silently for what must be as much as for what had been. She must have dozed off for a while because she was suddenly aware of the cold in her limbs. Her sister's voice called up the stairs to her.

"Eliza? Are you all right up there?"

That was what had started the whole business about going to the service in St Pancras, the morning after: Hetty Arkwright's haughty tone, sensing perhaps that something elemental had changed in Eliza Drew's demeanour.

The truth was that a London Sabbath was a different matter altogether from an Aghadoe Sabbath. Different even from the London Sabbaths of her youth. It might have been more casual still, but for the fact that the dread of cholera had moved the whole population to great fear. The notice from the Saturday *Evening Post* was fresh in Eliza's mind when she awoke the following morning.

Day of Humiliation Called
From Southend to Sunderland
Prayers to be offered for the alleviation
of the miseries of Asiatic Cholera

It was the vanity of the whole thing that got to Eliza Drew as she drew the brush through her hair, the following morning, with Theodora chattering away beside her. Theodora looked up at her.

"Are we going with Aunt Hetty and Uncle Charles to service?"

"I . . ."

"To the special service?"

What vanity! To seek to do deals with the Almighty, like an improvident gambler. As though the Holy One of Israel were about to wave a wand and dispel the cholera just because some titmouse of a rector in a Suffolk village bade Him to. It was all too silly! Eliza Drew considered herself in the gilded mirror. Yes, she had changed. The woman who had walked into the tap room, a few miles down the road, was not the woman who had walked out an hour later.

"Are we, Mama?"

"No, Theodora. We shan't be going to the service."

"But why?"

"Because I have decided so."

Charles and Hetty and little Albert were all down in the dining room, decked out in their best. Albert Arkwright was wearing the plum-coloured suit with the little lapels. Hetty was got up in the emerald dress the reading circle had so admired. Charles Arkwright was the image of a real city gentleman in a serge coat that made no allowances, unfortunately, for girth or age. They might have been a family off to a matinee show instead of a little threesome off to cajole the Almighty into staying his hand from further smiting London and the provinces. When she stood with Theodora in the dining room, her sister's eyes met Eliza's.

"Are you not dressing, Eliza?"

"We shan't be going, Hetty."

"Why? Are you not feeling well?"

"I think this ridiculous Day of Humiliation is just Hottentot superstitition!"

"Eliza!"

The front door practically came off its hinges as Hetty Arkwright slammed it shut behind her. Charles Arkwright had more sense than to protest.

Eliza sat down to breakfast and set to the papers of the previous day with gusto. The *Evening Standard* was still full of the Bermondsey murder, tales of the bodies pulled from the Thames each week and suicides by prussic acid. There was talk of the great gold digs in California and talk that Australia, where the Fenians and other convicts from the hulks were sent, was full of gold too. Cholera was alluded to here and there. Yes, perhaps that was the price of empire. A new curse on the white man who dared cross another's frontiers. An evil *jinni*, straight from the East.

Eliza Drew pictured men in dark clothes standing in pulpits, the length and breadth of England, clenching their tiny fists in the face of fate. The image made her smile as she chomped on her toast and marmalade. The truth was, she felt that the ministers of the cloth were behaving like the most superstitious of Catholics back in Aghadoe, thinking that a few fine words would forestall more deaths.

Mr Chadwick's Sanitary Investigations Continue

The answer was in the water. She was sure of it now. The dread disease was carried into the houses by befouled water. God was innocent of all charges.

Suicide by Prussic Acid

How many poor souls had snuffed out their lives in the past week? Wasn't life a maze of miseries, when you thought about it? Scarlatina, measles, smallpox and whooping cough to still a child's life. Cholera waiting around the corner to add to the terror. And the political agitators on the streets. The Chartists just waiting for another bite at the cherry. In Ulster, the Dolly's Brae petty sessions were trying to make some sense of the murderous capers of both sides. When Theodora brought over her book, Eliza Drew took out the little purple bottle from her handbag and tipped a couple of drops of valerian into the murky tea to settle her nerves, as Mrs Tours had recommended. She settled the child down with a tablet and chalk before taking up pen and paper to drop a note to Judith in Aghadoe, to remind her daughter to have Bridget Doheny give the house a good going over before their return.

Make sure you have everything in order for your return to school. This is your final year, Judith, and you must come out of it with credit. Make sure Bridget Doheny is keeping a fire in as I don't want to find your father with a bout of ague on my return.

It was about two hours later that Hetty Arkwright appeared back with Charles and Albert. You could tell by her eyes that she was in a tizzy. They always took on a certain sort of weariness on such occasions. The pitch of her voice jumped a whole octave, Eliza swore to herself. Hetty smiled at Eliza at the foot of the stairs.

"Kitty, we're back. Can you see to Albert and sort out the vessels?"

Eliza Drew and her sister walked around one another for the rest of the morning. There was scarcely a word said about the service. The stench coming from the cholera graveyards alone was probably enough humiliation for one day, Eliza Drew thought to herself.

Hetty Arkwright affected to be busy, in the way of a woman on the point of boiling over. But matters did not reach a head until after dinner, which was a sombre enough affair. The pheasant seemed tougher than an Irish one and even the pudding—Kitty McCormack had put together a trifle with vanilla essence—was nothing to write home about. When dinner was done, Charles Arkwright found a fresh excuse to leave the house to the women and took off for a constitutional and a couple of hours in the club. When the children took to playing out in the garden, the two sisters were left quite alone. Only the sound of Kitty McCormack singing to herself as she tidied up in the scullery could be heard. Hetty Arkwright sat down at the sitting room table, writing a long-overdue letter. From time to time, she glanced over her reading glasses at her sister in the easy chair.

"Eliza, it wouldn't have cost you much to come to the service this morning."

"I made up my mind, Hetty. I think it is morbid nonsense."

"Nonsense? A service to God for deliverance is nonsense? If Father could only hear you!"

Eliza left the novel down on the chair beside her.

"Father isn't here any more, Hetty. We are all on our own now, Hetty."

"I'm only saying, Eliza."

"And we should make up our own minds about things."

Hetty Arkwright laid down her pen. All pretence of continuing the letter was now dispensed with.

"Do you know what I think, Eliza?"

"What do you think, Hetty?"

"I think this Mrs Tours woman has put some strange notions in your head."

"Mrs Tours is like a sister to me, Hetty."

"And am I not your sister any more then? Tell me that."

Then the deluge of tears started. It was an old game for Hetty. Eliza just sat there, watching her sister sobbing and keeping one eye on the children out in the garden. Hetty Arkwright dabbed her eyes with a handkerchief. When the little storm subsided, there was silence for a moment. All they could hear was the distant shouts of the children as they played and Kitty McCormack humming to herself. Hetty's voice dropped now, just in case anyone but her sister might hear.

"I get very frightened sometimes, Eliza."

"I know, Hetty. So do I. So does everyone."

Eliza Drew made no stir to cross over to her sister, and Hetty Arkwright stayed where she was, staring into the sodden face of the writing paper.

"I get frightened for Albert and Charles."

"We all get frightened, Hetty."

"But most of all . . ."

"Yes?"

"Most of all, I get frightened that I will develop Mother's melancholy. That I will end up like a madwoman in bed, with my hair unbrushed and people whispering about me behind my back."

Eliza Drew lifted up her novel again and flicked over a couple of pages.

"That won't happen, Hetty."

"How can you know?"

"Because you have a good husband, a house and a child. And you're a good woman."

Hetty Arwright looked up into her sister's face. She had suddenly lost the look of a 'managing woman' now and seemed, to Eliza, no more than a frightened child.

"And do you not worry, Eliza?"

"I have come to realise, this week, that worry will help nothing. That we are all creatures of fate. We can only do so much."

"And that is why you wouldn't come to the service?"

"There are no deals to be struck with the Almighty, Hetty. Even Mr Palmerston or Queen Victoria cannot manage that."

"Is John Drew as sure as you are?"

"You must ask him yourself, the next time he is in London."

Hetty Arkwright stood up to look out at the children. Then she glanced back over her shoulder once more.

"You know I think the world of you, Eliza."

"I know that, Hetty."

"So, why are you so hard on me?"

But Eliza Drew made no reply.

When the two sisters made their way across Russell Square for Mrs Meredith's reading circle, later that evening, a sort of ease had settled in between them. All the same, Eliza kept her thoughts to herself in case her sister might take offence again. It was about ten o'clock when the cab arrived to take them back to Gower Street. The frost of the previous night was back. A farewell frost on leaving London felt right to Eliza Drew. She was now ready to return across the angry Irish Sea to Aghadoe. As she placed her hand on her breast and felt once more the spot where the locket had lain, she knew that things could never be the same between herself and the world again. She had changed—that much Eliza Drew knew to be true. She wondered how John Drew would greet her, on her return. Would he recognise her at all? Would they really have the burying of Edward, as he had suggested in his letter? She hoped so. Edward: The name suddenly seemed to come softly to her lips. There was no fear behind it now, only love. Love and life.

As she turned for sleep, Eliza Drew caught the pungent smell of the little cholera fumigators Kitty McCormack had placed on the downstairs windowsills. Another delusion, as vain and suspect as a Day of Humiliation or the fake East in the book she had confiscated from Judith Drew, a while before.

> The bazaars and the souks of Old Araby were as nothing compared to this. Animals hung in cages from the vaulted ceilings. Sacks of spices lay full to the brim against the stalls and the eyes of the pedlars and merchants darted about seeking business from all and sundry. The dragoman by Lorna's side spoke only when spoken to. That is to say, when Lorna had a query of her maid as to the nature of this spice or that. This was the East. Spices and silks and the mysterious ways of the Mohammedans. And Lorna, not a little fearfully, realised that this might be her lot for ever more, in the harem of her tormentor.

Eliza Drew was no longer afraid to meet her son in sleep now. If that was to be the only time she would see him again in this life, then so be it. She was only vaguely aware of the clip-clopping of horses' hooves on the street outside as she slipped into slumber. Because Eliza Drew was no longer afraid of the little death that is sleep.

XXIV

DAWN IN TULLYROE

A sour odour of stale whiskey and tobacco came to John Drew's nostrils as the hammering died away. He lay there a while, listening to the chatter of the women below in the kitchen. They were talking about the priest and making sure everything was ready for the procession to the grave-yard. There would be no chapel or church as the priest himself had come in from Callan. When he finally rose, John Drew felt as though he had scarcely slept. The noises of the wake had obvi-ously infiltrated their way into his sleep. Eliza would have received his letter in London by now. He wondered if he had been too forward with his wife. That sort of thing could go awry with women. Many marriages were founded on a sensible dis-tance between a man and his helpmeet. Too much sensitivity towards women unnerved them and made their moods even more mercurial. It was the same thing with horses.

Fox Keegan's mother greeted him at the foot of the ladder.

"Will you have a mug of stirabout itself, Mr Drew?"

"Thank you kindly."

Fox Keegan's sister Ann, with her long, auburn hair, eyed him curiously from the corner where she was darning socks. He nodded to her and, peering over his glasses, beheld Fox Keegan still asleep in the settle bed by the fire.

"Your brother seems to have slept well, anyway."

"Faith and I'll rise him out of it now, so I will. Wake up there, Fox!"

The drowsy, bloodshot eyes opened. There was a semi-toothless smile.

Fox's mother nodded her head.

"Get up and get washed, you. Have a show of decency about you today, at least."

The words trailed off into oblivion. A sermon long spent, John Drew saw. He sat himself down on the long bench and took up a spoon when the mug of stirabout was set down in front of him. Rough, stomach-churning oats with the musty scent of warm milk that had come straight from the cow's udder.

"That'll set you right for the day, Mr Drew."

The women went off about their business. Cleaning and fetching and making sure everything was right for the moment the priest arrived. By the time Fox Keegan rose, John Drew had finished his mug of stirabout.

"Are they treating you right, Dr Drew?"

Fox Keegan's sister crossed the flag floor to John Drew.

"I think this is yours. It fell out of Fox's pocket and he drunk last night."

The hand reached out to John Drew with the crumpled dog collar. John Drew glanced over at Fox Keegan's sister, who was standing in front of the fire. She had a half-smile on her face.

"You had right to tell us you were a minister. We wouldn't have ate you, so we wouldn't."

"I didn't want to complicate matters."

"Sure didn't Fox there work above in the Protestant school, once upon a time."

"So I've been told."

"He could read better than the minister himself, they say."

"That's very possible."

Tom Keegan arrived into the kitchen, having milked the cows and seen to all the other chores that had to be attended to before the man in the side room was laid to rest. He sat down at the table, elbows on the mottled surface, and glanced at Fox as he chewed on a heel of bread.

"Fox was never a great one for milking cows. The cows do be nervous of lads that reads too many books."

Fox Keegan said nothing, just stared ahead of him and sipped his black tea. Tom Keegan smiled.

"There's some bread soda above in the press, Fox. No extra charge."

The neighbours started to arrive back. John Drew could see them through the kitchen window that gave out on to the lane. Men and women in their funeral finery. Well-worn frieze coats and hats and long skirts that came out only on state occasions. Slowly the little kitchen began to fill until John Drew decided to slip out into the haggard to get some air. He strolled over to the stable to see how the horse was doing. It whinnied when it felt his familiar hand as though sensing the strangeness of the place and the people. A Protestant horse for a Protestant minister. As he stood there patting the animal's damp flank, the sound of a well-shod animal with a steady gait came to his ears. He looked about in time to see the priest ride into the haggard. The priest was a well-built man in his forties. A solid-looking type who knew his standing and would know when to speak and when to listen. He dismounted as Fox Keegan's mother appeared out in the haggard.

"Is it yourself, Father?"

"Aye, Mrs Keegan. A sad occasion for all of us."

"Musha, sure God is good."

"It was a release for poor Jeremiah in the end."

"S'é Dia an fear is fearr."

Fox Keegan's mother turned to face John Drew.

"This is Mr Drew, Father Nolan. He's a manager above in the brewery in Aghadoe, where Fox used to work."

"Pleased to meet you."

"And he's after being kind enough, so he is, to bring Fox home for the burial."

"You're a long way from home, Mr Drew?"

"London is my real home. Further still . . ."

"I hear tell London is a great city altogether. Trains and steamships and the Lord knows what."

"It is, I suppose."

John Drew fiddled with the bright brass of the horse's bit. He struggled but could find no small talk to offer. He remained outside in the haggard when the priest was led into the house. As he put the tackle on the horse, he heard the hymnic chanting of the rosary start up.

Holy Mary, Mother of God
Prayer for us sinners
Now and at the hour of our death
Amen

More people started to arrive. A couple of traps clattered around by the chicken house. They all nodded solemnly to John Drew as they passed. Some went on into the house while others stood outside, listening to the praying from a distance. It was mostly the women, John Drew observed, who were eager to get inside for the prayers. Not for the first time, he said to himself: their religion is a religion of women, with men at the helm. John Drew imagined the whispered questions, scattered in among the prayers.

"Who's the strange chap with the spectacles, abroad in the haggard?"

"Something in the brewery, above in Aghadoe."

"Is that right, now."

"A pal of Fox's."

Eyes like these were the eyes of Ribbonmen and Whiteboys and Shanavests, John Drew thought. Eyes that could sense a stranger arriving in the valley a mile away and know on which farm a dog would bark, when they were haughing cattle or burning out bailiffs. John Drew felt the chill of the alien sweep over him again now. A sense of being altogether other than the people around him, in their rough jackets and shawls and their heavy boots. It was only as he glanced back towards the house again, that he noticed Fox Keegan standing a few yards from him, aloof to all that was going on around him. True, he was chatting to the neighbours as they arrived. Making the sort of harmless chitchat that he, John Drew, could never make. But that didn't save him from appearing removed from those around him.

John Drew caught Fox Keegan's uneasy eyes a moment and he wondered to himself: was he born unsettled or did something throw him askew? Because it was as clear as day, in that moment, that Fox Keegan could be at rest nowhere, being caught between the two currents, the planter and the peasant. Was it the likes of Keegan who paid the real price for conquest? But the thought was too unsettling, and John Drew turned back to smiling politely at the neighbours as they passed by.

When the buzz of prayer had died away, a path was cleared through the crowd and a cart was drawn up near the door. There was an awkward moment when the coffin had to be manhandled around the doorway before it was loaded on to the cart. A man in a tall hat led the horse and cart down by the chicken house while the crowd assembled behind it. The couple of traps filled up then and John Drew brought his own beast around behind the gathering. A Protestant minister at the tail end of a Roman funeral. There was a great hubbub at the door. John Drew caught the eye of Ann Keegan as she made her way through the crowd. Tying the ribbon under her black bonnet as she spoke, she smiled up at John Drew.

"Fox would like for us all to go in your trap, if that's all right, Mr Drew?"

"Of course. Of course."

The little procession set off then, with the long cart and the coffin at the head, followed by John Drew's trap with the Keegans in it and all the rest walking behind. The priest, on horseback, kept pace with the coffin. They passed along by the lily-choked river, emerging on to the road for Tullyroe by the bridge. All along the rough road into the village, people emerged from their houses. As they approached the graveyard, the rosary started up again, the words passing along the line, from mouth to mouth. John Drew tied up the trap a little further down the road, against an old fence, then followed the Keegans into the graveyard.

"Mr Drew, would you be ever so good as to give a hand here?"

With that, John Drew set to shouldering Jer Keegan's coffin, along with Fox, his brother and a red-faced neighbouring man. They settled the rough deal coffin down beside the grave and stood back as the priest began the service.

In nomine Patre et Filii et Spiritus Sancti . . .

Dead words from a dead language. The ruined Norman chapel, in the middle of the old graveyard. Dust to dust, water to water.

He wasn't sure afterwards when or how it started. But it was sometime after the priest had sprinkled the holy water that John Drew experienced a presentiment of ill-will. Just as that awful keening sound began to break from Ann Keegan's lips. He became aware, suddenly, of cross-glances that meant no good. From people who had sniffed the air around him and thought: *Gall.* Foreigner. Invader. The two gravediggers were readying themselves for the committal. The gaping maw of the grave was

fully opened. Jeremiah Keegan was slowly lowered into the earth
from whence he had come. The first sods of damp earth met the
breast of the coffin with a brutish thud. John Drew glanced over
in the general direction of the ruined church. He had not been
mistaken at all. A youngish man, with a cap pulled down over his
eyes—an oddly disrespectful thing at a funeral anyway—was staring menacingly at him. A couple of other men beside him
seemed to be watching him too. What did they see in him? he
wondered. A process-server or a justice of the peace who had
wandered into their territory? Did it count for nothing that he
was a companion of one of their own? But John Drew was too far
away from Fox Keegan to catch him by the cuff and say, "I have
to go now."

He was swept back from the graveside as people arrived to pay
their condolences to the family. It might have been better if he
had lingered where he was and not made for the little stile. He
had it in mind to sit out in the trap until such time as Fox Keegan
appeared. But he had hardly reached the big rowan tree by the
wall when he felt a heavy hand on his shoulder.

"What's your hurry, mister?"

"I beg your pardon?"

"He begs me pardon, lads!"

There were three of them. God knows who or what they were,
Ribbon or some other rough brigade. He swallowed hard. What
harm was he doing, attending the funeral of his companion's
father? Hadn't he brought Jeremiah Keegan's son to his father's
burial in a spirit of Christian kindness?

"Faith and you're not from these parts?"

"Aghadoe, in the Queen's County."

"And you're not from there either, so you aren't."

"London, actually."

"London, actually, lads!"

He gazed nervously over his spectacles at them. It would do

no good denying his station anyway. If they took him aside, they would beat it out of him in a flash. Empty his pockets and find the Protestant dog collar to incriminate him. No, it wasn't valour that made him tell the truth, or even fear itself. It was more the awful understanding that what was going to happen would happen, regardless of what he said. John Drew said it to them out straight and declare his rank and station.

"He's a minister, bejaesus! Do you hear that, lads? An Orangeman in sheep's clothing."

"I'm a friend of Mr Keegan's."

"Fox do have quare friends all right. Tinkers and fiddlers and ministers. His own was never good enough for the likes of him."

Out of the corner of his eye, he could see Fox Keegan's sister, at the edge of the grave, looking across at him with a frown on her face. She disappeared from view. The taller of the three men stepped forward.

"I think you're here to make game of us, so you are."

"That's not true . . . I assure you it isn't."

"Do you know the Hail Mary itself?"

"His sort doesn't believe in that at all."

"We'll have to learn it to him then, won't we, lads?"

They were edging closer now. Smell of cheap Parliament on the breath of the smaller, more aggressive one.

"Come on! Say the Hail Mary then, Mister Minister!"

They were pushing him back towards the far end of the graveyard, into a corner. What did they intend to do? His lips found the words then. It was an irrational thing to do. A thing born of hysteria and foreboding. Words Fox Keegan had taught him, many years before, when they were first engaged in antiquarian pursuits around Aghadoe. Irish words in an English mouth. John Drew, in a voice pitched high with terror and his own lilting accent, began to recite the Pater Noster in Gaelic. He was calling their bluff. In their own, dying tongue.

Ár n-athair
Atá ar neamh
Go naofar d'ainm
Go dtaga do ríocht . . .

The eyes before him narrowed further. The taller of the three cocked his eye at him.

"I'll not suffer a Protestant minister making game of us!"

Suddenly, Fox Keegan and his brother Tom appeared out of nowhere. Tom Keegan pushed his way through and grabbed the leader of the mob by the shoulder.

"Are ye all right there, lads?"

"Nothing wrong at all, Tom."

"This is me father's funeral, boys. I wouldn't like for it to be upset, so I wouldn't."

The smaller of the three smirked nervously, glancing between Fox Keegan and his brother.

"Jaesus, aren't the Keegans getting rale swanky now, axing Orangemen to their funerals? Why don't you have them bury you as well?"

Tom Keegan leaned forward and seized the little man by the lapels of his frayed jacket. The other two suddenly stood aside.

"We'll axe who we fuckinwell likes, Nolan. Do you hear me, you gimpy little go-be-the-wall, you!"

"I was only remarking."

"Well and if my father's funeral is disturbed, there'll be another few fuckin' funerals to follow it, so there will."

There were shouts from over by the graveside, women's voices, shrill and declamatory, on the cold morning air. A whisper ran through the crowd that Fox Keegan's Aunt Mary, the one who ran the bit of a farm near the crossroads, had taken a turn. Tom Keegan leaned forward into the face of the dark-eyed leader of the group. He nodded towards the road.

"Go on with ye'erselves and leave us alone to look after our dead."

Fox Keegan and his brother and John Drew headed back over the stile. The women could tend to the women. Aunt Mary, a heavy-set woman in a black hat, was helped out of the graveyard and into one of the other traps. Fox Keegan nodded at John Drew. The fear faded away now.

"Will you leave me down by the crossroads, Dr Drew?"

"Of course. I think I should be on my way though."

"I'm sorry about what happened. They're just stookawns."

"But dangerous ones."

"All big lads when they have drink taken, Dr Drew."

Tom Keegan eyed his brother.

"When are ye off back to Dublin, Fox?"

"This afternoon. I'm going to get into Kilkenny and take a car from there. Or the train."

"Would ye not stay another night with us?"

"I'll be out on the street with no job if I do."

"Why don't you give up the Dublin caper altogether and rest here for a while?"

John Drew made his way to where the horse was tethered. There was no place for him in the complicated colloquy of brothers. He patted the horse on the forehead.

"We'll be off home now soon. Don't you worry."

He led the horse back down towards the two men. From the look on Tom Keegan's face, it was clear that he was only doing his mother's bidding in asking his brother to stay. Both knew well their roads were already set and that there would be no meeting of minds in Tullyroe. Fox Keegan was out over the stile now. The trap swayed as he hauled himself up into it.

"Down by the little boreen, near the pump, Dr Drew. I have to pay a visit to someone before I go back to Dublin."

The trap gathered pace as it pushed its way through the

mourners streaming out over the second stile. The little group of mischief-makers had vanished, but it was as well not to look around, just in case. At the pump, Fox Keegan turned to shake his companion's hand.

"Thank you for your help, Dr Drew. Let you go on now."

"You can thank me by taking more care of yourself, Mr Keegan. Don't you think you should. . ."

Fox Keegan smiled through broken teeth and, with that, he was off down the lane. John Drew waited until his companion disappeared in through the gap in the ditch before snapping the reins and setting off through the crossroads towards Tullyroe. All the time, as the beast picked up speed and nosed the road, John Drew felt something troubling his thoughts. But it wasn't until he reached into his pockets that it dawned on him that he had left his wife's locket in the care of Fox Keegan. He brought the trap to a halt and searched about in his pockets. Then he did a quick scour of the trap, just in case. But there was no sign of the silver locket. There was only one thing for it. He pulled the horse around and began to make his way back. When the trap reached the boreen near the pump, there were still mourners making their way back towards Tullyroe. John Drew avoided their eyes and goaded the beast carefully down the rutted road.

The gap in the hedge Fox Keegan had vanished through was really a concealed gateway that gave on to a track leading up to a neat cabin where a clatter of chickens were pecking at stones. A black dog barked in the distance as John Drew tied the horse up against the gate post and made his way into the haggard. The green half-door of the house was open and he could smell the fire burning inside. Voices came to him as he walked along. Fox Keegan's heavy voice. Then a young woman's voice cutting across his. Beneath both voices, he could make out the words of an old couple. The woman's parents, it must be.

It was dark inside the house, even with the half-door open,

and John Drew's eyes could find no purchase on anything until
he was practically on the doorstep. The old man had taken up
the talk now, mumbling through a mouth with few teeth left.
John Drew couldn't make out the words, struggle as he might,
until he realised he was listening to the other language. A warm,
mellifluous stream of slurred consonants and rich vowels. He
could make out the odd Gaelic word, here and there. *Tá* and *tusa*
and *dúirt and créatur.* He stood, looking in over the half-door, for
a full minute, before he realised that the old man facing him in
the chair had no sight in his eyes. John Drew coughed to
announce his presence. He heard feet shift inside as he leaned
over the door.

"May I come in? Mr Keegan, are you there?"

"Come in, sir, till we get a good look at you."

John Drew opened the half-door and stepped into the
kitchen. He stood a moment, allowing his eyes take in what little
light there was. Slowly, he made out the figure of the old woman
he had heard, to the right of her husband. Over in the corner, at
the foot of a settle bed, Fox Keegan was sitting with a younger
woman.

"This is Dr Drew. He was good enough to bring me here for
me father's funeral, so he was."

"Will you have a sup of tea itself, sir?"

It was at that moment, the unfortunate creature in the settle
bed stirred itself. John Drew stood a moment, catching his breath
in surprise. Was it man, woman or child? His eyes found the corner of the room and fixed on the face of what seemed to be an
older boy or a younger man. One with a malformed face, sightless eyes and the features of an idiot. The child's mother—for
who else would tend to such an unfortunate soul?—reached out
her hand and placed it on the boy's forehead.

"Whisht, alanna . . . whisht . . ."

"Want tae . . . want cupán tae, Mamó . . . cá bhfuil tú?"

Fox Keegan stood up slowly. His face looked suddenly haggard and the weight of his forty years and more seemed etched indelibly into his features. John Drew realised he had seen too much altogether. Seen something he hadn't expected to see: a strange warmth between Fox Keegan and the woman who was the mother of his crippled child. You couldn't hide it. It was like a luminescent presence between them. Yes, this was Fox Keegan's wife and that was Fox Keegan's child. The woman and child that Mrs Tours had mentioned to Eliza Drew. That he had supposedly reneged on. The boy spoke again.

"We go wallye, Mamó . . . we go wallye now, Mamó."

The old woman entreated John Drew once more to have a cup of tea but he declined. He could scarcely find words to fit his own thoughts.

"The locket, Fox . . . do you still have it?"

Fox Keegan reached into his jacket pocket. His fingers found the silver locket and chain.

"There you go, Dr Drew. Sound as a bell."

"Thank you. Thank you. I should be on my way now."

"Aren't you going to see that man out, Fox?"

John Drew bowed slightly to the old couple and nodded at Fox Keegan's wife. When they were back out in the haggard, it was John Drew who spoke first.

"I'm sorry, Mr Keegan. I had no intention of intruding."

"Well, now you have the story, so you have, Dr Drew."

"I won't be gossiping, I assure you."

"Well, the way it is now, it's all the one to me because I'm for the high road in a short while anyway. I do come down here every now and again with a few bob."

"I see . . . I see . . . and the boy?"

"Bad luck, Dr Drew. His mother caught the measles and she carrying him. Bad luck, so it was. Like your own bad luck. Bad luck trumps all cards. Did you know that, Dr Drew?"

John Drew's eyes narrowed. Then, feeling for the locket in his pocket, he thought the better of saying too much.

"Thank you for all your help, Fox. Now and in the past."

Fox Keegan's eyes stayed on John Drew until he had turned the trap around and passed back through the gateway. Then he disappeared back into the farmhouse. John Drew was a mile or more down the road before he breathed easy again as the road began to rise up out of the valley of Tullyroe, from where it would eventually descend to the flat, featureless bogplains of the Queen's County and Aghadoe.

It was early afternoon when John Drew, in the horse-and-trap, breasted the green hill of Moonavrone. As the horse plodded on, the first line of the Persepolitan inscription slipped in among his thoughts again.

His mind seized on the final sign as he read the line yet again. "Da-ri-ia-a-mush-LUGAL. GAL."

The language-within-a-language taunted him, like the muddled mixture the child had spoken, back in the cabin in Tullyroe. By the time he had reached the outskirts of Aghadoe, a few hours later, John Drew could no longer ignore the moment of his own musings. It was getting towards dusk when he climbed down out of the trap, at the first bridge over the river. With the horse chomping the fresh grass on the verge beside him, John Drew fumbled in his pocket for a pencil to score his thoughts into the notebook he always carried with him. But his fingers failing to find anything, and the march of his thoughts becoming too much for him, he picked up a sharp stone and scored his message into the lichen-shrouded parapet of the bridge.

LUGAL. GAL. He spoke the words softly to himself: *the great King.* He still wasn't sure what the final sign meant. Whether it was a case ending denoting the nominative or a class-sign signifying, perhaps, the use of a royal term. But he now sensed one thing: that the ideographs for King and Great were meant to be read in either language—in Babylonian, or in that earlier, much more ancient language. The language of Sumer, perhaps. The men of Darius had not written the tokens in syllables because the concept of King was too ancient and too sacred. So, accordingly, the word which had been written in the ancient ideograph could be read as the ancient Sumerian word LUGAL or the Babylonian *Shar,* like Hebrew. Signs could be syllables or ideas. Ideographs that could be read in two tongues, like Chinese ideographs in Japanese. Which must mean that the sign at the end of the line was a sort of reading cue. John Drew ran his fingers over the rough inscription into the stone face of the lichen-covered bridge and read *sotto voce.*

Jer Dooley was driving the cattle back out the road after milking as John Drew stood there. The cattle were almost upon him when he turned to see the blackthorn stick chastise one of the wayward beasts. The old drover raised his cap.

"Are you doing your sums there, Dr Drew?"

"I beg your pardon?"

"Your sums . . . is that what you're writing on the stone?"

"Yes, yes, I follow you now. Sums, indeed."

Yes, nice story that would be, down in Gordon's of the square, that night. *I spotted ould Drew and he writing some quare stuff on the bridge, beyont at Nan Cassidy's.*

John Drew watched the cattle clatter along the road until they had passed the bend. Then he pulled himself up into the trap and, with a flick of the reins, continued on for Sackville Square. LUGAL. GAL. Now he really had the key. A language wrapped in another language. A language badly written in the writing system of the earlier language. Like English written in Gaelic characters. Or vice versa. Sumerian words stuck into Babylonian sentences. The Babylonians had stolen the system of writing from the older, race, twisting and turning it so that it became an odd mixture of syllabic words and ideographs. With clumps of the older language appearing here and there, sticking out like sore thumbs. Or a Protestant minister at a wake.

His mind was lighter than it had been for weeks, because now he was sure he could read sign and syllable and he was ready to commit to a translation of the words of the Persepolitan inscription of Darius and a rational commentary. To translate and gloss the vainglorious words of the Achaemenid tyrant who was now as dead and buried as poor Jeremiah Keegan, late of Tullyroe. As dead as poor Edward Drew. As dead as he, John Drew, would one day be. A shade among all the other shades. As insubstantial as the stone-on-stone scrawling he had left behind on the bridge. But though all would fade away, did that give us the right to reject life? Surely not. That was the lesson of Job and Ecclesiastes. To live life to the full, in the shadow of the shadows, before fading away.

XXV

MRS TOURS SPEAKS PLAINLY

*T*he light was just up and you could hear the cock crowing as we passed in by Jack Deegan's. There was a great clanging and clattering going on in the brewery with the men working at the machines. The smell of the ale near knocked me out in the morning air. There wasn't a soul stirring on the square. Even Waxie Daly's dog was asleep. I could hear Bridget Doheny humming to herself in the scullery, when we pulled up in Willie Hill's car. I gave Madam Judith beside me a little puck in the ribs. Her eyes got very foxy then. She pulled the shawl around her and grabbed a hold of the little muslin bag. She looked up at Willie Hill and the big tears started. Men are eejits, of course. Willie Hill was nearly going to give into her until I spoke.

"This young lady will be resting here tonight."

"And if Dr Drew doesn't return from Kilkenny?"

"Well and I'll stay the night with her and get a good fire going. Eliza Drew will be back tomorrow evening, anyway."

"I really do think . . ."

"And that's that sorted, so it is."

I nodded and got madam down out of the trap. We went in by the back door. Bridget Doheny's chap was mending the gap in the hen house.

"Is your mother inside, Tadhg?"

"She is, Mrs Tours."

"Make sure you fix that right now, the way Mrs Drew will have a few fresh eggs left when she gets back from London."

I hunted Judith Drew in ahead of me. She didn't as much as bid Bridget Doheny the time of day but raced on up the stairs and threw herself down on the bed. We could hear the roars of her from down below, like all belonging to her was dead and buried. Bridget Doheny had her hand in a basin of suds and was working away at the washing board. She wiped her forehead and looked at me.

"That one upstairs is a great hand at crying."

"Lave her be. The more she cries, the less she pisses."

When you have to make water, you have to make water, no matter which end it comes out of. I didn't say another word to Bridget Doheny before I sat into the long armchair by the fire to have a little snooze. The next thing I knew, wasn't it ten o'clock in the morning. The young Doheny chap had built up the fire, and I asleep, so that the whole place was as hot as the halls of hell. I nodded over at him.

"Would you ever wind them clocks too, like a good man?"

Bridget Doheny came in from the kitchen. She looked fit to drop from all the work.

"Are the eggs and the other yokes all done away with, Mrs Tours?"

"They are, faith."

"Because if it was a thing they were still there. . ."

"All gone. Ould Drew has had a bit of sense knocked into him."

We sat there then, the two of us, drinking sweet black tea and eating curranty cake with the little chap.

I decided to go up to missie. But I took me time. I had another slice of curranty cake and had a little think to myself. Life is very queer, says I, in me own mind. Ould Drew is gone to bury Fox's father, Eliza Drew is gone to mind her sister, and the minister's daughter is caught with her drawers dropped for the blackguard son of a bigger blackguard. God send, says I to meself, there hasn't been any damage done in that quarter. A few sweet words, at that age, and they'll let the biggest bollox in the world bull them. I took a deep breath and called up the stairs.

"Are you awake at all, up there?"

There wasn't a sound. I knew well she was awake though. It was all I could do not to race up the stairs and give her a few choice flakes on the backside for herself. But I had to find out the truth. If there was any damage done, Mrs Tours had the potion to fix it, if it was got in time, so that Eliza Drew and that stook of a husband of hers need never know. Mrs Tours knows the plants to boil to clear the belly out. She'll not bring any of the Hennigans' bastards into the world, says I, in me own mind, and ruin the lives of all around her, for a moment's mischief.

"Are you awake up there, I said?"

I slipped up the stairs as fast as I could, so as not to give her too much time to compose herself. The sniffling was all over now. She had cried enough, God knows. Women are all water, one way or the other. Water in, water out. I pushed open the bedroom door. A grand room it was, with pink frills on the curtains and little porcelain dolls lined up on the window and all kinds of bits-and-bobs lying around the place. Beside the two hairbrushes on the dressing-table, with pictures of Queen Victoria on the back, lay a lovely jewellery case. I sat down at the dressing table, fiddling with the little jewellery case, trying not to look at her ladyship, and she lying there in her shift, staring at the wall.

"You and me has to have a little chat, so we do, Judith."

"Go away! You have no right to be here at all!"

And she sits up with that cheeky Protestant snout on her, like she was Queen Victoria herself. I shouldn't have done it, God knows. And if Eliza Drew had seen me, I'm sure she would have swung for me. But that snout got to me, when she said, "I'm not taking correction from . . . from a seamstress!"

It was done before I knew it. She got the back of my hand, three times across the face. She put her hand to her cheek and she squinting through her eyes at me. I leaned over her and says I, "There'll be another few to follow that, my dear, if you ever speak like that to me again, you little streep, you!"

I grabbed her by the shoulders then and I gave her a shaking that put the heart crossways in her.

"A minister's daughter out in the ditch, with the dirt! Now, you can have it two ways, missie . . . either you do as I say or your mother will get to hear every detail . . . from the seamstress!"

That put a stop to her gallop. The vexed looked turned back to tears again. She carried on crying for God knows how long. You could hear her from one end of Sackville Square to the next. When she finally quietened down, says I to her, "Women has to look after themselves, alanna, the way men doesn't. They have to look after each other."

Water running into water, that's what I was thinking of. All the women of the world, like all the seas of the world, on the big globe John Drew has in his study. I stroked her hair, the way I once used to stroke my Paddy's hair, who's over in California, with the other madmen, looking for gold.

"Whisht now, alanna. Your mother won't be back until tomorrow. There's still time for us to do whatever needs to be done."

The eyes opened and she let on to be puzzled. No wonder the Hennigan fellow fell for her, those beautiful nut-brown eyes of hers.

"But you have to tell me the truth, Judith, so you have. Now, I'm going off up the town for a few messages. You have time to think about it and you'd want to come clean with me, when I come back. It's just between the two of us it is. I won't tell another soul, so I won't."

She gave a little sniffle. I handed her my lavender handkerchief.

"If you tell me the truth and there's harm done, old Mrs Tours has the cure for it. But you have to tell me."

And I left it at that, so I did. I left orders with Bridget Doheny not to let her stir from the house till I got back, in case she got any quare notions.

It must have been near twelve in the day and I getting back to my own house. Says I, I'll get the bit of mending done and let out that frieze coat for Timmy Phelan before I go back up to the Drews'. I was expecting John Drew back soon enough anyway. He would hardly stay another night in Fox Keegan's country. I'm sure he didn't love him that much. Biddy

Reilly dropped in, in the afternoon, and we had a cup of tea together. She didn't notice the pot boiling away with the herbs, or, if she did, she didn't pass any remark.

Miss Judy must have thought things over back in the house. Of course, she probably wasn't sure herself what way it was with her, but I had made up my mind to give her the dose anyway, just in case. The only way I could do that was in my own house. I threw the scraps from the lodgers' dinner out to the cats in the backyard and put on my bonnet to go back up to the square. I passed Jack Ryan of the hill and I going over the Beggar's Bridge.

"That's a cold one, Mrs Tours."

"Them that's near hell doesn't feel the cold, Jack."

"We're all saved so, Mrs Tours."

Gordon's house was doing good business at the bottom of the square, as I passed. I could see old Nick Hynes through the window and he holding up the bar with his big talk and bullshit. Cremate him, they should, says I to meself, like the Hindoos, down in India, and leave his ashes on the counter beside a bottle of whiskey. I left in Dan Brady's boots to Waxy Daly, in his little box across from Gordon's.

I bought a couple of pounds of hairy bacon in Terry's for Bridget Doheny to cook the next day. Then I nipped over to the house. It was only when I turned the corner that I recognised the Hills' pony-and-trap tied up by the gates. That humpy little man of theirs was filling his pipe and standing by the trap. He told me Violet Hill was inside. I slipped in by the back door.

"Is there anyone in?"

"We're in the parlour, Mrs Tours."

I left the bacon in the safe, in the scullery, and took me time arriving in the presence of her ladyship. Violet Hill was all got up in a dark skirt and a jacket affair that wouldn't have been out of place at a wake. If Protestants weren't too mean to have wakes, that is. She must have given Judith Drew a piece of her mind because they were sitting across the table from one another.

"*I have been making Judith aware of the seriousness of her conduct.*"

"*Serious is right.*"

"*And the scandal it would cause, for the whole community, if word got out.*"

Says I, in me own mind, one mickey is much the same as the next, Orange or Green. But I just let on to be real impressed like.

"*You're right there, faith. But no one knows only us.*"

"*So, I want Judith to pack her things and return with me until her father arrives home.*"

Judith Drew looked at me under her eyelids. There was fear in her eyes.

"*Sure she can stop up with me until her father comes home this evening.*"

"*Mrs Tours, I would prefer Judith to come back home with me. What if her father doesn't make it back tonight?*"

"*No fear of that. Won't Mrs Drew herself be back tomorrow, anyways?*"

"*Even still . . .*"

"*And can't she give Bridget Doheny a hand to get the house ready in the morning? A little elbow grease would do this young lady no harm at all.*"

"*The truth is, Mrs Tours, I'm afraid to take my eye off Judith, because of her deceitful behaviour.*"

Aye, says I to meself. No one ever wanted to throw the leg over you that badly, you stiff ould bitch. Missie started up with the tears again, but one woman can always see through another woman's tears. I stood up and rose the kettle from the hob. Then I turned around to Violet Hill, as I wet the tea.

"*There'll be no straying for you in my house, girl, so there won't.*"

"*I still think, Mrs Tours . . .*"

"*And, as well as that, if you'll pardon me saying so, Mrs Hill, I don't think them two girls is fit company for one another. Think of the example to Cassandra.*"

Cassandra, my tit. Cassie Hill, another one with a snout on her.

Mind you, that gave Violet Hill a way out, do you see. She was happy enough to get shut of little Lorna Lovegrove, behind it all.

Judith Drew started the whining again. It was time for me to put in me spake.

"Whisht, out of that, will you! If you done a bit more praying, my girl, there'd be less tears now."

Violet Hill left down her cup of tea. She was pleased to see that Judith Drew was afraid of someone, at last.

"Perhaps you're right, Mrs Tours."

"I grant you, Miss Judith here won't be giving her mother any trouble for a long time to come."

The dark brown eyes looked up at me. I couldn't let Judith Drew down.

Violet Hill dropped us off in the trap at my house. I let on to Violet Hill I would call John Drew in to take his daughter as soon as I saw him pass in by the window, but I had no notion of doing any such a thing. I hunted Judith Drew into the kitchen and left her at the big table while I put the pot back on the fire. The lodgers weren't back in from the brewery yet, so we had a little peace and quiet. I looked at her from the corner of my eye, as I stirred the pot.

"You haven't been in your woman's way for a while, would I be right about that, now?"

There was no answer, just that scowl again. But underneath it was fear. Fear of a big belly and the bastard she was going to present to the world if I didn't work fast. There was no knowing if she really was in the family way though. Old May Callanan would have known by just leaving her hand on her belly. But, says I to meself, Judith Drew isn't long that way, if she is. A seamstress has a sharp eye for a figure.

"Since when, Judith. Tell me, alanna?"

"Since a month or two."

"And no more?"

"No more."

I strained the mixture through a muslin cloth, the same way I always do. You have to make sure to take the bits of dock out because it can push things too far, so it can. The first cup of it, she brought up in the back yard, but the next stayed down. I got her to lie down on the couch then and did the first massage with the hot compress to loosen things up. I put her up into the little bed in my own room and spread the gutta-percha sheet under and left a chamber pot by the bed.

"Every hour or so, I'm going to get you up."

Her big eyes looked out at me from the corner of the room. The boldness was gone out of them now.

"Mrs Tours . . . might I die?"

"No fear of that, cratur. Ould Mrs Tours knows what she's doing."

I didn't tell her about Dinah Somers, the coachman's wife beyond in Abbeyleix, who took a turn ten years ago, when she was under May Callanan. Or the Maloney one they brought in one night to me, a few Christmases ago, and she nearly bleeding to death. I sat on the bed beside her and cradled her head in my arms. It's an easy thing for men. A minute's pleasure and a lifetime's worry. Sin in haste and repent at leisure. But Judith Drew is a hardy girl, says I to meself. Well-fed Protestant stock. No cause for panic. I hardly had her in bed when the lodgers arrived in and I had to put the dinner out for them. There was no point in trying to hide that I had a visitor upstairs so I just dressed the yarn up a little.

"I have the minister's daughter above in the bedroom."

"Have you taken the soup then, Mrs Tours?"

"'Deed and I haven't. She took ill and her father isn't home from Kilkenny yet, so I said to Bridget Doheny, she could stop with me until her father arrives. So, if you hear any roaring above, lads."

"Well, with the help of God she'll be all right."

"It must have been a chill she got."

"Easy get a chill at this time of year."

Chill where the sun never shines, says I, in me own mind. I left them to tuck into the mutton stew and went back upstairs. It had started quicker than I expected. Maybe that was on account of her age. I had left towels and a nice bar of Dublin soap for her, but I couldn't let her drink any water yet and go and weaken the mixture. I looked at her face then and thought to meself: what a pretty girl you are. No wonder every dog and divil in Aghadoe cocks his leg at you. She got a bit feverish then. I kept on taking away the soiled rags and leaving them in a little sack by the far bed, just in case anyone strayed in. It was nearly dark when she fell asleep, but I knew I would have to wake her again soon. You had to keep things moving, just in case there was a sudden thickening of the blood or the heart or the kidneys started to give trouble.

I was out in the scullery when I heard the knock at the door. I nearly fell out of me standing when I opened the door and the dog collar stared back at me. Wasn't it ould Drew himself, his wife on the high seas from England, Fox Keegan on his way back to Dublin after burying his father and his own daughter up in bed. His face was tired. They must have dragged him into the wake, above in Kilkenny, says I to meself. I opened the door and put my finger to my lips.

"Whisht!"

"Mrs Tours . . ."

"Whisht, will you!"

"I was told Judith had come in from the Hills and was with you. I'm afraid I don't understand."

"Come in and don't let the whole town hear you, will you?"

He muddled his way in and stood there with his spectacles hanging off his long Protestant nose. I sat him down near the fire. I could hear the lodgers laughing away over the card game in the sitting room. Tim Delaney was probably robbing the both of them blind, as per usual.

"Is there something the matter with Judith, Mrs Tours?"

"Divil a thing much. She took ill when she was in with Mrs Hill and I said for to leave her here until you got back, and now she's fast asleep."

"Well, we shall have to wake her then."

"Oh, I don't think you'd want to go waking her, Dr Drew."

"And why is that, now?"

"She looks like she needs a good night's sleep, before her mother gets back."

"Mrs Tours, I really must insist on seeing my daughter."

"Well and if she catches a chill on the way up to that house of yours, I'll thank you kindly to explain it to Mrs Drew that it was your doing, Dr Drew."

He blinked a minute. That stopped him in his tracks. I lit a candle from the fire and made my way upstairs with bossy boots behind me. I made a great racket going up the stairs so Judith Drew would know who was with me. But she was half-asleep when we entered the bedroom. For good luck, I had moved all the vessels to the far side of the bed. Ould Drew could hardly see his own daughter in the lamplight.

"Is that you, Judith?"

"Yes, Father."

"Are you all right, child?"

"Just a stomach illness. Mrs Hill said I could wait with Mrs Tours."

"Well, I'm back now. Let's get a move on. Chop! Chop!"

"I don't feel well, Father."

"Shall I fetch Dr Prescott?"

"I just need to sleep, Father."

I whispered into the eejit's ear.

"Let her rest easy here and I'll hunt her up to you first thing in the morning."

He stood muttering to himself for a while, like a little child trying to remember something.

"First thing in the morning now, Mrs Tours."

"I'll have her ladyship packed off at first light. I have a big basket of mending to get through anyway."

"I'm much obliged, Mrs Tours."

It must have been near nine when I finally got shut of him. The lodgers were whispering among themselves. Jack Nolan, of the cottages, arrived in to play another couple of hands with them. I said nothing to anyone but I kept an eye on Judith Drew, going up and down every so often to give her another little sup of the mixture. It was around midnight and the lodgers were well asleep when I heard her give a little yell in her sleep. I slipped up fast as I could. When I held the rushlight over her face, I could see she was only half-awake.

"That's the worst of it over now, alanna. It's almost gone now."

I didn't tell her how sick she would be, the following day. That she would have to drink a lough of nettle soup to settle her blood back. She had enough to think about now, the poor divil. I sat down beside her on the bed, wiping her forehead with the wet towel, like she was one of my own. When Judith Drew fell into a heavy sleep, I quenched the rushlight and settled myself into the far bed. But the truth is, I hardly slept a wink for worrying about the Protestant minister's daughter, in the bed opposite.

XXVI

THE FOX'S FAREWELL

Fox Keegan noticed the berries in the bushes, most of all. The blackberries and the fraughans and the little purple flowers that peeped out of the ditches at him, in between the ferns. He found himself puzzling over their strange colours and longed to climb down off the ass-and-cart and grab a handful of the little flowers. But he just didn't seem to have the energy. There was a chill on the air that said autumn and the turning of the year all right, but it was a different sort of chill that seemed to be in his bones. A chill that seemed odd, in light of the raging fever in his head. There wasn't much point in lingering in Tullyroe though. His brother Tom had seen him right for a few shillings to get himself back to Dublin. And he had promised Mr Dawson, in Pim's, that he would return to Dublin immediately after the funeral. It was just that it all felt stranger than he had expected. But maybe that was the fever. It had come on him suddenly, when they were a couple of miles out of Tullyroe, after he nodded off in the cart that had picked him up at Nolan's bridge. Whether he had carried it down from Dublin with him, or picked it up along the road, there was no telling. The driver, a comical little cut of a man who was bringing a churn of butter to some farmhouse along the way, remarked on his high colour.

"You have a face on you like a turkey cock, Fox. Did you make a meal of the wake or what?"

The odd, disconnected sensation hadn't seemed much different from the aftermath of many another night's drinking at first. But, after a little while, it began to feel like his innards were burning up. In Kilkenny, he took a car to Carlow. It was a heavy yoke, badly sprung and he felt every rut in the road. The driver wasn't at all impressed when the car had to stop every now and then, for Fox Keegan to relieve himself behind a ditch.

"Can't you hould it like a man, mister?"

When they changed horses, it was all Fox Keegan could do to drag himself back into the car. He dozed off at one stage, dreams dancing in and out of his mind, like the detritus of a hundred daft designs. The stories he hoped to tell in *The Irish Peasants' 1001 Nights*, with each yarn to be prefaced by a little comment.

> *Journeymen have the best stories of all. Pedlars and tinkers and travellers especially, like a good tailor, they take in a bit here and let out a bit there.*

Of course, the people would have to be allowed speak in their own words. Not the nicely buttered language of the Tullyroe primer, which he had taught from, but the colourful tone the real people used.

> *There was a man used to visit this town once. A fine cut of a man. As broad as a barn door and as big as the oak tree, beyond in the haggard. Anyway, this day, didn't he . . .*

He gazed out at the damp streets of Dublin as the car made its way up the quays in the dark of the autumn evening. His thoughts felt even more jumbled now. If he hadn't known better, he would have thought he was still drunk from the night before, though a drop hadn't crossed his parched lips since the wake. It took all his will-power to get as far as Clanbrassil Street and, from there, to Sam Parker's little two-up-two-down, in Malpas Street. With the fever raging in his head and his loins on fire, he was scarcely in the door when he made a run for the outhouse and discharged whatever was left of the previous day's food and drink. Sam Parker looked at him oddly when he came back into the house.

"I'm thinking you're not a well man, Fox."

"I caught an ould chill on the way down. In Abbeyleix, maybe."

"Is that it?"

"I need to lie down, Sam. I need to lie down."

It was sometime around midnight when Fox Keegan awoke to the roaring flame behind his eyes and the stiletto jab in his gut. He wanted to cry out in his misery but there was no one around to hear him. Water was what was needed. He stumbled down the stairs and made for the little pitcher of water near the safe. The water flowed down his gullet like honey but still it did nothing to quench the flame darting about his head.

"Oh, Jesus! Jesus, stop it!"

If only he could get to the fresh, cool air, to feel the cool damp on his cheeks. This would bring down the burning and let his thoughts cool down again. And that was where Sam Parker found him, a short while later, grunting and groaning and lying across the threshold.

"Come on, Fox! Get back into your bed, like a good man. I'll get the medical officer up for you in the morning, so I will. Come on now, like a good chap."

In the bed, Fox Keegan was only faintly aware of his brow being mopped by the older man. He couldn't follow his own words as he lay there. His thoughts seemed to be running into one another, like a frenzy of wild dogs after a hare. When his mind cleared a little, in the late morning, it was to see Sam Parker and another man whispering at the bedroom door.

"I can tell you now, sir, by the look of him and the go of him."

"You're sure?"

"I've seen dozens of them, so I have."

A light drizzle was falling as Sam Parker helped Fox Keegan up into the car he had requisitioned from the swillman, at the end of the street. Fox Keegan shivered in the warm, autumn air. His eyes were bloodshot now and the sound of the ass's hooves on the cobblestones thrummed through his head like a thousand hammers on a thousand rivets. He didn't pay much heed to the direction they took. In fact, the only way he realised they were crossing Cork Street at all was when he caught the foul stench of O'Keefe's, the knackers. He jerked his head up and looked into Sam Parker's sharp, northern eyes.

"Am I on the way out, Sam? Am I?"

"Not at all, Fox. Few days inside and you'll be rightly, so you will."

The fever had swallowed him up again, by the time they reached the fever hospital. He scarcely remembered passing through the gates. But he did remember the first sight of the ward when the sickly sweet smell of other men's faeces came to his nostrils. He understood, vaguely, that he was lucky not to be out in the makeshift tents at the back. Sam Parker's intervention had seen to that. Then he fell into a deep sleep on the little pallet assigned to him and Sam Parker was no more. This wasn't a place for casual visitors but one where the quick and the dead were sorted out in short order. Where the names of the dead were printed in the newspapers as numbers only, ciphers to hide the truth from prying eyes.

His father's face was the first one to come to Fox Keegan as he lay there. But it was a vision from the previous time he had been down home, the year before. Around harvest time. They were both sitting at the long table, on a Sunday morning, slurping stirabout in great big mugs. His mother was feeding the hens out in the haggard and Tom was milking. It was just the two of them. His father left down the large discoloured spoon on the table.

"I'm afraid you'll never get sense, John, will you?"

"I'll never be a farmer, anyways."

"Why couldn't you have stuck to the teaching job itself, above in Minister Rodgers' ould school? Or the job in the brewery? You have the brains for it. More than Tom, there."

"Brains isn't everything."

"By Jaesus and it mustn't be."

His father stood up and put on his hat. He had the same round, grizzled face as Tom. Plain ways and plain talk. No thinking or talking too much. Just the seasons, the beasts of the field and the price of oats. Jer Keegan pursed his lips and looked down at his son.

"I met a chap at the mart in Callan, last market day."

"Oh . . ."

"And he says to me, says he, 'Are you the father of that Keegan fellow, the poet?' Says I, 'I'm married to his mother, anyway.'"

"What was it he wanted?

"Says he, 'I can quote you every line of "The Lament for Redhill", so I can.'"

"Is that a fact?"

"And didn't he stand there, again the counter, and recite the whole bleddy poem for us . . . from beginning to end . . . he did."

His mother arrived in with the empty bucket in her hand and glanced at the two of them. Then she crossed to the fire and began stirring the pot.

"Tom's having trouble with that heifer again."

Jer Keegan shuffled out the door and off across the haggard. Fox Keegan sat there for a while, staring into the empty mug, knowing it was the first and the last time he and his father would ever mention such matters. Knowing too, that it was the closest he would ever get to a commendation.

The proctor called out
The tithe, it is due
And the bailiffs they gathered
Their mischief to do
But Malone he did rally
The men, for he knew
That no tithe would be taken
For no tithe was due.

Redhill. Knockroe. It might have been yesterday. They had gone over to Knockroe, at the far side of the hill, himself and his father and Tom, over a stallion that was to service the mare. At least, that's what his father told him, years later. His father, after all, wasn't the sort to go looking for rows or confrontations with tithe-proctors and Protestant ministers. He recalled sitting in the ass-and-cart with Tom and his father, as they passed through the little village of Knockroe—that the papers insisted on calling Redhill, after the incident. He recalled seeing the crowds gathering at the far end of the village and his father speaking to a small man in a battered black hat.

"What's all the stir about?"

"They say they're going to turf the Sweeneys out of their home, over the tithe they haven't paid to that black bastard, James."

"Is that so?"

"And that they're going to tumble the house, along with it."

His father nudged the ass on, but, in no time at all, they were stuck in the middle of the crowd. He could see military men in front of the house, their carbines raised in the air. There were shots and then shouts. A wild-looking man, with a slashers in his hand, was standing in front of the local crowd.

"Leave them go, ye bastards, ye!"

It seemed to quieten down then and it looked like they might pass through without mishap. His father was walking alongside the ass-and-cart now, holding the reins tightly and leading the beast forward, along *the fringes of the crowd. He heard his father confide to Tom, "All piss and wind. It'll be over in a minute, so it will."*

Tom had big, frightened eyes, but he, Fox Keegan, wanted to see all. That was the difference between himself and Tom. He had to see. He needed to see, despite his fear. Or, maybe because of his fear. They were just at the far end of the crowd, near the big horse trough with the fancy crest, when a great shout went up.

"Come on, lads! Lay into the whores!"

The crowd surged forward then. There were wild screams of anger and pain and the sound of stones clattering off skulls. Shots were fired in the air over their heads. Their father pushed them down in the cart.

"Lie down, will ye, for the love of Christ!"

There were women screaming and children hiding under their cloaks and the mad shouts of big, red-faced men, with slashers and sticks and pitchforks. Fox Keegan, sticking his head up for a moment, saw a rock fell a militia man and the carbine slip from his hands. As a couple of his companions turned to help him, more rocks flew. Now the crowd was on them and a couple of the carbines were seized. There were more shots and the crowd drew back. A tall local man, with blood streaming down the side of his long, frightened face, broke through the crowd in their direction. He stared at them a minute, as though waiting for directions, then clambered up into the ass-and-cart before falling on top of Tom. Jer Keegan dragged the ass by the reins, goading it away from the mêlée. There were more shouts and the screams of women and children.

"Take them, lads! Break their fucking heads for them!"

The swell of the crowd was pulling them this way and that. Then, all of a sudden, the mood of the mob seemed to turn again, like the mind of some aimless monster that, a moment before, had been cowering under the buckshot and bullets and had now been seized by an urge to charge forward at its tormentors. People began to run by the cart for Sweeneys', the eviction house. There were shots fired directly into the crowd. Fox Keegan saw a woman fall at the right flank.

"Jesus, Mary and Joseph, help me! Someone!"

It was Tom Keegan who wiped the blood from the mouth of the man lying in the cart at their feet. Fox just sat there, staring into the groggy face of the dying man. At the pale, quivering skin and the terrified eyes. He glanced over his shoulder as they reached the bend in the road, where the road rose out of the village. To the left of the houses, Fox Keegan saw a group of locals dragging away one of the militia men. First the helmet was knocked off, then the gun was taken from him and broken across his back. And now they had him up against an oak tree and were laying into him with sticks and stones. The man just leaned against the tree, dazed with concussion and knowing that his end was near. A couple of men made a dart at him, kicking and punching him. Each time he fell, he dragged himself up again. He was like the man in the cart, life blood seeping away through his mouth and his nose and his eyes even. A little man at the head of the crowd raised his hand.

"Finish the bastard, lads!"

The main group of militia men had rallied in front of the cottage now and a few more shots were fired. Horses were mounted. They either couldn't see their companion or had given up the ghost.

"Oh, Jesus! Jesus, help me!"

Fox Keegan looked down into the face of the dying man, then the cart gave a little lurch and they were around the corner and the whole show disappeared from view. There were people running around the corner and down the hill now to catch a glimpse of the proceedings, as if to a pattern or a fair. An old crone stuck her head out of a doorway.

"Is it over yet? Is all the shooting stopped?"

But Jer Keegan didn't say a word. Instead, he shouldered the dying man from the cart and laid him inside the old woman's house, on the little settle bed in the corner. They all scurried inside then, with the door bolted and the ass tied up at the side of the cottage. Fox Keegan watched the old lady fill a basin of water from a big enamel jug. She wrung out a bit of a cloth and began wiping the sick man's brow. She mumbled to them through gapped teeth, without even looking at them.

"Musha, God is good. God is good."

A few minutes afterwards, as they heard hooves galloping past the door, the dying man's eyes went still and the last breath left his body. The old lady nodded at Jer Keegan.

"Let you take them two boys home to their mother now, sir. You've done your business here, so you have."

"Do you know him?"

"He's one of the Mitchells of Clooneen. The poor fool."

Fox started at the word. Fool. Why was the man a poor fool? Hadn't he been doing no more and no less than what he, Fox, had often heard the men suggest, and they gathered around the fire on a winter's evening? The old woman left the cloth on the man's forehead and looked into Fox Keegan's eyes.

"He have only himself to blame, for being in the thick of it."

"He got caught up in it."

"The same chap, God be good to him, would rise a row at a wake."

Fox scanned the crinkled skin of the old lady and her narrow mouth. Her hand reached out for a shawl on the back of the settle bed and drew it over the dead man's face.

"I had five and I buried four of them, sir. I seen it all before."

Jer Keegan nodded to the boys. The old woman blessed herself. Then they all blessed themselves.

"Let you take them children home to their mother now, is what you'll do, sir."

Fox Keegan's father nodded to them both. In a minute, they were back out on the street, pushing their way through the remnants of the crowd, gazing at the stones and sticks littering the road. Jer Keegan bade them lie down in the cart, covered them both with a couple of sacks and warned them not to look out until they were out of the town again. Only the sharp curses of his father kept Fox Keegan from sticking his nose up to inspect the scene. All the time, his brother lay there, with his face to the rough boards of the cart, pretending that nothing had happened. That no one had been hurt or killed and that all was well with the world.

It was late afternoon when the cart was heeled up in the haggard in

*Tullyroe. Their mother was washing the vessels in the basin when they got
home. She looked up at them oddly.*

"What kept ye?"

*They boys were sent inside to get a cut of bread and a mug of tea from
their sister. The only words Fox Keegan could make out, from the far room,
were whispered ones.*

"There was a bit of bother above in Knockroe."

"What sort of bother?"

"There was ructions over an eviction."

"Was anyone hurted?"

"A few all right . . . a few . . ."

"Badly?"

"You wouldn't know, so you wouldn't."

*There wasn't a word said on the matter by Jer Keegan after that. Each
time the issue of the eviction or the unrest was brought up, he sat in stony
silence until the matter was dropped again. But, late that night, when the
candles were quenched, their mother sat with them in the dark, repeating
over and over again, as she stroked their hair*

"God is good, boys. God is good."

Fox Keegan opened his eyes slowly to the clanging of a bell. A
large, jowled man with a top hat and a sick-nurse were walking by
the foot of each pallet. They stopped here and there, to comment on one patient or another. The man gazed over at Fox as
the woman whispered in his ear. That sickening smell came to
Fox's nostrils again. His own smell and the smell of those around
him. It was the smell of flesh and blood reduced to pestilence
and putrefaction and fouled water. Fox Keegan eased himself up
slowly on his elbows. The cramps in his stomach seemed to have
flared up again now but he didn't have the energy to call an
attendant. There didn't seem to be any point. All he wanted to
do was to sleep and to hide from the cramps and the fire in his
head and the dryness in his throat. He somehow managed to tilt

the pitcher of water on the floor beside the pallet to fill a mug of water. But most of the water spilled out over his shirt. He lay back and let his turbid thoughts find their own way again.

> *The Fox is a clever animal*
> *He lives in the wild.*
> *He feeds on fowl and small rodents.*

He heard the voice of one of the Marshall boys reading from his primer. It was an early spring morning, in the little schoolhouse, up on the hill. The rain was beating against the long windowpanes. His mind was drifting from the thirty little faces in front of him.

"Mr Keegan . . . Mr Keegan, sir . . . we're all finished reading, so we are."

These weren't the pinched little faces of the Dublin poor he would see ten years later, but the hardy faces of young boys and girls whose playground, bad and all as it was, was the fields. Fresh air and potatoes— when they weren't maggoty with blight—and buttermilk and the sun beating down on the harvest. Not like the withered, woebegone eyes of the children in the Dublin tenements, with their dazed, soulless complexions and their lightless eyes. Intelligence dulled by sheer hunger and want.

"Violet Grace . . . you carry on there, like a good girl."

It hadn't been such a hard life. There was shelter from the rain and a turf fire that the little scholars kept tended. But the tedium of the company of children finally began to gnaw at him, with their constant chatter and the need to have someone in authority to chafe against as their minds hardened. Sometime into the third year of the post, he began seeking solace and stimulation in the big talk in the two public houses in Tullyroe. There were rows up and down with Minister Rodgers too. Strange location for a Protestant school and chapel, anyway. Must have taken the wrong turning in Abbeyleix. Belonged more in Queen's County, with all their talk of Queen and Country and the Good Book. Still, better than the lot up north. Less Bible and Sword and Wrath-of-God and

Assyria smiting the Israelites and all that sort of silly shagology. And Rodgers wasn't too harsh on him either, seeing as he was one of the few, within an ass's ride of the school, who could teach the little swaddlers their tongue and their prayers and their precious Holy Book, at least half of which, as Casey was wont to point out after a few drinks, they had lifted from the Jews and claimed as their own. As if the great Jehovah was a portly-looking Englishman, taking the quarter-past-eight train to London from some little hamlet along the railway line. And to be fair to Minister Rodgers, it wasn't until the day he came in and found Fox asleep over the desk and the children running wild all around him that the axe fell.

That Saturday morning, when he heard the tidy clip-clop of the minister's pony-and-trap crossing the haggard, Fox knew it was all over. His mother called him out of the bed.

"Minister Rodgers wants a word with ye, Fox."

It was all very civilised, of course. Rodgers was decent enough to do the business in the kitchen, with none of the family around to hear him.

"I'm afraid you have the mind to be a monitor and a teacher, Mr Keegan, but not the temperament. I fear that will always be the case."

"You may be right."

"It has nothing at all, you realise, to do with party spirit."

"I understand that."

"So, it grieves me to tell you this, but I will have to let you go at the end of the month."

There was no place on the farm for him either. He couldn't turn his hand to the plough or the cattle and he wasn't bringing in any coppers either. And there was no going back to the wedding bed he had vacated, not a year before. So the only solution was the hard road, over the hills, out of Tullyroe. On a whisper from Rodgers himself, and a letter of recommendation, he presented himself at the brewery in Kilkenny, the following week. But there was no hope of a post there, despite Rodgers' sweetly written missive. In the coopery office, a heavy-set man with a rough English accent said they were taking on people in Aghadoe, in the Queen's County.

"How do you know that, sir, if you don't mind my asking?"

"Have to keep an eye on the opposition, lad."

So it was Aghadoe, then. The big brewery, at the foot of Sackville Square, where he sat in a little office overlooking the pond and toiled away on accounts and schedules and invoices and costs.

He recalled the first meeting with John Drew again. That blazing summer Sunday afternoon, on the lawn of Captain Neal's house, East-holme, with its turrets and fancy gables and solid, red-brick front. Long tables had been laid on out on the lawn for the midsummer brewery managers' party. Fox Keegan was swamped by the English voices of the foremen and clerks all around him. Mr Terry was standing on the steps of the grand house with Captain Neal and his wife next to him. There was a sprinkling of local Catholics, in among the planters and their English overseers. He, Fox Keegan, had been brought to the party, on a nod and a wink from Crowley, the senior clerk.

"Do you good, lad, to be pals with these people."

"I suppose it would."

"Oh, yes. I'll be home by Christmas but you'll still be here, if you follow me."

How was it he had met up with John Drew exactly? The memory seemed to be quite muddied now. That was it—the accident at the tea-table, when one of the children's toy carriages sent the whole lot careering down on to the lawn. Women ran to the scalded boy who was unceremoniously dipped into a nearby horse trough to cool his burns. Fox Keegan was helping tidy up the mess when a small, perky voice at his shoulder butted in on his thoughts.

"I suppose that's the last of the tea, so."

He looked around to see a short, smiling man squinting through ill-fitting lunettes, an otherworldly look in his eyes. Maybe that was what had attracted Fox Keegan to John Drew, in the first place. The distance behind the eyes. It was neither cunning nor craft but something more like the absence that he felt himself, from time to time. Fox Keegan remembered looking up from the debris of broken cups and saucers.

"I'm sure there'll be more along in a minute, so there will, sir."

"Your accent isn't a local one, is it, Mr . . ."

"Keegan . . . John Keegan . . . I'm a clerk in the brewery . . . from Kilkenny."

"Ah, well I'm John Drew. Dr Drew, as my parishioners call me. But, then, I suspect you're not one of my parishioners. Not that I know them all, of course. One tries."

"I often seen you walking around town, Dr Drew."

"Really?"

Fox Keegan gathered up a pile of broken pottery and heaped it into the wheelbarrow that was left beside him.

"You see, Dr Drew, the servant does always know more about the master than the master does about the servant."

"You're my servant then, are you, Mr Keegan?"

"You could do worse, so you could."

He left John Drew to chew on that, spending the rest of the afternoon sipping tea and chomping on seed cake as he strolled around the gardens. At one stage, he wandered into Captain Neal's house, along with Crowley.

"Let's see how our betters live, shall we, Mr Keegan."

"Fair enough."

This was their life, then. Captain Neal's castle, with its two drawing-rooms and its servants' quarters and the little room where, rumour had it, Captain Neal liked to practise physical exercises, from his time on commission in Afghanistan. But there was the scent of a woman about the house too. Not the stale, insipid smell that clung to quarters that saw only males. It was the scent of a woman who was waited on by other women. There were fancy high-backed chairs in the dining room, a great oak table, a grand upholstered chaise-longue and a gaudy portrait of the Battle of Waterloo over the fireplace with a brass motif appended to it that said

Semper Fidelis

Fox Keegan looked out through the dining room window on to the lawn. In among the ladies' hats and the gentleman's sombre coats, he could see John Drew bumbling about with no one much to talk to but himself. Fox Keegan made his mind up to speak to the little minister again, if only to bait him more. In the end, they found themselves cast together, under one of the willow trees by the pond, discussing matters of local history and the stirrings of the new antiquarian society of Ossory.

"The past is essential for understanding the present, Mr Keegan."

"So is the present."

"True, true. Perhaps you might be able to help me with some of my scholarly endeavours."

"What would I know about all that now, Dr Drew?"

"I could do with an amanuensis."

"Would that be a class of secretary?"

"A thinking secretary. Also, my eyesight is getting weaker."

Fox Keegan had a presentiment of someone watching them from afar then. Eliza Drew was over to them in short order. Fox Keegan felt himself bristle instantly in her company. There was an arrogance in her eyes that made him watch his tongue and his thoughts. A well-calibrated snooti-ness. And something else too—that waspish jealousy certain women felt when their man was befriended by another man. Eliza Drew appeared ready to nip the air of domestic sedition in the bud.

"I haven't been introduced, John?"

"This is Mr Keegan. He's a clerk in the brewery."

"Pleased to meet you."

"Some people do call me Fox."

"I see. Fox in name . . . and in nature too, Mr Keegan?"

"You wouldn't know, so you wouldn't, ma'am."

She laid her thin hand on John Drew's shoulder. A motherly, wifely, threatening hand.

"John, the Hills are waiting for us, over by the punch bowl."

"Oh, are they?"

"Enjoy the rest of your day, Mr Keegan."

Fox Keegan watched them beat their way across the lawn to where Willie Hill and Violet Hill were sitting at a long table. He didn't stay long after that but slipped away quietly up to Mrs Tours' house, where he had lodgings.

It was John Drew who approached him the next time, there not being too many amanuenses to be found hanging around the Beggar's Bridge. And so their relationship began, in the study of the rectory, under the sharp eye of Eliza Drew and the bemused, haughty smiles of her daughters. At first, John Keegan helped John Drew with local place-names and the like. Then, one winter's evening, John Drew handed him a little list of signs that had been taken from a squeeze of a stone inscription.

"You're not expecting me to learn these, are you?"

"Well, the stonemason who inscribed them probably couldn't read them either. I just want you to do what he did. Copy them faithfully. This is work for the Academy."

Over the next four or five evenings—the effort was scarcely worth the few coppers John Drew could pay him—Fox Keegan transferred the little pictures of birds and snakes and the like from the squeeze.

"This one is called the key-of-the-Nile, Mr Keegan."

"Is it, faith?"

Their encounters brought them closer, as time went on. There was the odd excursion, in the pony-and-trap, to some rath or long-forgotten stone set in the middle of a boggy field. It was at the rath out past the Burrow, that Fox Keegan brought up the subject he had first mentioned at the garden party in Major Neal's. It was the sort of awkward moment that Fox Keegan was always drawn to whenever things were going too well for comfort.

"You know, Dr Drew, it was your own crowd that tumbled the rath that used to be in Aghadoe. There's a bit of antiquarian news for you."

"Yes, you told me that before, I believe."

"Like you say, the past is important. Do you know what they built on the rath, do you?"

"Yes, I think you told me that too."

"They built ye'er church up there."

"Isn't that history, Mr Keegan? One superior group comes and topples the battlements of the lesser group."

"Superior?"

"You know what I mean . . . in technology . . . trade . . . learning."

"Aye, I know what you mean, all right. Ye came with guns over ye'er shoulders and books in ye'er satchels and a sack of guineas."

John Drew looked out over his lunettes across the lawn. Then he turned back to Fox Keegan.

"In a manner of speaking, yes. That is the truth, I suppose."

John Keegan knew, at that moment, that this was John Drew's weakness. The flaw that marked him out from the rest of the flock. Now, where has that wound come from? Fox Keegan found himself wondering, at the time. And why is there none of it visible in his wife? It was only later, through Mrs Tours' talk, that he came to hear of the dead child. Maybe that was what had happened: the same wound that had soured Eliza Drew had opened her husband's heart to the hurt of others. Eliza Drew had pulled into herself, in order to assuage any further pain. And yet, even with this knowledge in mind, Fox Keegan's despair at the woman's contemptuous gaze never waned.

Another bell sounded, somewhere in the distance, outside the sick room. It was followed by the sound of doors opening and of heavy-booted feet. The orderlies' shift was changing. Fox Keegan heard the sound of a cart crunching on the gravel, at the back of the building. A rough voice said, "Stop there! Nice and easy now!"

He heard the sound of wood meeting wood and of the rough, cheap coffin sliding into place on the cart. Fox Keegan opened his eyes painfully. A man in a long coat was pushing the water trolley along by the foot of the pallet. His eyes met Fox Keegan's for a minute, but there was nothing to see in them. Neither fear nor favour. The stomach cramps had eased a little from the laudanum concoction they had given him but the headache and the dryness was still there. He was almost too weak to think now. Things that had happened years ago seemed to have happened only the other day. He was even becoming unsure of who had done what to whom. It was as though everyone was everyone else. As if there was just one commonality of pain and pleasure. The bell sounded again and the cart moved off across the cobble-stones.

"We'll be back by eleven."

Eleven? Day or night? Day, because of the light streaming in through the torn drapes. Days were told by light; nights by darkness. You learned this early on. Light could be stronger or weaker and so could darkness. A song passed through his mind.

> *Night is always darkest*
> *Just before the dawn . . .*

The cart was back in the yard now. But it could scarcely have been more than an hour, could it? The cart was back and so too were the loud voices of the attendants with their heavy Dublin vowels. Never trust the vowels, that's what John Drew always said. The fever seemed to have subsided now. Yes, the fever would pass now, he knew that. Just as he would himself. Drifting out into space and time and mingling with other thousands of pictures and thoughts and stories.

"Water! For the love of Jesus, give me some water!"

His own voice seemed curiously distant and disembodied now. The water would count for nothing, he knew well. Just ease the fever in the last moments, as his thoughts sank below their own weight. In the final moment, when the bell and the voice seemed to torment him the most, he glimpsed little vignettes through his bloodshot eyes. Mary Macken, sitting by the settle bed, tending to their son. She had an odd, half-smile on her face, like she was about to say something. He heard himself speak then. He felt his lips move slowly as he looked at her in the dream.

"I'm sorry, Mary."

His eyes opened now. But he could still see her sitting there, across from him. The smiled had broadened now. Her soft skin. That sheen in her hair. She rested her hand on the child's head. Then she stretched out her hand to touch him.

"We're all right, Fox, so we are. You get good bed rest, now."

Good bed rest. He could feel his parched lips break into a dry smile now. An odd sort of warmth began to suffuse his whole body. Mary Macken seemed to fade and drift away into the distance.

John Drew was staring up at him over his lunettes. A question on his lips, as always. His father, was looking at him from the doorway, the hat pulled down over his forehead, calling him on, calling him on, into the next room.

"Come on now, like a good man. There's work to be done here."

One of the lines John Drew had given him to copy out, a few nights before, began burning brightly in his fevered mind. He could see each of the shapes as though they were right there in front of him, on the rubbing he was copying from.

It was the line that was made up of signs for kings. He heard John Drew's voice speaking the strange words. LUGAL. LUGAL. MESH. LUGAL. KUR. KUR. MESH. John Drew was telling him to be sparing with the ink and to mind the direction of the little triangles he was copying. The line had burnt itself so deeply into his brain that he could still have copied it out, there and then, if only he had the strength. He couldn't read it and he couldn't reckon it. But still the signs winked at him, in his fever. From the deserts of Persia, from the East, to where he was now following the light. Because home was in the East. That was where the light came from. East was home.

XXVII

HOME IS WHERE THE HEARTH IS

A sour wind cut across Sackville Square. It broke in squalls across the dry face of the square, rising dead leaves and twigs in its wake. Waxy Daly's dog, Prince, cowered behind the horse trough by the barracks wall. When the Hill's pony-and-trap appeared at John Gordon's corner, the horse instinctively shied away from the little maelstrom. Willie Hill's man flicked the reins impatiently.

"Go on, there! On with ye!"

Violet Hill glanced at the portmanteau she had brought with Judith Drew's clothes. She nodded to the driver.

"I won't be long."

"Right you are, Mrs Hill. I'll wait down by Waxy Daly's cabin, if that's all right with you."

Violet Hill pushed open the gate of the rectory. Although it was midday, there was scarcely a sinner to be seen on the square. Autumn was well in now. The darkening of the days would come soon. A harbinger of winter, with its cold, sleety skies. God send it didn't bring the ague and the quinsy that had struck down Mrs Harry Peters, a year in October, her throat closing up with the infection so that she practically suffocated. Warm weather brought cholera in the cities; cold, damp weather brought chills to the throat and chest. Violet Hill wondered, as she had wondered a thousand times before, why her forebears had sought to plant such a wicked and inhospitable land. Would they not have been better staying on their little plot in Suffolk in gentler, warmer, more welcoming climes?

A lamp was burning in the study. The curtains were still drawn on the bedroom windows above. Violet Hill caught a glimpse of John Drew as he sat at his desk but he didn't mark her feet on the gravel as she approached the house.

John Drew had a puzzled look when he answered the door. His dog collar looked dishevelled and the red blush of his skin revealed the marks of hasty shaving.

"Mrs Hill?"

"I've dropped by with some of Judith's things. I thought I might go out with her in the trap to meet Mrs Drew and little Theodora."

"Well, you can't really."

"I beg your pardon?"

John Drew nodded vaguely at the ceiling.

"Judith is a little off-colour, it seems. Mrs Tours had to give her some sort of potion or other."

"Is that so?"

"Of course. . ."

"Yes?"

"I disapprove of these sorts of folk remedies. But I'm only the girl's father, after all."

"May I step in?"

"Of course! Of course!"

There was the look of a woman's hand about the house now, Violet Hill thought. Sense and order and warmth. Mrs Tours had obviously coached Bridget Doheny well. The fire was holding in the grate. It was a cosy house to come home to now. Not the cold, damp place it had been, over the previous days.

"Should I throw some more wood on the fire, Dr Drew?"

"No, please! Let me . . ."

In the end, they managed it between them, until the flames of the fire were rising up the chimney, bathing the walls of the parlour in a roseate glow. Violet Hill adjusted her hat. She stood there a moment, as though she had forgotten her lines. There was an awkward pause as she waited for John Drew to offer her tea. It was still too early to meet the Dublin train.

"Tea, Mrs Hill?"

"That would be wonderful, Mr Drew."

When John Drew had wet the tea and run out of small talk, he left Violet Hill with a couple of back copies of the *London Evening Standard* which her husband had brought down, earlier in the week. He was scarcely aware of the desultory turning of pages in the living room for the beat of his own thoughts. Even when the latch lifted on the back door and Bridget Doheny appeared in with her boy and the women began talking, their words weaving in and out of one another in a crochet of jumbled conversation.

"It's fierce wild out there, so it is, Mrs Hill."

"What can we expect for this time of year, Bridget?"

"It's true for you. I want to put on that bit of bacon and have a bit of soda bread ready for them."

"You're kept busy, between two houses."

"Don't be talking!"

"Has all the difficulty been sorted out, Bridget?"

"We're all right as rain, so we are now, ma'am . . . right as rain."

John Drew closed over the study door and began drawing an image on a sheet of blotting paper. First, he drew a picture of a tree, then one of a river. He wrote the names of the items in Gaelic, underneath their images.

crann + abann   =   cr + own = crown

Consonants

Initial consonants + whole word

Gaelic ideographs = Gaelic/English syllables = English word

He smiled to himself at the crude drawings then turned back to the charts and tables all around him. The Urartian material, from Lake Van. The squeezes taken from Nineveh, and the brick, baked by a heathen sun, with the inscription nabu-ku-du-ur-ri-usur. To his side, on the smaller table, notes from London, Leipzig, Vienna, Paris and Berlin lay piled. His head jerked up as he heard Bridget Doheny's coarse knuckles rapping on the study door.

"It's me, Dr Drew . . . Bridget."

John Drew stood up slowly and made for the study door.

"Yes, Bridget?"

"I'm only after getting here. Mrs Hill is gone off to meet the train, so she is."

"Fine, so . . . fine . . ."

Bridget Doheny wiped her hands in her apron and glanced over at the drawing on the desk.

"Begor and that'll be a great game for little Theodora, when she gets home."

"Yes, indeed . . . a great little game."

A great little game for the men of the Academy, in their tight shoes and frock coats, thought John Drew. When Bridget Doheny retreated into the parlour, John Drew stood staring through the window. When a sheet of squally rain slapped the pane in front of him, he turned back to the page and wrote, firmly and forth-rightly.

> *The principle of polyphony is one I shall elaborate upon, at a later date . . .*

Over the next hour or so, John Drew stalked his own thoughts assiduously, ducking and feinting until he had foxed them into a corner. The smell of bacon fat came to him from the kitchen. He could hear Bridget Doheny and the boy speaking to one another. But their words were like tunes played randomly on a whistle and he took no meaning from them.

"Build up that fire for us, like a good boy."

"Can I go then?"

"When you have the rest of the wood chopped."

Persepolis. John Drew tried to picture again the platforms in the desert and the trilingual inscriptions. The vain palace of a vainglorious king, built to impress and intimidate. Craftsmen drawn from all regions of the known world. Darius the Great scion of a civilisation that was already old when the inhabitants of these islands were living up trees. Of course, now there was coal, steam and iron. The shoe was on the other foot, you might say. He was suddenly tired now. He heard his eldest daughter moving about in the bedroom upstairs and Bridget Doheny call-ing up to her.

"Are you all right up there, Miss Drew?"

There were then footsteps on the stairs. The secret redoubt of women's words, a place no man was wanted. He considered himself as he sat in the chair. A stooped man of fifty now. What did it mean? What did any of it mean? But as quickly as the thought had come, it lifted. Because the house would be warm again, one again, with the women around him. He felt as though he were back in himself, all of a sudden. His hand reached for the pen and dipped it into the ink well. He swallowed hard.

London, Leipzig, Vienna, Paris, Berlin. A small town in the Queen's County. Fresh horse dung on a cobbled pathway. The catcalls of young men on an autumn evening. He took a sheet of writing paper out from one of the little bureau drawers. Syllables and ideographs, sound signs and pictures. He realised, with not a little amusement, that his own scribblings would one day seem as archaic as those in Persepolis now did. As he gazed out the window at the dazed lime trees in Sackville Square, he understood that he was on the right track now, Westmacott or no. Of course, tackling all the ideographs inserted in between the Babylonian syllables would take a very long time and many hours perusing other sources and inscriptions, because the remote, clinical tongue concealed in the ideographs was the ancient inheritance of scribes and stonemasons who themselves might scarcely have been able to read what they wrote. He wondered again at the genius that had driven some ancient to move from writing in pictures to writing in syllables. Could it all have happened one searing, soul-shrivelling day, on the great Persian plateau? Or in the Land Between the Two Rivers, the very cradle now, it seemed, of civilisation and literacy? For a moment, he fancied himself as just such a scribe. Toiling away at a clay table under the Mesopotamian sun, with the sound of dogs barking in the background and dust in the air. An overseer was looking down on his work from above. Was this how it had really happened? He grinned at the notion that he, John Drew, was somehow kin to an ancient scribe, squatting in a loin-cloth before a clay tablet.

John Drew was still sitting there, over an hour later, when he became aware of Willie Hill's pony-and-trap clip-clopping up Sackville Square. Bridget Doheny called out to him from the parlour.

"That must be Mrs Drew and little Theodora."

"Yes . . . yes . . . here I come."

In the brief moments before the trap pulled up, he managed to write, on a piece of bonded paper, the words:

The Rectory
Sackville Square
Aghadoe
Queen's County
September 25th, 1849

My Dear Westmacott,
I hope this letter finds you well. I was, of course, most upset to hear that you would not be able to partake in our joint cuneatic endeavour, in Queen's County, as planned. Nevertheless, I fancy I have made some progress in the matter-at-hand. I refer you to the pictographic element of the third language of the Darius inscription. My conjectures, of course . . .

The study door opened. Theodora Drew, in a purple bonnet that set off her translucent skin, rushed across to the desk. Behind her, Eliza Drew brushed dust from her dress, then undid her bonnet.

"Everything all right, John?"

"Splendid. And yourself, my dear?"

"Theodora and I have had a wonderful time in London. Hetty and Charles send their regards. Where is Judith?"

"She's still in bed, I'm afraid. Some sort of tummy upset . . ."

Eliza Drew ascended the dark stairs to the bedroom. Below, in the parlour, John Drew heard the muffled words of mother and daughter, then a door close over as Eliza made her way back down again. She crossed back into the parlour and spoke, as though to herself.

"I think I'll send Bridget for Dr Moore"

"Can't be too careful"

Bridget Doheny was at the parlour door. Red-faced, she wiped her hands in the polka-dot apron around her waist.

"I have the meat just on, Mrs Drew, and there's some fresh soda bread. Maybe yourself and Miss Theodora and Dr Drew would care to try?"

"Thank you, Bridget. Would you see to Theodora for the moment . . . Violet?"

Violet Hill's thin voice echoed from the far room. "Yes, Eliza."

"I shall be out in a minute."

A mottled light suffused the skies over Sackville Square that afternoon. A type of grey-green that seemed to bar all other light. It was a light that stung the eyes and unsettled the mind. John Drew turned away from the window as his wife approached him. He took out the silver locket from his waistcoat.

"I thought it was lost for ever, John."

"I kept it warm here . . . all the time."

"And how is Mrs Tours?"

"Well, she has been a great help to me, actually."

"I'm glad to hear that. I always knew I could count on her."

Eliza Drew's eye fell on the scattered sheets of paper on the desk. She pursed her lips and frowned before speaking.

"We must talk, John . . . about everything."

"I know."

"I mean, in relation to poor Edward."

"I have come to that conclusion too."

"I believe I have finally laid Edward to rest in London, John, over these last few days."

John Drew kept his mouth. He continued holding his wife until the pain had subsided in her voice.

"So, let us sit and talk tonight, John."

"All right, my dear."

"When the children are in bed and we have the parlour to ourselves."

They went into the dining room then and sat to the tea and soda bread while Bridget Doheny told all the news around the town, since Mrs Drew had been away. Eliza Drew and Theodora spoke of Regent's Park and the Diorama and the Soho Bazaar. There was no talk of illness from any quarter.

In the late afternoon, John Drew took a catnap in the easy-chair, in front of the fire. He was only faintly aware of Judith Drew descending the staircase. When he awoke to see the three women sitting around the great dining room table, he was minded, for a moment, of the night in Fox Keegan's house, in Tullyroe. He would have to speak of the wake to Eliza, sooner or later. She would find out about it anyway. Jer Dooley's cows were passing out towards the Coneyburrow and Waxy Daly was shutting up his little booth at the far end of Sackville Square when John Drew finally opened his eyes and stretched himself. He noticed vaguely how pale his eldest daughter was but put no pass on it. Her mother was home.

"Look what we brought you back from London!"

Theodora Drew handed him over a little booklet of pressed flowers. He opened it slowly and beheld, in gentle amusement, a collection that included Vetch and Valerian, Herb Bennet and Herb Robert. Each flower had its name, date of collection and location neatly inscribed in ink.

"Thank you, Theodora. It's very beautiful."

John Drew left the women among themselves and made his way out to the haggard where Bridget Doheny's boy was tap-tapping away at the chicken coop. What was the blessed child's name again?

"Martin . . ."

"I'm Tadhg, Dr Drew. I have it finished for you. I got an ould plank out of the coachhouse, so I did."

"Mr Reynard won't be at the hens tonight, so."

"What's that, Dr Drew?"

"You know, the fox. We'll have plenty of fresh eggs."

"Lashins and lavins, Dr Drew."

"Indeed . . . indeed. Lashins and lavins, as you say . . ."

John Drew glanced over his shoulder towards the house. Through the dining room window, he could see Eliza and the girls poring over a book. This evening. Yes, this evening they would talk.

John Drew smiled to himself, for a moment, at the notion of the all-powerful Mrs Tours, in her little palace, in Pound Street. Provider of hems and darts and patches to both high and low. Sometime apothecary for colds and quinsy and God-knows-what-else. He forgot about the boy at his feet and made for the coach-house. In the fading light, he patted the horse's flank and muttered something to him about oats and the harvest and the new slates on the church roof. What about the Sunday sermon? Habbakuk could scarcely be resurrected a second time. Job, per-haps. Job and his midden. The great gourd and the Eastern sun beating down on the poor, vain fool. *Nil desperandum.* That was the sort of thing he would speak about.

He took a deep breath and pushed further into the coach-house. The ledges where he had stored the skulls and eggs were now bare. But the little booklet in which he had noted down details of dates and location was still in the study drawer. Mrs Tours had done her job well. Over in the right-hand corner, near the old wardrobe, he unwrapped the three bricks in the burlap sacking and ran his fingers over the syllables: *nabu-ku-du-ur-ri-usur.* Nebuchadnezzar, King of Babylon. Westmacott was to have taken the bricks back with him, for lodgement in the museum. Not that they didn't have enough of their own material, of course. John Drew understood, as he marked the tiredness of his own thoughts, that, like Job, he had come down from his own midden. He had been within an ass's roar of burning half a life-time's work, had buried the father of an erstwhile companion and had emerged, shriven, into the light. Over the next week, he would prepare the paper for the Academy.

A Translation of the Third Persepolitan Inscription with Copious Comments on Ideographs, Polyphony, Syllabification, Class-Signs and the Relationship of this Language to the Ancient Hebrew

Westmacott would struggle to find fault with the emended translation, though certain supposed authorities in London might carp.

1. Darius the Great King
2. King of Kings King of all the lands
3. Of all tongues entirely
4. Son of Hytaspes
5. The Achaemenian
6. Who built this palace

He would begin formally writing up the commentary, with the syllable and ideograph lists, at the weekend after Eliza had had time to settle back first.

John Drew became aware, just then, of a movement over by the coachhouse door. At first, he thought it was Bridget Doheny. The woman standing there had a pail in her hand. He looked over his spectacles and then slowly recognised his wife. Eliza Drew's voice had an odd girlish giddiness about it.

"I'm going to fetch water from the well, John."

"I'm sorry?"

"From Campion's well . . . water . . ."

"Can't that Doheny woman do it?"

"Would you like to walk with me?"

John Drew turned back slowly to the workbench and re-wrapped the bricks against the cold night. He stood a moment, puzzled, not knowing what to say to his wife. Not sure, in fact, whether he had correctly understood her invitation. Then he coughed embarrassedly to himself and followed in Eliza Drew's wake. Over his shoulder, as he passed out of the coachhouse, he spotted Bridget Doheny with her hand on Theodora's shoulder, as she gazed out through the scullery window. He plodded along after his wife, ducking his head as he passed under the apple trees in the little orchard. When they emerged into Campion's field, Lyons' donkey, tethered to a post at the far side of the field, brayed as it saw them coming, fearful, perhaps, of a blow from a stick or the torment of being hitched to a cart. A couple of children were playing close to the Pound Street cottages. Though John Drew called out after her, Eliza Drew paid no heed and strode on through the heavy grass in her purple dress with the floral bows, the empty pail swaying in the air by her side. When she reached the well, Eliza Drew turned to face her husband who paused, breathless, on the rutted little track before the well.

"Eliza, what is the matter?"

"Help me, please, John."

With his wife holding the pail, John Drew winched the well-bucket up. Then he poured the cold, clear water into the pail, taking care not to spill a drop on to the dry earth. When the pail was full, Eliza Drew set it down at her feet and wiped her hands with a little crimson handkerchief. They stood quietly for a moment, John Drew wiping his spectacles, Eliza Drew drying her hands, as the children from the cottages scampered about in the high grass that ran along the ditch. Neither of them marked Mrs Tours watching from the yard nor did Mrs Tours hear the words that passed between them.

"John . . ."

"Yes, dear?"

"How . . ."

"Yes?"

Eliza Drew wiped her lips and looked over her husband's shoulders towards Sackville Square.

"John . . . how do we know that our Edward . . ."

"Yes?"

"That he will be there for us . . . waiting for us . . . when we pass over?"

"Eliza . . . I don't think . . ."

John Drew stooped to take up the pail of water but his wife restrained him.

"How?"

He pulled himself up slowly and gazed about Campion's field. At the trees on the Sackville Square side, at the rude beast tethered to the post and the children playing along by the Pound Street ditch. He spotted Mrs Tours this time but he made no mention of it to his wife.

"We know, Eliza . . ."

"Yes?"

"We know . . . the same way we know there will be water in this well for us tomorrow. What we take from the source goes back to the source."

"Faith, you mean, then?"

"Yes, I suppose so. There will be water in the well tomorrow. And, one day, all the waters of the world will be as one again. In the end."

Eliza Drew didn't pause to reply. Instead, she took up the pail of water, sharing the load with her husband, and they both began walking back across Campion's field. Mrs Tours waited until they had passed into the little orchard before turning back to her house. Before she did so, however, she let a little shout at the children, over by the ditch, telling them to steer clear of the ass tethered at the far end of the field, for fear it would kick one of them. In the orchard, Eliza Drew gathered up some early windfalls in her apron and made for the house, leaving John Drew to follow behind with the pail.

"Just a minute, Eliza . . ."

Then they both made into the house together, for the warmth

of the parlour and the soda bread that Bridget Doheny was cutting into thick, doughy slices.

SOME OTHER READING
from

BRANDON

Brandon is a leading Irish publisher of new fiction and non-fiction for an international readership. For a catalogue of new and forthcoming books, please write to Brandon/Mount Eagle, Cooleen, Dingle, Co. Kerry, Ireland. For a full listing of all our books in print, please go to

www.brandonbooks.com

EMER MARTIN
Baby Zero

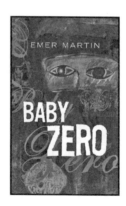

"An incendiary, thought-provoking novel, like a haunting and spiritual ballad, it moves us and makes us care." Irvine Welsh

From an award-winning writer, a darkly comic novel about a family caught between East and West. In an unheard of country, each successive Taliban-like regime turns the year back to zero, as if to begin history again. An Irish-born woman, Marguerite, imprisoned for fighting the fundamentalist government, is pregnant. To retain her sanity she tells her unborn child the story of three baby zeros – all girls from a family that has been scattered across the globe, some to Los Angeles and some to Ireland, all born at times of upheaval. Despite its unflinching portrayal of extreme oppression, *Baby Zero* constantly bubbles with humorous incident and characters, presenting a compelling and entertaining satire on both East and West.

ISBN 978-0-86322-355-6; paperback original

MARY ROSE CALLAGHAN
Billy, Come Home

"At the heart of this innocent-seeming novel lies a scathing critique of attitudes to mental illness. Mary Rose Callaghan's velvet-gloved hand wields a pen as sharp as a razor. An honest look at how we really are, this is not a novel to forget in a hurry."
Éilís Ní Dhuibhne, Orange Prize shortlisted novelist

A thirty-year-old woman travels to London to identify a body that has been fished out of the Thames; it is believed to be that of her brother, Billy. The narrative flashes back to the brutal murder of a teenage girl when Billy is regarded suspiciously by the neighbours, one of whom sends poison pen letters. This moving novel is about a mentally ill man and his need for a home. It is also a mystery novel, set in present day suburbia.

ISBN 978-086322-366-2; paperback original

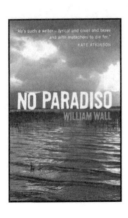

WILLIAM WALL
No Paradiso

Evocative, haunting short fiction by the 2005
Booker longlisted author

"In addition to the author's alert, muscular style, his
painlessly communicated appreciation of obscure
learning, his vaguely didactic pleasure in accurately
providing a sense of place, many of these stories are
distinguished by a welcome engagement with
form . . . In their various negotiations with such
tensions, the stories of *No Paradiso* engage, challenge and reward
the committed reader.
The Irish Times

"Irish writer William Wall's total command of words is demonstrated
again . . . There is something painterly about the way William Wall draws his
characters, using just two or three deft strokes to bring a character to
life . . . The reader cannot fail to be mesmerised by the quality of the prose
and the poet's gift for the perfectly chosen word." *Sunday Tribune*

ISBN 978-0-86322-355-6; paperback original

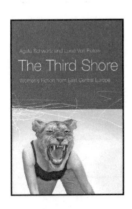

**AGATA SCHWARTZ AND
LUISE VON FLOTOW (EDS)**
The Third Shore
Women's Fiction from East Central Europe

A rich compendium of fiction by twenty-five women
from eighteen different nations: stories of illness and
death, love and desire, motherhood and war,
feminism and patriarchy.

The Third Shore brings to light a whole spectrum of
women's literary accomplishment and experience
virtually unknown in the West. Gracefully translated, and with an
introduction that establishes their political, historical, and literary context,
these stories written in the decade after the fall of the Iron Curtain are
tales of the familiar reconceived and turned into something altogether new
by the distinctive experience they reflect.

ISBN 978-0-86322-362-4; paperback original

DRAGO JANČAR
Joyce's Pupil

"Jančar writes powerful, complex stories with an unostentatious assurance, and has a gravity which makes the tricks of more self-consciously modern writers look cheap [. . .] Drago Jančar deserves the wider readership that these translations should gain him." *Times Literary Supplement*

"Elegant, elliptical stories." *Financial Times*

"His powerful and arresting narratives leave the reader in no doubt as to the fragility of the human condition when placed under the stress of political, historical and ethnic conflict." *Sunday Telegraph*

"[A] stunning collection . . . ambitious, enjoyable and page turning." *Time Out*

ISBN 978-0-86322-340-2; paperback original

NENAD VELIČKOVIĆ
Lodgers

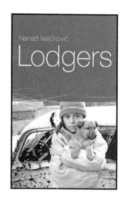

"Excellent... *Lodgers* supplies one of the best examples of 'war literature' . . . More literarily convincing and existentially urgent than numerous current-affairs books, newspaper reports, and travel writing, *Lodgers* stands out as a poignant document of a turbulent era." *World Literature Today*

"In deploying his curious cast of 'lodgers,' Veličković reveals an artistry that defeats the forces of brutality with wit, indirection, and boundless good humor." *Review of Contemporary Fiction*

"In equal measure of farce and tragedy, Nenad Veličković's novel offers a wry take on the siege of Sarajevo, a place where an accreditation badge gives more protection that a bullet-proof vest." *Guardian*

"Nenad Veličković offers a beautifully constructed account of the ridiculous nature of the Balkans conflict, and war in general, which even in moments of pure gallows humour retains a heartwarming affection for the individuals trying to survive in such horrific circumstances." *Metro*

ISBN 978-0-86322-348-8; paperback original

DAVID FOSTER
The Land Where Stories End

"Australia's most original and important living novelist." *Independent Monthly*

"A post-modern fable set in the dark ages of Ireland. . . [A] beautifully written humorous myth that is entirely original. The simplicity of language is perfectly complementary to the wry, occasionally laugh-out-loud humour and the captivating tale." *Irish World*

"I was taken by surprise and carried easily along by the amazing story and by the punchy clarity of the writing. . . This book is imaginative and fantastic. . . It is truly amazing." *Books Ireland*

ISBN 978-0-86322-311-2; hardback

CHET RAYMO
Valentine

"Such nebulous accounts [as we have] have been just waiting for someone to make a work of historical fiction out of them. American novelist and physicist Raymo has duly obliged with his recently published *Valentine: A Love Story*." *The Scotsman*

"[A] vivid and lively account of how Valentine's life may have unfolded… Raymo has produced an imaginative and enjoyable read, sprinkled with plenty of food for philosophical thought." *Sunday Tribune*

ISBN 978-0-86322-327-3; paperback original

BRYAN MACMAHON
Hero Town

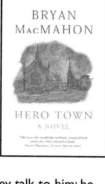

"*Hero Town* is the perfect retrospective: here the town is the hero, a character of epic and comic proportions. . . It may come to be recognized as MacMahon's masterpiece."
Professor Bernard O'Donohue

"For the course of a calendar year, Peter Mulrooney, the musing pedagogue, saunters through the streets and the people, looking at things and leaving them so. They talk to him; he listens, and in his ears we hear the authentic voice of local Ireland, all its tics and phrases and catchcalls. Like Joyce, this wonderful, excellently structured book comes alive when you read it aloud."
Frank Delaney, *Sunday Independent*

ISBN 978-0-86322-342-6; paperback

JOHN B. KEANE
The Bodhrán Makers

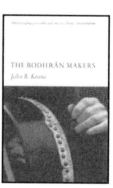

The first and best novel from one of Ireland's best-loved writers, a moving and telling portrayal of a rural community in the '50s, a poverty-stricken people who never lost their dignity.

"Furious, raging, passionate and very, very funny."
Boston Globe

"This powerful and poignant novel provides John B. Keane with a passport to the highest levels of Irish literature." *Irish Press*

"Sly, funny, heart-rending. . . Keane writes lyrically; recommended."
Library Journal

ISBN 978-0-86322-300-6; paperback

KATE MCCAFFERTY
Testimony of an Irish Slave Girl

"McCafferty's haunting novel chronicles an overlooked chapter in the annals of human slavery . . . A meticulously researched piece of historical fiction that will keep readers both horrified and mesmerized." *Booklist*

"Thousands of Irish men, women and children were sold into slavery to work in the sugar-cane fields of Barbados in the 17th century . . . McCafferty has researched her theme well and, through Cot, shows us the terrible indignities and suffering endured."
Irish Independent

ISBN 978-0-86322-338-9; paperback
ISBN 978-0-86322-314-1; hardback

KITTY FITZGERALD
Small Acts of Treachery

"Mystery and politics, a forbidden sexual attraction that turns into romance; Kitty Fitzgerald takes the reader on a gripping roller coaster through the recent past. In *Small Acts of Treachery* a woman of courage defies the power not only of the secret state but of sinister global elites. This is a story you can't stop reading, with an undertow which will give you cause to reflect." Sheila Rowbotham

"[It] is a super book with a fascinating story and great characters . . . all the more impressive because of the very sinister feeling I was left with that it is all too frighteningly possible." *Books Ireland*

ISBN 978-0-86322-297-9; paperback